BEYON

The Sto

JOSEPH AMAEZE

DARUDAN PUBLISHING

First published in 2018
by Darudan Publishing

Milton Keynes, Buckinghamshire, U.K

ISBN: 978-0-9935860-2-6

Printed in Great Britain by Lightning Source UK Ltd

Cover design: Vikncharlie

To Grace-Julia on your jubilee

THE FIRST WORD

The story of Joseph is a fascinating account of how one person's faith enabled him to access all God had in store for him and persevere in the face of adversity. The triumph of accomplishment in the midst of trials is a popular theme because we can all relate to it in some way. Joseph's journey from the pit to the palace has encouraged multitudes over the years because it reveals God's faithfulness to us, regardless of our circumstances. Even when our afternoon appears gloomy, we are assured that, behind the clouds of adversity, the sun is still shining.

When God reveals His will for our lives, He expects us to internalise the vision and let it become the light that guides our feet and the lamp that brightens the darkness around us. The prophet Isaiah commands us to arise and shine because the glory of God has been bestowed on us. The true value of light lies in its ability to obliterate darkness. God will reveal our destination, but the route has to be discovered. For Joseph, that route was discovered over a thirteen-year period. His story teaches us not to fret about the route, but to focus instead on the destination.

I must thank my soul mate and able assistant – my wife, Isoken – for the inspiration that birthed this book. Following an engaging discussion of Joseph's journey, which was seasoned with my improvised narrative and dialogue, she asked me to write an account of Joseph's story, incorporating those features.

Where necessary, I have relied on literary licence to amplify the lessons and experiences in the biblical account. I also researched historical and archaeological sources in an effort to capture the story's epoch without diminishing its essence.

God wishes to have a transformational encounter with each of us through His written word, and I believe this version of Joseph's story provides a medium for such a process.

Finally, this book tells the story from Joseph's perspective presenting an uncluttered view of the events that shaped his journey. In all other respects, however, it remains faithful to one of the most profound literary experiences in Scripture.

Joseph Amaeze
Milton Keynes, UK
20 May 2017

THE HOUSE OF CARDS

Mark 3:25

The view over the Nile at sunset is a rich composition of orange, grey and yellow shades. It provides a visual delight unrivalled by any other in Egypt, particularly when beheld from the panoramic terrace of my home in the city of Waset. It forms a magnificent backdrop to the silhouettes of the slender palm trees, sculptures and buildings, and I easily forget the day's challenges. Listening to the distant laughter of the local women, who gather every evening on the riverbank to wash their clothes, is another highlight. Laughter is like music to the ears of the weary.

Each evening, I find myself drawn to the same spot; the brilliance of the scenery surpassing even the artistic beauty of Egypt's finest tapestries or murals, feeling privileged to be here. The view is therapeutic and free of charge – there to be enjoyed by anyone who has the capacity to look beyond their challenges. I should know, I've had my fair share.

This is my twentieth year in Egypt. On the eve of my thirty-seventh birthday, I still feel isolated here and my environment, although familiar, still looks strange. I am home, but feel as though I am in transit, like a nomadic shepherd in search of green pastures to graze my flocks. My beautiful, intelligent wife Asenath, the daughter of the priest of On, has borne me a gorgeous son named Manasseh, yet still I feel empty. I named him Manasseh, because I believed God had helped me forget my troubles and the treachery that led to them. But, despite my best efforts, I struggle to escape my sense of injustice or ignore the scars of my exploitation.

Let me explain. I am of Hebrew origin, born into an old and revered family line, but I was forcibly transported to the greatest Kingdom in the world, Egypt. I am an alien in this country – part of the vast immigrant workforce that contributes to Egypt's wealth and prosperity. I have been well rewarded for my diligence and loyalty, but material gifts no longer satisfy me. Like many immigrants before me, I am homesick. I love the view here but still long for home.

My story is a complex one. You may find certain aspects of it familiar. Life is going extremely well for me here in Egypt, but it's not my home. I have no family – no, I should rephrase that. I have no extended family network here. I love my wife dearly, and we have grown closer over the past seven years. She's one of my strongest advocates and has grown to understand me. Our son is my delight and I am grateful for him.

After the rigours of my daily shift, I love to see him rushing out of the house, into the courtyard, when he hears my chariot. We are a close family and do everything together. Our home is full of laughter and love, but why do I still miss my father's house?

Don't let my earlier bout of nostalgia give you the impression that I am ungrateful. Reminiscing about a bygone era in a place I vaguely remember is a regular pastime for me, one that is almost always dismissed as wishful thinking, because I don't believe that after all this time I will ever see my home country again. Even if I was able to make the journey, it is doubtful that I would be able to locate where my father's tents were pitched. My family is nomadic, and would undoubtedly have moved from the spot in Canaan where I last saw them. It is tortuous to put myself through this, but I do it because a tree without roots is dead.

While I may not be able to navigate my way back across the Arabian Desert to locate my roots, I have very vivid memories of my ten relatives who played a part in my journey to Egypt. These ten are my siblings. Our father, Jacob, had thirteen children, of whom I am the twelfth, although I was the first child born to my late mother. Even now, tears well in my eyes as I remember how she was taken away from me when I was very young.

My father's home was a collection of tents, fabricated from animal skins and tough fabrics woven together and set around a central quadrangle, which provided some security and an area for socialising. I can clearly recall the layout of my familial community and the vast expanse of patchy land that surrounded it. I remember the well my father dug to provide us with a constant source of water, but which ended up being a constant source of bickering between his wives and children. The polygamous family I grew up in was more intimate than most, but we still had our problems. Where there are multiple wives, there will inevitably be divisions. Despite her place as my father's second wife, my mother – Rachel – acted like his first wife. She made sure I was not exposed to the hostility and simmering turbulence of his other wives. For a short while I was shielded from this divisive family culture … until the day my world fell apart.

My mother, the most beautiful of all my father's wives, had been barren for many years. She told me that when I was eventually born, my father threw a grand feast to celebrate the event, as my birth was an answer to his prayers. Aunty Leah, as we called her, my mum's older sister, had given birth to seven children – six boys and a girl, my half-brothers and half-sister. My father's two concubines Bilhah and Zilpah, who had formerly been maids to my mum and Aunty Leah, each had two sons for him. During our residence in Bethel, my mother unexpectedly became pregnant again, with my younger brother Benjamin. I recall that my father was exceedingly happy and that he again threw a party in celebration.

I don't remember all the details, but I was told that, as we travelled from Bethel to a city called Hebron, near a town called Bethlehem, my mother went into labour and developed complications which put her and the baby at risk. The midwives informed my father that the baby had not assumed the birthing position and was distressed. Despite the midwives' best efforts to encourage the baby to assume the correct position, my mother's weak heart failed and she passed away soon after giving birth to my brother, who she named Benoni, which means 'son of sorrow'. My father, however, took a more positive view and renamed my brother Benjamin, which means 'son of my right hand'. It appeared that my mother's sorrow had become my father's strength.

From the moment my mother died, my father became much more protective of me and Benjamin, which I never fully understood. I knew that he had loved my mother very much and that her death was a crushing blow, but his level of protection over my brother and me bordered on obsessive. Our movements were heavily restricted and we were not allowed to fraternise freely with our other siblings. As a teenager, I was aware of my father's favouritism towards Benjamin and me, which created an even greater division between Benjamin, me and my other siblings. For example, my father erected an additional tent in our community where Benjamin and I slept, along with the maid he had assigned to attend to us. The maid's role was to ensure that Benjamin and I had everything we wanted.

Looking back, I can see how that level of blatant privilege would engender bitterness within my brothers and hatred for Benjamin and me. Although I didn't think about it at the time, my father's conduct towards them was occasionally fairly harsh, especially when dealing with Reuben, Simeon and Levi. I recall asking him once, just before the events that led to my sudden change of circumstance, what my brothers had done to make him so cross and short-tempered with them, but he didn't answer. Frustrated by his silence, I turned to Joram, a servant who tended to my father's flocks, and he told me that Reuben had slept with my father's concubine, Bilhah. Bilhah who had been my mother's maid was the mother of Dan and Naphtali, my half-brothers. It is taboo in my culture for a son to sleep with his father's wife: it is irreverent, and it's the same thing as a son uncovering his father's and mother's nakedness.

It was clear that Reuben had been reckless and that, like our Uncle Esau, he had allowed his lust and greed to rob him of his status as first son. It explained why my father always bypassed him and preferred to deal instead with Judah. Simeon and Levi had committed a different offence. It was harrowing. As Joram told me about their violent and merciless actions, my blood ran cold. This explained why my father was so distant from my half-sister Dinah, Aunty Leah's daughter, who was withdrawn and reclusive and very rarely seen outside her mother's tent.

According to Joram, while we lived at a place called Shalem, Dinah was violated by a young man named Shechem, whose father was the ruler of the country. However, after the violation he fell in love with her and regretted his actions. In an attempt to right his wrong, Shechem tried to marry Dinah, with his father's support. Simeon and Levi, acting on my father's behalf, pretended to agree to the union, with one condition: that Shechem and all the men in Shalem circumcised themselves, in accordance with Hebrew custom. All Hebrew men are circumcised at eight days old as a mark of the covenant that God entered into with our ancestor Abraham.

When the men of Shalem were incapacitated due to the soreness associated with the circumcision, Simeon and Levi invaded the city, killed all the men and rescued Dinah who was still being held captive. When my father found out what they had done, Joram told me, he was livid with them, despite their protestations about what had been done to Dinah. I got the idea, from what Joram said, that my father was less worried about Dinah than he was about his own safety, and this worried me.

Simeon and Levi had merely tried to restore honour to our father's house after Dinah's trauma and disgrace, but they had clearly gone about it in the wrong way. Our father had raised us to be God-fearing; he was never vengeful or vindictive. Simeon and Levi had, however, grown up to be quick-tempered, impatient individuals like Uncle Esau, who had plotted to kill our father when he was younger. My half-brothers were always involved in heated family disputes and their hostility towards me was apparent. I believe they resented the fact that my father was more openly affectionate to Benjamin and me than he was to them or their mother. I suspect they blamed me for their poor relationship with our father, which may explain why they wanted to get rid of me.

These days, I mull over my past, while gazing at one of the greatest splendours of God's creation. The beauty of the Egyptian sunset is a palliative for my sorrow. I am homesick, yes, but struggle to sift through my catalogue of painful memories for one that draws a fond smile or a warm feeling. The emotional and psychological instability in my family meant that, rather than enjoying a tranquil family life, my father was always wading in to resolve disputes that he was indirectly the architect of.

As always, whenever I think about my past, I find my thoughts dipping towards the pit of heavy-heartedness and despair. At such times, like a person waking from a deep slumber, I shake myself awake and blink to clear my blurry vision. I shake off all thoughts of ingratitude and try to be grateful instead. Not many people are fortunate enough to live through adversity and emerge reasonably unscathed, but I'm a survivor. I have a story to tell: a tale of rejection, betrayal, injustice, abuse, and exploitation. It is a story I never thought I would experience. Standing here on the terrace of this magnificent house in the city of Waset, which is second only in architectural splendour to Pharaoh's palace, I can't stop marvelling at the chain of events that have brought me to this place.

I turn at the sound of shuffling feet behind me, and the delicate, curvaceous form of Asenath's dark-skinned Nubian maid greets my eyes. In her placid face and demure brown eyes I read nothing, no clue to the content of her message. Her name is Kiya, which means 'jovial lady'. She is always smiling and full of joy. Kiya is not her original Nubian name, but her Egyptian name, because every foreigner living and working in the country is given a name that the locals could pronounce. An Egyptian name leads to societal integration and acceptance.

My Hebrew name is Joseph but Pharaoh named me Zaphnath-Paaneah, meaning 'discloser of secret things'. I chuckle when I think of the irony of my name. If I could indeed disclose secret things, surely I would have foreseen what would happen to, but I did not. Only God can disclose the secret things that have been and that always shall be.

As Kiya draws near she bows from the waist, in keeping with protocol. In every Egyptian household, a servant girl must curtsy when approaching the master of the house, but because of my status, Pharaoh passed an edict that all men should bow to me from the knee and all women from the waist, depending on their attire. Kiya is clad in a long linen garment that covers her from just below the breasts to the ankles. Unlike many other households, where women go bare-chested, I insist that all my female servants cover their upper bodies with a broad necklace woven from thick beads to preserve their dignity.

'My master, may your days be prolonged like the crocodiles of the Nile and may your stature rise higher than an eagle's,' says Kiya, addressing me in the flamboyant manner that I had reluctantly become accustomed to. It was an edict from Pharaoh which could not be broken.

'What news do you have for me of Asenath's condition?' I ask, trying to quell my anxious thoughts.

'Master, she has given birth to a baby boy. The

midwives assure me that both are doing well,' answers Kiya, still looking at the floor.

My instant reaction is to give thanks within my heart because both baby and mother are in good health. According to the Canaanite calendar, Asenath had been due to give birth in a month's time, but as I left for work that morning she had complained about cramps, prompting me to send for the midwives just in case. While I was inspecting the granaries in the Lower Nile area, I received word by a messenger in a fast chariot that my wife had gone into labour. My first instinct was to rush home, in case the labour was short, but my sense of duty prompted me to carry on with my task. Even though I have appointed regional overseers to ensure that the grain is stocked according to the agreed allocation, I still conduct impromptu inspections to ensure that corrupt officials are not holding back grain to trade on the black market. I had therefore sent a message back that I would return as soon as I could.

As I hurry after Kiya, walking briskly but with measured strides befitting a person in my office, I begin to think of names for the new arrival. To be honest, after my first son, I was rather hoping for a daughter whose beauty would surpass my mother, Rachel's, and whose personality would mirror Asenath's. Isn't it every father's dream to have a daughter who combines the best features of the most important women in his life? For a moment I fantasise.

Sensing the weeds of ingratitude sprouting in my soul, I flush them out with a noiseless song of praise: one that overflows from my heart but never strays from my lips. I am determined to convey ecstatic joy when I see my wife, lest she feels that she has offended me, for it is an ancient Egyptian belief that the woman determines the sex of the child, just as Mother Nature determines the quality of the crops. Displeasure from me would be a rod across Asenath's back.

Walking briskly through the cool, high-ceilinged chambers of the upper floor of my house, ignoring the colourful hieroglyphics inscribed on walls and columns and the exquisitely woven tapestries that act like partitions, we arrive at my wife's chamber. A group of my servants and officials are gathered outside at a respectful distance, and they bow in unison as I arrive. As I walk into the chamber, little Manasseh, who was nestling in the arms of his maid, leaps off her lap and runs towards me with a delighted shout. I scoop him up and hoist him onto my shoulder. In the middle of the room, resting on the bed with midwives surrounding her, is the woman whose love has been my anchor and helped me to partially forget the loss of my mother.

Approaching the bed, I see the tiny brown form of a new-born baby feeding from his mother's breast. A piece of white linen covers his lower body. I stand there, mesmerised by the spectacle of new life functioning instinctively without any tutorial. Who teaches a baby how to suckle his mother's breast? Who instructs a baby on the art of breathing through lungs that have been redundant in the womb?

My eyes meet Asenath's. Concern flashes across her face and she smiles hesitantly, as if waiting for my approval. I give her a broad smile, and she reciprocates. Handing a reluctant Manasseh to a midwife, I lean over to kiss my wife on the forehead before placing a gentle hand on the back of the new-born. His skin is smooth and tender, and I try to picture my own birth, imagining my father's joy when he first touched his long-awaited son.

I turn to the midwives and dismiss them. "My wife and I wish to be alone."

It is customary for babies to be named in a more formal setting, but I am determined to give my son a name that has not been selected by a committee.

'Do you have a name?' Asenath's voice catches me off guard.

'I've thought of different names, both Hebrew and Egyptian.'

'And have you chosen one?'

I ponder this for a moment. I do not have a name for our son because I have only been considering girls' names. I study my son as he rests placidly, taking a break from feeding, and my thoughts stray to the theme of my meditation whilst out on the terrace. Suddenly, a name leaps out at me.

'His name will be Ephraim,' I reply, a resolution in my voice conveys the depth of deliberation behind my choice of name.

Asenath's expression betrays the merest hint of a frown. 'Ephraim,' she repeats softly, sampling the sound and texture of the name. 'What does it mean?'

'God has blessed me and caused me to be fruitful in the land of my affliction.'

'Yes, He has been good to you,' she confirms with a gentle nod.

I study her oval face, high cheekbones, dimpled chin and the dark brown eyes that softly caress my face, and feel blessed. God has indeed blessed me. Every time I mention my second son's name, I will be proclaiming that fact. It is my testimony of God's faithfulness.

Asenath's expression slowly morphs into a smile and she nods slowly. It is clear that she has made the connection and approves of my choice. Admittedly, it is an unusual name, but one rich with meaning.

'Manasseh and Ephraim,' she murmurs.

'Yes. Because God first delivers us from the pain of our affliction, this paves the way for our blessings and fruitfulness.'

Asenath appears to be happy with the name and her glowing face confirms this. For me, however, it is a growing realisation. I chose the name Ephraim as a memorial. I wanted a name that conveyed my gratitude. Ephraim was my way of silencing the voice of ingratitude in the most meaningful way. But it is becoming clear that both of my sons' names tell a story: they define a journey. Manasseh should always precede Ephraim, because God's healing will always precede His blessing. This is my story.

FAMILY TIES

2 Corinthians 6:14

Twenty years earlier

'Joseph!'

The sound of my name spoken by a familiar voice prompted me to look up from my meal. I had barely got halfway through my lunch of bread, roasted lamb and lentil stew. After hours of sheaving wheat in the harvest fields, I was famished, but my father had summoned me. I turned to Benjamin, who sat beside me in the tent, facing the rectangular communal area between the other tents. Benjamin and I always ate together. Because he was not yet old enough to join us in the fields, he would wait for my return before eating.

'I'll be right back,' I said, getting to my feet, nibbling on a piece of bread. 'I haven't finished eating yet, okay?'

Benjamin waved a hand in acknowledgement, but I didn't trust him not to make a beeline for my bowl the moment my back was turned. I contemplated stuffing my mouth with lamb, unwilling to forfeit the highlight of an otherwise ordinary meal.

'Joseph!'

The second summons shook me out of my thoughts and I hurried across the quadrangle towards my father's tent. Along the way, I paused to greet Bilhah and Zilpah, who sat outside their tents, grinding grain by hand with a quern – a milling tool made of rough stones. Both women saluted me in the traditional manner and blessed me, even though I knew they probably hated my guts. Bilhah and Zilpah were responsible for overseeing food storage, a task previously undertaken by my late mother. But, judging from the amount of food spoilage we experienced, they clearly weren't very good at it.

Approaching the entrance to my father's tent, an inexplicable feeling of apprehension gripped me. I hoped he was not going to reverse his promise that I could go out to graze the flocks with my brothers when I was seventeen. My seventeenth birthday had been several months ago, but my father had not yet issued permission. He was obsessively protective towards Benjamin and me and it felt stifling; I was keen to explore the world beyond our home.

Taking off my sandals at the doorway to the tent, I stooped to enter, bowing to my father as I stepped inside. Like all the other tents in our community, the ground was covered with light mats and rugs that smothered the grainy sand beneath, which somehow still managed to seep through. Apart from the pile of rugs that acted as my father's bed, the only other furniture in the tent was a collapsible wooden chair and footstool where he sat, and a flimsy wooden table on which rested a ceramic jug of water. A basket on the floor contained some of his clothes, but I knew that his ceremonial attire was kept in Aunty Leah's tent. Aunty Leah was responsible for making most of our everyday clothes, which were made of fabric she wove out of goat's hair and sheep's wool. She also created linen fibres out of fibrous plants and used them to fashion fabrics on her loom, which all the women used to craft their garments. With my half-sister Dinah's help, Aunty Leah also kept our clothes in good repair.

I looked up at my father's wizened, lined face. As our eyes met, his affectionate smile embraced me. Jacob, my father, was well over a hundred years old, and these days he rarely ventured out of his tent. I glanced at the wooden staff he used to support him, which was resting between his legs, and recalled the fascinating story he had told me about how he had wrestled with an angel of God – but lived. It had left him with a severe limp, as a result of God's angel putting his hip out of joint.

'You sent for me, Father?'

'Yes, son.' My father's smile slowly evaporated and his expression became pensive.

His change in expression was troubling.

'Dan, Naphtali, Gad and Asher are at the plains near Shechem with some of the flock,' my father said, 'but they have sent word back that they have run out of food. I need someone to replenish their supplies.'

'Send me, Father!'

The eagerness in my voice was matched by my exuberant body language. I was like a horse raring to go. My father's smile broadened and he nodded gently.

'Okay, my son,' he said in his gravelly voice, 'you can go to them, but I will send Joram with you as it is your first time.'

Joram was my father's personal aide, a servant who had been with him since his sojourn in Mesopotamia at the house of my maternal grandfather, Laban. Joram had grown up under my father and had become like a son to him. He was entirely trustworthy and loyal, but I was troubled.

'But, Father, I am of age,' I protested gently, 'and I can find my way to the plains of Shechem without assistance.'

'Joram goes with you,' said my father, with an air of finality. 'I need you to set off right away so you can return tomorrow evening.'

'Will my brothers also be returning tomorrow?' I asked, knowing the answer.

'No. They will stay on for a couple of days, making the most of the terrain before the rains come. That's why they need more food to sustain them.'

'Why can't I stay there with them?'

'Because I need you to come back to me tomorrow, son,' said my father, sounding increasingly fatigued. 'You know I cannot bear to be without you that long.'

I was tempted to rise up and leave his tent in anger, but my conscience stopped me. His obsessive care for my safety was frustrating, but I knew he meant well.

'Father, do you trust in God?'

The question appeared to rattle my father. 'Of course I do!' he said.

'Then prove it,' I said, leaning closer to him until I was able to place both my hands on his feeble knees.

There was a weighty silence. He avoided my gaze and uttered a series of grunts and sighs, along with the occasional tongue-clicking. I could tell he was wrestling with the decision. I felt for him, but my thirst for independence kept me rooted to the spot, gazing at him intently, waiting for an answer.

'Joram will stay with you,' he said at last.

'But Joram is your aide,' I said, my eyes widening. 'How will you cope without him?'

'Judah and his brothers are due back this evening,' my father answered, 'so I will not be alone. The only condition on which I will let you remain with your half-brothers is if Joram remains there with you.'

I nodded demurely. At least he had met me halfway. Joram was as much of a control freak as my father and would hover over me like a shepherd. I suspected that my father could detect my disappointment because he leant forward till the tip of his white beard almost made contact with my forehead.

'You might think I am being over-protective,' he whispered, 'but I know my sons well, and I do not have confidence in the sons of Bilhah and Zilpah. They are generally well behaved, but I sense a jealous streak in them concerning you. They behave more like servants than the sons of my loins, whom I circumcised myself on the eighth day with a flint knife. '

Dan, Naphtali, Gad and Asher were the sons of Bilhah and Zilpah, my father's concubines. They had become his wives thanks to an ancient Mesopotamian tradition that permitted a wife who was either barren or past childbearing age to offer her maid to her husband to bear children for him. Any children borne by the maid typically belonged to the wife who had offered her, and even though the maid was elevated to the status of concubine and was at the beck and call of her master whenever he needed her company, she was not a wife in the legal sense and was entitled to no inheritance. Her sons were also perceived as being inferior to sons born to legal wives, and were at the bottom of the succession line.

In accordance with status, my father divided my brothers into two teams of shepherds, with Aunty Leah's sons – Reuben, Simeon, Levi, Judah, Issachar and Zebulun – charged with looking after the more prestigious flocks, comprising cattle and camels, which were more expensive but fewer in number. Bilhah's and Zilpah's sons, however, had drawn the short straw and looked after the more mobile herds of sheep and goats. Occasionally, the teams of shepherds collaborated to herd the entire flock when they located particularly fertile grazing ground.

'I understand, Father,' I answered. 'I'll be careful.'

I felt my father's dry lips press gently against my forehead, and I reached up to embrace him. I knew that it was a difficult decision for him to make, and wanted him to know that I appreciated this.

My father said a brief but passionate prayer over me, as was his custom. I rose to my feet, my heart thumping loudly in anticipation of the adventure ahead. Then I remembered someone and my excitement diminished. Benjamin! This would be the first time we would be apart since his birth, and I worried about his welfare. Would he go on hunger strike till I returned?

'Will you make arrangements for Benjamin?' I asked.

'I have already thought about that. He will sleep in my tent.'

My enthusiasm returned and I bowed to my father before departing his tent, a spring in my step.

* * * * * * *

The journey between Hebron and the plains near Shechem is a tedious one: it's almost a day's journey, the terrain is difficult, and the heat of the sun intolerable. Travelling by camel or donkey – the most durable and reliable animals for such a journey – is therefore essential. Our caravan, made up of four donkeys, wound its way along the brutal path at a slow and steady pace. Riding on the donkey beside me was Joram, and tagging along behind, attached to a length of rope, were two other donkeys laden with food and other supplies, including warm clothing, because the open plains get extremely chilly at night.

I had never been to the grazing ground, which is a frequent destination for the sons of Bilhah and Zilpah, but from the stories they've shared, it seems to be well suited for grazing flocks, having grass and an oasis that never seems to run dry. Apart from the occasional threat of wild beasts – large desert cats and hyenas that preyed on lambs which had strayed from the flock – it was relatively safe. The valleys were surrounded by hills that provided a formidable fortress and many clear vantage points from which to spot threats. There was also the threat of skirmishes with other shepherds who used the region, but since the events in the city of Shalem, when Simeon and Levi slew all the men, my half-brothers had acquired a reputation that induced fear in the hearts of other shepherds.

My excitement about this trip was linked to my desire for independence, plus my desire to make a valuable contribution to the way my father's business was run. I also longed to engage in other activities with my brothers, including swimming, fishing and hunting. Most mornings, I was woken by the sound of my father's shofar, an instrument made from a wild ram's horn, which prompted my brothers to get ready for the day's work. I would sit watching enviously as they set off with the flocks, leaving behind their wives and children. Every time they departed I became the man of the house, but I was fed up with bundling sheaves of wheat and assisting the women with all the domestic tasks that needed male assistance. The day I had been waiting for had finally come.

Several times during the journey I had tried to strike up conversation with Joram, but he was a man of few words and our discussions fizzled out almost as soon as they had begun. A large man with a permanently pensive expression, Joram was not renowned for his interpersonal skills. Instead, he was a highly effective administrator who ran my father's business.

'There they are, Master Joseph,' said Joram, pointing at a cluster of trees at one edge of a valley.

Squinting in the direction he pointed, I saw tiny figures moving about among the trees and wondered how he could be so certain of their identity. I said nothing but, as we drew near, I recognised Naphtali and Asher speaking to a bearded stranger wearing the elaborate robes and headgear of a trader. Traders were easy to identify: their headgear was wound around their heads, a loose end dangling over one shoulder. My father told me they wore such headgear to protect themselves during sandstorms as they crossed the Arabian and Western desert trade routes. Traders often stopped over at our home in Hebron, selling their wares from Egypt and Mesopotamia, which included spices, trinkets, fabrics, precious stones, sandals, leather goods and knives, among other things.

Beyond the trees I saw a valley where dozens of sheep, rams and goats grazed on the undulating patchy fields. Meandering around the fields at the base of the valley was a narrow stream where even more livestock had gathered, quenching their thirst.

Hearing the sound of our caravan, Naphtali turned toward us, looking startled. He quickly whispered something to Asher, who responded by steering the trader away from the cluster of trees to a field beyond, where there were at least a dozen heavily laden camels and a number of other traders, speaking to Dan and Gad. I alighted from my donkey, dismayed by the lukewarm reception, and waited for Naphtali to approach us. He now wore a pleasant grin that contrived to assure us that all was well, but it was clearly an act. He had something to hide; they all did.

'Joseph!' he exclaimed affably as we embraced. 'What made Father send you along with the supplies?' He turned to Joram, who stood silently beside me, his gaze on the ground. 'Is everything all right, Joram?'

'Yes, Master Naphtali,' answered Joram, who had always extended the respect he had for our father to all his sons.

'So why are you here, Joseph?' asked Naphtali.

'Because I want to get more involved in the family business,' I answered.

I noticed Gad leading some sheep away from the rest of the flock in the direction of the traders' camel caravan, and counted them. There were seven sheep in all and, from their size, they looked like the cream of the crop.

'That's interesting,' said Naphtali with an awkward chuckle, 'but if you're here, who's bundling the sheaves of wheat and helping the women with their chores?'

'Father sent me,' I said resolutely, making it clear I would not be deterred.

'Okay. I guess you'll be heading back home this evening? You know he can't bear to be apart from you.'

'Actually, I'm staying for the next couple of days so I can understudy you.'

My casual response elicited a surprised stare from my half-brother. That was not the answer he had been expecting. Naphtali had never been any good at hiding his feelings. He was an innovator who had a great imagination and many great ideas that he used to improve the quality of life in our family. He hated repetitive tasks and had a lust for freedom, which meant he was wasted as a shepherd.

'Maybe I should tell the others,' he said, walking briskly away in the direction of the traders' caravan.

'You wait here.'

I was tempted to follow him, but had no desire to complicate matters. Whatever they were up to could not be legitimate. Noticing my other brothers staring at me, their faces unwelcoming, I turned toward Joram with a quizzical stare, silently soliciting his opinion.

'Midianite traders, Master Joseph,' said Joram, studiously avoiding my gaze. 'Your brothers are trading some of the flock in exchange for trinkets and fabrics.'

'Does my father know about this?'

Joram's sideways glance confirmed my suspicions.

'So what do they do with the goods they purchase?'

'They exchange them for alcohol and the pleasures of the Canaanite women in the brothels at Dothan and Shalem, Master Joseph.'

I reacted with wide-eyed horror and observed the dishonest transaction in stunned silence. It became clear why Bilhah's and Zilpah's sons preferred to graze the sheep so far away from home, pretending that they were finding a land overflowing with milk and honey. Part of me wanted to confront them and frustrate the illegal deal, but caution urged me to do nothing. Instead, I remained a silent witness as my father's sheep were handed over to the Midianite traders in exchange for what looked like jars of fragrances and a handful of colourful textiles. As soon as they had taken possession of my father's flocks, the traders mounted their camels and departed in the opposite direction.

'How long has this been going on?' I asked, squinting at my brothers, who were huddled together, conferring.

'I cannot tell you exactly, Master Joseph, but it has been going on a while.'

'And you have never mentioned this to my father?'

I tried hard to suppress the indignation that was rising within me.

'I am mindful of my status, Master Joseph,' said Joram softly. 'Who do you think Master Jacob is likely to believe?'

I grudgingly accepted that he was right. Which servant would have the audacity to accuse their master's heirs of theft? Even if the servant was so bold, he would probably meet with a fatal accident at the hands of the culprits. Then another thought occurred to me: what if Joram was on their payroll and also benefited from their dealings? The possibility gave me goosebumps and gripped me with paralysing fear.

'Do they know that you know?' I managed to ask haltingly.

'Of course, Master Joseph,' answered Joram, 'but they are convinced that my family ties with Bilhah will prevent me from betraying them.'

'Family ties? What family ties?'

'We are first cousins. Our mothers are siblings.'

This was the first time I had heard this, and I wondered if my father knew.

'Master Jacob knows about my relationship to Bilhah,' said Joram, reading my mind.

'If my father knew what was going on here, he would be livid. He needs to know.'

'You tell him,' said Joram soothingly.

'Me?' I stared at Joram incredulously.

'Yes, Master Joseph. Your father trusts you. He will believe whatever you tell him.'

I noticed Asher heading towards the cluster of trees and froze. I waited with trepidation as he drew near, and when we were finally face to face, I met his suspicious stare with the most angelic expression I could produce. My every instinct was compelling me to confront him, but I took the safe route.

'Are you still planning to stay out here?' asked Asher, stroking his silky beard. I could smell the alcohol on his breath.

Asher was well known for having a taste for the good life. He loved to entertain and be entertained. While he was quite hospitable, he was not very charitable, and he spent any wealth he managed to accumulate in looking after himself. I could easily imagine him being at the centre of the illegal transactions.

'Yes,' I answered, glancing at Joram, who casually looked the other way.

'This is not a safe place,' said Asher, looking around him as if he had suddenly detected danger. 'It would be better for you to return home. We cannot guarantee your safety – and you know Father worries about you.'

'That's why I'm here, Master Asher,' interjected Joram in a subdued voice.

Asher's face paled and his furtive eyes darted around. I was clearly an unforeseen obstacle to his plans.

'Joseph, can I have a word with you?' asked Asher, a steely glint in his eye. He steered me towards my other brothers with a firm hand. Despite my resentment at being patronised, I allowed him to usher me away from Joram.

As we strolled away, Joram made as if to follow but Asher glanced back and shook his head.

'This is a private discussion between brothers,' he said menacingly. 'You start unpacking the supplies and prepare the donkeys for the return journey.'

We continued walking towards Gad, Naphtali and

Dan, who were huddled together observing us. From the corner of my eye I noticed my father's servants who worked under the sons of Bilhah and Zilpah herding the flock into a makeshift paddock, indicating that they were stopping work for the day. I found this strange, because the day was still bright enough for the flock to keep on grazing.

'Joseph,' said Gad, smiling warmly as we arrived, 'how was your journey? I see you've come to pay us a visit.'

While he spoke, Naphtali and Dan nudged him. That was my first cue that all was not as it seemed. Gad is not one who initiates; he is a man who always procrastinates and takes a defensive perspective on all issues. He needs a good prod to provoke him to take action, but when he steps forward, he is an effective negotiator, very much like my other brother Judah. It was clear that he had been elected as spokesman for the quartet, and I sensed a deal coming.

'I am here to help out with the flocks,' I said quietly.

'Look, Joseph,' said Gad, who always got to the point once he had scaled the hurdle of procrastination. 'I'm going to be straight with you, okay? We're planning to spend a couple of days in Dothan, so this is not a good time for you to be here.'

I resisted the temptation to ask whether they were going to a brothel. Instead, I asked, 'Are you taking the flocks along with you?'

'The flocks will stay here till we get back,' explained Gad. 'We just need to unwind and relax after what has been an extremely challenging period for us.'

'Can I come?' I had no intention of going but wished to test them.

'No,' answered Gad, fixing me with a benevolent

smile. 'It is a pretty rough place and our father would never forgive us if anything happened to you. However, we hope that we can count on your discretion.'

As Gad spoke, his eyes searched mine and he reached for the leather purse strapped to his waist. He opened the purse and withdrew a couple of gold pieces, which he held out to me.

'What is this for?' I asked, determined to convey my displeasure. 'My silence? So I won't tell Father what I have seen? About how you mismanage his flocks so you can go and have a good time?'

'Look, Joseph,' said Dan, stepping forward, 'we all do it. Even Reuben, Judah and the others fiddle the inventory every now and then.'

'That's right,' chipped in Naphtali, 'you know how stingy Father can be.'

I had heard enough. Even though I had realised that some sort of deal was being done, I had no idea that they would be so brazen. I had half expected them to be remorseful, which would give me an excuse to keep their confidence. A promise from them never to do it again would have sufficed, but in the current circumstance they left me with no choice. I was duty bound to do the right thing.

I stormed off to the cluster of trees where Joram was unloading the donkeys, determined to return to Hebron that evening.

'What if we increase it to six pieces of gold?' I heard Gad call out.

'You should have let him come along with us!' I heard Dan snarl.

'Okay, Joseph, you can come along!' called Asher.

* * * * * * *

Our journey back from the plains of Shechem was a silent one, apart from the occasional braying of the beasts. Before leaving the area, Joram had fed and watered the donkeys for the journey while I ignored my brothers' solicitations and increased bribes. My main annoyance was their failure to show remorse and, as I subsequently discovered, their utter lack of reverence or regard for our father. As our caravan rolled out of Shechem, with Joram leading the way, I could have sworn I heard Dan say something about me receiving a harvest of the seeds I had sown. Throughout, Joram had not said a word or made eye contact with me. Even now, as we trotted downhill into the plains of Hebron, he kept his steely gaze on the path ahead.

Night arrived more quickly than expected, and the star-filled sky and half-moon lit our path. The cool night breeze hinted at the lower temperatures ahead, and I contemplated spending the night sleeping outside my tent after the heat I had endured on the journey. Desperate to be reunited with Benjamin, I hastened.

'They will never forgive you, Master Joseph.'

Joram's first words in almost five hours were startling, despite his soft voice.

I jerked my head around to look at him. 'Are you suggesting that I do not report the matter then?'

'No, I am just informing you, so you can take the necessary precautions.'

'I'm not afraid of them,' I answered defiantly. 'They can't do anything to me.'

'I imagine that's what Abel thought about Cain.'

AN APPOINTED TIME

Habakkuk 2:3

'I don't believe it,' muttered my father, staring morosely at the clay plate laden with pomegranates, olives, grapes, figs and dates that was set before us.

Benjamin and I had joined him for the evening meal and he seemed ecstatic to see me, apparently believing that my early return was evidence of my inability to be parted from him for longer than a couple of days. I had found Benjamin in my father's tent when I arrived. Both had already eaten, but my father insisted in joining me for a snack before we turned in for the night. Seated in the courtyard in front of his tent, the moon shining its luminous beam on us, I eventually informed him of the day's events concerning the sons of Bilhah and Zilpah. Determined that my father should be fully acquainted with their folly, I held nothing back.

'I should have known,' said my father, reaching for a date. 'There have been too many tales of wild beasts attacking the flocks, or of disease striking at the best of my rams and sheep. Even though I had my suspicions, I always believed it was misfortune because I could not prove otherwise.'

'So what are you going to do, Father?'

My father stared at the date between his fingers and then thrust it in his mouth as if that were the response to my query. For the next couple of minutes we ate in silence. Presuming that in his old age he had forgotten my question, I did not repeat it. He was an alert, wise old man, but an old man nonetheless. In the background, a tinkling of bells and a chorus of melodic

---

34

female voices singing songs that I vaguely remembered from our stay in Mesopotamia punctuated the tranquil night. Every evening, the women and girls gathered in the communal tent and practised songs and dances for festivals and ceremonies.

'Nothing,' said my father after a long pause.

The delayed answer took me a while to process. 'But why?' I asked. 'If you do nothing they will continue, and your profits will eventually suffer.'

'Then they will only be using up their inheritance.'

'I don't understand, Father.'

'It is a sensitive issue,' said my father, stroking his beard with his index finger and thumb in a manner that reminded me of my brother Asher. 'If I take immediate action based on your report, I will expose you to more hostility, but they will find other ways to carry on with their activities. They will not stop until they realise that they are stealing from themselves.'

I pondered my father's wisdom and struggled to understand how he could be so calm in the face of such blatant dishonesty. Surely he should be enraged and consider punishments to kick the reprobates in line. A part of me also felt foolish for bringing the report to him. If I had known that he would take it in such a casual manner I would have held my tongue.

'I see you are upset,' he observed, surveying me.

'I had expected some form of punishment.'

'Every seed sown in fertile soil produces a harvest,' answered my father. 'I have told you of the time when, for almost twenty years, I served your grandfather, Laban, looking after his flock.'

I nodded, even though I could not figure out where the story was going.

'Over that period he renegotiated my wages

downward at least six times, but kept increasing my workload. I would have been justified to make up the difference in my wages by selling the animals he placed in my care, but as the God of my father Abraham is a witness, I did not compensate myself using his livestock. Even when one died or was taken by a wild beast, I bore the loss out of my own wages, and even when I was hungry I never killed one of his animals to feed myself. I was totally loyal to him even though he did everything he could to frustrate me. However, when it was time for the God who spoke to me at Bethel to bless me, He turned the tables on Laban and I – legally – dispossessed him of all his wealth. I have since learnt that there is a time to sow and a time to harvest.'

I mulled over my father's words and marvelled at his wisdom as well as his faith in the God of Abraham and Isaac. It was an unshakeable faith, and one that I desired to share.

'I would give anything to have an encounter with God,' I murmured to myself.

'You want to meet an angel?' asked Benjamin innocently.

'Yes.' I laughed.

'I see angels when I sleep,' said Benjamin, picking up some grapes in his tiny fists and squashing them before eating the pulp. 'I'll ask one of them to visit you.'

My father laughed boisterously and patted Benjamin's head. 'Yes, my son, angels visit innocent ones like you because of your clean hands and pure heart.'

'I guess that disqualifies me, then.' I chuckled.

'No, son, but they also visit those who have faith in God,' said my father.

I absorbed this and noted the candour in his eyes,

even though he was smiling. My father really believed that God visited people who had faith. But I didn't know if I had enough faith to attract Him.

*　*　*　*　*　*　*

Harvest-time – three months later

Harvest-time in my father's household was a collaborative effort that required all hands on deck, and it was my role to supervise the bundling of sheaves by my brothers. My father reckoned that, since they were responsible for tending the flocks, the wheat harvest should provide me with my first taste of leadership. I relished being given responsibility like this because it meant I could use my ideas and show my organisational ability without being criticised by my brothers.

To ensure that none of the harvest was wasted through carelessness, I produced a harvesting plan engraved on a tablet, using the standard Canaanite script. The plan called for the family to be divided into teams of four, including all adult men and women. Several teams would scythe the wheat, gatherers would walk behind the scythe teams gathering the wheat into piles, and the sheave teams, made up of men, would follow the gatherers and bundle the piles into sheaves. The stock team, made up of the older women who were renowned for being meticulous, would then walk through the fields, counting the bundles of sheaves.

It was a simple harvesting model but, to succeed, it relied on organisation – and that is what I enjoyed. I made provision for the resident poor to come and glean the fields of all the wheat and grain that was not harvested.

I shared my plan with my father, who studied it

carefully and averted his gaze briefly to dab at the corners of his eyes. I could tell that he was overcome with emotion and that he approved of my harvesting model. While all the harvesting activities were in common use, they had not been combined in the way I had outlined in my model. Before giving me a thumbs-up, my father suggested that I include another team responsible for sifting the sheaves into food and fodder. The poorest quality wheat would become animal fodder, while the better quality would be reserved for personal consumption and sale.

My brothers and their mothers did not welcome the changes represented in my harvesting model but, in deference to my father, they grudgingly complied with the process. I tried to motivate my workforce with the promise of a reward for good work. I had persuaded my father to buy fragrances, fabrics and trinkets for women, Midianite swords and Egyptian sandals for men as rewards. Excitement about my proposed reward scheme spread to neighbouring families, who offered to assist us in the harvest in the hope of receiving a reward. My father grudgingly agreed that a limited number of closely vetted outsiders should be included in the workforce, and purchased even more gifts to ensure there would be enough to go around.

On the first day of harvest, a large workforce was present in the field at the crack of dawn. Working on the belief that a motivated workforce was a productive one, I also offered to provide lunch for the outsiders, much to my father's dismay. My brothers sniggered, particularly the sons of Bilhah and Zilpah, and told me that my strategy was doomed to failure. I ignored them and pressed ahead.

Armed with one of my father's shofars, I got my

teams into position and officially opened the harvest with a long blast on the horn. As the day wore on, everyone worked steadily. To ensure that we had people in reserve in case of fatigue or injuries, I created a roving reserve team that would fill in for any team that was short of workers. My strategy ensured that the harvesting continued until sunset. After the stock teams had done their rounds, they announced that we had accrued the largest daily harvest ever. At this stage my sceptical brothers were no longer sniggering. Those who had deliberately tried to frustrate my efforts by digging in their heels or dragging their feet were instantly replaced with workers from my reserve team, and in this way five of my brothers were sidelined.

At the end of the first day, I handed out rewards for effort. Only Judah and Issachar of all my brothers earned a new sword or sandals. I had had an inkling that Issachar would excel because he was a hard worker who was diligent, disciplined and principled. His industrious nature had come into its own, provoking a response from Judah, who was keen not to be outdone by a younger sibling. Because Benjamin was too young to be an active player, I had asked him to serve water to the thirsty and food to the hungry. I also got him to hand out the rewards as I called out the names. My father sat in his chair at the edge of the family commune watching proceedings from beneath a specially constructed shade fabricated from palm fronds and wooden beams. Although he didn't interrupt, I could tell that he was proud of me.

Later that day, I was heading back from the fields with Benjamin. We had spent some time gazing at the setting sun from a vantage point on top of a nearby hill and soaking up its beauty, and now we were famished and in need of dinner. The sight of all the sheaves of wheat standing upright in the field was inspiring. As we headed back, we were met by some widows from neighbouring communities who carried baskets full of the wheat they had gleaned from our fields. They greeted us exuberantly and bowed many times to thank us for our generosity. I had planned my strategy so that none of the teams scooped up any wheat that fell out of the bundles, and had insisted on them providing more residue than normal so that the poor could have enough. I had replaced Dan with a reserve worker because he refused to leave any wheat for the gleaners but picked up whatever fell out of his bundles.

At the border of the camp, I saw a group of four people standing on the footpath, and we slowed our pace. Drawing nearer, I recognised the sons of Bilhah and Zilpah. They looked defiant. None of them had been rewarded for their efforts, and Dan in particular was looking extremely upset by what he might have perceived to be my deliberate attempt to humiliate him.

'Here comes the pride of Jacob,' said Asher, stroking his beard. He raised the beer jug and took a swig of beer in an ironic toast to me.

'You must be chuffed,' said Dan, stepping forward with his arms folded across his chest. 'I guess things have worked out for you just as you planned.'

I didn't answer. I felt that they were out for trouble and was determined that they wouldn't drag me in. On the outskirts of the camp were armed servants on patrol. It was their job to protect the family. Joram, their commanding officer, was near the entrance, watching us. I therefore felt reasonably safe; besides, I knew none of my brothers would dare lay a finger on me for fear of incurring my father's wrath. They fought among themselves, but none of them had ever threatened me.

'You think you're better than us, don't you?' asked Naphtali, whose innovative strategy for irrigating the land had previously been rejected by our father.

'Yes, he wants to rule over us,' said Gad.

I wanted to say something about working as a team but, realising it would be wasted on them, I held my peace. To my relief, out of the corner of my eye, I noticed Joram approaching. I wondered what had taken him so long. My brothers spotted Joram as well and turned to face him.

'Master Joseph, your father wants to see you,' said Joram when he drew near.

'No doubt he's got a reward for you,' sneered Dan.

Holding Benjamin's hand tightly, I pushed between them and continued towards the camp, Joram beside us. For the first time, I was concerned about my brothers' behaviour, which was borderline aggressive. For a moment, I considered mentioning it to my father. However, recalling his reaction when I had mentioned the sheep theft, I decided not to bother.

'Thank you,' I said, turning to Joram. 'That was quick thinking.'

'Your father really does want to see you, Master Joseph,' answered Joram. 'I guess it was just good timing.'

'Why were they being so mean, Joseph?' asked Benjamin as we walked.

'Because they've drunk too much beer,' I answered, unwilling to trouble one so young with the facts of life.

We arrived at our father's tent, which was the closest to the entrance of our community. Joram headed back to his post. Benjamin and I slipped off our sandals and

I clapped my hands twice to announce my presence, then waited for my father to summon me. As we stepped into the tent, I saw Aunty Leah, her back to me, holding up a garment for my father's inspection. As always my father sat on his wooden chair. He was feeling the fabric of the garment. It looked like a shepherd's coat, but instead of being made of animal skin, it was fashioned from multiple coloured textiles. Even in the dim light emitted from the dung-fuelled lamp, the garment looked magnificent. It was unlike any other I had seen before.

Benjamin and I greeted my father and Aunty Leah, bowing respectfully in the customary manner, and they responded warmly. Glancing sideways at Benjamin, I could see that his eyes were widened in awe at the splendour of the garment in Aunty Leah's hands. I wished it was daylight so that I could more clearly see its patterns and fabrics and fully appreciate the workmanship. I wondered if this was my father's new ceremonial coat.

'Come closer, Joseph,' said my father, beckoning to me with a bony finger. 'Your mother has something for you.'

My father always insisted on calling Aunty Leah my mother. I never protested, even though I knew about the rivalry between her and my late mother. Having said that, Aunty Leah was the gentlest soul in the household and she had never been hostile towards Benjamin or me. If not for the history between her and my mother – her younger sister – I would have no qualms about adopting her as my mother. However, as things stood, I could never see her in that light.

'Yes, Father,' I said. I drew near, my heart beating in anticipation. The robe was really for me? I looked at it:

an exquisitely sewn long-sleeved robe, such as I had seen worn by regional rulers, with ornamental stitching and multi-coloured textiles.

'This is your new coat, Joseph,' said Aunty Leah, with a faint smile that didn't quite hide the pain that flickered across her eyes.

I took the ornamental coat from her, one hand covering my open mouth, too amazed to speak. The fabrics appeared to have been dyed. Knowing how complex the dyeing process was, I could only guess at how expensive the garment had been.

'Go on, put it on,' urged my father. 'Your mother designed and made it especially for you.'

'Actually, your father designed it and got me to make it,' said Aunty Leah in her soft voice.

'Wow!' said Benjamin, as I slipped on the ankle-length coat.

The coat was a perfect fit. I couldn't wait to get back to my tent to admire myself in my late mother's polished copper mirror.

Aunty Leah excused herself, saying that she had chores to attend to. I thanked her again as she walked past me towards the entrance. She responded with a tender, modest smile, disarming me with her humility. I felt a lump in my throat as she left the tent, and wrestled with a pang of guilt about my hesitance at accepting her as my mother. There could surely be no more dignified woman living in Canaan.

'My son, your future will be more colourful than that garment,' said my father, 'and the Lord's rainbow shall provide a banner over you all the days of your life.'

I bowed before my father in submission to his authority, so that his prayer would fall upon me like the morning dew falls on the grassy fields.

'You made me very proud today, son,' said my father, 'and I see in you the greatness of your fathers Abraham and Isaac. May the Lord reveal Himself to you and confirm the brightness of your star, which shall shine a path for all to see.'

I remained where I was until I felt the tip of his staff touch my shoulder.

'It has been a long day, my son,' he said, 'and you need to get some sleep. May all your dreams be pleasant ones.'

As I rose to my feet, an inexplicable sense of purpose came over me, but I couldn't tell what had caused it, the coat or my father's prayers.

*   *   *   *   *   *   *

I stood in the fields around Hebron binding a sheaf of wheat with all my brothers around me, including Benjamin. The sky above was unusually red, like a vivid sunrise. After I had completed my task, I stood in the field next to my sheaf, gazing at the sky. I was mindful of my brothers labouring all around me to bind their sheaves but I felt a strong sense of accomplishment, as you do when you have finished a task and are enjoying a well-deserved rest. The cool breeze that precedes rainfall wafted across my face, lifting my hair. As I lowered my gaze to watch my brothers, to see how far they had got with their task, I noticed that my sheaf, which had been lying on its side, was now vertical, standing proud and noble. All my brothers' sheaves were bowing to mine! I marvelled at the spectacle, wondering what was responsible for it. Then I opened my eyes.

*   *   *   *   *   *   *

Peeping through the thick curtains that covered the

entrance to our tent, I saw that it was almost dawn, so going back to sleep was pointless. When I rose from my bed, Benjamin was still asleep. I took care not to disturb him. My dream had been so vivid that I was able to relive all the details, scene by scene. I even recognised the field I had been standing in – it was the one where, just a day earlier, I had been organising my family to harvest the wheat. It was so surreal: I could recall the exact spot in the field where I had stood.

Driven by curiosity, I hurriedly put on my multi-coloured coat, which was draped over a makeshift wooden rack by the doorway, and emerged from the tent into the deserted moonlit quadrangle. It was still relatively dark, although a hint of sunrise had started to penetrate the gloom. In about half an hour, the shofar would be sounded to awaken the workforce for the second day of harvesting. This was my time for reflection and meditation and I aimed to make the most of it.

I slipped my feet into my sandals and hurried across the open space between the tents, clutching my flapping coat to be as noiseless as possible. At the entrance to our nomadic community, I slowed down so the servants who stood guard with their swords and javelins could identify me. The two burly young men recognised me and bowed. I passed through and headed towards the fields. Making my way between the bundles of sheaves, I tried to locate the spot where I had stood in my dream. When I found it, I looked around to see if the scene replicated my vision. To my dismay, all the sheaves were lying sideways, just the way they had been left the previous day.

I stood for a while surveying the area, noting that the sky looked nothing like it had in my dream, being both greyish blue and moody. I closed my eyes and pictured the scene in my dream, trying to relive the experience and understand what it meant. In the midst of my reverie, I heard the shofar being blown in the camp. In a while, I would no longer be alone. I headed back across the fields towards the camp, pondering my dream. I could not be sure whether it was my imagination or whether I had actually been in this field observing my brothers' sheaves bowing to mine, but it seemed so real that I had goosebumps. Had the dream come from God? This was the first time I had experienced such a vivid dream, or vision. Even though the facts around me didn't corroborate it, I still believed it was real.

A small crowd had gathered around the well to fetch water. From their bickering, I recognised the shadowy figures as my ten brothers. Because their tents were on the periphery of the community, close to the entrance, they had easy access to the well. From the look of things, they were arguing over access to the well. The well was the lifeline of the community, providing water for domestic purposes, for the livestock, and for irrigating the fields. Seeing all my brothers together for the first time in weeks, I hurried over, determined to share my dream with them in the hope that someone would be able to interpret it. I was hoping to see Judah, who was the wisest of my siblings and who often shared nuggets of wisdom with us.

Though day had begun to break and the sun was making an effort to pierce the early morning gloom, it was still too dark to recognise faces from a distance. I therefore slowed my pace to a brisk trot to make it easier for them to identify me. As I drew near the well, all activity stopped abruptly and they turned towards me.

'Who's that?' asked a voice that sounded like Simeon's.

'It's me!' I answered breathlessly. 'Joseph!'

'You can put away the sword, Simeon,' I heard Reuben say.

I heaved a sigh of relief. Simeon carried his sword everywhere because he feared reprisals from kinsmen of the men he and Levi had slain at Shalem. His fear made him alert to potential threats even when none existed and, as my father had observed, it made him dangerous.

'What are you doing out in the fields so early?' asked Zebulun, who was the most charitable and hospitable of my brothers, and the most caring. 'You know there have been reports about a pack of vicious hyenas prowling the area.'

'I know,' I said, scanning their faces for Judah, 'but I had a dream last night. It seemed so real that I had to come out here to share it and hopefully better understand its meaning.'

My remarks drew guffaws and sniggers, but I was determined not to be discouraged by their mirth. I was sure that if I told them about my dream, they'd understand.

'Whoa!' exclaimed Reuben, stepping forward, gazing at my colourful coat. 'What's that you're wearing?'

'Looks like a rainbow!' said Asher.

'So that's where it went.' Dan chuckled, holding his sides. 'No wonder the last rainfall seemed to last forever.'

'Maybe Joseph's been employed by God to show up whenever we have a torrential downpour,' scoffed Levi.

'I like it,' said Issachar, nodding his approval. 'It looks like the coat I saw Mum sewing the other day.'

'Actually, it was your mum who made it for me,' I said without thinking.

A deathly silence descended. For the best part of half a minute, nobody spoke. The day had brightened considerably by this time, so I could see their faces more clearly. My brothers all bore variations of the same expressions – surprise coupled with disbelief. Even Issachar, who had seemed so enthusiastic a moment ago, looked stunned.

'Mum made that for you?' asked Levi, who was usually on the quiet side.

'Yes, it was a gift from Father,' I answered, without pausing to consider the reason for their strange reaction.

'Father asked Mother to make that coat for *you*?' The indignation in Simeon's voice betrayed his strength of feeling, inflaming an already emotionally charged atmosphere.

There was a rumbling of discontent from my brothers, although none of them was overtly hostile or abusive. I registered the mood, but struggled to make sense of it. Why were they so upset that my efforts had been rewarded? After all, father always rewarded them and their families at the end of every harvest for their contribution.

'Come, come, brethren,' said Judah, wading between me and my antagonists with a benevolent smile, 'this is no way to behave. Joseph is our brother and a valuable member of this family. We know how devastated our father was when Rachel died and how he mourned her for many months. We need to appreciate that, to our father, Joseph represents a memorial of his late wife. Any gifts he gives to Joseph are a feeble attempt at preserving that memory.'

Judah's persuasive words had an immediate calming effect on the gathering. While I did not agree with what he had said, I could not deny they had worked to quell a potential lynch mob. I was in no danger of being physically attacked, but from their hostility I felt there was a real threat of being ostracised, something I dared not think about. I loved my brothers and I was grateful for Judah's support.

'We'd better assemble in the fields,' said Reuben, coming up beside Judah. 'The women are already on their way.'

My brothers finished washing their faces and rinsing their mouths. I waited for them to depart, before hurriedly attending to my hygiene and then following them into the fields, where the rest of the workforce had already gathered.

I organised them into teams, rotating people so that some who had carried scythes the previous day went into the gathering teams and some who had been in the sheaving teams moved to the scythe teams. My harvesting model was geared towards building capability across the workforce so we would have a multi-skilled team, ensuring that those who had been engaged in the most physically demanding chores were well rested to avoid succumbing to fatigue and burn-out.

The second day of harvesting was relatively uneventful. To ensure that morale was sustained, I introduced slightly longer breaks and more healthy refreshments for the workers' lunch. And, we beat the previous day's yield by a considerable margin. To ensure that the workforce was well rested, we stopped an hour earlier than the previous day and provided locally brewed beer and a selection of delicacies which went down very well with everyone. I also used the opportunity for some bonding with my brothers, creating an area in the fields where we could be alone with our own refreshments.

Although I rarely drank the Canaanite beer, on this occasion I decided to let my hair down and enjoy my brothers' company; and so I drank. The beer was from our father's personal stash. It was potent, and needed to be treated with respect.

In this relaxed environment, tensions eased, jokes flowed, teasing and frolicking was rife, and laughter was not in short supply. To the casual eye, we looked like a close-knit family who enjoyed each other's company. After a while, even I began to believe the alcohol-fuelled illusion of unity, and my laughter rang out as loudly as anyone else's. My inhibitions gone, I told stories of my own foolishness, to the amusement of my brothers, who readily supplied their own tales. Someone produced an Egyptian board game – one which my father had forbidden us to play because of its links to the pagan worship of other gods. But, in our inebriated joviality, we took turns to play for prizes – and my coat was nominated as a prize. Ensnared, I could not afford to gamble away my coat. I played with intensity and was elated when I was crowned the winner of the tournament.

As we sat back after our entertainment, a fire keeping us warm and keeping wild beasts at bay, I noticed Reuben leave our group and head back towards the camp. Along the way he met a woman whose face was shrouded with a scarf. Despite this disguise, I knew who she was and shook my head sadly. They headed off, hand in hand, for some secret rendezvous, giggling as they went. What I had previously thought to be a one-off was an ongoing affair. Lying on my back alone, looking up at the twinkling stars and the moon that presided over the night sky, I thanked God for paving the way to reconciliation.

'Tell us about your dream, Joseph.'

Simeon's voice shook me out of my rumination and I turned to find him squatting beside me, his eyes glinting. Next to him was Asher, who had a jar of beer in his hand and looked the worse for wear, a dreamy grin plastered across his face. I was considering how best to frame it when out of nowhere Judah appeared with Levi in tow. They squatted down beside me expectantly.

'Yes, Joseph, tell us about your dream,' said Judah gently, 'and maybe we can help interpret it.'

I studied their faces in turn, wondering about their sincerity, but a part of me wanted to speak, to maintain our newfound camaraderie and rapport. With the golden glow of the dying fire providing the lighting, I described in vivid detail how we had been bundling sheaves and how my sheaf had stood erect while theirs had bowed to mine. As I spoke, more of my brothers joined the audience until all nine – except Reuben – were present. As I finished my story I noticed their quizzical frowns and wondered if they had understood a word I said.

There was a thunderous silence that amplified all the night sounds; crickets chirping, owls cooing, dogs barking, hyenas laughing, camels grunting, distant voices chattering, and the nearby fire crackling. Then Judah burst out laughing. All my brothers joined in, and there was a raucous chorus. I sat staring at them, disheartened that they appeared to be making fun of something that had seemed so meaningful to me. As the chortling and sniggering continued, Reuben turned up, looking bemused.

'What's going on?' he asked Judah, who was struggling to control the tears streaming from his eyes. 'What's all the laughter about?'

Judah turned to our older brother, still shaking with mirth, and jerkily told him about my dream, contriving to make it sound as far-fetched as possible. Rather than seeing the funny side, however, Reuben looked pensive. I sighed with relief as I perceived in him an ally – someone who understood the significance of dreams. Maybe I had misjudged Reuben. I looked at him longingly in the hope that he would intervene.

'And why are you all laughing?' he asked sharply, in a voice like the whip across a donkey's back. 'Don't you get it? Don't you understand what it means?'

Judah was the first to sober up. The others followed suit until their laughter had died down and their faces were serious.

'His sheaf standing erect while ours bow down to it means that he is going to rule over us!' snapped Reuben, eyeballing each member of his captive audience before turning to me, looking appalled. 'Do you really believe that, just because you are our father's favourite, that I, his eldest son, will bow down to you?'

The indignation in Reuben's voice spelt out loud and clear that my dream was offensive. I was embarrassed by my inability to see the meaning of my interpretation. What other meaning could it possibly have?

'So, you think you'll rule over us and have dominion over us?' asked Simeon, slurring his words. 'And when is this supposed to take place?'

'After our father dies, most likely,' suggested Asher, stroking his beard.

'Maybe it's not a dream at all,' said Dan, eyeing me like a lion prowling around a stray lamb. 'Has our father promised to leave the greater share of his estate to you?'

'But he can't do that,' protested Levi. 'Reuben's the eldest!'

'Well, our mother was his first wife and the older of the two sisters,' observed Issachar, 'but that didn't stop our father promoting his second wife over her, did it?'

'How many times have we heard him tell the story of how God promoted him over Uncle Esau and how he took the birthright of the first son?' asked Zebulun, shaking his head. 'Maybe he wants to promote Joseph over us in the same way. Look at how he's let him organise this year's harvest!'

Zebulun's comments triggered general murmuring, and the hostility that had reared its head earlier in the day resurfaced. As my brothers filed away from the fields in disgust, I wondered what to do. How could I persuade them that I had no personal ambition to rule over them or receive the portion reserved for the first son?

'Master Joseph!'

Recognising the voice, I turned towards Joram, who had appeared surreptitiously.

'It is not my place to speak,' he said, crouching down beside me so that our faces were at the same level, 'but my heart prompts me.'

'Please speak,' I invited him. Right now, I welcomed any counsel.

'The God of Abraham, Isaac and your father Jacob does not lie,' said Joram, looking me firmly in the eye, 'and so what he has shown you shall surely come to pass. For all things, there is an appointed time.'

I thought about this. Joram had been worshipping

idols in the house of Laban, my grandfather, before serving my father and abandoning those gods in favour of the one true God. He had sturdy faith and was a firm believer in God's plans.

'What do you think I should do?' I asked.

'Tell your father that you wish to spend some time with your Uncle Esau.'

'Why would I want to do that? You know how things are between them, even though they've formally made peace.'

'I believe it would be safer for you if you did.'

'Thank you for your suggestion,' I said dismissively, 'but my father would never agree – and to be honest, I don't want to do that.'

Joram nodded, rose to his feet, bowed and walked away. I watched him until he was out of sight, and then laid on my back with a sigh, staring at the stars. While I believed Joram was exaggerating how much danger I was in, I knew that I had to do something to nip my brothers' hostility in the bud.

THE LAST STRAW

John 15:25

I woke up to find myself lying on my back in a harvested field, staring at a clear sky in which all the great lights were present at the same time. The sun took possession of one sphere while the moon took possession of the other. To see both great lights occupying the same space was a marvel indeed, and I soaked up the splendour as if I had just been served the very best wine. So bright was the light that I could see every star in the universe clearly outlined, yet there were eleven stars that shone more vividly than the rest. Despite the blinding brilliance, it did not hurt my eyes and I was able to stare without blinking, which in itself was a unique experience.

As I studied the fiery surface of the sun and contrasted it with the luminescent surface of the moon, I sensed movement and stared in awe as the globes began to gently glide closer together like two shy lovers on a first date. I watched this spectacle of nature with an open mouth, for never before had any man been blessed to witness what was unfolding right before my eyes. The planets kept drawing close to each other until some invisible hand arrested their progress. As if on cue, the eleven stars drew closer together, as if being drawn by an invisible leash, and they became more prominent until all of them had bunched themselves beneath the moon and sun.

The resulting image looked like a smiling face that was missing its nose. I felt an unspeakable joy sweep over me and settle in my soul, erasing all heaviness and evaporating all weariness. I had never felt better, and my feeling of wellbeing gave me emotional buoyancy that threatened to elevate me above the earth. Out of nowhere another star appeared brighter than all the others, almost matching the combined brilliance of the sun and moon in intensity and growing more prominent than all the other lights on display. The new arrival took up the foremost position and appeared to be elevated above the sun, the moon and the eleven stars, which in unison began to rotate forward and backward as if bowing to this exalted star.

In wonder, I rose to my feet and stood up, still gazing up as the elevated star directed its ray of light towards me, bathing me in its ivory splendour. The star hovered above the place where I stood while the sun, the moon and the eleven stars kept bowing to it. Basking in the glow of my eminence, I stood with a regal bearing, believing that I was worthy of this adulation. Then, without warning, I heard a familiar voice call out my name several times, and darkness flooded the field.

* * * * * * *

'Joseph!'

I opened my eyes at the fourth shout and yawned expansively.

'Were you dreaming?'

I looked around me, blinking furiously, I could see through the gloom in my tent, which was in total contrast to what I'd just seen. Hovering over me was Benjamin's concerned face, his features illuminated by the dull glow of the small oil lamp in his hand. To have been wrenched from a place of such extra-terrestrial splendour to the reality of my earthly surroundings was discouraging.

'Yes, yes, Benjamin, I was dreaming,' I said groggily. 'How did you know?'

'You were talking in your sleep.'

'What was I saying?'

Benjamin's handsome face cracked into a smile.

'You were saying "I can see it now, it's so clear", over and over again. It woke me up.'

What could I see that was so clear? I thought about this while Benjamin left my bedside and went to light the larger lamp. We had two lamps – the smaller for venturing out of our tent at night to the area reserved for our toileting, and the larger for lighting up our tent.

'What did you see, Joseph?'

The question thrust me into the spotlight of inquisition.

'I saw the universe displayed before my eyes,' I began slowly, trying to order my thoughts, 'and I saw the sun and moon more clearly than ever before. Both planets were so vivid that I could virtually see their core without being blinded by their brilliance. But then something strange happened.'

'What?' The eagerness in Benjamin's voice encouraged me.

'I saw the sun and moon draw close together, as if they were about to collide.'

'Did they?'

'No – they drew close enough to occupy the same space but did not touch.'

'Weird.'

'Yes, but it was very harmonious.'

'Hmm, so what happened next?'

'Eleven stars appeared and arranged themselves below the sun and moon so that it looked like the universe was smiling.'

'And one of the stars formed the nose.'

I chuckled. My baby brother had a vivid imagination.

'No – all were neatly arranged below the planets and then another star appeared, one that shone more brightly than the rest, and it stopped in front of them. I don't quite know how to explain it, but it was with them … while also being apart from them.'

'And was that it?'

I hesitated. Benjamin drew nearer with the larger lamp. I cleared my throat.

'The bright star hovered over the spot where I stood … and the sun, moon and eleven stars bowed down to it.'

'What does it mean?'

The words came tumbling out before I could stop them. 'I think it means that I'm going to be greater than all of you.'

Benjamin's eyebrows rose slowly into an expression of disbelief. I could understand this because, as I spoke, somehow, I had received the interpretation of the dream and I knew it was controversial. The sun was my father and the moon was presumably Aunty Leah – my father's sole surviving wife. Bilhah and Zilpah had never been elevated to the status of wives, which would explain why they hadn't featured in my dream. There were no prizes for guessing the identity of the eleven stars – my brothers, including Benjamin.

'I know this must be weird for you,' I began.

'Does this mean you're leaving us, Joseph?' asked Benjamin. 'Are you going to leave me?'

His words threw me. For a lengthy moment I had no response. I hadn't realised that his overriding concern was about losing me. What had given him the idea that I would be leaving home? Had he seen something in my story that I had failed to see?

'Don't be silly,' I said, trying to make light of it. 'Whatever gave you that idea?'

'Your star was apart from ours.'

The answer struck a chord with me. It was a

plausible interpretation.

'No, I am not leaving you,' I said, injecting as much conviction into my voice as possible. 'Why would I? This is my home.'

'But people leave home and they never come back – Mum didn't come back.'

'That's because Mum is with our fathers Abraham and Isaac and with our mothers Sarah and Rebekah, waiting for us to join them in heaven.'

My answer seemed to quell his anxiety and his shy smile returned.

'I'm not leaving,' I said, rising from my bed to hug him warmly to my chest. The joy on his face moved me close to tears.

I headed out of the tent, slipping on my sandals as I went. Outside, in the deserted courtyard, I gazed up at the night sky, looking for the eleven stars and brighter lone star. Though there were distant twinkling stars creating a backdrop for the pale moon, I could not see any prominent stars in their midst. I thought about the interpretation I had received, and my heart thumped with excitement. My father had taught us that dreams were a window into the future and that visions were God's way of revealing things to come. My father had also taught us that a recurring dream or vision, repeated with different images but the same theme, would definitely come to pass. I believed him.

My two dreams had occurred over two nights. Although the images in the dreams had been different, the theme was the same. In each dream my brothers had bowed to me, but of equal significance was the fact that my father and Aunty Leah had featured in the second dream.

This element scared me, as I couldn't imagine a

situation where I would let my father – or even Aunty Leah – bow to me, no matter how elevated my status. I then began to consider what sort of position would place me above members of my family, particularly in a place like Canaan, which was littered with diverse pagan cultures. Was I going to make my father's house greater than it was? Was I destined to expand my small family setting into a city of significance in Canaan? God had promised my father that he would produce a mighty nation and that a line of kings would come from him. Was I the one who would establish this nation? As these ideas revolved in my mind, I became breathless with excitement at the infinite range of possibilities. As my father liked to say, *greatness is written in the stars by the one who created them.*

I strolled across the courtyard towards the entrance to our camp, intending to go to the well to fetch some water for my bath. As I passed Aunty Leah's tent, I heard gentle sobbing. I stopped dead. I had never been one to eavesdrop, but this morning my curiosity got the better of me. Leaning closer to the tent door, I strained my ears.

'My son, you should not harbour such wicked thoughts.'

I recognised Aunty Leah's voice.

'The God of your father frowns on such ideas – do you not remember the story of Cain and Abel? It did not go well with Cain.'

'But at least I shall derive some satisfaction, Mother.'

I recognised Simeon's hoarse voice.

'Reuben is our father's first son and he is the rightful heir. The sons of Rachel will not rob him of his birthright, like Father did to Uncle Esau.'

'And will having his blood on your hands bring you

peace? Cain knew no peace.'

'In time, I shall find peace from seeing order restored in this home.'

'A cursed man finds no peace, Simeon – even his sleep is filled with torment.'

'Then what should I do? Sit still and watch Joseph become our lord and master? Wait until he climbs upon our heads and ascends to greatness?'

'Lower your voice, my son! The stillness of night carries sound and its breeze amplifies the whispers of men.'

What I heard had shocked me to the core. I covered my mouth with my hand to prevent myself from crying out.

'Keep your hands clean and your heart pure, my son,' said Aunty Leah, 'and the Lord will guide you and your brothers into your own seasons of greatness. Just because a naive young lad has a dream, do you think that stops you from fulfilling your own destiny?'

'And what is my destiny? To be a slave?'

'You are one of Jacob's sons. His greatness shall be apportioned to you.'

'Just like he apportioned it to you and Rachel?'

There was silence.

'I am still here,' said Aunty Leah finally, 'and even though I no longer occupy his bed because of age, he respects me as his wife.'

'Like when he asked you to sew that coat for his precious son? Did that make you feel privileged?'

'You forget your place.' Aunty Leah's tone was soft but stern. 'The privilege of childhood is ignorance.'

'I'm sorry, Mother,' said Simeon. 'I was out of line. I'm just so angry at the injustice.'

'Your father is already upset with you because of the

atrocity you committed at Shalem; don't give him cause to disinherit you. Now, you'd better go. It will soon be daylight, when all eyes see and all ears hear.'

I hurried away from the doorway but, rather than head out of the camp, I made my way back to my tent, deeply troubled.

* * * * * * *

The workers showed up in even greater numbers than the previous day. My methods had been tried and tested, the workers knew what they were doing, and there was a seamless flow to their approach. The teams organised themselves according to the pattern of the previous two days, and I was able to delegate responsibility for some of the oversight functions to others, freeing up my time.

As the day wore on, I noticed that my brothers were less involved than they had been the previous day. Some of them would wander off for long periods without explaining where they were going – or why. It occurred to me that they were trying to affect the morale of the workers in the hope that it would slow the rate of progress. They clearly wanted to show that my plan was not working, to discredit me, but I was determined that they would not succeed.

Upset by their general lack of cooperation, I began to replace them with workers from the reserve team, something my brothers resented, and so managed to keep the work on track. By evening, none of my brothers was anywhere to be found. Work progressed. By sunset, we had matched the previous day's harvest, even though it had taken longer to achieve. The mood of the workforce was upbeat because of their achievement, and I distributed even more rewards to those I had seen to be working diligently and those who had been praised by their team leaders.

By the time I left the field I was beaming, elated with the pace of progress in the harvest, planning to report back to my father with the daily record. As I headed to the well to fetch some water, I spotted my brothers assembled around it, which meant I'd have to pass among them to reach it. Undaunted by their menacing presence, I marched forward defiantly, keeping a straight face. If they sensed fear, they would capitalise on it, and I didn't want to give them any leverage. As I meandered my way through them, Dan stuck out a foot, tripping me up so that I stumbled, but managed to regain my balance. I turned to him, anger in my eyes, but he and the others merely sniggered. They were being childish and I was minded to tell them so, but held my peace because of the servants present. I had no desire to shame my brothers in front of them.

I lowered the clay pot into the well, scooped up water then hauled it back up. All the while my brothers watched, mumbling among themselves. I knew their behaviour had to do with my first dream. Having heard Simeon and his mother talking earlier that day, I knew there was no love lost between us. Simeon's great fear – like my other brothers – was of me taking over the reins when our father passed away.

'Hey, dreamer!' called Simeon, as I splashed water over my face and neck to cool down. 'Have you had any more dreams lately?'

I ignored him.

'Has God stopped speaking to you in dreams and visions?' asked Levi.

'What makes you think God spoke to him in the first

place?' asked Dan, chuckling coarsely. 'He's so desperate to convince us that he has a great destiny, because of his rainbow coat that his imagination has run wild.'

'Maybe his coat has magical powers that allow him to live out his fantasies while he sleeps, and when he wakes he believes they're real,' said Asher, joining the rabble.

'Stop deceiving yourself, dreamer!' called Naphtali. 'Your dreams will never come to pass.'

'You're destined for insignificance, just like your mother!' spat out Simeon.

Unable to contain myself any longer, I turned and slammed the clay pot against the side of the well. The pot shattering grabbed their attentions.

'I *am* going to be great!' I insisted, my eyes flashing. 'And I shall be greater than my father's house! Last night I had another dream confirming the first, where the sun, the moon, and eleven stars all bowed down to me. Just in case you are all too slow-witted to know what that means, *you* are the eleven stars!'

I stormed off, upset by their jibes and by how Simeon had dishonoured my mother, and headed straight to my father's tent. I intended to tell him what had happened – and highlight the insult to my late mother's memory – in the hope that it would get them into trouble.

Arriving at my father's tent, I clapped my hands to attract his attention. After I heard his summons, I headed in, still seething. As I went in, I turned to see if my brothers had followed, and saw them making their way into the courtyard behind me. Determined to present my case first, I hastily bowed to my father, who reclined on his bed while Zilpah massaged his legs with balm. Without waiting for him to invite me to speak, I began. I told him about my first dream and my brothers' reaction to it, then told him what had happened today in the fields, including my encounter with my brothers by the well, and how I had been forced to inform them of my second dream. At the end of my incoherent rambling, my father had sat upright and his face had clouded over.

'What sort of dream is that?' he asked, fixing me with a livid stare. 'Are you suggesting that I, your mother and your brothers will bow before you?'

'But, Father, that is what I saw in my dream,' I protested, 'and it was so vivid.'

'No! The only thing that is vivid is your effrontery, for which I must bear the blame.'

His rebuke impaled my heart. This was not the response I had expected. The tables had been turned on me. As his stinging words wormed their way through my thoughts, I was silent. Gradually my anger began to dissipate.

'Is that all you came here to say?'

The question snapped me out of my thoughts. I knew I was no longer welcome in his tent.

'I am sorry if I offended you, Father,' I said, then turned around and headed for the tent door, trying hard not to cry.

He did not respond. His silence told me that he would need time to process the information, then take the appropriate action. I had noticed an evil smirk on Zilpah's face and knew that she would gossip until everyone in the camp knew the details of my dream – and, more importantly, how I had fallen out of favour with my father because of it.

Outside in the courtyard I found my brothers

gathered, all staring at me, their expressions ranging from scornful to hostile. I walked between them, ignoring them, and headed back to my tent. My heart was heavy. With a superhuman effort I firmed my trembling lips, which would have given away my emotional state. I was determined that they would not see me weak and discouraged, lest I fuel their confidence. As I walked away, I could feel their eyes boring through me, drilling holes in my heart. Conscious of their eyes on me, I controlled myself and walked steadily to my tent, where I kicked off my sandals and went in.

It was fortunate that Benjamin wasn't inside the tent at the time; he would have seen my pain and subjected me to endless questions until I broke down and gave in to my fragile emotions. Alone, I took off my colourful coat, folded it neatly on my clothes basket, then laid on my bed, my face buried in the linen sheets, and unburdened my soul with noiseless, heaving sobs.

THE BEST LAID PLANS

Proverbs 19:21

One month later

The month that followed was easily the most hostile time of my life. Buoyed by my father's rebuke, my brothers tried to make my life as miserable as possible through endless baiting and taunting calculated to break my spirit. Looking back at this, I can see that it was one of the defining moments of my life, but at the time it seemed so intense and unbearable. Had I been a weaker person, I would have become a nervous wreck. But I survived. I believe my resilience in the face of adversity is a quality I inherited from my parents – and now it was being refined by God.

My father had served in the household of his father-in-law, Laban – my maternal grandfather – and had endured years of hardship and exploitation. My mother had been barren for most of her married life, and was forced to share her husband with her older sister, as a result of Laban's trickery. Neither of them broke under pressure. Using their lives as my inspiration, I was resolved to enduring anything that my brothers hurled at me.

My father's anger with me regarding the dream subsided as quickly as it had arisen. Though he never apologised for his outburst, his behaviour towards me did not change. I was left in charge of the harvest. My father continued to invite Benjamin and me to his tent for evening meals. He didn't mention the dream again. His manner led me to believe that the matter was well and truly buried and that, as long as I did not share my dreams with any member of the household, life could carry on as usual. Even though I didn't talk about it again, I dwelt on it privately. The fact that my dreams had revealed me to be better than my brothers fuelled my imagination; I imagined myself as a mighty ruler in Canaan who would establish righteous rule in the land and destroy all forms of pagan worship. These thoughts sustained me.

Concentrating on my vision also kept me from giving in to my brothers' needling. I kept busy with my duties in relation to the harvest and stayed out of my brothers' way as much as possible. This was not always possible; some tasks required us to work together. I always maintained a cordial, but distant, relationship with each of them, even though I could sense their hatred for me. Simeon seemed to be their designated ringleader, and he relished having fun at my expense, such as getting the servants to give me misleading messages supposedly from my father, only for me to subsequently find out that they were a hoax.

My father, who seemed to understand what was going on, never took offence, but instead issued a strong caution to my brothers. However, his words carried little weight: my brothers were already set in their ways and determined to cause me as much discomfort and embarrassment as possible.

One day, I woke up to find that my brothers had stolen my coat. I spent the whole morning searching for it, until I finally found it wrapped around the body of one of our sickly donkeys, which was no longer in service. The old donkey had been quite stubborn and the incident had provided my family with much entertainment as they watched my feeble efforts to retrieve the coat from the ancient beast.

If their intention was to break my will, they did not succeed, though there were moments when I felt really down and considered leaving my father's household to learn a trade from one of his trading partners in the city of Ur in Mesopotamia. Ur was a modern centre of commerce where many men went to seek their fortune. I fancied my chances there. There were schools in Ur that groomed traders, who went on to become regional entrepreneurs. The problem was, I didn't think my father would approve of such a career.

My other alternative was to head to Egypt, but that was a daunting prospect because my father had no trading contacts there, and it had an excessively pagan culture that influenced everyone who lived there. I recalled my father speaking about how most Canaanites who migrated there had lost their identity, shaved their facial and body hair, changed their diets, and even adopted their gods.

So, with few options available to me, I decided to seek opportunities at home. With the harvest ended and all the wheat sheaved and being processed, I was redundant. My father kept me at home, away from my brothers, and I grew bored. I longed for a new project to sink my teeth into, but the predictable routine of our family life meant that there were none. I began to spend more time with Benjamin and to share my dreams with him, painting a picture where I was an influential ruler and he was my chief of staff. I am not sure if he believed my fantasies but he certainly seemed to go along with me and was enthusiastic about seeing me fulfil destiny.

* * * * * * *

'Joseph!'

I looked up from the board game I was playing with Benjamin to see my father limping towards me across the courtyard. I sprang to my feet and headed over to meet him. It was the first time he had ventured out of his tent in a long while and it concerned me, because I imagined that he was going to speak to me about something important. As I bowed before him, I began to conjure up all sorts of scenarios. Had someone mentioned to him that I was filling Benjamin's head with fantasies based on my dreams? Had he been informed that I'd been complaining about the lack of activity around the camp? Had he read something in my body language during our evening meals that suggested I was no longer committed to supporting the family because of my dreams?

'Yes, Father?' I enquired as I straightened up.

'How are you?' His eyes searched my face.

'I am well.'

He didn't look convinced, but kept on speaking. 'I sent your brothers to Shechem to graze the flocks several days ago, and now I need to send you to them.'

Mixed emotions scuffled vigorously within me. I was glad to escape the humdrum atmosphere of the camp but sceptical about why he had chosen me to run an errand to visit my brothers, who despised the very ground I walked on.

'Are you up for it?' he asked.

I wrestled with my response. 'Yes, of course, Father, I'm ready and able.'

'Good.' He sounded satisfied. 'I need you to go out there and confirm that everything is well with your brothers and the flocks, then report back to me.'

'Certainly, Father,' I answered. 'I'll go right away. Will Joram be accompanying me?'

My father's eyes drilled into mine. I could see a struggle taking place inside him.

'You'll be going alone,' he said after a while. He reached out his right hand and placed it on my head. 'May the Lord go with you, keep you and guide you.'

After these words, he turned around and limped back to his tent. I waited where I was until he had vanished inside. Part of me suspected that he was trying to find a way of addressing my boredom by sending me on a fairly mundane assignment which could easily be accomplished by a trusted servant like Joram. Another part of me, however, wondered if he was seeking a way to reconcile me with my brothers.

I headed back to my tent to change my footwear to more durable sandals. As I arrived at the door of the tent where Benjamin sat with the board game, I noticed his troubled expression.

'What did Father want, Joseph?'

'He wants me to check on the welfare of our brothers and the flocks.'

'Is that all?'

'Yes, that's all,' I answered with my most reassuring grin. 'Why do you look so apprehensive?'

'I thought for a moment he was going to approve of you leaving for Ur.'

I thought about the conversation we had had a while ago when I shared my second dream with him.

'I'm not leaving home, Benjamin,' I said, holding his gaze.

'Promise?' His face still conveyed his foreboding.

'Absolutely,' I said, crouching down next to him to reassure him. 'That day may come but today, I'm only going as far as Shechem.'

Benjamin's face relaxed and he smiled. We hugged briefly but warmly, and I could not recall a time when I had felt more loved. It is a moment that I continue to cherish.

*　*　*　*　*　*　*

My donkey grunted as we climbed uphill. Digging its hoofs into shallow grooves between the stones to give it traction, it plodded up the treacherous dirt path. I considered dismounting and leading it, but it doggedly fought on until we had reached the top. We were a short distance from the field in Shechem where the flocks were being grazed; I had used the uphill route to shorten the journey and save a couple of hours. The journey was a lengthy one, lasting almost a whole day: my intention was to locate my brothers and the flocks as quickly as possible, check on their welfare, then head back. I hoped to be back in Hebron late tomorrow.

Leaving home, I had been in two minds about wearing my colourful coat. At the last moment, I decided to wear it, reckoning it would make me more visible to my brothers from a distance. Trudging along at a steady pace, we eventually arrived at the cluster of trees where I had been embroiled in the incident with Asher and Naphtali. I dismounted, gave the beast a healthy portion of fodder and a bowl of water, then headed to the valley where the fields were. I looked down into the fields. Even though there were a number of flocks grazing, my brothers were nowhere to be seen. I headed down into the valley, using my staff for support, paused halfway to look all around for my father's servants among the shepherds.

After failing to recognise any of the shepherds, I headed back up to the cluster of trees. There, I walked about the area, scanning every field for signs of my family. As harvest season had ended and watering spots were few, my father had sent all my brothers to graze the flocks. Therefore I was looking for a group of about ten men plus servants and a sizeable flock of sheep, rams and goats. For about an hour, I wandered about the countryside, calling their names through cupped hands, but received no response. Finally, I turned and headed back to the cluster of trees, wondering what my next move should be.

'Hello!'

I whirled around, startled by the voice, and saw a lone figure approaching, riding a single-humped camel. He had seemingly appeared out of nowhere. I waited for him to draw near. He was a middle-aged, dark-skinned man and his camel was a local breed. His local accent was also a dead giveaway.

'Are you lost, friend?' he asked. 'What are you looking for?'

'I'm looking for my brothers,' I answered. 'Ten of them and five servants have come all the way from Hebron and ought to be pasturing a large herd of goats, rams and sheep in this area, but I see no sign of them. Do you happen to know where they are?'

'Ten brothers, you say?' said the man, looking around him slowly. 'Yes, I saw a large company of shepherds here yesterday. In fact, I had a chat with some of them and recall them saying that they were going to Dothan.'

'Dothan?' I enquired. 'Why would they go there?'

'Lush plains,' answered the man. 'The green pastures are great for flocks and there are a good number of watering holes.'

I thanked the man and, after ascertaining the fastest route to Dothan, unwilling to overburden my donkey, I tugged its lead rope and headed north, according to the directions I had been given. My plan was to walk as far as I could before remounting the beast. The man, who turned out to be the owner of the flocks I had seen grazing in the valley at Shechem, seemed knowledgeable about the area and described the geography in fine detail. According to him, trade routes from Mesopotamian and Midianite cities passed through Dothan on the way to Shechem.

The late afternoon sun beat down on me callously and my skull cap bore the brunt of its fury. Thanks to that and the dry, dusty air, I felt dehydrated and had to sip water from my skin flask a number of times. I tripped on the rocky terrain a couple of times and would have fallen, but for the support of my shepherd's staff. Behind me, the donkey, probably grateful to be spared the additional burden of my weight, complied with my every command; this enabled us to make good progress. After walking a considerable distance, I remounted my well-rested beast and trotted on at a brisk pace.

Arriving on the outskirts of Dothan, I noted the gently swelling hills interspersed by vast green fields and a healthy population of trees. Most of the fields resembled large well-kept gardens where even the wild plants and flowers seemed to grow in an orderly fashion. There were species of trees and plants here that I had not seen in Hebron, and the diversity of vegetation had a planned feel. Unlike the undulating terrain in Shechem that had tasked my donkey, the ground here was mostly even and our progress was a lot easier. The man I had met in Shechem had given me directions to a valley where he said most shepherds went to seek pasture for their flocks when the fields in Shechem were too busy or too dry. He was confident that I would find my brothers here because of the accessible water sources.

His directions were easy to follow and I soon found myself approaching a valley with fields demarcated by watering holes, hedged around by shrubs and other overhanging vegetation. As I drew near, I saw my father's flocks spread out in the fields, goats and rams grazing among the sheep, and marvelled at how many there were. This was the first time I had had a bird's-eye view of my father's wealth, and I wondered whether he knew how vast his herd was. Between the fields were clusters of mustard trees with short trunks and low-hanging leafy branches that provided shelter. Behind the fields I could see grey stone buildings rising above the hills in the distance, and figured out that this had to be the city of Dothan.

Looking around me for signs of human life, I spotted my father's servants and a handful of my brothers – Dan, Gad, Asher and Naphtali, guiding the flock to the watering holes. Further away, gathered beneath one of the mustard trees, were Aunty Leah's sons, on the ground, chatting. Neither group had seen me yet making me wonder how best to announce my presence. Though the sun was on the verge of setting, there was still enough light to see, so I reckoned I would still be able to conduct my audit of the flocks and compile my report before nightfall. My plan was simple – leave first thing in the morning and head back to Hebron, bypassing Shechem to save time.

Finding a convenient tree surrounded by healthy-looking grass, I dismounted from my donkey, tied it to the tree, and continued on foot towards Reuben, Simeon, Levi, Judah, Issachar and Zebulun. As I approached the watering hole where the sons of Bilhah and Zilpah were watering the flocks, I called out a greeting. When they saw me, they abruptly abandoned their activity, huddled together and stood staring at me venomously, leaving the servants to carry on with the task. My presence had clearly rattled them and rekindled their animosity to me; however, I had a strategy for damage limitation. Before leaving Hebron, I had made up my mind that I would only talk to Reuben and Judah – the most reasonable and least hostile of my siblings.

'It's the dreamer!' grunted Asher as I walked past. 'What's he doing here?'

'And he's wearing that coat!' hissed Dan.

I ignored the comments and continued walking towards Aunty Leah's sons, who had seen me and were slowly rising to their feet. They didn't look any happier to see me. I noticed Simeon lean towards Levi and say something to him before turning around and doing the same to Judah, Issachar and Zebulun. I yearned to hear what they were saying but was too far away. Reuben, who was in front of the family gathering suddenly turned around and began to address them, gesticulating as he spoke. From his body language, I worked out that there was some sort of argument going on, and slowed to a halt, unsure whether to continue towards them or wait to be summoned. As I watched Reuben address my brothers, Dan, Gad, Asher and Naphtali strolled up from behind and brushed past me to join the others. I wanted to respond with indignation, but held back, recalling my strategy to minimise contact. The sons of

Bilhah and Zilpah joined the other six and the discussion immediately grew heated, with Levi, Simeon and Dan seeming to argue with Reuben. Despite my burning curiosity, I remained where I was, worried that, if I joined their discussion, I might make things worse. It was best for them to resolve their differences.

At what appeared to be the end of the discussion, which was signified by lots of nodding and thumbs-up, Reuben broke away from my other brothers and signalled to me. I walked briskly towards them, smiling pleasantly in the hope of tearing down the walls of division. As I neared the trees, Reuben stepped out to meet me with open arms. His warm-hearted gesture brought a lump to my throat and I responded in like manner, my arms open wide to embrace him. We hugged and kissed each other lightly on the cheek, as was our custom, but as we came apart I felt two sets of hands grip me firmly around the upper arms and yank me away with a force that made me momentarily go airborne.

Simeon and Levi had come up behind me, unnoticed, while I was hugging Reuben. They had positioned themselves, ready to grab me once they received the signal. The hug and kiss were probably the cues. Before I could ask what was going on, Simeon ripped off my colourful coat and tossed it to the ground. Shocked, I struggled to compute what was happening while I searched for an ally in the sea of dispassionate faces that surrounded me.

'Reuben, what's going on?' I asked my eldest brother, who had begun to back away.

His shrug gave nothing away. He was clearly part of the plot. Maybe he was even its architect. I was on the brink of panic, but still too stunned to succumb to full-blown anxiety. Standing, clad only in my loincloth and sandals, my bare torso exposed and vulnerable, I shuddered. What were they going to do to me? I wondered if they planned to thrash me, as I had so often seen them do to stubborn donkeys. Another part of me wondered if they would take turns to punch me, like they did to each other when their arguments escalated. Neither of the options was attractive. Maybe they only wanted to humiliate me by ripping my coat and sending me back home half naked. I prayed this was all they had in mind.

Simeon and Levi frogmarched me forward, each keeping a painful grip on my upper arms, making escape futile. Even if I was minded to escape, my pulverised thoughts were too mangled to construct a sensible plan. Like a lamb to the slaughter, I was propelled forward, the tips of my toes painfully scraping the ground. They walked past the trees and headed towards a stone quarry at the base of the hill leading to the city. The sun had begun to set and the area, which had initially seemed so inviting and pleasant, felt sinister. I was frozen with fear. What lay in store for me? I would have screamed if my senses had not been dulled by the horror of my predicament.

Near the quarry was a cistern – a manmade pit with a circular opening, carved out of stone, usually containing water. As we drew closer to it, their intent became clear. They were going to throw me inside! This realisation triggered my survival instinct and I began to struggle vigorously, digging my heels into the rough ground, trying in vain to halt our progress. Recognising my tactics, Simeon and Levi literally lifted me off the ground and carried me so that my feet no longer made contact with it, even on tiptoe. My wrestling was futile;

they were too strong for me. We were at the edge of the pit now. My heart began to beat more loudly and vigorously, giving me a headache. The circular mouth of the pit was not much wider than my shoulders, and claustrophobia added itself to my fear. I shoved backwards, trying to overbalance them, but their grip remained resolute.

'Please, Simeon,' I implored as my fate stared me in the face, 'Levi, do not do this! You have to let me go!'

I felt their grip slacken, then they let go of my arms. I opened my mouth to express my gratitude but the pull of gravity sucked me downwards with an aggressiveness that was breath-taking. As I slipped through the mouth of the pit into the abyss below, I let out a yell that was swallowed up by my rapid descent. Light became darkness and hope turned to despair. I couldn't see a thing, and I wondered if I would hit water at the bottom. The thought of drowning ramped up my fear and paralysed me.

Without warning, my feet hit solid earth and I fell backwards against one of the rough stone walls that lined the pit, ending up in a seated position. Too traumatised to scream or shout, I sat where I was, looking up at the small circle of light above me and the two shadows around it which I knew were my brothers.

My aches and pains told me I was bruised, the light above me spoke of betrayal, and the depth of the pit told me that I was in a helpless, hopeless situation.

* * * * * * *

After a while – a few minutes? An hour? I have no idea – my curiosity prompted me to take stock of my environment. Gingerly, I felt around the dry, sandy ground beneath me, with a slow probing hand, afraid that I might touch some poisonous reptile or other creature that had made the pit its home. The drop had been sudden and the landing hard, but I could see that the pit wasn't as deep as I had first imagined. I knew I couldn't climb out; the plastered walls afforded no grip. But it meant that my cries for help could be heard by a passing stranger.

I felt around the entire pit. I was relieved to note that there were no other species of residents beside me, and there was no water in it because it was the dry season.

I was in a man-made cistern, carved out of stone. These sorts of cistern were essentially pits that usually contained water which was used for industrial and commercial purposes. In the rainy season, the water gushing down the hill above would follow a man-made gully designed to deposit the water in the cistern. Depending on how heavy the rainfall was, it would be filled in a matter of hours. Because the cistern's mouth was narrower than its below-ground width, the water would be partially shaded from the sun and would not evaporate.

After taking stock of my surroundings, I gradually began to acclimatise. Despite my confusion at my brothers' reckless actions, my fear began to subside. If their plan had been to kill me, Simeon and Levi would have used their swords to get the job done rather than throwing me into a dry pit. Clearly, they wanted to punish me in some way or teach me a gruesome lesson, but their ultimate aim wasn't to kill me. For that, I was strangely grateful. I wondered if Reuben's words to them had anything to do with my predicament. Perhaps he had intervened in some way. Simeon and Levi looked up to Reuben, even though our father favoured Judah over him because of his indiscretion.

Reuben was sensible enough to know how much our father valued me. He knew they could not return home without me. What explanation would they give for my disappearance? I considered this for a while and my courage withered. I imagined they would lie and say that they had never seen me and that I had either got lost or been attacked by robbers. If they could persuade my father that they hadn't seen me, he would organise a search mission, relying on the expertise of Midianite hunters who were expert trackers. They would search the region until they found me, dead or alive. The possibility of them finding my corpse was alarming, and I quickly shut the thought out of my head. Instead, my thoughts drifted to more immediate help in the form of Reuben, who had intervened to spare my life.

I nursed the secret hope that Reuben would come back for me after they had decided that I had suffered enough. This thought gave me a degree of peace. As inhospitable as the conditions were, light at the end of the tunnel – or, in this case, light at the top of the pit – reassured me. Alone with only my thoughts for company, I began to recall the stories my father had told me about when his brother Esau had tried to kill him and he had to flee home under the guise of going to look for a wife. However, many years later when they reunited, all hatred and bitterness were gone and they were able to reconcile. I prayed that my story had a similar ending. Despite their cruelty to me, I did not hate my brothers, and wished above all else to reconcile with them. However, I still firmly believed in the vision that God had revealed to me.

I sat back, closing my eyes, and began to replay my

dreams in my head, going over every detail. Why would God make such an astronomical promise to a man who was condemned to death by his brothers? My father had often said that it was impossible for God to lie, and always gave the example of my great-grandfather Abraham. God promised he would be a father of a great nation, even though he was old and his wife – my great-grandmother Sarah – was barren. The seed of that promise was Isaac, my grandfather. All my great-grandfather had to do was believe God, and his faith was accepted as the evidence of his righteousness. Likewise, all I had to do was believe God.

This reassured me that, one way or the other, everything would work out in my favour. If God did not lie, then I would survive this pit and go on to fulfil the great destiny He had revealed in my dreams. It was clear to me that the ripping of my coat and the trauma of the pit represented a seismic shift in my situation and that things would never be the same again.

Once my father heard about what my brothers had done to me, his punishment would be swift. It would create an even greater rift between me and my brothers. Even if Reuben and Judah persuaded me not to tell my father about the incident, things had changed. My life would never be the same again. Never again could I live with brothers who wanted my blood. I resolved to plead with my father to send me north to Mesopotamia to learn commerce like my great-grandfather Abraham. If he refused to let me go, I would trouble him night and day until he caved in.

I don't know when I drifted off to sleep, but I was startled into consciousness by the scraping sound of something making contact with the walls of the pit. Opening my eyes abruptly, I looked up and saw the bright circle of light above. Initially, I thought it was natural light but as I squinted, I realised it was the artificial light of multiple lamps held around the mouth of the pit. The mystery of the scraping sound was resolved when a thick object struck my left shoulder, hard. I sprang back in terror, wondering what strange creature had assaulted me, and banged my head against the wall. In the distance, I could hear faint voices, and my heart began to beat hard with anticipation.

I reached around me with cautious fingers, trying to determine whether I was alone at the bottom of the pit, even though I could sense no movement or hear any sound. My fingertips brushed against something coarse. I withdrew my fingers again – more instinctively than with any conscious fear. It didn't feel like a living thing, so I reached out again to feel for the object. My heart jumped – it was the thick end of a rope. Someone above had lowered a length of rope to me – help had come! It had to be Reuben!

I scrambled to my feet with nervous exhilaration and hurriedly wrapped the rope around my chest, under my arms, tying it into a knot at one end, then tugged vigorously on the rope to alert them that I was ready. The rope tightened around my chest, making me suck in my breath, and I reached up to grip the rope above me as tightly as I could. As I felt myself ascending, the rope started to sway, making me spin around and crash into the walls of the pit. I placed my feet against the sides of the cistern and hauled myself upwards. As I ascended towards the circle of light, a sense of relief and gratitude gripped me, drawing tears.

My brothers had made their point. In the end it was more than likely that Reuben and Judah had prevailed on them. As upset as I was about their humiliating treatment – which, but for the grace of God, could have resulted in me sustaining a serious injury – I resolved not to confront them about it until we were back in Hebron. I was also determined to report the incident to my father, regardless of what Judah said. Right now I was just relieved at not being left in the pit to die – which, from the look in Simeon's eye, could well have happened.

As I ascended through the circle of smelly, oil-fuelled lamps into the cool evening air, the first face I saw was Judah's, then Simeon's. They gripped the thick rope with both hands, but neither made eye contact with me. Looking all around, I noted the sun was setting fast and a sinister-looking twilight was creeping in. Then I saw them! All around the mouth of the well they stood, impassively, like statues, watching in silence but projecting sufficient menace to make my relief evaporate.

Their faces were bearded, their hook-shaped noses dominated their angular features, and their eyes were unfriendly. There were at least a dozen men. Around their heads was the sort of headgear worn by desert dwellers and traders. Several hands reached for me as I was hauled out of the well, and I noticed – to my relief – some familiar ones. Judah and Simeon helped me out, both avoiding my gaze, then stepped away from me.

Looking around at the faces of the audience, I saw that they were not locals. Their elaborate caftans marked them out as Midianites but their language identified them as Ishmaelites. The sound of camels grunting caught my ears and I saw the long caravan of camels, around thirty of them, loaded with goods and provisions that stretched back to the city of Dothan.

As my brothers stepped away, two of the strangers

began to examine me roughly, using their lamps to aid them. One of them examined my limbs and even had the effrontery to lift my loincloth to examine my private regions, much to my embarrassment. What was going on? I wondered. Why was I being assessed like a slave? As these questions flashed through my mind, the two Ishmaelites continued their rough assessment of my person, examining my mouth and teeth, my eyes and ears, and checking my hair by yanking at it. I longed to shout at them and ask what they were doing, but was too paralysed with fear to utter a word. Several times I had to avert my face due to their odious breath, which was no different from that emitted by their camels. Throughout, Judah and Simeon stood watching, neither meeting my gaze nor protesting.

'He is in excellent condition, Hadar,' said my examiner to another man who was observing from the side-lines. 'You can conclude the deal.'

'Thank you, Tema,' said Hadar, a tall, grey bearded man whose robes did little to hide his fondness for good food.

It was at this point that I realised what was going on. I was the subject of a transaction!

'Judah?' I cried. 'What is going on?'

My brother turned away, focusing on the man named Hadar.

'What is this?' I asked the Ishmaelite named Tema in my own dialect, unwilling to hint that I understood their language. 'Why are you examining me in this way?'

Tema stepped away from me as if he was leaving then without warning he struck me hard across the cheek. The blow almost knocked me back into the cistern from which I had just been extracted, but somehow I managed to stand my ground. I wanted to cry out, but my vocal cords failed me.

'That's enough, Tema!' called Hadar. 'He's not our property yet.'

I noted the single earring in Hadar's right ear which marked him out as the owner of the caravan, and my heart skipped a beat. I had learnt the Ishmaelite tongue from my dealings with them through my father, and I knew a bit about their culture. Most of the traders from Midian were Ishmaelites who had settled in that region and extended their base to the city of Gilead. They traded between the cities of Mesopotamia and Egypt and I had often seen slaves being dragged along as part of their caravans. I watched as Hadar took out a small cloth bag and began to count out a number of glittering pieces, which looked like silver, which he passed to Simeon.

Simeon counted the pieces. Once satisfied, he nodded and tossed the bag to Judah, who transferred the silver to his pockets. I was so amazed by their betrayal that I barely heard the jangling sound – until I felt something cold and heavy clamp around my left ankle. Before I could react, one of the Ishmaelites had fastened another manacle around my right ankle and clamped it shut. The manacles were linked by a length of heavy chain. I thought of trying to resist but, looking at the sheer numbers of the traders, I realised it was pointless.

'Why?' I cried out as Judah and Simeon strolled away and an Ishmaelite fastened copper manacles to my wrists. The copper dug painfully into my flesh. 'Why are you doing this to me?'

Judah and Simeon walked to where my other brothers waited at the border of the quarry; their sardonic stares showed no remorse. I searched desperately for Reuben, but there was no sign of him; maybe he was too cowardly to see the fruit of his handiwork. As the Ishmaelite traders dragged me towards their caravan, I took one last look at my brothers. Bitterness smothered my soul like an avalanche. Realising that I might never see my father or Benjamin again, heartache joined in, jostling for supremacy. I let out an agonising roar from the depth of my soul; then my tears fell.

FROM HERE TO ETERNITY

Psalm 105:13–15

Fifteen days later

Traders from Midian often quote an old proverb regarding the relationship between the first step and the last step of any journey. They say that the journey to the unknown always starts from the known. My father explained the meaning of this proverb to me: if we are to make progress in life, we start from what we are familiar and comfortable with and progress to what is unfamiliar and uncomfortable. The destiny we crave is always located in what is unfamiliar and uncomfortable. I don't know the origin of this proverb, but I've heard it said on many occasions and each time, I think of my father. He left the familiar comfort of his home to travel to the unfamiliar discomfort of his Uncle Laban's home.

There is another proverb, however, that I know the origin of, and it is one that my father used often. He always says that intention starts a journey but determination finishes it. This resonates with me because it speaks about purpose.

My father has always lived his life intentionally, and this is how he tried to raise all his children. In my short life I have therefore tried to live intentionally, rather than indifferently. An indifferent lifestyle produces indifferent results. My Uncle Esau lived indifferently and led a commensurate lifestyle. My father always taught us that success is not an accident; rather, it is the product of a deliberate investment of time, energy and commitment. He emphasised that no shortcut to wealth ever produced a lasting legacy.

Traders are a resilient bunch. They have to weather challenges and obstacles in their quest to earn a living. They are restless by nature, incapable of spending any length of time in one place. One can imagine that, as children, they were the sort who found it difficult to stick to parental instructions that ran contrary to their nature. They also live their lives intentionally. Traders are not the sort to leave things to chance: they don't believe in accidents, coincidences or luck. They take calculated risks that are geared towards maximising their profits and every investment, like a seed sown in good soil, is intended to yield an excellent harvest. Successful traders rarely invest in anything they do not think will produce a healthy return. They trust their instincts, but rely mostly on experience and knowledge.

The Midianite traders are a curious community because of their great diversity. Of all the traders in our region, they are the most successful because they refuse to stick to one trade. There are no specialists; they diversify. A merchant who trades in spices, fragrances, textiles, gold, ivory and trinkets will at the same time trade in livestock, grain or slaves if he thinks there is a profit to be made. This is not a random commercial model, but a highly flexible and profitable one that allows traders to hedge their bets, thus protecting themselves against uncertainty. It is for this reason that Midianite traders prosper in the midst of famine, while others flounder. The key to their success is a diverse population. Their cities attract people from all over the region, who settle there and pool their collective wisdom into building a more economically dynamic environment. The Ishmaelites are just one of many tribes trading under the Midianite banner. Their trade networks are varied and their versatility enables them to switch trades fluently without breaking sweat.

Hadar's caravan fit the mould of the Midianite trading model. As I was later to learn, Hadar didn't own the caravan to which I was now chained; rather, he was the caravan's manager. The owner of the caravan was a Midianite entrepreneur who had leased the camels to Hadar and owned the trading contacts between Mesopotamia and Egypt. He had been a caravan manager who eventually earned enough to go into partnership with other former caravan managers and build a successful business. My knowledge of these affairs came courtesy of Tema – the Ishmaelite who eventually became my friend.

The transformation from tormentor to acquaintance came on the seventh day of our trek across the trade route to Egypt when one of the caravan's hands, a young Ishmaelite named Massa, forgot to remove the key from the lock of the manacles that bound the slaves together.

I'd better explain.

I was not the only slave in the caravan; there were a good number of healthy young men and women who had been purchased along the coastal slave trade route from other parts of the world. They included bronze-skinned Assyrians and Sumerians, lighter-skinned Anatolians and others whose origin I could not make out, both male and female. They were picked up along the way after our departure from Dothan and kept in the human cargo section of the caravan. In addition to the copper manacles around our wrists and ankles, we were linked by chains fastened to the manacles around our necks. This considerably impacted on our pace, despite some of the more fatigued slaves being rotated and relegated to the back.

The rotation cost us time, as we were soon almost half a day behind schedule. As I subsequently learnt, we were heading for an auction in a city known as Men-nefer in the region of Lower Egypt, where we were due to be sold. The caravan was incredibly well organised, with every trader or trading hand being assigned a specific task as well as leadership roles. Massa – the Ishmaelite trading hand I mentioned earlier – was a pleasant enough young man who treated the slaves well, despite the boisterous nature of a handful of the Sumerian slaves.

Sumerians have a proud history – for instance, they invented the twelve-hour day – but today they are greatly diminished in significance and population, due to the ravages of war. Survivors dwell in poverty-stricken rural communities where they earn a living plying the northern end of the Euphrates–Tigris river basin.

From the moment the Sumerians joined the caravan on the second day of our journey, I sensed there would be trouble, judging from their cuts and bruises and the challenging behaviour they displayed, both to the traders and to other slaves. They complained loudly in guttural dialects that I barely understood. I later discovered that they were skilled sailors who had been sold to repay debts owed by their families. They would be sold in Men-nefer to work on Egyptian galleys that patrolled the Nile, as there was a high demand for their skill.

On the evening of the sixth day, the Sumerian ringleader became tired and had to be rotated to the back of the caravan. Massa suffered a momentary memory lapse. When he rotated the ringleader, he forgot to remove the metal key from the lock of the man's neck manacle. This enabled the ringleader to loosen his neck manacle. During the night, as we camped in the desert under the dark, moonless sky, he undid the manacles around his wrists and ankles. His freedom secured, he then proceeded to liberate a handful of other Sumerians who, like him, had feigned fatigue, to be rotated to the back of the caravan. Rather than sneak away from the caravan with stolen camels, they instead prepared to attack the Ishmaelites, but I happened to spot them and instantly alerted Tema.

I was exhausted from walking all day in the heat, and had become weak. From walking, I regressed to shuffling, staggering and eventually crawling. After being dragged on my bruised knees for a short distance – to the great discomfort of others around me – I had to be rotated to the back of the caravan along with the Sumerian conspirators. When their ringleader rescued his comrades, he also liberated me; he had no choice really, because I was chained to them by the neck. At the time, I was borderline delirious because water was in short supply and we had not drunk for hours.

In my semi-conscious state, I saw them get ready to attack. Fearing that I would be implicated with them if their plans failed, I yelled for Tema with my last ounce of strength. Tema, who happened to be several camels ahead of us, about to settle down for the night, reacted instantly, drawing his sword and rushing to the back of the caravan. There was a brief scuffle, which I heard rather than saw, followed by a couple of bloodcurdling screams, then silence. The following morning, when I regained full control of my senses, I was informed that the ringleader and another Sumerian had been beheaded and left in the desert for vultures and hyenas to feast on. The others had surrendered. After being suitably chastised with a whip as a lesson to others, they were re-shackled and threatened with death if they slacked in pace again. They didn't.

From that morning, Tema became my friend. The perks of having the lieutenant of a trading caravan as your new best friend were considerable. For instance, my diet was improved and I was given a selection of dates and exotic fruits, along with a better supply of water than the other slaves. On a couple of occasions, Tema even shared chunks of meat from his rations with me. While I was still manacled at the ankles and wrists, and therefore painfully restricted in my movements, I was no longer chained to other slaves. This meant that I could slow down to rest whenever I felt like it, and walk alongside Tema's camel. At each oasis, I was allowed to drink my fill before other slaves. The ultimate privilege, however, was the length of linen cloth that Tema gave me to wrap around my head during the worst of the afternoon heat.

As we approached the outskirts of Egypt, travelling along the coastal route, where the surface was more sandy than rocky and more generously endowed with oases, Tema restored my neck manacle and slotted me in with the other slaves, but away from the Sumerian contingent, who still blamed me for the deaths of their fallen comrades. I didn't mind. Over the last ten days I had enjoyed an overwhelming sense of God's presence. My trip had been far from pleasant – I had blisters on the palms of my hands and the soles of my feet, as well as bruises from the manacles where the metal dug into my flesh – but it could have been worse. There had been a sandstorm on the tenth day that almost buried us, and resulted in the death of a camel. Also, a couple of slaves had died along the way, one Assyrian woman and an Anatolian man, one from dehydration and the other from disease. Even as we abandoned their bodies for the scavengers, I couldn't help thanking God that I wasn't one of them. It wasn't my determination to survive that had preserved me, but God.

* * * * * * *

We arrived at Men-nefer almost twenty days after my brothers had hauled me out of the pit and sold me to the Ishmaelites. For the last four days I had marvelled, despite the grimness of my circumstances, at the cosmopolitan modernity of Egypt. The architecture was breath-taking, as were the pyramids and monuments that adorned our route to Men-nefer. I was especially impressed by the gateway to Men-nefer, which was dominated by two massive statues of a seated man and woman, carved from dark grey stone. The statues cast long shadows across the sand, and there people took refuge from the blistering heat. Neatly planted palm and date trees lined the roads, as well as the banks of the all-important River Nile, which was always visible. At one point, our journey took us along the Nile's banks and we saw boats constructed from reeds, carrying people in different directions. The mood of the Sumerian contingent became animated as they saw the tools of their future employment, and it seemed for a moment that they had forgotten their fallen comrades. The Nile has a very pleasing ambience, with trees overhanging the river at points, along with colourful, gorgeous plants that reminded me of my precious coat.

As for the people who passed us – on foot, on horse, in mule-drawn carts or chariots – their appearance could not be more different from that of the conservative people in Hebron. They were all well-groomed, and both men and women used kohl to line their eyes.

I marvelled at the fact that men were typically hairless and clean-shaven. Most young women I saw paraded around with decorative wide collars over their breasts, and close-fitting garments covering the lower part of their bodies, while older ones wore full-length garments that covered them from chest to ankle. The men wore kilts and left their hairless chests exposed. Some men wore decorative jewelled broad collars and a handful wore longer garments, like tunics. The more prosperous wore sandals of leather or reeds, but the majority were barefoot. The contrast with my community in Hebron was striking as I wasn't used to seeing people clothed in such delicate fabrics. As I trudged along in the caravan, I couldn't help noticing the variety of ethnicities we passed. There were dark-skinned Nubians, whose athletic strides captivated me. I had only seen a dark-skinned person once before – a muscular man during a trip to Shalem with my father – but I'd never forgotten my first impression of his beautiful dark brown skin. I also identified a number of Cushites by their bronze complexion. They were a shade lighter than the Nubians, but their dress code was very similar, with men in loincloths made from animal hides and wearing necklaces fashioned from beads and precious stones. I even saw a couple wearing leopard skins across their torsos. Their women wore long, colourful, close-fitting garments, their silky black hair either plaited or braided and decorated with beads. Nubians and Cushites wore gold or bronze armbands, bracelets and anklets that glistened in the sun. Some of the women also wore nose rings.

Compared to Hebron, Shechem, Dothan, Bethel and other Mesopotamian cities I know, Egypt is on a completely different scale. Its infrastructure is much more advanced. I could see evidence of the Mesopotamian influence: the buildings were similar in appearance – flat-roofed and constructed of mud and clay. All buildings were single-storey and built close together. We walked past other suburbs where there were huge grand white houses which I later discovered were made of stones and granite. These homes, which had several storeys, were close to the Nile and were obviously for the very wealthy.

The caravan slowed to a halt at a major road, where mule-drawn carts and horse-drawn chariots streamed past in either direction. We all watched Tema's hand, waiting for his prompt. My gaze strayed from his hand and drifted to the other side of the road … and my heart skipped a beat. Walking towards us with the aid of a shepherd's staff was an elderly white-haired man with a pronounced limp. From his clothes, I could tell he was from either Hebron or Bethel. The nearer he came, the more I began to see my father's face superimposed on his. The resemblance was uncanny. Convinced beyond all reasonable doubt, I opened my mouth to shout 'Abba!' But the words died in my throat as the man came close enough for me to see that he was blind in one eye. His nose was also misshapen, and his forehead was the wrong shape. My heart sank, dragging my mood down to the depths of the pit in Dothan.

I felt a sharp prod in the small of my back and realised that it was the Anatolian male slave behind me. The caravan had begun to move and I quickly shuffled forward to keep up with the smelly, slow-moving camels ahead. From this point onwards, my fragile frame of mind dampened my enthusiasm and, despite the fascinating sights we passed, my thoughts centred on my father and Benjamin. I started to feel guilty for neglecting to think about them and for being overawed by the magnificence of Egypt. I remembered my new status and the circumstances leading up to it, and fresh tears of self-pity, mingled with despair, trickled down my dusty cheeks till they made contact with my fuzzy beard.

So engrossed was I in my sorrow that I barely noticed the point at which the caravan split in two and the traders with camels laden with spices, fragrances and other goods headed along a different route under Hadar's command, while Tema and some of the trading hands guided us in the opposite direction. It didn't occur to me to enquire about the reason for the separation, but I later understood that it was because the goods had to be placed in cool storage in a different part of town.

Our long trek concluded on the outskirts of Men-nefer at a large fortress-like building with a gated entrance. Images were engraved on the walls, depicting bare-chested figures in loincloths, engaging in all kinds of manual labour under the watchful gaze of a figure carrying a whip. On the walls bordering the entrance gate were hieroglyphs engraved in smaller script. I read them slowly, mouthing the words to myself, unaware that Tema, who was riding on a camel just ahead, was watching. When I was much younger, I had learnt to read and understand hieroglyphs from a roving Sumerian scribe who had studied the art and visited homes in Hebron teaching it for a living. I became quite proficient in the art and memorised at least two thousand signs before the scribe left for Mesopotamia, where he could earn a better living. Though two thousand was less than half of the actual number of hieroglyphs, it was enough to allow me to read most basic text. The inscription on the wall announced that this was the Great Slave Auction House, then went on to set out guidelines for sellers and purchasers visiting the place.

'You read Egyptian script?'

I looked up at Tema, who had stopped his camel and was staring down at me. His pensive eyes triggered an imp of fear within me. What should I say? Was it forbidden for slaves to read?

'I saw you,' said Tema with quiet persistence.

'I'm sorry,' I said gently, lowering my gaze. 'I promise it will not happen again.'

'So you do read?'

I considered his question. Why was he so interested in whether I could read hieroglyphs? From deep within me, a boldness emerged. 'Yes, I do, but I still have a lot to learn.'

'How many scripts?'

'Just over two thousand.'

'Are you a fast learner?'

'Yes,' I answered without thinking. I was a quick learner but I had no idea what standard I was being measured against.

Tema dismounted and walked back to me. Taking the key out from beneath his robes, he unlocked my neck manacle and gently tapped my upper arm for me to step out of the line. I obeyed his prompt and stood to one side, struggling to understand what he was doing. I didn't feel like I was not in trouble, but his face gave nothing away. He drew out two other slaves – an extremely attractive, olive-skinned young woman and a powerfully built, bronze-skinned young man, both of Assyrian origin – then waved on the caravan. The young man and woman had been picked up at an oasis along the way from another caravan that was heading towards the Red Sea. Tema signalled to Massa.

'Stay with them,' said Tema, aiming his thumb in my direction.

Tema left us to attend to the caravan. I watched him go over to the gates and bang on them repeatedly with his fist until one opened. He walked in ahead of the caravan and spent a while inside before coming out with four bare-chested Egyptians clad in loincloths, wearing striped headscarves. He stood aside as the four Egyptians took charge of the slaves, leading them into the fortress-like building. After the gate had shut behind them, Tema returned to where we stood and his features became relaxed.

'You will fetch a higher price than that lot,' he said, looking pleased. 'Very rarely do we purchase a slave who can read hieroglyphs. Reading is a highly valued skill in this society because literacy is reserved for the scribes and other privileged people.'

His remark began to give me a glimmer of hope. If he sold me to a scribe, I could prove a useful assistant. Working for a scribe would ensure that I avoided manual labour, and this gladdened me.

I was led back to the caravan with the Assyrian man and woman. As we reached it, to my surprise, he unshackled my manacles, freeing my wrists and ankles from the agonising pain that had plagued me all along the route. However, while the young Assyrian woman was also unshackled, the young man was left in chains. I concluded that it was probably because of the man's size that Tema saw him as an ongoing threat. Because of the heat in the desert and the temperature of the ground, my feet had swollen and started to blister. Likewise, my wrists had increased in size so that the close-fitting manacles dug into my tender flesh, branding me with their mark.

'The camel at the back is yours,' said Tema. 'Do you know how to ride a camel?'

I nodded quickly, even though I was more familiar with donkeys and mules. The fast pace of events had caught me unawares. What was going on? Why had my shackles been removed, and why was I being upgraded to riding on a camel?

I went towards the camel and stood there, staring at my new mode of transport, wondering if this was a test, expecting Tema to change his mind. Massa, recognising my hesitance, gave a command to the imposing beast, which slowly went down onto its haunches, tucking its limbs beneath it. I mounted the camel and took hold of the reins as the Ishmaelite repeated the command and it rose to its feet. Behind me, the Assyrians were seated on another camel, the woman holding the reins. Ahead of us, Tema mounted a hairy two-humped camel. As he rode towards me, he grabbed the reins from my hands, steering my beast in the direction he was headed.

With Tema leading the way, our lighter ten-camel strong caravan made its way into the heart of Mennefer. From where I sat, I had a commanding view of the city. Thoughts of my father and Benjamin tried to seep in again, but I pushed them out, recalling the unbearable sorrow I had experienced earlier that day. The sun was beginning to set over the city, and the hustle and bustle had calmed down.

As twilight settled over the city, we arrived at a

nondescript building in the shadow of a colossal statue of a majestic-looking man with a slender goatee, wearing an imposing head-dress and seated on what looked like a throne. All around the statue were huge, strategically placed copper-plated oil lamps that brightened the statue, making it clearly visible throughout the city. As we rode into the courtyard, I kept looking back at this marvellous sight, fixated by its arrogant splendour.

'That is Pharaoh,' said Tema, following my gaze. 'He is ruler of all Egypt and the most powerful man in the land. He is like a god to the people and his word is law.'

I nodded slowly. I had heard about the king of Egypt from passing traders who told us tales of his lavish lifestyle and awesome power. The stories had almost sounded mythical at the time, but the statue behind me was undeniable evidence of their reality.

We dismounted our camels in a specially designated area of the courtyard where some men were stationed, as if waiting for us. They immediately took away our camels, leading them to stables. It was clear that this place was to be our stopover for the night, and I deduced that it had to be a guesthouse. There were eight of us in the caravan and I wondered whether there would be enough accommodation for all of us. My concerns were, however, laid to rest when I stepped into the building and noted the number of doors along corridors set over two floors. If each door represented a room, then there was more than enough space.

Tema seemed to know his way about and was also quite popular with the guesthouse proprietor and his wife, who welcomed him – and other members of our entourage – warmly. From their appearance, they were not Egyptians, but I couldn't place them until they began to speak. Tema conversed with them in the dialect familiar to people living around the Euphrates–Tigris basin, which I understood because it is derived from Hebrew. I therefore guessed that they were Midianites. The guesthouse owner assured Tema that they had reserved the whole of the top floor for us, along with a communal room where we would be fed. Tema asked the man's wife to arrange for a local physician to come over, as I was in need of urgent medical attention. Hearing this alarmed me because I did not feel ill and had fully recovered from my dehydration.

As we climbed the stairs, I relayed my concerns to Tema who had a good laugh and explained that the physician was coming to attend to the bruises and cuts I had sustained from my manacles during the journey. I cast my mind back to Tema's earlier remarks when he discovered that I could read hieroglyphs, and realised that I was being prepped for sale. My value would undoubtedly increase if I was well presented and had an appearance to match my purported pedigree. No doubt I would be sold as the child of royalty to some scribe who would pay the asking price in the belief that he was getting something unique.

I was reunited with the Assyrian slaves and we had a bath in a communal washroom where servants waited with containers full of cool water. They repeatedly splashed water over us as we rid ourselves of the dirt and grime of our long trek. Once we were clean, the servants provided us with white loincloths then we reunited with Tema and the other traders, who led the way to another room, furnished with benches made of tough bamboo and covered with thin cushions. Here we sat, while another set of servants trooped in carrying platters and trays laden with food.

Despite the hostility of our situation, to my surprise we were served bread seasoned with seeds and fruit, succulent meats flavoured with spices, figs, dates, exotic fruits, lentils, cucumbers and melons. I was reminded of the fattened cows that my father bred to entertain his special guests and became wary.

Initially, I had little appetite and merely picked at my food, while my companions stuffed themselves with anything they could fit into their mouths. Sudden homesickness gripped me, affecting my mood and ruining any appetite. My gnawing hunger dissipated. Eating felt like a betrayal of my father. As the evening progressed, however, my resistance gradually wore down, and as my hunger resurfaced, I ate my fill of meat. Although I ate guiltily, this did not rob the meal of its savour. The more I ate, the guiltier I felt, till at one point I was prepared to repent and confess my sin. I despised my weakness.

After dinner, some scantily clad women arrived, accompanied by men carrying instruments that included lutes, lyres and harps as well as drums and stringed instruments. I learnt from Tema that the women were dancing girls who had been hired to entertain the traders. At this point, Massa ushered us to our quarters.

My room was small, furnished with a single bed, a narrow window overlooking the courtyard. There was an empty spot on the floor where a rug had been placed. As I prepared to lie down on the bed, my escort curtly informed me that the bed was for him and the rug for me.

I had barely closed my eyes when a knock on the door destroyed my hope of an early night. The elderly, stooped man in traditional Egyptian attire was the physician. I surrendered to his care, watching as he unfurled a papyrus which he studied for a moment before opening his bag and taking out several jars containing lotions. The physician applied lotions and ointments to my bruised flesh, particularly around the wrists and ankles, until my skin began to respond.

Ignoring the disagreeable odours coming from the medication, my aches began to ease so I had greater mobility and dexterity in my limbs. The quick-acting potions had done the trick, providing almost instantaneous pain relief. The physician was still attending to me when I drifted off.

CASH & CARRY

Psalm 22:1, 2

When I woke the following morning, I was permitted to have a lavish bath to remove the last traces of desert debris from my person, and thereafter my teeth and tongue were cleaned with a strange potion which was applied with a sponge made of Nile reeds. I was also subjected to a facial, where my beard and eyebrows were trimmed. I was presented in a white linen tunic and sandals made of tough reeds. By the time they had finished sprucing me up, I felt more dignified, despite the gruesome nature of my situation.

Tema inspected me. Only when he was happy did he instruct that a new set of chains be placed around my ankles, but not my wrists. The new manacles were slightly larger, allowing my circulation to flow unrestricted. I was then taken to a waiting room and reunited with the young Assyrian slaves who, like me, had been groomed for sale.

Unlike many of the nations between the Red Sea and the Euphrates, I learnt that Egypt doesn't have a slave market – at least, not one in the accepted sense. In these nations, slaves are stripped naked and sold in bazaars where interested customers bid for them like livestock.

In Egypt, low-skilled slaves are taken to the Great Slave Auction House. It is like a prison for slaves, who are housed in large cells that are leased by the sellers. Most slaves are brought to the auction house a day before the sale and placed in the cell leased by their owner.

There are different categories of slaves at the auction house, including those who have voluntarily offered themselves for sale to settle their debts. Indentured slaves – those who are legally bound to their masters or mistresses – are not transferred via the auction house. Transactions involving indentured slaves are dealt with via the legal system, which also caters for those who are enslaved because of their failure to abide by the terms of their apprenticeships. I have also learnt that some extremely poor families sell their children into slavery to raise money to feed their other children.

The sale itself is a private affair and is strictly by invitation. A person cannot just turn up to the auction house to buy slaves. The sellers already have interested buyers on standby and notify them once their cargo is in the country.

Once the slaves are sold, the seller pays an auction fee to the Great Slave Auction House and the purchaser also pays a revenue fee which is collected by the auction house on behalf of the Pharaoh. Under Egyptian law, the Pharaoh gets a cut of every transaction of human resources – as they are known.

My own experience revealed that there are various tiers of slave auctions, and that skilled slaves are dealt with in an even more private arrangement that may take place in a person's home depending on that person's wealth and status. Because my skill in reading and writing hieroglyphs was in great demand, I was not taken back to the Great Slave Auction House but to the courtyard of our guest house, where Tema was convening a private viewing.

The young Assyrian slave woman's hair had been braided and she wore a long white linen gown. She was also wearing make-up, but this did nothing to lift her downcast expression. The young Assyrian man only wore a loincloth, but his powerful body had been polished to perfection with scented oils so that every muscle was clearly defined. I tried to guess what his role would be. What was his skill? When Massa was not occupied, I cornered him and enquired about the Assyrian.

'He is a skilful lion tamer,' whispered Massa. 'His new owner will use him to train leopards and other wild cats for sale to the wealthy.'

'And what about the woman?' I enquired, since I had his attention.

'She is a seer – one who communes with spirits. She will be sold to someone who will make much money from using her as a fortune teller.'

After he'd departed, I marvelled at how inaccurate I'd been. I had figured that the man would be a bodyguard, due to his size, and the woman would be a courtesan, because of her great beauty. My father had always cautioned me against judging the taste of a fruit by its appearance. It was clear that Tema was arranging a highly skilled slave auction. Despite my misgivings, I grudgingly acknowledged the brilliance of his strategy. He was clearly an astute businessman. Scribes, lion tamers and seers possessed rare skills that guaranteed more money for whoever purchased them.

'You carry a presence.'

I swung around to the Assyrian prophetess who had just spoken.

'You carry what we call the unseen presence,' she explained, her unwavering gaze resting calmly on my face.

Her casual voice did not seek to persuade me, but her

tone had a compelling quality..

'The unseen presence? What are you talking about?'

'I perceive that there is more to you than the eye can see, and it has to do with the spiritual presence surrounding you like a wall – fortifying you.'

'You're making no sense,' I said, waving a hand dismissively.

There were seers in Canaan who dabbled in the dark arts and went from city to city, reading the fortunes of men in exchange for a fee. Most of those who dabbled in mystical matters communed with dark spirits and worshipped idols. My father had labelled them con artists and warned me never to have anything to do with them. These prophets, or seers, went around gleaning information about a person then offered their services to him. They asked their unwitting victim a series of questions, then gave a prediction of his future life. However, even my father acknowledged that there were a handful of genuine seers who had been given a rare prophetic gift by God. This made them valuable to those in authority. The gift in the seer responded to whichever spiritual path they chose to follow: if they followed the God of Abraham, then their gift would be exposed to the light, but if they submitted the gift to the pagan gods then it would be exposed to darkness. I sensed that this woman belonged to the darkness, but had no way of proving it.

'I am simply relaying what I perceive,' she said quietly. 'I carry a strange gift that was in my mother and her mother before her. It opens my eyes to the elements and draws my attention to certain phenomena.'

'I don't believe in that sort of thing,' I answered scornfully.

'And I suppose you don't believe in dreams.'

I hesitated. I did believe in dreams, but only the ones I was confident were given to me by God. Because I regularly commune with the God of Abraham through prayer and meditation, I can tell when He is speaking to me. As my father has taught me, God is not visible to those who are outside the covenant, except when He chooses to reveal himself to them, as he did to my grandfather, Laban, who was pursuing my family with an evil intent towards my father. God appeared in a dream to my grandfather, who was a pagan, and warned him not to harm my father.

My father had also shared with us previous incidents where God had appeared in dreams to two pagan rulers who wished to violate my great-grandmother. In the dreams, God warned them not to touch her. As I pondered the seer's words, a voice I recognised penetrated my thoughts, warning me not to respond to her, so I held my peace. It was a voice I trusted.

'You believe your dreams will come true,' she continued, her lifeless hazel eyes boring through my thoughts, 'but you do not even know what they mean. How do you know that your interpretation of the events you saw is correct?'

This time, I did not hesitate. 'Because the one who revealed them to me also assured me that He would bring them to pass.'

'And you still believe him?'

'Yes, because He never lies and nothing is too hard for Him.'

'But what about the betrayal?'

'What betrayal?' I feigned ignorance.

'The betrayal that brought you here.'

'He never betrayed me,' I said staunchly. 'I was

betrayed by those who repaid my love with hate – just as you were.'

The intensity of my answer appeared to have silenced her, because she averted her gaze for the first time. Her head lowered, and she studied her chained wrists in the subdued manner of one seeking a new source of inspiration.

In a strange way, I felt sorry for her, because she was controlled by forces that dictated what she should think and say. She was in two types of bondage – first, to the spirits possessing her, and then to those who were exploiting that state of affairs for financial gain. If I had the power to liberate her, I gladly would have. In Canaan, there were people who specialised in exorcism and performed rituals to cast out devils from those in bondage. My father wrote them off as charlatans who cast devils out of a person only to unwittingly invite others in to take their place. With no hope of liberty, bondage for the seers is a carousel of misfortune.

We did not speak again. I spent the time mulling over the events of the past twenty days, wondering whether my father had organised a search party for me yet. I recall my father once sending us out to search all the neighbouring fields for a missing donkey – we had no rest until we eventually found it. If my father could kick up such a fuss about a missing donkey, a beast of burden, was I his beloved son not more deserving? Would my father's search party be able to track the Ishmaelite caravan's route?

From the waiting room, I had a good view of the courtyard. Massa, who was going back and forth between the courtyard and waiting room, informed me that a large ceremonial hall adjoining the guesthouse was where the actual auction would be convened. An hour after my discussion with the now subdued seer, prospective purchasers started turning up on camel, in horse-drawn chariot or by mule-drawn cart. One person even turned up in a stylish ceremonial litter with an elaborate canopy, carried by four muscular Nubian men. There were at least thirty people in all, a mixture of men and women, although men outstripped the women two to one. From their appearance, they were all obviously Egyptians, and from their attire I could tell they were rich. The women were more elegantly attired than the men and their jewellery and headgear more exquisite. I watched Tema ushering the prospective purchasers into the adjoining hall and noted that Hadar, who had been conspicuously absent the previous evening, had also shown up. Although Hadar came into the waiting room to inspect us, he remained very much in the background, leaving all the arrangements to his lieutenant.

A growing apprehension enveloped me as I watched our prospective owners arrive. I engaged in a private game of elimination which involved singling out the people I least desired to serve, based purely on appearance. In the labyrinth of my convoluted thoughts, I had a mental image of the kind of master or mistress I would be most comfortable serving, and that person resembled my father. I wanted an employer who would treat me humanely and reward my efforts, one who would respect my right to worship my God, not their gods, and one who would also give me a guarantee of freedom if I were to fulfil certain requirements. In return, I would serve such an employer to the best of my ability and would ensure that, by the time we parted company, I left him – or her – better off than when they first engaged me.

Shortly afterwards, Massa turned up with another of Tema's servants, a burly Nubian fellow, even larger than the lion tamer. Massa winked at me and tried to grin reassuringly, but he ended up looking awkward. Like me, he was a servant, albeit one with more freedom. In reality, his situation was no better than mine.

As they led us to the ceremonial hall, my anxiety increased. Before the end of the morning, I would be heading off to a strange home in a strange land. In all probability, I would be valued no higher than a good or chattel, and be used in service until my value depreciated to zero. More agonising was the thought that I might never see my family again and that when I died, it would be in some lonely cold grave where the memory of me would fade away faster than the maggots could erode my flesh. With these negative thoughts flooding my mind, my heavy heart prompted tears to spill out of the corners of my eyes.

* * * * * * *

A rotund, dark-skinned Egyptian with fat, greasy fingers prised open my lips as if he intended to rip them from my face, and began to crudely probe my mouth. His rough appraisal of my tongue and teeth made me feel sick, and his foul breath worsened my condition. I tried to avert my face, but when that failed I switched to breathing through my mouth. Having concluded his inspection of my face, he started to examine my limbs, squeezing my upper arms as if he expected me to miraculously sprout biceps. He continued to violate me in this manner, treating my thighs and knees to similar crude exploration. He then stepped back, shaking his head, clearly not thinking me good value for money. I was elated. He approached Tema and spoke in quiet tones, gesticulating as they conversed. My heart rate decelerated as I noticed Tema shake his head. No deal.

The auction had begun as soon as Massa had arranged us in the centre of the room. One by one the invited bidders came forward to inspect us. I had been expecting Tema to make a short speech introducing us, but apparently the prospective purchasers had already been briefed. Each held a papyrus in their hands which no doubt contained our details. It was an organised affair, with none of the mobbing that occurred at slave markets, where several people would typically tug and pull one slave at the same time. The dark Egyptian with the rough hands was the fifth person to inspect me, and it made me wonder whether he had even bothered to read the papyrus which outlined my skillset as a scribe. What had my physical condition got to do with my abilities to read and write hieroglyphs?

A sixth purchaser stepped forward. I heaved a sigh of relief. She had been one of those on my list of preferred bidders. Her shoulder-length silky black hair crowned a slender face with kind-looking brown eyes and the sort of mouth that looked as if she was permanently smiling. She was a middle-aged woman and wore minimal make-up. It blended well with her jewellery, which was restricted to a broad necklace. Her ankle-length sleeveless gown displayed modesty in its simple cut, and she exuded an aura of being refined and educated. She looked me over, but made no physical contact. Her eyes conducted the inspection. When we eventually made eye contact, there was a benevolence there that reminded me of my mother. I began to earnestly pray that she was the winning bidder.

At the conclusion of the visual assessment, she raised her left hand. In it was a rolled-up papyrus which looked to be of the highest quality. Under my father's tutelage I had learnt that there are various grades of papyrus and just by looking at a sheet, I can tell its quality from its colour and texture. The whiter, finer, smoother and more refined it is, the higher its quality.

She unravelled her papyrus sheet and held it up before my face. The papyrus was littered with neatly ordered hieroglyphs set out in two columns. While the etchings were not the handwork of an expert, I was able to slowly read through the text. The wonderful thing about hieroglyphs is that even though they originated from Egypt, they can be understood by educated Canaanites, who translate or interpret them in the relevant Canaanite language. I therefore started to read the hieroglyphs in the general language spoken in Shechem and Bethel, but a quarter of the way through my task, the lady cut me short with a raised hand then summoned Massa, who hurried over. She then signalled me to resume. Realising her difficulty, I started from the beginning while Massa translated. As I read, she smiled and nodded. The document simply set out various recipes for meals and their origin, but I recognised that if I was to be her slave I would need to quickly learn the local language.

At the end of my reading, the lady beckoned to Tema. When he came over, she drew him to one side and they spoke in hushed tones. From the way Tema was nodding, combined with the smile on his face, I was confident that a deal was being struck. I was so focused on their discussion that I failed to notice the tall, elegantly built man with the cold expression who came up beside me, studying me intently. As I spotted him out of the corner of my eye, I turned and started. He was one of the people on my list of undesirables.

Even though he was a good-looking man, his face was cruel. He was slightly taller than me and had an athletic build. His hairless torso looked like it had been baptised with glistening oil, and his colourful kilt barely hid his loins. He had a single lock of hair dangling down the right side of his otherwise shaven head, with the obligatory kohl under the eyes. His upper arms were adorned with brass bands, and similar bands graced his wrists. He had an arrogant profile with an upward-tilting chin so that he looked down his nose at me, forcing me to look upwards.

'You read very well,' he said suddenly in the native Canaanite tongue.

'Thank you,' I said quietly, trying to mask my disappointment.

'You are from Bethel?'

'Hebron,' I replied without thinking.

'And you can also write?'

'Yes, but I am a bit rusty.'

'No problem. You will have plenty of opportunity to practise. Are you familiar with accounts ledgers?'

I nodded cautiously. I had been responsible for keeping my father's books in relation to his livestock and was also in charge of collating the figures produced by the women who supplied the harvest inventory. I did not know whether the Egyptian model was more complex than the Hebrew one, but was confident that I could quickly learn it.

'Good, I think I can use you.' He turned to Tema, who appeared to be concluding his discussion with the elegant lady, and said, 'Send this boy to my house.'

As Tema saw him, he bowed low and the lady with

him also.

'Yes, Captain Potiphar,' said Tema fawningly.

I watched my preferred purchaser leave the auction room, and my heart sank as I realised that I wouldn't be leaving with her. Clearly, the man next to me had to be someone of significance to elicit that sort of reaction. Without even putting in an offer he appeared to have bought me, and with a single instruction had reduced Tema to a humble serf. Tema snapped his fingers at Massa, who hurried over, bowing to the prospective purchaser.

'Captain Potiphar has just bought the boy,' clarified Tema, 'so I need you to arrange for him to be transported to his house in Men'at Khufu – you know where it is?'

'Yes, on the way to Waset,' replied Massa. 'Last year I took two female slaves there.'

'Good,' said Tema urgently. 'Leave the boy in the care of Onamun, the head servant.'

As Tema finished speaking, he turned to the man named Potiphar and bowed again.

'Captain, the boy is highly skilled,' said Tema slavishly, 'and it is quite difficult to find slaves as literate as him. The cost of locating such a slave, in addition to his exorbitant purchase price, means that I need to sell him at the right level so as not to be out of pocket. I was therefore hoping we could agree a sensible price that represents a modest profit for me and value for money to you.'

'How much?' asked Potiphar. 'Name your price.'

'Well, Captain, the lady was about to pay me fifty shekels of silver,' he said quietly as if he expected to be rebuked.

'Then I shall pay you fifty shekels,' said Potiphar,

removing the cap from his signet ring. 'Payment on delivery; bring me the bill of sale.'

Tema produced a papyrus on a short wooden plank. Potiphar affixed his signet ring to it, leaving the impression of his seal at the bottom of the sheet. A lip-splitting grin worked its way across Tema's face as he saw the seal. Even without knowing how much Hadar had paid my brothers, it was clear to me that he had made a huge profit. As Massa led me out of the auction and back to the empty waiting room, a fresh set of tears began to drop – not tears of anticipation, but of revelation.

RITE OF PASSAGE

1 Corinthians 13:11

Potiphar's house was in the upmarket southern suburb of El Akhet on the outskirts of Men'at Khufu. As the mule-drawn cart carrying me approached the house, I marvelled, in spite of my heavy heart, at its architectural splendour. It was a vast white complex with a grand entrance that stood out in the sea of other imposing homes in the area. Unlike homes in the heart of Men-nefer, which are compact and built close to each other, those built in Men'at Khufu are spaced out and occupy more land.

El Akhet is an area reserved for very senior government officials and priests, and it boasts an impressive array of communal features, including wide palm and date tree-lined boulevards, generous enough for four chariots to ride abreast with dedicated areas for pedestrians, which is not seen in Men-nefer. There were also a number of water fountains and pools, statues of Pharaoh and various Egyptian gods, scaled-down replicas of pyramids and a prominent obelisk carved out of dark basalt that towered above all the buildings. Being set close to the Nile meant river views. The banks were lined with beautiful flowers whose colours were complemented by the colourful hieroglyphs painted on many residential and communal walls. As I later came to learn, painting hieroglyphs on walls attracted significant rivalry as neighbours tried to outdo each other in the artistic stakes.

The people commuting – on foot, in horse-drawn chariots, mule-drawn carts or litters carried by men – all looked physically healthier and stronger than those I had seen at Men-nefer. Their clothing and jewellery proved their affluence, and their arrogant profiles provided insight into a class structure that, as I was to learn, pervaded Egyptian society. The rich and poor don't mix, and the difference in their respective living standards is staggering. Even the servants in El Akhet looked better fed and presented than their social equivalents elsewhere.

Before setting off on the long trip from Men-nefer, Massa removed my chains and instead bound my wrists with thick ropes woven out of coarse dried-out papyrus. Fortunately, my ankles were spared the indignity of being bound, so I was able to walk rather than shuffle. It did occur to me that with my ankles unrestrained I could make a bid for freedom and hope to find mercy under the protection of some influential stranger, but another part of my brain cautioned against such a foolhardy enterprise. I was in a strange land whose culture and customs were alien to me – even if I succeeded in escaping, it might be to a worse situation than the one I now found myself in.

For the journey, I was bundled into the back of a mule-drawn cart driven by Massa. For company I had an athletic dark-skinned Cushite slave named Abali who seemed to permanently stare into the middle distance. He avoided eye contact, despite my efforts to catch his attention, and unlike me he was still bound in chains around the wrists and ankles. I later came to understand that this apparent discrimination in treatment was a precaution due to the fact that Cushites are excellent hunters and skilled in a variety of weapons as well as hand-to-hand fighting. I also came to learn that Cushites were at the forefront of almost every uprising by servants or slaves in Egypt – a statistic that meant that they represented an ever-present threat. They were mostly used in construction and farming where their ability to navigate a cattle-drawn plough was incomparable.

As we travelled through El Akhet, I noticed Abali's reclusive mood change: his eyes seemed to glitter in fascination at the beautiful surroundings. A semblance of a smile graced his lips and his tense limbs seemed to relax slightly. For the first time, we made eye contact. Even though no words were exchanged, the atmosphere was more affable. Upfront, Massa had acquired the status of a tourist guide and made it his duty to describe the areas we were passing through, explaining the significance of some of the religious and cultural landmarks. It was not clear whether Abali understood the Canaanite tongue, but his intelligent eyes reflected a level of comprehension.

Potiphar's house was the most outstanding in an ocean of outstanding buildings in the El Akhet area, and this communicated his level of influence in Egyptian society, more than rank or title. It was a magnificent complex of glistening white stone buildings, mostly single-storey, built around the central residential building: an elegant villa with four columns supporting the protruding balcony above. The white building was bordered by palm trees and the entrance to the double front doors was a grand affair, with a wide stairwell leading upwards from the shaded porch.

As I later discovered, it also had a large pool to the rear, in which Potiphar reared exotic species of fish. The palatial building was home to Potiphar's family and was divided into quarters: women occupied one section and men occupied the other. There was a dedicated area for the stables, where Potiphar bred various types of horses, and another sectioned area with stacks of bundled straw and wheat where his mules and camels were fed. The servants' quarters, as I came to discover, were in a separate building above the stables. Like the main building, it was divided into male and female quarters. The servants shared rooms as well as communal bathing facilities. Though there was no running water, there were at least two wells that tapped into subterranean water from the Nile, and these supplied water for cooking, washing and bathing. All this I discovered in my first day at the complex.

When we arrived at the gateway, we were halted by two Egyptian soldiers, each armed with a sword and javelin. While one of them kept the tip of his javelin aimed at Massa, the other came around to the back of the cart and climbed up to inspect Abali and me before poking around the straw around us with his javelin, as if expecting to find some form of contraband or harmful weapon. Only when he was satisfied were we given the all-clear and allowed to proceed into the complex. Rather than heading for the front door, Massa guided the cart around the side of the main building towards the stables and servants' quarters, where we were unloaded.

We were met by a fit middle-aged man, whose unsmiling eyes surveyed our faces. He towered over us, compelling us to look up at him. His dark leathery skin, shaven head and kohl-adorned eyes could have passed him off as an Egyptian, but his features appeared to be mixed race. Like most men in the El Akhet area, he wore a white kilt, but his torso was bare and his upper arms and wrists bore engraved brass bands.

It appeared that we were expected, because no

words were exchanged between him and Massa. From a leather pouch around his waist, the man produced a small hide-skinned pouch which he handed to Massa. Massa spilled the silver pieces into the palm of one hand and counted them. Satisfied, Massa placed the pouch in his own bag and handed the man a long metal key. The man clapped his hands twice and two young, tanned men in white loincloths appeared. They loosened my wrist bonds and Abali's wrist chains, providing a partial feeling of freedom. As Massa climbed back up onto the wooden bench at the front of his cart, he smiled congenially at me.

'It is going to be all right, Joseph,' he said softly. 'Potiphar's a good man. He treats his slaves well and rewards loyalty.'

I wanted to say something. I wanted to tell Massa how meaningless his words were to someone who had no hope of ever seeing his family and homeland again, but I held my tongue because I didn't believe he had the emotional intelligence to appreciate my predicament. My words would be wasted. The reality of my situation was now vivid. I had to adapt to the first day of the rest of my life.

I watched Massa steer his cart towards the front entrance, feeling as if my past was drifting away from me. It was only a firm grip on my shoulder that snapped me out of my reverie. I turned towards the owner of the grip and looked up into his frosty gaze.

'I am Onamun,' he said, in a tone that radiated the same wintry temperament.

I nodded, not quite sure how I was expected to respond.

'I oversee this household on behalf of our master, Potiphar,' he went on, 'so that means you work for me.'

I nodded again.

'I will give you a tour of the areas of the house you have access to, explain the rules, then show you to your quarters. Your induction begins tomorrow.'

My third nod was curt. It seemed to meet with his approval, because his face softened a smidgen. He was clearly a man who loved to wield authority. I registered this detail and knew that if I was to survive under him, it would require a substantial degree of subservience. As long as I kowtowed enough and performed his instructions to the letter, I wouldn't have any problem with him.

As Onamun escorted Abali and me around the stables, the servants' living quarters, the administration building where the hired scribes worked, and the ground floor of the palatial main building, he explained the house rules. Servants were confined to the areas of the house relevant to their functions; servants worked from sunrise to sundown with two half-hour breaks during the day; servants were not permitted to speak to each other while working; servants could not speak their own language on the premises; servants were not allowed to receive visitors at any time, even when they were off duty; servants had to eat what they were given and could not help themselves to food; servants were confined to their quarters after sundown; male servants were not allowed to fraternise with female servants at any time; Cushite and Nubian servants did not share sleeping quarters with other servants; the consumption of beer or wine by servants was strictly prohibited; and servants were not allowed to openly worship their gods.

Despite the clarity of the house rules, one of them bothered me so, in spite of all my instincts screaming at me to keep silent, I spoke.

'Why aren't we allowed to serve our gods?'

'Because it is the house rule,' he retorted, 'and all servants must comply.'

'Does that mean we have to worship the Egyptian gods?'

'The master does not insist on it,' he answered, much to my relief.

I resolved to continue worshipping the God of my fathers in the privacy of my quarters. Another question came to me as I processed the house rules, and again I ignored my instincts.

'Why are the Cushite and Nubian servants not allowed to share sleeping quarters with the others?'

'Because they are inferior,' answered Onamun without hesitation.

Part of me was offended by this response, and wanted to inform him that my God had created all men equal, but I knew that I would be pushing my luck, so I bowed to my instincts. A slave had no voice in Egypt.

We were shown around certain areas of the ground floor of the house. I was captivated by the amazing artwork on the tapestries and murals as well as the skilful hieroglyphs etched by first rate artisans. The flooring was of polished precious stone, as were the internal columns, and though the chambers we were allowed to view were sparsely furnished, everything was tastefully done. In all, we viewed about ten chambers, although I later discovered that there were fifteen on the ground floor and another fifteen upstairs in the private living quarters. The delicate-looking carved wooden furniture was of the highest quality, with the chairs in particular incorporating ornamental artwork.

At the end of the tour, Abali and I were taken to the courtyard near the servants' quarters, where all the servants ate. When we stepped in, it was clear that the servants' practices exceeded the stringent house rules, as female servants sat in one corner and male servants in another. In addition, the darker-skinned servants sat apart from the others. I was immediately uncomfortable with this arrangement. When we walked in, the buzz of voices died down and all eyes were upon us: some curious, some disapproving, others indifferent, but none admiring or friendly. They were the eyes of those who had seen it all and who had given up on the prospect of seeing anything new. When Onamun invited us to join the other servants, Abali whose ankles were still chained, shuffled towards the other dark-skinned servants, but I reached out to touch his arm. He turned to look at me with an enquiring gaze, and I inclined my head in the direction of a space between both groups, then squatted on the ground like the others.

Abali hesitated for a moment then, to the disappointment of most of them, he squatted next to me. His bold action triggered a fresh bout of murmuring among our audience, and I imagined that they were talking about our audacity, which flew in the face of the domestic protocol. Abali's tense expression relaxed into a faint thin-lipped smile and his eyes softened.

My father was against racial discrimination and had brought us up to understand that all men were descendants of one ancestor, Noah, who was the father of all the families of people upon the Earth. My father had also reminded us that because of our father Abraham, we were one day going to be part of a larger community comprising people from all the families on the face of the Earth.

'Thank you,' said Abali in a thick accent. He spoke the Canaanite dialect from the Red Sea area, hinting that he was well travelled, despite his appearance.

'What do you do?' I asked as a light-skinned servant girl set a platter of food and bowl of water before me, giving me a dirty stare as she departed.

'I am a farmer,' he answered quietly. 'I used to grow grapes and produce wine.'

Seeing that the girl did not return with food for my companion, I proffered my platter to him and he helped himself to some of the dried fruits and vegetables. We ate silently and shared the bowl of water until the same servant girl turned up some time later with a platter for him, which contained far less food than mine, as well as a smaller bowl of water. Abali received his platter then tipped its contents into mine so we could continue eating from the same platter.

'So, what do you do?' he asked, growing in confidence.

'I have been a herdsman, a farmer and a trader,' I said, 'but I have been brought here to work as a scribe.'

Abali smiled grimly. 'You are a privileged servant then,' he remarked. 'As a scribe, you will avoid all hard labour.'

I didn't respond, because I knew what he said was true. While he would be breaking sweat ploughing Potiphar's vineyards, I would be indoors crafting documents. At the end of the meal break, the other servants filed out of the room and Onamun returned for us. As we stood to meet him, his frown spoke volumes.

'Are you not familiar with the protocol for meal breaks?' It was a rhetorical challenge.

'We are,' I said, meeting his cold stare unflinchingly,

'and that is why we did not sit with the female servants.'

'And what about the division between dark-skinned and light-skinned men?'

'But I thought that only applied to the sleeping arrangements.'

My response caused him to do a double-take, and he stared intently at me, as if searching for signs of impudence. He opened his mouth to speak, but then shut it abruptly and led the way out of the courtyard at a brisk pace so that we struggled to keep up. With his ankles chained, Abali gradually fell behind, and I had to slow down several times to wait for him as he shuffled along. Onamun navigated a path that brought us to a rear entrance. Once outside the walls, we found ourselves in a vineyard where some of the servants who had been eating in the courtyard a short while ago were manning cattle-drawn ploughs.

'This is where you will both work,' he said flatly, gesturing to the vast expanse of land.

Believing that he had made a mistake, I spoke up. 'But I am supposed to be a scribe, Master Onamun.'

'You will be working in the fields,' said Onamun brusquely, 'seeing that you enjoy the company of Cushites and Nubians.'

It became clear to me that I was being punished for having the effrontery to disregard the house rule.

'But that was not what Master Potiphar said,' I protested.

I had barely finished speaking when the back of Onamun's hand struck me squarely across the face. I staggered back under the impact. He followed up with an open-handed slap that nearly knocked me out. The force of the two strikes drew blood from my nose and my split upper lip. As tears welled in my eyes, I learnt a valuable lesson: in this house, Onamun was my master.

'You will work alongside Abali,' said Onamun, turning his attention back to the vineyard with a nonchalant air.

In spite of my pain and the blood trickling into my mouth, I muttered an affirmation.

'You will also both study and master the Egyptian language,' said Onamun, strutting around with his arms behind his back. 'From tomorrow, I will stop speaking to you in the Canaanite tongue.'

Wondering at the impossibly high hurdle he had placed before us, I was minded to protest that no one could start speaking a new language overnight, but the pain in my face jogged my memory and I held my peace. Abali, who had been silent all this while, spoke, but in a language that I could only presume was the Egyptian dialect. I watched Onamun's reaction to Abali's words: he flinched, then stiffened, clearly caught unawares by the Cushite's revelation.

'It would seem that our dark-skinned friend already speaks the Egyptian tongue,' said Onamun after a momentary silence, 'so he can be your teacher.'

I nodded and continued to soothe my upper lip with my tongue while gently tweaking my nostrils to stem the flow of blood.

'You have a month,' said Onamun, glaring at me contemptuously.

We were led back to the now deserted courtyard where we had eaten our meal, and left there under the watchful gaze of one of the residence's Egyptian guards. While we sat in silence, leaning against a wall, another servant showed up with a long metal key and unlocked Abali's shackles. With the chains removed from his swollen ankles, Abali's mood improved and his expression brightened considerably. This incident opened my eyes to the universal truth that no person was born to be in chains. I truly believe that chains bind our souls and produce greater rebellion than the potential insurrection that they were installed to prevent.

'If you are smart, you can learn the basic dialect in a month,' said Abali once we were alone again. 'Onamun is just trying to put you in your place because he feels threatened by your education.'

'I realise that now,' I said with a deep sigh, 'but doesn't Master Potiphar have the final say on what happens to us?'

'In wealthy Egyptian households, the head servant runs affairs. The master does not interfere because he trusts his head servant to manage the others.'

'So I could be in the fields for as long as Onamun decides?'

'Yes – it is how they tame you, in the same way that a wild horse or camel is subdued. The intention is to break your spirit and mentally force you to your knees.'

'But I am already on my knees.'

'Not yet you're not,' muttered Abali wistfully. 'Not until any rebellious instincts have been purged from you and subservience becomes your new nature.'

The same words spoken less ominously might have been less unnerving, but I began to suspect that they were not merely speculative and that Abali had already been in the system. His knowledge of the local dialect should have alerted me.

'How long have you been in Egypt?'

'Too long,' he answered, once again gazing into the distance.

My enquiring gaze spurred him on.

'I was a prisoner of war aged ten and sold to the Aegean Isles, then to the Mesopotamians, and then to an Egyptian.' The pain in his eyes filled in the gaps. 'I have been resold within Egypt three times. Even though I escaped from my last master, a brutal beast who castrated me, I was recaptured by some Nubian bounty hunters and resold at the Great Slave Auction House, where Potiphar purchased me.'

Bounty hunters were the bane of every slave as they were ferocious and fastidious in their efforts to recapture a runaway slave. My father had never used their services because all the servants in our household were treated as part of our extended family, but we had heard tales of woe from neighbours in Hebron who had fallen victim to such bounty hunters.

'I am sorry,' I said quietly, wishing I had never probed.

'I have been in good households and I have experienced bad households,' he went on as if he had not heard me, 'but, whether they treat you well or badly, at the end of the day you are a chattel – property to be used and discarded or resold at will.' He looked deeply into my eyes and I felt naked and exposed. 'I lost my humanity at the age of ten.'

His final words pierced my soul. It was such a profound statement that it reverberated long after he had spoken.

That night as I slept on my narrow wooden bed frame, struggling to shut out the sound of my Sumerian roommate's snores, I thought about Abali's story and replayed his words in my mind. It was hard enough being a slave, but being one from an ethnic minority aggravated the problem. I could only guess Abali's age, but as I imagined myself in his situation, fear gripped my soul. I tried to combat my anxiety by recollecting my prophetic dreams, but even these became hazy in the light of my present reality.

Before closing my eyes and succumbing to much-needed sleep, I prayed for God to reveal His unseen presence to reassure me. It was a short, weary prayer, but one imbued with depth of emotion. My desperation clashed strenuously with my faith as the silent words escaped my lips, but in the aftermath of the struggle, I felt a peace that seemed to cocoon me. That night, I dreamt that Onamun bowed to me, then took off Potiphar's signet ring and placed it on my finger. When I woke up, I replayed the dream over and over until I felt strong enough to tackle any challenge that came my way.

* * * * * * *

Seven months later

I guided the ox-drawn wooden plough across the field, at the border of Potiphar's vineyard, creating grooves in the soil, taking care to follow the path I had made earlier that morning. Trailing behind me, Abali held a bag of the finest seedlings, which he was scattering into the grooves. This was planting season, when the seedlings and plant stems that would give birth to plump grapes were sown. Through a process of sowing and propagation those grapes would in turn be processed into the finest wine. Potiphar's wine was famed throughout the land for its full-bodied texture, fruity taste and exotic aroma, which were all to do with the quality of grapes he used. The original grape vines and seedlings were imported from islands in the Aegean Sea and had been specially chosen by Anatolian wine merchants who sailed across to trade in the Nile basin. The grapes were chosen for their ability to survive in Egypt, which was less humid than the Aegean Isles.

Potiphar's wine was so revered that it was reputedly, so I was told, the only brand that Pharaoh and his vizier drank. It was also in much demand by the elite, mostly scribes and priests. Onamun oversaw the whole wine production process from start to finish. Because quality control was stringently enforced, barbaric sanctions awaited anyone who contributed to a drop in the expected standard. Field servants, as we were known, were routinely whipped, starved, imprisoned or resold as galley slaves if Potiphar's important clients ever complained about the wine.

In the six months since my arrival at Potiphar's house, I had seen the master of the house probably no more than five times, and never face to face. I was mildly surprised that he had never asked about me – why I was not serving in his administrative office alongside his other scribes. How could someone pay such an exorbitant price for a slave and then simply forget about their existence? I was gradually acclimatising to life as a chattel, and growing accustomed to being seen but not acknowledged. It was as if I had ceased to exist, except in my own imagination. If this was Onamun's idea of an induction, it was brutal because it contrived to strip me of my personality, dignity and identity. I eventually came to realise that this was all part of a deliberate process by which a free man became a slave, psychologically.

Potiphar's household was structured along severely diverse lines, incorporating a hierarchical framework of authority and privilege. The structure ensured that every person knew their place, and there were clear lines of responsibility. At the pinnacle was Onamun, who oversaw all servants and other staff and literally ran the household, enforcing Potiphar's rules. There were only two teams of workers: indoor and outdoor workers.

The indoor workers were domestic workers or 'house slaves', while those – like me – who worked in the fields were outdoor workers or field slaves. Onamun was forever racing backwards and forwards between the house and the vineyard to micro-manage his workers. As a result of his huge remit, he was often physically and mentally burned out, which I believe contributed to his foul moods.

I often wondered why he didn't have the good sense to establish a domestic committee composed of team leaders for the internal and external divisions. The committee would meet to discuss the affairs of the household and report any areas of difficulty that needed to be escalated to Onamun. The committee would oversee all projects carried out by the internal and external divisions and be responsible for deciding who delivered them. I thought about this in my first week there, but I dared not share it with Onamun, who would most likely misconstrue my intentions and resist the change that was so desperately needed.

The other thing I noticed from day one was that almost all the field slaves were dark-skinned Nubians and Cushites. As a result, I stood out like a torch among them, and for a while felt very self-conscious. They seemed to find me quite novel and I caused quite a stir for the first week, but thereafter, my celebrity status wore off and I was accepted as one of them. Abali stuck beside me like a shadow to protect me and to teach me the Egyptian dialect. For some reason, I learnt rapidly. Within three weeks, I was speaking a basic degree of Egyptian that surprised even my tutor. Onamun could not conceal his surprise when, in my third week, I deliberately started a conversation in Egyptian with another field slave in close proximity to him so that I had the opportunity to show off my skill. Within six months I was able to speak fluently enough not to be derided. The language made information more easily accessible, because I could eavesdrop and pick up useful snippets which I pieced together to give me an idea of what was happening in my world.

Thoughts of my family had started to fade, although I still dreamt of reconciliation with them. There were nights when I turned my face to the wall, ignoring the aches and pains racking my body from my work in the fields, and wept silently, but bitterly, as memories of my father and Benjamin filled my thoughts. At such moments I battled with self-pity, anger and despair – self-pity for myself, anger with my brothers and despair about my situation. I wondered whether God would ever step in and reverse the injustice and betrayal that I had suffered – and, if so, when? I wrestled with negative thoughts that painted a picture of eternal servitude in Egypt; thoughts that blocked out the voices that mocked my fragile faith in the God of my fathers.

Through no fault of mine, I had been separated from the umbilical cord of familial comfort; like a baby aborted before full term, I had been ripped out of the security of my family's womb. I wondered what lies my treacherous brothers had told my father when they returned home from Shechem, and imagined them wailing and beating their chests as they lied to him about my fate. Would they say I had been kidnapped? Murdered? Had an accident and fallen to my death?

Would my father believe them? Was he grieving for

me? What about Benjamin? How was he taking the news? Every day, for the first four weeks, while ploughing the fields I considered my father's state of mind and wondered whether he had given up on being reunited with me. Now my thoughts of Hebron were fading ones: like twilight giving birth to darkness, I was gradually losing hope. Unless something happened to change my situation, I didn't know how long I could carry on hoping, carry on believing—

'Joseph!'

My startled reaction to the sound of my name affected my ox, which briefly wandered from the clearly defined line I had been guiding it along. I turned in the direction of the shout and saw Onamun strutting towards us, clad in full ceremonial attire incorporating an ankle-length stripy patterned piece of cloth, fastened at the waist, and matching headgear. The length of his robe impeded his progress making it hard for him to walk and he had to gather up the cloth in one hand to avoid tripping over it. I glanced at Abali, who shook his head in exasperation.

'I wonder what he wants,' he muttered.

I left the ox-drawn plough in Abali's care and headed towards the overseer. Since I had joined Potiphar's household, he took delight in striking me with his fists or an improvised whip whenever he felt like, often on the pretext that I had either failed to respond to his instructions or not carried them out to the expected standard. I could see that this was his way of taming the imaginary jackal within me and subduing a potentially rebellious slave. My anticipation of pain kept me on my toes.

'I need you to change your clothes,' he said urgently as I came within striking distance of his fists. 'You're coming with me to the farmers' market.'

I was tempted to ask why I was suddenly being summoned to perform a task reserved for the house slaves, but good sense arrested my lips. I had half expected him to comment on my pace of ploughing the field and find an excuse to start pummelling me, so the request, as awkward as it seemed, was welcome.

'What about the crop?' I asked, glancing back at Abali. He had taken over the ploughing, but was scattering seed with some difficulty.

'Abali can manage on his own,' said Onamun, turning around and striding away. 'I need you dressed appropriately and seated in the cart within the next ten minutes.'

Without further prompting, I raced out of the field, overtaking him, and headed towards the servants' quarters. I had very few clothes, and nothing I could call decent or appropriate. Having never been to the market before, I had no idea what to wear. Along the way I located my roommate in the courtyard and briskly explained my dilemma. Over the past six months we had grown close, due more to the fact that we shared the same nocturnal space rather than having any interests in common, and it was through him that I learnt about the affairs of Potiphar's household. My roommate, who was privileged to be a house slave, generously lent me a simple cotton tunic which I wore over my kilt and slipped my feet into my only pair of sandals, the ones Tema had given me ahead of the auction.

I found Onamun seated on the bench of the cart next to another servant, who was our driver. I clambered into the back of the cart, taking care to sit out of range of the overseer's whip. Despite my precautions, Onamun reached back and grabbed one of my wrists, yanking it towards him. Unsure what was going on, I prepared for the worst, but was mildly relieved when he fastened a manacle, which was chained to the cart, around my wrist. I was clearly not a trusted slave yet, because most slaves in the household were allowed to venture out without chains. As the cart rolled out of the premises, I felt elation: this was my first time outside Potiphar's house since my arrival, and I soaked up the atmosphere.

Roads in El Akhet are probably the most advanced and organised I have seen. There is an orderliness to the way traffic flows, unlike in other parts of Men'at Khufu where chaos seemed to be the order of the day. In El Akhet, traffic heading east stayed on the left while traffic heading west stayed on the right. People typically walked on either side of the wide roads, although some occasionally strayed into the roads, disregarding the chariots, carts, horses and camels. There also seemed to be a speed limit. I was particularly grateful for the steady pace of our cart because it allowed me to observe everyone we passed.

As we left the wide, tree-lined boulevards of El Akhet and arrived in the southern districts of Men'at Khufu, I had a completely different perspective of life in Egypt: this was where the poor and destitute lived. There were decaying mud brick houses, built close together, their gutters cluttered with refuse. A pungent odour hung in the air and unkempt-looking stray dogs roamed freely, nosing around rubbish heaps. Little children ran around naked, laughing and shouting, oblivious to their poverty, and domesticated livestock wandered here and there. The people here looked more emaciated and shabby, and as we rode past in our cart drawn by well-fed mules, we attracted attention.

About half an hour after we left El Akhet, we arrived at a busy bazaar in the southern part of Men'at Khufu where traders advertising their wares and chattels at the tops of their voices and hordes of bargain hunters moved slowly between stalls. There were carpenters exhibiting samples of their ornamental chairs and three-legged tables; merchants selling metalwork including swords, javelins and shields; jewellers selling trinkets and gold objects; traders selling textiles of different patterns and fabrics, alongside dye makers who offered to dye white linen or cotton fabrics; and physicians selling potions and medicinal cures in jars. One section was devoted to the sale of livestock, including camels and horses, and another to fruits and vegetables. The busiest areas were occupied by multi-ethnic caterers offering a wide variety of aromatic spicy dishes from strategically located carts and stalls.

'My regular aide has taken ill,' said Onamun, glancing back at me, as we pulled up in a space reserved for carts and chariots, 'and I need someone who is literate to help me carry out my transactions.'

I nodded. It was all beginning to make sense. I had been informed by an Egyptian house servant that Onamun could neither read nor write hieroglyphs. For this reason he relied on the services of scribes within the household, and one – a bright Midianite scholar – had been appointed his personal aide. I reasoned that he had only sent for me because there were no other scribes available to accompany him, but I didn't let this detract from my enjoyment of the trip.

Onamun uncoupled my manacled wrist and I clambered out of the cart, stretching my limbs as my sandaled feet made contact with the ground. The sight of the crowds distracted me and I began to feel an artificial sense of liberty. The rough grip of Onamun's hand on my arm reconnected me with reality as I followed him through the crowds towards the area where livestock were being sold. On arrival, Onamun was quickly surrounded by several traders whom he seemed to know. Left on my own, I started to survey my surroundings. All the livestock were kept in wooden pens, and Onamun seemed to be interested in the donkeys.

As I watched him haggling with the livestock traders, an idea crept into my mind: escape! Make a bid for freedom. Onamun's eyes weren't on me, he was too engrossed in his discussion, and in a crowded marketplace fleeing wouldn't pose much of a challenge. I was about to give in to my instincts when something more powerful urged me not to attempt it. It was a trap. I don't know where the idea came from, but the more it lingered, the more uncomfortable I felt about it. From the fluid way Onamun engaged with the traders, I began to wonder whether he really required the services of a scribe.

Wisely, I stood my ground, keeping my eyes on Onamun, who seemed to have forgotten about me. When he did eventually turn around, his gaze betrayed mild surprise at seeing me in the spot he had left me; it was then that I realised it really had been a trap. It made no sense. Why would Onamun subject me to such trickery? But I was glad that I had not fallen for the bait. I was determined to secure my freedom, but not at the risk of recapture and torture by ruthless bounty hunters. Having finished his haggling, Onamun beckoned to me. As I approached, I detected disappointment in his eyes.

'I have just purchased these donkeys,' Onamun grunted, aiming a thumb at the two docile donkeys behind him, 'and I want you to take them back to the cart and wait there for me.'

Without a word, I took the donkeys' rope from him. As I did, I noticed that one donkey was lame in the left hind leg. It didn't have a pronounced limp, but my keen eye spotted it and it was enough to signal alarm bells. I had purchased donkeys for my family many times at the markets in Bethel and Shalem and had always examined them thoroughly for any signs of ill-health. Having spotted a defect in one donkey, I examined the other, starting with its legs and moving to its face. I immediately noticed the yellowish colour in the whites of its eyes and realised that it was jaundiced. The jaundice was a sign of probable liver disease, which could occur if the animal had been allowed to graze on poisonous plants. This called into question the care these poor beasts had received from their previous owners.

I wondered whether I ought to alert Onamun about the defects, but was concerned about how he would react. How was he going to take it if I pointed out that the donkeys he had haggled so hard to purchase were in such poor condition? Part of me also wondered how he had failed to spot such obvious signs of neglect, especially as he had purchased donkeys and mules for Master Potiphar in the past.

'What are you waiting for?' asked Onamun, glaring at me.

I opened my mouth to speak, but his hostile stare dissuaded me. If I said anything now, he would blow his top and possibly even assault me. I nodded demurely and led the two sickly beasts back to the allocated spot. I decided to tell our cart driver about the donkeys and ask his advice. Being an Egyptian like Onamun, he would probably know how best to communicate the matter to him. Arriving at the cart and chariot rest point, I located our cart, but there was no sign of our driver. I looked around for him, but could not see him. I considered tying the animals to a wooden pole then going off to search for him, but worried about their security.

Determined not to see Master Potiphar swindled by rogue traders, I decided to head back to Onamun and run the risk of telling him. Even if he chose to curse and assault me, he could not ignore the evidence. I headed back to the livestock area of the bazaar, walking as briskly as the two beasts I was tugging along would let me. Because of the crowds ahead of me, I decided to work my way around them, following a path I believed would get me to my destination more quickly. When I arrived at the livestock area, approaching from the opposite route to the one I had taken earlier, I saw Onamun sitting with two of the traders, sipping beer from a jug. All three were laughing, and their camaraderie made me halt. I had learnt from my father that socialising with traders was the surest way to get a bad deal.

As I watched them, Onamun opened a leather pouch and poured some silver pieces onto the ground. He then divided these three ways, keeping back the largest portion, which he returned to the pouch. It was clear that there was some sort of scam going on here, where Onamun's partners in crime provided him with poor-quality livestock and gave him a bill of sale for far more than they were worth; they then shared the ill-gotten profits, with Onamun retaining the lion's share. The animals would eventually die or be conveniently stolen and Master Potiphar would be none the wiser. How long had Onamun been swindling Master Potiphar? How much profit had he made from his scam? The situation reminded me of the incident in Shechem involving my brothers.

I sighed. I had several choices. I could confront Onamun and his crooked partners and reveal the defects in the beasts, which would be hard for him to ignore; I could search for the cart driver and report my discovery to him; I could wait until we were home, then find a way to report the matter to Potiphar; Or I could mind my own business and turn a blind eye to something that had been going on before I arrived, and would most likely continue long after I left Potiphar's household.

I analysed the options. Option one could either cost me my life or make life in Potiphar's household more unbearable. Option two was a risk, because the cart driver might be part of the fraud. Option three would bring me into direct conflict with Onamun, who would probably arrange to have the donkeys swapped and label me a liar, which might see me sold to the quarries. Option four would maintain the status quo.

I quickly chose option four and headed back to the rest point with the two donkeys in tow. If I turned a blind eye, things would hopefully not get any worse for me. While I felt this course of action was morally wrong, I was more concerned about my wellbeing: in the face of potential aggravated affliction, my survival instinct kicked in. I had to survive this ordeal if I ever hoped to see my father and Benjamin again. On my arrival back at the rest point, I found the driver had returned and, from the perfume flirting about his garments, I suspected that he had popped into one of the many brothels dotted around the bazaar.

While we waited in silence for Onamun, the driver secured both donkeys to the rear of the cart. When Onamun returned, we made our way to another part of the bazaar where tablet engravers plied their trade. Leaving me unshackled in the back of the cart, Onamun went into a store belonging to an elderly hieroglyph engraver. Part of me desperately wanted to believe that his decision to leave me unchained meant that I had now earned his trust, but a more sceptical part suspected that he was still hoping I would make a bid for freedom, so that a manhunt would ensue. He returned about half an hour later with an engraved stone tablet for Master Potiphar along with a thick bundle of papyrus sheets, assorted reed brushes, and coloured ink dyes. Glancing at the tablet, I noted that it contained a revised list of rules for the house slaves. From there, we trundled along the road back to El Akhet. Although I was prompted to ask Onamun why he had gone to the trouble of bringing me along without using my services, I kept quiet. Sitting in the cart, I considered my next move, realising that I needed to stay one step ahead of my persistent antagonist.

THE UNSEEN PRESENCE

Psalm 37:23

I sat eating my meal in the courtyard, aware that my silence was bothering Abali. Mealtimes were usually an opportunity to catch up and discuss life in general. Most evenings I had talked to Abali about my family, culture and religious beliefs, and listened to his own vague recollections of life before slavery. This evening, however, I was in no mood to talk. What I had witnessed at the bazaar still bothered me and I was worried about whether Onamun knew that I knew what had gone on. I began to conjure up a range of scenarios where, despite my precautions, Onamun had seen me spying on him and was deciding how to punish me. I had wrestled with my conscience about my decision and, despite my trepidation, finally convinced myself that it was the right one. I had no choice. Despite my stance, however, the voices in my head kept accusing me of cowardice.

'You are troubled,' observed Abali, breaking the silence in his calm, meditative way.

'I cannot speak about it,' I said morosely, 'but even if I could, it is best if you did not know. No slave is ever punished for ignorance.'

'When one keeps silent, knowledge and ignorance are the same.'

I considered his words and nodded. He was a wise man. What he lacked in cognitive ability he made up for with experience, and what I lacked in experience I made up for with cognitive ability.

'My father says that silence can be a shield.'

'Some of us have learnt that it can also be a sword.'

My enquiring gaze sought clarity.

'It pierces your soul.'

'I'm sorry, but I can't tell you,' I said resolutely, ignoring my screaming instincts.

'That is your right,' said Abali, 'but it is my right to worry about you.'

'As long as I keep silent, you have no need to worry.'

Abali nodded. My answer seemed to have appeased him. We kept eating in silence.

'Joseph!'

Startled, I dropped the date I was eating and looked up with apprehension. Two of Master Potiphar's fearsome-looking Egyptian guards stood there; armed with javelins, their expressionless faces were like fatal hieroglyphs. My fragile nerves fell to pieces. It was not normal for guards to invade the space reserved for slaves and servants; they had their own quarters at the rear of the house. As captain of Pharaoh's palace guard, Potiphar always had a detachment of men, armed and ready, in case the need ever arose to defend the throne. Every morning the guards could be seen training and going through all kinds of combat manoeuvres, and their chants and roars sent shivers down my spine.

'Yes?' I asked timidly.

'Captain Potiphar wants to see you.'

The spokesman was the larger of the two guards, and his gravelly voice struck my heart like an arrow. I rose quickly to my feet and glanced at Abali, who was looking more curious than concerned. He was probably trying to figure out how much trouble I was in to warrant such a high-level summons.

The guards flanked me before marching towards the

house. I struggled to keep up. As we vanished out of the courtyard, I turned to steal a glance at Abali. Would I ever see him again? His reassuring gaze did nothing to restore peace to my soul, but it was the most emotional I had seen him in our seven-month relationship. Keeping in step with my armed escort, I was led to the building that housed Master Potiphar's administrative section. My heart pounded so vigorously that it was deafening.

Master Potiphar's offices were sparsely furnished. Each room contained a series of long tables and stools in the middle and lacquered wooden chests around the walls. The chests served as storage for papyrus documents. The walls of each room were plastered with neatly presented hieroglyphs. At this late hour, they were lit by oil-fuelled lamps that hung from special brass brackets.

I was escorted to the largest of the rooms, which was lit with more lamps than the others. Sitting on a stool at a large table, surrounded by a handful of scribes in white linen tunics, was the master of the house. Since our first meeting at the private slave auction, this was the closest I had been to him. I had often seen him from afar as he inspected the vineyard while I laboured, and I wondered if he even remembered who I was.

'Joseph,' said Potiphar. My armed escort left my side and took up position by the doorway, their javelins held out menacingly in front of them.

I did not know how to respond or whether I ought to, so I bowed.

'I need you to interpret a document,' said Potiphar, glancing sideways at one of his scribes, who stepped forward with a papyrus sheet which he handed to me.

I bowed again, still unsure what protocol demanded.

I glanced at the document, which was inscribed with hieroglyphs that were scrawled across it by an unsteady hand. The scribe who had given me the document detached one of the wall-mounted lamps and held it close to me so that I could read more clearly. I held my breath. The text was familiar. It was drafted in the Egyptian-inspired hieroglyphs common to Canaanite dwellers, using a mixture of red and black ink. Some of the characters were warped, making them difficult to read, but I recognised it.

I started to read the text slowly, nervously at first and then with increasing confidence. It was a short document that had clearly been written in a hurry, judging by the quality of the hieroglyphs. When I finished I handed it back to the scribe standing beside me. I searched Potiphar's face with apprehensive eyes, sensing what he was about to ask next.

'Did you write this?' asked Potiphar, fixing me with a beady stare.

'Yes,' I replied. Deception was futile. I had written it.

Left alone in the back of the cart at the market with writing materials, I had prepared the document. I had used red and black ink as used by Egyptian scribes, but because my mastery of the hieroglyphs was limited I was forced to rely on the Canaanite style.

At the time, my efforts were driven by necessity, but it was my limited literacy that had eventually identified me. Even though I had taken precautions to secrete my document within the blank sheets in such a way as not to smear or smudge the wet ink, and had discarded the used brush beneath the hay at the back of the cart, it had still been traced back to me. My attempt at anonymity had unravelled. I sighed. With hindsight, I should have expected this – it would have been easy to narrow down the author to someone who had accompanied Onamun to the bazaar that afternoon. The document had been written in a hurry by someone who was clearly not Egyptian. I was therefore probably the only suspect.

In the document, I had written that the donkeys purchased at the market were not worth the money that had been paid for them, and urged Potiphar to have them inspected before putting them into service. I had deliberately not mentioned anything about a conspiracy to defraud or even pointed a finger at Onamun, because I had no intention of getting him into trouble. At worst, he would be labelled incompetent for failing to carry out proper quality checks on the beasts.

'How did you discover that the beasts were substandard?'

'I inspected them after purchase.'

'And why did you not bring this to Onamun's attention?'

I hesitated. How could I tell him that his chief of staff was a cheat and had been probably ripping him off for years?

'I was afraid that he might perceive me as challenging his authority and punish me.'

My answer seemed to satisfy Potiphar, who nodded gently. The tension that was building around his eyes dissipated.

'Had he been drinking?'

'Yes.'

'That would explain it,' said Potiphar. 'It is not the first time.'

I said nothing, but it felt as though he could read my thoughts.

'Why did you take the risk?' asked Potiphar, studying

my face. 'You could have kept quiet and said nothing and I would have been none the wiser.'

I said nothing.

'After my scribes discovered your document among the stationery,' went on Potiphar, 'I had the donkeys inspected and confirmed that they did indeed have defects. As a precaution, I also arranged for several other animals to be inspected – camels and horses that had been purchased within the past year. They also have various physical defects, so there is clearly a pattern emerging.'

I nodded, but kept my gaze averted so he could not read my expression, fearing that my eyes would betray the truth.

'I have not yet confronted Onamun about it,' said Potiphar ponderously, 'as first I needed to know whether it was a case of negligence or fraud. But now I know it is a case of negligence, I intend to put in place better quality control to ensure it does not happen again. However, the defective animals will have to be disposed of at a loss.'

'Master Potiphar,' I interjected, momentarily forgetting my position, 'you do not have to dispose of them.'

When I remembered my place, I stopped speaking, but Potiphar's eyes invited me to keep on speaking.

'I can restore the animals to good health,' I said recklessly.

'How?'

'By using livestock rehabilitation techniques.'

Potiphar's gaze became inquisitive.

'My father taught me and my brothers how to use diet and herbal remedies to restore animals back to health so that we could sell them on for a profit.'

'And these techniques work?'

I nodded. I was confident about what I was saying. My father had used these methods while looking after my grandfather's flocks in Mesopotamia.

'Okay Joseph, wait outside,' said Potiphar. 'We wish to confer on the matter.'

I started walking towards the doorway but, halfway there, I turned around, to see the master of the house huddled with his scribes.

'Please do not mention my role in this to Onamun,' I mumbled.

'Why not?' asked Potiphar.

'Because I fear that he will make my life in the vineyard even more miserable.'

'Well, there is a process that has to be followed,' he said with an indifferent expression that gave me no comfort. 'Now wait outside until we send for you.'

I nodded in resignation. Outside, I waited on the veranda, under the intimidating gaze of the two guards at the doorway, silently praying that Potiphar would be gracious and grant my request for anonymity; I could not afford to cross paths with my brutish overseer, who would definitely exact his revenge despite my best efforts to protect his reputation. Finally, one of the scribes appeared in the doorway and beckoned to me. Heading back into the room I felt as if my legs were about to give way.

'We have reached a decision,' said Potiphar as I approached, 'and we all agree that you should no longer work in the vineyard.'

My bulging eyes searched his face to ensure that my ears were not deceiving me.

'From now on you will be responsible for livestock quality control,' said Potiphar, 'and even though you will still be under Onamun, you will report directly to this office regarding all matters relating to my livestock.'

I stared at him, mouth agape.

'Don't look so stunned,' he said, rising from his seat and strolling towards me with his arms behind his back. 'It is our policy to put all new slaves through a two-year induction before reassigning them. You have just been reassigned.'

I had served less than seven months in the vineyard. I was overawed. What kind of mercy was this? What kind of extraordinary grace was at work here? It was truly humbling.

'Thank you,' I gasped.

'As part of your new responsibilities you will be given an office in this building and two other slaves of your choice to help you to develop a new quality control standard for livestock. Your new posting is effective immediately.'

I bowed in gratitude. As I straightened, I felt his hand on my shoulder. Looking into his eyes, I saw a benevolence that was reassuring.

'This is not a random appointment,' said Potiphar. 'We have been watching you for a while and have been impressed with your conduct and work ethic. I sanctioned Onamun's decision to assign you to the vineyards. You never complained, but threw yourself into the tasks you were given. If you keep it up, you will go far. Now you may leave us.'

I bowed again and withdrew from his presence, still struggling to come to terms with what had happened. As I left, I saw the two Egyptian guards marching Onamun towards me. He paused to glare at me before continuing on to the room I had just exited. My euphoria was temporarily quelled. How would he react when he learnt of my elevation? I headed back to the courtyard to share the news with Abali, but found the place deserted. It was well past mealtime, and twilight had been replaced by moonlight. Standing alone in the courtyard, looking up at the sky, I praised the God of my fathers, who had once again been merciful towards me.

* * * * * * *

Sharp pain inflicted by the palm of a calloused hand striking my bare back shattered my sleep, thrusting me awake. Befuddled, my eyes still groggy with sleep, I struggled to focus on the shadow hovering over me. Was it a nocturnal apparition? Was I dreaming?

'Wake up!' hissed a familiar voice.

I roused from my semi-conscious state and sat up, looking at Onamun's face, which was becoming clearer in stages. The moonlight shining through the window gave him a ghoulish appearance, but despite my initial surprise at seeing him, I was not afraid. The previous evening's events had done much to boost my confidence. If Onamun thought that he could exert the same kind of aggressive and violent influence over me as he had previously done, he would have to be more discreet because I was no longer a field slave.

'What do you want?' I asked, resisting the temptation to react with indignation.

'I wish to talk.'

I considered his request. Despite the late hour, I nodded and sat up.

'Let's go outside,' he said.

I rose and followed him outside onto the veranda in front of the servants' quarters. We sat down on the low wall bordering the veranda. For a moment he said nothing, choosing instead to gaze up at the moon.

'The master told me what you did yesterday,' he began in his grouchy manner.

I steeled myself for what was about to come next, but said nothing.

'He also informed me about his decision to make you responsible for quality control of all livestock,' went on Onamun, shaking his head in disbelief. 'According to him, I am to have nothing more to do with buying or even selling livestock.'

Anticipating that he still had more to say, I remained silent.

'I am powerless to reverse his decision, but I believe you set me up to get back at me and improve your prospects.'

'That's not true,' I began.

'Then how do you explain your promotion from field slave to head of quality control?' asked Onamun, spreading his hands abruptly. I flinched.

'Master Potiphar needed to know about the condition of those animals before he put them to work,' I said. 'One had a fractured leg and the other was jaundiced.'

'You should have pointed out the health issues to me first, rather than going behind my back to report me.'

'I didn't report you,' I cut in. 'I never even mentioned your name.'

'But you knew that I would be blamed.'

'I felt it was better for you to be found to be negligent rather than fraudulent.'

'What do you mean?' His eyes bored into mine, but I did not flinch.

'I saw you sharing money with those livestock merchants and realised that the bill of sale they gave you was fake. It means you have been deliberately buying substandard livestock and sharing the difference in price with your partners in crime.'

'Are you accusing me of dishonesty?' His belligerence escalated.

'I am not your judge,' I said quietly, 'but I know what I saw.'

His proud shoulders slumped and his haughty expression melted away. 'Why didn't you tell the master?' he asked hollowly after a tense silence.

'Because I knew the penalty.'

Onamun's silence was profound. I could see he was struggling.

'I-I do not know what to say,' he said at last.

'There is nothing to say.'

'It seems I am in your debt,' he said, his voice stripped of the last vestiges of dignity.

'You owe me nothing,' I murmured 'No man should ever be in another's debt. I did it to free you, not enslave you.'

It took him a while to understand but, when he did, his face brightened and his shoulders lifted.

'Thank you for giving me a way out,' he said, getting down off the wall.

I watched him shuffle away, less of a man than he had been the day before. Despite my assurance, I knew he would still feel indebted to me, and that made me uncomfortable.

*   *   *   *   *   *   *

Two years later

'Joseph!'

I looked up from the table, where I had been counting the pieces of silver I had received from the part-exchange of some elderly camels, and saw Master Potiphar. I immediately rose to my feet and bowed. He very rarely came to my section of the administrative building, but he relied on me to provide him with the profit and loss accounts at the end of every month. His unexpected presence triggered panic.

'Master?' I responded.

'I have just been examining the books,' he said, halting beside me, his eyes unsmiling.

'Is there a problem, Master?' I asked, fearing that there had been some discrepancy in my figures, and knowing how fastidious he was.

'There has to be. The entries cannot be right,' he said, shaking his head.

My heart began to perform an Egyptian folk tune. What would the repercussions be for making an accounting error? Even though it had greatly improved, my writing was still far from perfect.

'Your figures don't add up,' said Potiphar, placing a bundle of papyrus sheets down on the table before me.

Despite my apprehension, I believed that there must be a simple explanation, especially as I had been collecting and counting all money received in person. I hadn't kept back anything for myself. I lowered my gaze to the accounts and scrutinised the entries carefully. Potiphar had an accounts scribe who always checked my entries, but he had never had cause to query my calculations before. Looking through the records, I noticed the slight decline in the previous month's sales figures and suspected that this was the problem, but I had an explanation.

Since taking over the quality control of livestock, I had introduced a system my father used, called part-exchange, where I rotated the flock and sold off animals that were more than three years old. I made deals with Anatolian traders who purchased livestock from the Aegean islands. The animals were generally larger than those found in Egypt, Midian or Mesopotamia. I paid part in silver pieces and the other part in healthy livestock aged over three years old. The livestock I part-exchanged were healthy and would give many more years of faithful service to their new owners, depending on how they were looked after. However, my plan was to ensure that half of all Potiphar's livestock was less than three years old. I therefore spent the first year rehabilitating and then selling the old livestock and the second year on consolidating the gains into a sustainable business model.

All the unhealthy beasts purchased by Onamun had been nursed back to health in a newly created animal nursery run by Abali, where I administered restorative medication and treatment learnt from my father. But, something amazing happened to the animals I was nursing; they recovered at a faster rate than I had expected. Even my father hadn't experienced such phenomenal results. I attributed this success to my prayers, and the faithfulness of the God who answered them. The rapid recovery of these beasts enabled me sell them off early at a profit and use the money to purchase new livestock, which I inspected myself. I also refused to trade with Onamun's Midianite partners in crime. Instead, I established a rapport with the Anatolian traders who bought animals for me according to my specification.

Last month, however, my part-exchange strategy had not brought in so much profit because I discovered that some of the animals I was about to sell still had minor defects, so I withdrew them from sale at the last minute. But I hadn't updated the records to reflect this. I prided myself on offering only the best-quality animals in part-exchange, and didn't want to lose the trust of my Anatolian trading partners.

'Last month was not so great for sales,' I began.

'I am not bothered about last month,' said Potiphar dismissively. 'It's the annual figures for your second year that concern me.'

A frown creased my brow but I quickly erased it. In Egyptian society a frown is a very serious thing, as it conveys displeasure or disapproval. A frown is the same thing as calling the recipient a liar. Slaves were not allowed to show displeasure to their masters, or even another Egyptian, for that matter.

'I can assure you that the calculations are correct, Master Potiphar,' I said, treading carefully.

'I know,' said Potiphar, planting his hands on his hips, 'and that's what bothers me.'

I said nothing, but studied his face instead. What was he accusing me of? But he looked baffled, not accusatory.

'I don't understand, Master, but I can assure you that I have been entirely honest in all my dealings,' I said pre-emptively.

'I know,' repeated Potiphar, 'but I am still amazed at how profitable the livestock side of my business has been.'

His response silenced me.

'This has been the best year ever!' exclaimed Potiphar, spreading his muscular arms expansively.

'How did you do it?'

I stared at him, wide-eyed, having lost the power of speech. What answer could I give?

'To experience a three hundred per cent increase in profit in a year is unprecedented,' he continued, 'and my accounts scribe who went over the figures is in shock!'

I had tried hard to perform well in my new role – not with an ulterior motive, but out of a sense of gratitude for the opportunity. I'd taken everything I had learnt from my father's experience and used it. Even then, I knew that without the intervention of the God of my fathers, who had given me favour with the Anatolian traders, the profits would have been far less. It was God who had answered my prayers for direction and had guided my steps. I recalled how all the sickly animals had recovered far faster than expected, and knew that something far more potent than my father's strategies and remedies had been at work.

'The God of my fathers has been merciful to me,' I answered gently.

Potiphar studied me and nodded slowly. 'I do not know which god you serve,' he said pensively, 'but the spectacular turnaround in my fortunes in such a short space of time can only be attributed to the intervention of a god.'

I said nothing, but registered his sombre mood.

'Before you took over the care of my livestock,' he continued, 'I had to contend with a higher than normal rate of mortality among the animals. I was losing money and my herds were diminishing. Despite our efforts to change things, it got worse. But you have been a blessing to me, Joseph – and to think that I only saw you as a slave I could train to be one of my scribes!' He paused, appearing to struggle to articulate his thoughts. 'You are worth more than ten scribes to me.'

His words produced tears from the corners of my eyes, but I furiously blinked them back, unwilling to show emotion. I reserved my feelings for moments when I was alone; tears from a slave were a sign of weakness and I had no wish for him to exploit it.

'I am considering an extensive restructuring of my domestic affairs,' he said, pacing around my office, his hands still planted on his hips authoritatively, 'and I am factoring you into my plans. I need to find a role for you that is worthy of your loyalty and integrity.'

I stared at him quizzically. What other role would he assign me to when my management of the livestock was working so well? I imagined being assigned to work with the scribes, who spent most of their days drafting edicts and decrees for Potiphar and occasionally also for Pharaoh, and shuddered.

'The affairs of my house are in need of an overhaul,' he continued, 'and I cannot think of anyone more qualified than you to take over from Onamun as overseer.'

As he spoke, I could not resist the temptation to frown. The past two years had been relatively peaceful because Onamun was still in charge of the house. However, I could foresee problems with Potiphar's decision, as it would awake old hostilities and fragment the fragile truce.

'Master Potiphar, that may not be advisable,' I said in a subdued voice.

'Why not?' He stopped pacing and turned to face me with his steely gaze. 'I sense discomfort in your voice. Do you not feel you are up to the task of managing my home?'

'I am, Master Potiphar,' I answered, averting my gaze, 'but I have no desire to conflict with Onamun. If you give me his post, he will believe that I am behind his demotion.'

'And why should that concern you?'

The question was weighty but rhetorical.

'I would find it difficult to instruct him,' I answered diplomatically.

'Don't worry about that,' said Potiphar, his voice softening. 'He will be retiring with effect from today.'

I processed the information slowly. I had learnt from Abali that Onamun was a mixed-race Egyptian whose father had been an Ishmaelite and his mother an Egyptian prostitute. He had been sold into slavery to pay off his mother's debts when he was about ten years old. He had worked for many years in the Nile ferry business, then the stone quarries at Giza, before being purchased by Potiphar. He had been a slave all his adult life, but tomorrow he would be a free man. I envied him.

'Have you told him yet?' I asked.

'He will find out this evening.' He flicked his wrist as if he were shooing away a Nile fly. 'But don't worry about him – he is gaining his freedom and enough money to buy land, build a modest house and live in reasonable comfort.'

I thought about all the years Onamun had been defrauding his master, and imagined that he would be living in much more than reasonable comfort.

'I am reassured, Master Potiphar. Thank you for the opportunity.'

'Good,' he said. 'Tomorrow Onamun will do a handover and you will become overseer in his place. You will be in charge of my whole household and every servant and slave will be answerable to you, apart from my wife and official scribes. You will attend to all my affairs. There are areas of this house that you have previously not had access to, such as my private quarters, but from tomorrow that will change. My clothes, food, transport, entertainment and ceremonial affairs are all part of your new portfolio.'

I bowed deeply, under my breath giving thanks to the God of my fathers, who had once again seen fit to elevate me to a status that I could not have attained without His help. As livestock quality controller, I had been content, but to be promoted to overseer was beyond my wildest dreams. In effect, Potiphar was giving me charge of his life. Even though I had resolved to devote as little time as possible to thinking about my father, so as not to make my sojourn in Egypt more tedious, I recalled my dreams in Hebron and wondered whether this was what they had meant. Was this the pathway to greatness that God had promised? Was the manifestation of His promise going to happen through such an unconventional route?

SCANDAL

Proverbs 2:16

My first day in office was an eventful one. From the moment I woke up in my new self-contained quarters – a room double the size of the room I had shared with my Sumerian roommate – I found a subdued-looking Onamun waiting outside my door. The previous night, Potiphar had instructed Onamun to vacate his sleeping quarters, and I had moved in. The room was unique in that it included a separate washroom with a raised slab where one could stand, or sit, while washing – or being washed. As I soon discovered, Onamun had a male slave whose duty was to douse him with water while he washed, a privilege I had previously believed was preserved solely for Potiphar. There was also a makeshift toilet fabricated from limestone which a slave emptied in a dedicated sandpit near the Nile. One of the other perks Onamun enjoyed was a proper bed carved from wood with an embedded wooden headrest and linen-covered mattress. That night I enjoyed the best sleep I had experienced in almost two years.

Each morning, I spend the first moments praying to the God of my fathers, who has been my guide. When I shared a room with the Sumerian I had performed this task on my bed, facing the wall for privacy. This morning, however, I was able to bow on the floor and pray more energetically. I was aware of Onamun's presence but, even though I was no longer answerable to him, I did not want to keep him waiting. To my surprise, when I eventually summoned him, Onamun bowed on entry, although I detected a stiff reluctance in his posturing. Nevertheless, it was a remarkable turnaround in fortunes and an experience that stayed with me long afterwards.

Onamun was accompanied by a slave – a young Cushite boy, Kaa, with an infectious broad grin. I had seen him around, but never talked to him. Apparently Kaa's duty was to bath Onamun and empty his waste, among other things. In light of the impromptu change of guard, Kaa was now my new personal assistant and had turned up to supervise my personal hygiene. Rejecting the luxury of being washed, I took care of my own hygiene, all the while resisting Kaa's efforts to help. He was probably panicking at the prospect of sudden redundancy.

Although I still wore my old clothes, Onamun told me that the family dressmaker had been instructed to provide me with a new set of tunics, more in keeping with my elevated status. As I finished dressing, Kaa showed up with my breakfast in a bowl woven from reed rushes, and a clay bowl of water. Egyptians typically eat twice a day. Breakfast is an assortment of fruits and grains selected to provide the right amount of energy required for the day. Unlike other servants and slaves, Onamun did not eat in the courtyard, but in his quarters, and I was accorded the same privilege. To my surprise, Onamun did not join me for breakfast, but waited outside with Kaa while I sat on the stool beside my bed and ate.

As was my habit, I did not finish my breakfast. In the past, Abali, who had a healthier appetite than me, had finished my portions, but today my unfinished meal was for my new aide, Kaa. It was my way of establishing a rapport with him, and a practice I had learnt from my father.

When Kaa came to remove my bowl, his eyes widened at the sight of the berries, dates and other exotic fruits nestling there awaiting another appetite to appease. He looked at me awkwardly. When I nodded, he scooped up the bowl and departed faster than a race camel in full flight. I laughed inside when I saw this: it was evidence that Onamun had never accorded him a similar privilege. As I rose to my feet, Onamun bowed stiffly again but, despite his conflicting body language, his facial expression was contrite.

'As part of the handover, I will escort you around the master's living quarters as well as the female quarters,' he said quietly. 'I will also show you where the wine, beer and grain are stored and give you a tour of the guards' quarters, introduce you to the head of the guard and show you the armoury. These are places you have previously not had access to, and there are many slaves and hired servants you have not met.'

I raised my eyebrows. I had believed that all the servants and slaves ate in the courtyard and that I knew each of them by face if not by name.

'I will also be introducing you to the master's wife.'

I raised my eyebrows again. In my two and a half years at Potiphar's house, our paths had never crossed. Even during my two years as head of livestock quality control, I had not been allowed to venture beyond my office into the main residential quarters. Any news about Potiphar's wife had filtered down from the house servants, who had described her as a paragon of beauty with a tempestuous manner. I was very much looking forward to meeting the woman who occupied my master's affections.

'Before I leave, I will hand you the master's signet.' He raised his hand to display his signet ring.

All senior Egyptian officials wore a signet ring, and each had a unique design. The signet stone, once dipped in ink and compressed against papyrus, was an official seal that converted the document into one carrying legislative authority. All Potiphar's documents were marked with his signet, but Onamun wore the ring on his behalf as there were many commercial transactions requiring its imprint which the overseer of the house was entrusted with. That was why Onamun had been able to operate autonomously, with no supervision or checking. This same privilege was now being extended to me.

'Thank you,' I answered, 'and I am glad that you are taking this well.'

Onamun grunted and led the way out of the room, clearly uncomfortable discussing the topic. Despite his grumpy manner, I sensed his relief. No doubt he relished the prospect of experiencing freedom and being his own master, but there would be a part of him that missed the perks of exercising authority over others, something he would most likely never experience again. As I followed him across the compound towards the main residence, I wondered if news had got round. I was the centre of attention, and all eyes were on me. Hired servants and slaves, male and female, paused in their tasks to stare at me, some in bewilderment, but others with genuine admiration.

My Cushite and Nubian friends went the extra mile and bowed as we walked past. This seemed to irritate Onamun, whose response was to clear his throat noisily in disapproval. I knew the field servants and could count on their loyalty, but could I win the loyalty of the Onamun faithful – all those who had benefited from his tenure?

We arrived at a set of ornate wooden double doors with massive brass handles, which I had never ventured beyond. Stationed at either side of the doorway were two of Potiphar's guards in full military regalia, armed with javelins and swords. Neither of them glanced at us, but we were under their close surveillance nonetheless. My heart thumped like the drums at a military parade as we paused in front of them, and I realised that this was a milestone: a changing of the guard. Onamun glanced at me then twisted both brass handles simultaneously to open the doors, and we stepped through the doorway into the splendour beyond.

The broad hallway we stepped into reminded me of the road to El Akhet in its vastness, and the turquoise stone flooring resembled the Mediterranean Sea, which I had briefly glimpsed on the way to Egypt. The walls were decorated with colourful frescoes of hieroglyphs. There were oil lamps mounted on the walls, and the doorways to the different chambers on either side were veiled with silk drapes. A perfume hung in the air. The servants who scurried past us, paying us scant regard, were well groomed and predominantly Egyptian in appearance. Some of them nodded at Onamun, but they barely glanced at me. Leading off the hallway was a large staircase fabricated from white polished stone. At the top of the stairs, another pair of guards waited.

Onamun took me in and out of different chambers along the hallway, introducing me to servants as his successor. Some expressed surprise or shock at the news that he was retiring, and he casually informed them that he had decided to retire with Potiphar's blessings and had personally nominated me as his replacement. He even had the effrontery to inform one attractive female slave that I was his protégé.

At one point, while he was introducing me to the head chef, a plump, middle-aged woman, I wished to protest, but felt it inappropriate to start an argument on my first day. Besides, I reasoned, this was Onamun's last day on the job so I could afford to cut him some slack. By presenting me as his protégé, Onamun was craftily turning the situation on its head so he came out with his dignity intact, while also taking the glory that rightfully belonged to God, who had shown me favour. That upset me.

Having given me an elaborate tour of the ground floor, he led the way to the first floor, avoiding eye contact – most likely, on account of his guilt. At the upper level, he paused outside a chamber with a silk-covered doorway and for the first time met my eyes. Something ominous in his eyes alerted me to an impending danger.

'I am about to introduce you to the mistress of the house,' he said quietly. 'She is the power behind the throne and in this house her word is law.'

'What is she like?' I asked anxiously.

'Like any other woman who was born into wealth and married into even greater wealth, she is conceited,' he replied furtively, 'and the master adores the ground she walks on. If she likes you, it will go well with you, but if she doesn't…'

'Are there any particular dos and don'ts?' I asked eagerly, determined to learn as much about her as I could before the introduction, knowing that first impressions counted.

'She doesn't like change,' he answered in the same hushed tone. 'She likes things to be kept the way they are, and she likes her servants to be seen but not heard.'

As I listened, I wondered whether I was being set up

to fail. Was Onamun telling the truth – or was he trying to smother my innovative approach to management, so as not to overshadow his own dubious legacy? This put me on my guard. Despite his words of caution, I was determined to remain authentic and true to myself.

He clapped his hands twice and waited until a female voice summoned him to enter. I followed him into the chamber, my eyes widening as they took in the scale of the place. Compared to the other chambers, it was colossal, and the fact that it was sparsely furnished made it seem even more cavernous. There was a vast wooden bed with legs carved in the shape of a lion's paws, a number of large lacquered boxes of the type used for storing clothes, a wooden table on which stood assorted beauty products, and a vast polished brass reflector which served as a mirror. The walls were plastered with colourful frescoes showing the master's wife in different settings. As my eyes roved over them, I could see that they told her life story, from infancy to her marriage. The perfumed atmosphere was pleasant, but less so than the paragon of beauty curled up on a padded recliner being attended to by three Egyptian maidens. As we approached, she casually glanced in my direction, then looked back at Onamun, who was bowing. I copied him.

Potiphar's wife had a perfectly symmetrical face, with angular cheekbones and almond-shaped hazel eyes with long lashes. She wore kohl and gold eyeshadow. Her prominent nose, which was very un-Egyptian, overshadowed her pert lips and her bold chin was blessed with a single dimple. I could not see her natural hair because of the elaborate braided wig she wore, adorned with gold beads and other jewelled ornaments. She wore a sheer white sheath dress embellished with gold embroidery. My first impression was of a powerful, sophisticated woman whose confidence sprang not only from her God-given beauty, but from her circumstances of birth, which had placed her at the top of Egyptian society. She looked like a woman who was unaccustomed to hardship and had never known poverty. I could not tell what sort of heart lay beneath her unblemished skin and golden complexion but, if appearances were anything to go by, I was prepared to endorse Onamun's assessment. She looked like a woman used to getting her own way.

'Mistress, as you know, this is my last day as overseer on the estate,' said Onamun in the fawning manner he adopted whenever he was speaking to anyone he deemed superior. 'I have come to introduce the *young* man who will be taking over my duties.'

Potiphar's wife glanced at me again. This time her gaze lingered for a fraction longer: her disparaging eyes swept me from head to toe. Even though I had only just turned twenty years old, my face and physique conveyed a much more mature presence.

'What do they call him?' she asked.

'My name is Joseph,' I interjected, unwilling to be spoken about.

Again she glanced at me and again her gaze lingered a fraction longer. However, this time her eyes were amused.

'One who can speak for himself,' she observed.

'I apologise, mistress,' said Onamun, bowing. 'He has always been a precocious one, but his heart is in the right place.'

Her eyes appraised me again. This time they rested on mine as if trying to stare me down. I was urged to lower my gaze, but some inexplicable bravado possessed me and I met her gaze unflinchingly. To my surprise, after a few seconds, her eyes dropped and her cheeks darkened. I had no idea what this meant, but considered it a victory. I was determined to be noticed in my own right, not as some substandard replacement for Onamun.

'I trust that you will prove to be as loyal and dedicated as Onamun,' she said in a wavering voice.

I felt like saying I would be even more committed than him, but wisdom prevailed.

'Thank you for your many years of loyal service, Onamun,' she said curtly. 'You have earned your freedom and I hope you will do everything you can to avoid reverting back to your family's legacy.'

'Thank you, mistress, for your kind words,' said Onamun, bowing again.

As we walked out of the chamber, Onamun leading the way, I processed her parting words and wondered why he had thought them kind. Was he so browbeaten that he could not detect the cynicism in them? She had thrown the circumstances of his birth in his face. She clearly had no regard for him. Did she have any regard for anyone?

Once we were a comfortable distance away from the chamber, Onamun stopped and turned to me, fixing me with such an intense stare that I thought he was about to forget his place and hit me.

'That was foolhardy, Joseph,' he said scathingly. 'The mistress is not a person to tangle with. You only speak to her when you're spoken to.'

'Well, I got tired of being perceived as your protégé.'

'I did that to give you acceptance!' said Onamun, grabbing my shoulders. 'I want everyone to know that you are taking over with my blessing so that you do not encounter any hostility or resistance.'

His words silenced me and my gaze dropped. He was right. People often hate change and need reassurance. I had misconstrued his actions and felt ashamed.

'You did me a favour some years ago,' went on Onamun, 'so I feel obliged to repay the compliment. Never resist the demands of authority.'

I thought about this under his watchful gaze, and realised that he was passing on the code he lived by. He had survived his journey by never resisting the demands of authority, but I wasn't sure if that was how I wished to live.

'From now on, you must become invisible,' said Onamun. 'Let your work be more prominent than you and it shall become your armour – your security. If you let your guard down, and start craving prominence, you may find yourself facing demands that conflict with your beliefs. I've finished my journey, now you need to go and live yours.'

I nodded even though his words were obscure. They were probably deep and at least deserved acknowledgement. 'Thank you,' I said quietly.

He nodded and let go of my shoulders. For the rest of the tour, I slipped into the role of protégé and behaved as he wanted me to.

* * * * * * *

One year later

The first year as overseer passed in a flash. It was only while attending the official opening of Potiphar's first brewery that I realised that it was the first anniversary of Onamun's departure. My first year had been a busy one, during which I persuaded Potiphar to diversify his business interests away from focusing on livestock, farming and small-scale wine production to the manufacture of bread and beer.

The multi-ethnic Egyptian population had a craving for assorted types of bread and beer, and traditional production techniques placed the focus on quantity to meet demand at the expense of quality, which was indifferent. I spotted this gap in the market and spent six months investigating the production of bread at bakeries in Upper and Lower Egypt, as well as beer production at the breweries. The production of these staple products was of the cottage variety – family-based, passing down from generation to generation. My Anatolian trading contacts put me in touch with bakeries in the Aegean Isles which, for a price, were willing to share their recipes with me, as well as their more modern techniques for producing and preserving the bread in a hot climate. By adopting their techniques, and using more modern kilns fuelled by coal, I was able not only to improve the quality of traditional Egyptian bread, but also to introduce a number of varieties that had not previously been available.

I tested my bread among a select consumer group comprising the elite and commoners. Everyone – apart from Pharaoh's chief baker – gave favourable reports. I subsequently learnt that Pharaoh's baker preferred his own recipes. Despite the lack of royal endorsement, we began production in a converted room in Potiphar's home, and within three months we were unable to cope with demand. We found new premises in El Akhet for a larger, more modern bakery, using imported kilns. This officially opened after I had been in the job for nine months.

The concept for the brewery was being developed alongside the bakery, and I followed the same route of exploration. We relied on Mycenaean and Mesopotamian methods to refine our beer production, experimenting with different grains and hops to find the best flavours. We employed servants from Mycenae to oversee the beer production and servants from the Aegean Isles to oversee the bread production, to ensure consistency in quality as well as train the Egyptians who would take over.

Now, twelve months after the day I took over as overseer from Onamun, Potiphar and his wife were attending the opening of their first brewery, also in the El Akhet district. We hoped the wealthy families and officials who lived in the area, as well as their influential friends in other cities, would buy the beer. As my Mycenaean brewery manager guided Potiphar and his wife around the facility, explaining the production techniques, I noticed my mistress stealing glances at me. Each time our eyes met, I bowed, having learnt my lesson from our first encounter, but when I lifted my head I noticed her still staring at me. On a couple of occasions, I could have sworn that I saw her smile approvingly. I took this as a compliment, that she was satisfied with the quality of my stewardship: after all, my God-favoured efforts had made her husband one of the richest men in the country.

* * * * * * *

Three months later

'Joseph, do you find me attractive?'

I hesitated. Potiphar's wife, my mistress, was not unattractive. To be honest, of all the Egyptian women I had encountered so far, she was the most beautiful. We were on the balcony that adjoined her chamber, which had picturesque views over the Nile. She reclined on a padded three-legged bench while I stood in the doorway, having just been summoned to her presence. While her beauty was not in dispute, she seemed to be indiscreet, judging from the provocative garments she wore that appealed to the baser instincts of men. I initially presumed that she was an attention-seeker who got a thrill out of teasing men, but in the months that I had known her, I began to sense something more worrying, something specific to me.

'My master is indeed very fortunate,' I mumbled.

'That is not what I asked.'

'My master has been blessed with a wife who is indeed beautiful and virtuous.'

Her hazel eyes flashed.

'So, you find me attractive then?'

It was not a question.

I cleared my throat to buy me time, and looked everywhere but at her face.

'I do not think I'm beautiful.' She sighed.

I was tempted to disagree, but held my tongue. Out of the corner of my eye, I noticed her rise up and walk about in her flimsy gown, admiring herself in the gigantic brass reflector.

'If I was beautiful, you would find me appealing.'

'My master is the envy of all the men in the city, who testify to the beauty and virtue of his wife.'

'I do not care what the residents of Men'at Khufu say,' she answered edgily. 'I want to know what you think, Joseph.'

'I think my master has chosen wisely.'

She giggled at my response, and gave me a mocking

smile.

'So, you believe your master, my husband, has chosen a wife who is both beautiful and appealing enough to provoke desire in men?'

I nodded curtly, unable to think of a more non-committal response.

'I want to hear it, Joseph.'

'Yes.'

'Yes?' Her enquiring gaze invited further detail.

'Yes, mistress.'

She laughed out loud, a throaty, full-bodied laugh that hinted at mischief.

'You are very naïve, Joseph,' she purred. 'I don't know whether it is an act but, if it is, then it is a very convincing one.'

Realising which direction she was headed, I kept my expression impassive.

She reached up a hand to stroke my cheek. I flinched instinctively, but made no effort to remove her hand. She was my master's wife, and I was wary of her. Any display of indignation would be construed as an act of aggression by a slave, and there would be consequences.

'Tell me, Joseph,' she said, drawing closer so that her perfume filled my nostrils, 'have you ever had any dealings with the maidens under your command?'

I drew back slightly, moving out of her reach. The discussion was straying into dangerous territory and I was seriously concerned. My actions, rather than repelling her, seemed to be spurring her on. She drew even closer so that she had me backed against the wall.

'Don't tell me that you've never taken advantage of a female servant. I am told they are so besotted with you that they secretly gather to watch you walk past their chambers, and become weak-kneed when you speak to them.'

'Mistress, if you will excuse me,' I said resolutely, 'I have urgent matters to attend to at the Southern Men'at Khufu Bazaar, and I am running late.'

I eased away from her encroaching presence, ignoring her mockery, which reverberated around the walls and seemed to chase after me as I hurried down the hallway.

* * * * * *

Four months later

I was supervising the unloading of the wagon carrying beer which had just arrived from the local brewery when Kaa showed up with a sheepish grin. Before he spoke I knew what he was about to say, and my blood ran cold. For the past four months I had found every excuse I could to work away from the residence. Having trained a trio of slaves to carry out tasks on my behalf, I was able to delegate work and spend time negotiating transactions away from the house, which required me to rise early and return late.

My strategy was to avoid my master's wife – but, realising my strategy, she had taken to bribing Kaa to inform her about my specific movements.

'The mistress requests your presence,' said Kaa, beaming effusively, much to my chagrin.

I was tempted to tell him to tell her that he could not find me, but I did not tell lies. Abandoning my task, leaving Abali in charge, I headed towards my mistress's chambers. This ritual occurred whenever Potiphar was away from home and she had received advanced knowledge of my movements – thanks to her spy. At these times I had to have my wits about me. My weary legs conveyed me to her chambers on the upper floor. As I entered, dreading the tedious verbal struggle that lay ahead, I found her reclined on her bed clad only in a revealing gown.

'Come and sit next to me, Joseph,' she said, patting a spot on the bed beside her.

'How can I be of service, mistress?' I asked, making no move to comply.

'Are you refusing to obey my instruction?'

I sighed deeply, but inaudibly, before moving closer to the edge of her bed, averting my gaze from her immodest attire. I did not, however, sit down.

'You have been avoiding me, Joseph.'

'Can I be of service, mistress?'

'Yes – come and lie with me.'

'But I am not tired, mistress.'

'Joseph!' She giggled, stretching one of her shapely legs towards me until her toes nudged my knees. 'You know what I want, and I believe deep down that you want the same thing, so why are you resisting it?'

'Resisting what, mistress?'

'Resisting the urge within you to take me in your arms and share the comfort of my bed.'

This was the most direct she had been. It marked a deeply troubling change to the cat-and-mouse game she had initiated. How could I respond?

'I am not comfortable with this discussion, mistress,' I mumbled through tense lips.

'Joseph, lie with me and satisfy my passion,' she said, rising to a seated position.

'No, mistress.' I shook my head firmly. 'My master trusts me with all his affairs and has placed the welfare of the household under my care. As you know, no one here exercises more authority than me because he has held nothing back from me except you, his beloved wife. How could I therefore do such a wicked thing? To even think of such a thing would be a great sin against God!'

'God? Which god? Osiris? Ra? Amun? Isis?'

'My God. The God of my fathers is righteous and disapproves of marital infidelity.'

'I do not worship your God.'

'But I do, mistress, and if I even conceive of such an act of wickedness his hand will withdraw from me.'

'Oh, Joseph!' she groaned, holding the sides of her head in despair. 'Leave religion out of this! You are not a priest. You are a man with immense power and you must choose for yourself! Be your own god!'

As she spoke she gazed up at me imploringly, soliciting sympathy, tears sparkling in her eyes, but I was not moved. In her posturing, I perceived only evil. I recalled how my brother Reuben had slept with Bilhah, my father's concubine, and this helped to reinforce my conviction about the wickedness that was being proffered. Weakening was therefore not an option.

'Mistress, I cannot with a clear conscience even consider what you suggest,' I answered, taking a step backwards. 'You are my master's most personal asset and one that he loves passionately and guards jealously.'

'And how do you know he loves me?'

'Because he never stops speaking about how much he loves you.'

This was not a lie. Potiphar, when inebriated by wine, would tell me of his passion for the woman who was his wife. If only he knew what fires burned within her bosom, he may have changed his mind…

'Why do you make up stories to mask your cowardice?' she asked, leaning forward provocatively. 'Why would my husband share such private details with you, his slave? Joseph, I am a woman with needs, and you are the man I am asking to share my bed! Me – a woman who has spurned the advances of influential and powerful men. Aren't you flattered? Does my passion not move you?'

'Mistress!' I cried desperately. 'What you suggest is impossible! I beg you to stop. I will never betray my master's trust. I am therefore blind to your beauty and deaf to your persistence regarding this dangerous venture.'

'Dangerous venture? Where is the danger?'

'Danger lies within the shadow of betrayal.'

'Are you calling me treacherous?'

'No, mistress, I am referring to the proposal.'

I could see the rage in her eyes and felt a cold chill run down my spine. How might she react? She was unpredictable and had a track record of attacking anyone who opposed her. Onamun's final warning – never resist the demands of authority – echoed through my mind.

'Leave now!' she bellowed, pointing at the doorway. 'You have angered me!'

I backed out of her chamber before she changed her mind, thanking the God of my fathers for intervening to rescue me. I knew, however, that I had had a lucky escape, and fully expected the temptation to continue.

* * * * * * *

Four months later

The Egyptians love festivals, as these are times when

people have an excuse to eat, drink and be merry. All the festivals have a religious relevance, and one of the most popular of these events is the Wepet-Renpet festival, otherwise known as the Opening of the Year or the New Year's Day celebration. At this time of year, all households take to the streets to dance, sing, eat, drink and observe the solemn processions – even servants and slaves are accorded a degree of freedom to join in the celebrations and for several days most labour is suspended.

Every year Potiphar's household immersed itself in the religious carnival. Under close supervision, some of the slaves were allowed to leave the residence and journey from El Akhet to the centre of the city of Waset where most of the celebrations were. I had never attended these festivities, even when invited by Potiphar, because I considered them pagan in nature and an affront to the God of my fathers. But, I looked forward to the New Year because it was the only time when I could truly experience privacy and enjoy a rest from my hectic schedule.

While there was still work to be done, it was mostly light domestic tasks that I could accomplish on my own, such as taking stock of supplies and assessing areas of the house in need of repair or refurbishment. This year I was especially looking forward to the short holiday because Potiphar always attended the festivities with his wife and they typically stayed away for the duration. I knew that they stayed in a guesthouse reserved for Pharaoh's officials, in Waset.

A three-day break from Potiphar's wife was the sort of reprieve I desperately needed, due to her increasing demands. From what had previously been a weekly practice – cornering me whenever I went into the private residential quarters to inspect the work of my domestic staff – her demands for me to satisfy her passion were now daily. To ensure that I was never alone with her, I always attended the residential quarters with Kaa, but she would often dismiss him on some pretext, such as having something important to say to me, and I would be powerless to refuse. To avoid this, I resorted to monitoring her movements remotely by getting one of her closest female attendants to alert me whenever she left the house.

I trained Kaa to carry out inspections and delegated the job to him, so that any day I knew she was in the house, I could avoid going there. In this way, I was able to stay out of her way most of the time. On a number of occasions she had sent Kaa or another servant to summon me to her chamber, but I always found a way to wriggle out by reserving some of Potiphar's most pressing tasks for moments such as these. When I said – through her emissaries – that I had urgent business for Master Potiphar, she would back down, but before I could catch my breath, she would be back with a fresh invitation.

On days like this, when the house was deserted, I would neither have to listen to her begging with me nor avert my gaze from her body, which was always clad in revealing attire, as part of the enticement. Not being able to confide in anyone else about what was happening was also a challenge, and there were moments when I wished I could share the psychological burden with another. Abali, who was my closest companion in the household, probably suspected what was going on – because of my mood when I was summoned to her presence – and Kaa definitely knew because he was her emissary, but I could not risk a scandal. Despite her demands, I bore my mistress no ill-will, considering her to be an instrument of mischief in Satan's hands.

The concept of a manipulating evil spirit like the devil is alien to the Egyptians, despite their belief in many gods, and as such, temptation is not something they are either conscious of or able to guard against. Life for them is a matter of choices which their gods either approve or disapprove of. I often wondered about the forces that drove men and women to engage in inappropriate relationships. For instance, I knew that some of my brothers indulged in all sorts of indiscretions with Canaanite women and that they often frequented brothels, despite having wives at home. On the other hand, my brother Reuben had spurned the advances of the Canaanite women, but committed an even greater indiscretion with one of my father's concubines. My father had warned us against succumbing to one of the strongest baits of Satan, lest we fall out of favour with God, but some of my brothers had capitulated.

At puberty I had made a covenant with my heart never to stray into an inappropriate relationship, but my resolve was being tested every day.

I gained access to the main building and went about my chores. While I was heading to the kitchen to take stock of food supplies, I recalled Potiphar mentioning he had some garments in need of laundering. The task of laundering was reserved for a couple of designated servants but, as they were attending the festivities, and this was only the first day of the event, I knew I could not wait for their return. I had laundered Potiphar's clothes on many occasions whenever the need arose and so was both familiar and comfortable with this task.

I headed upstairs to his chamber, humming an old folk tune to myself. His chamber was directly opposite his wife's, and I was the only person apart from his wife who had unfettered access to it. Like many prominent Egyptians, he chose to sleep separately from his spouse, reminding me of my own nomadic dwelling in Hebron where my father slept in a separate tent from his wives.

I was about to step into Potiphar's chamber to retrieve his clothes when I saw his wife lounging in her doorway. I froze where I stood, paralysed in limb and thought, unable to react to her unexpected presence. She was clad in a transparent sheath dress that clung to her curvaceous body, and her hair was woven into shoulder-length braids that flattered her symmetrical face and accentuated her neck. She wore little make-up, restraining herself to the obligatory kohl liner and golden eyeshadow, but her beauty was not impaired. To crown it all, there was an impishness dancing in her eyes, complemented by an arched eyebrow that was extremely provocative.

As I regained my mental capacity, dozens of thoughts fought their way through my head, jostling for position. What was she doing at home? Had I not witnessed her departing with her husband for the city of Waset that morning? When had she returned? Why did I not know about this? It was unusual for her to be alone at home without her maids for company, so where were they?

'Hello, Joseph.' Her voice was husky and thickly laced with syrupy seduction.

'Aren't you supposed to be at Waset with the master?' I asked, making no effort to mask my agitation.

'Yes,' she purred, 'but as we departed El Akhet I

became curiously faint and had to return. I wonder why.'

I knew why, but my respect for her status prevented me from saying.

'Where are your maids?' I asked, looking around me anxiously.

'I told them I just needed to rest and asked them to take the day off. I am not expecting them back until evening.'

Goosebumps shivered over my vulnerable skin and my heartbeat sounded in my ears. From her present appearance and past conduct I was in no doubt about her motives, but extricating myself this time would be trickier.

'I just came to get some of the master's garments for laundering,' I stuttered in confusion. 'Do you have anything that needs cleaning?'

I suddenly realised my error and stopped speaking, but it was too late. I had played right into her hands and the twinkle in her eyes confirmed it.

'As a matter of fact, there is,' she said, reaching out to clasp my wrist and draw me towards her.

I considered pulling away but all the while I thought about the implications of unintentionally hurting her, as I was well capable of. Like a lamb to the slaughter I let her draw me into her chamber. As I arrived at the side of her bed, she started to giggle in a manner that I found tortuous. What was I doing? Had she not made it clear what she wanted from me? We were alone in the complex. Apart from two guards outside the main building, there was no one present to pose a threat to her evil intentions. This was no chance encounter, but a carefully orchestrated and choreographed strategy aimed at destroying all arguments I might have against giving in to her erotic desires.

I noted her dilated pupils and the heaving of her chest and realised that she was becoming crudely excited. All my senses screamed at me to do something, to say something, but I was frozen, the palms of my hands clammy. The sheer ripples of her dress were like an open gate to a city about to be invaded, and the intensity of my righteous thoughts, coupled with my desire, made me dizzy with confusion.

'Joseph, I want you,' she said hoarsely, tightening her grip on my wrist. 'Just take me – I'm yours.'

'No,' I said anaemically. 'I can't.'

She pulled me down towards her as she fell backwards onto her bed but I reached out for the headrest to balance myself. Noting my resistance, she tugged more forcefully and I strained, refusing to be drawn down beside her.

'I want you to lie with me!' she said with escalating aggression. 'Take me in your arms and quench my drought!'

'No,' I muttered, pulling backwards, not wishing to move too suddenly and hurt her. 'No, mistress, I cannot do what you ask. Please let me go.'

'What are you afraid of?' she asked, in a voice smothered with desperation. 'There is no one here but us!'

'No, mistress, we are not alone,' I gasped. 'There is one who sees all things and He is watching us right now. It is not too late for us to halt this madness and for you to depart with your dignity!'

'What dignity?' she shrieked, gripping my wrist with both hands and tugging me towards her with such unexpected force that in spite of my efforts I fell down on the bed beside her. 'The dignity of rejection?'

'Mistress, I cannot reject something I can never have,' I said firmly.

'But you can have me!'

'No, mistress, you belong to my master and to him alone.'

'Joseph, don't defy me,' she hissed, sounding like one of the Nile serpents that her people worshipped. 'You do not want me as an adversary!'

Realising that she was already my adversary, I wriggled out of her grip, taking care not to injure her. Taking advantage of my freedom, I scrambled to my feet, but she reached out and grabbed my knee-length linen kilt which, due to the intense heat, was the only piece of clothing I wore. I felt the kilt start to slip from my waist and had to grab it to prevent myself being stripped bare. The frenzied look in her eyes was, bizarrely, accompanied by tears, but whether of sorrow or ecstasy I could not tell. Intense fear gripped me even more tightly than she was gripping my kilt. Inside, I screamed out to the one who had been my guiding star in every storm.

'Yield to me, Joseph, and I will not rest until my husband has given you your freedom and recommended you to a place of prominence in his administration!'

As she spoke, a mocking voice inside me urged me to avail myself of the privilege that was presenting itself to me so I could fulfil my dreams of greatness and rise to influence in Egypt. However, I knew that voice: it was the one I had been trained from youth to resist.

'Please, mistress, let me go, do not do this!' I implored, as she reached a hand beneath my kilt with an intent that was too despicable to contemplate.

I knew there was only one way she could compel me

to be a willing partner in her sordid adventure, and she would stop at nothing, even if it meant physically enticing me. I was a man, with the capacity for carnality like all men, and the longer I remained with her, the greater the chance that I could be seduced by a need that I had been suppressing from puberty. Maybe it was the horror of her intention that was the trigger, but it caused a reckless surge of energy within me, enabling me to tear away from her. Without pausing, I raced towards the doorway of her chamber and down the hallway towards the stairs. It was only when I reached the top of the stairs that I realised I had left my kilt in her hands.

'Joseph! Joseph!'

I heard her shriek in agony like a wounded animal as I bounded down the stairs, unclothed.

THE MIDNIGHT HOUR

Proverbs 4:18

I stared down at the manacles around my wrists, bound together by a thick length of chain, then at the manacles around my ankles. I heaved a sigh. It had been almost four years since I had last been in chains of any sort but, as excruciatingly burdensome as they felt, the weight around my heart was heavier.

I was standing in the courtyard of the servants' quarters with two of Potiphar's Egyptian guards either side of me. In front of me was the husband of my alleged victim. Behind him, sobbing gently, with a tear-stained face, besmeared make-up and dishevelled hair, was my accuser, holding my abandoned kilt in her hand like a trophy.

To call the chain of unfolding events 'dramatic' would be an understatement. My head was still reeling from the speed at which everything had happened. One moment I had been sitting alone in my quarters, wearing a replacement kilt, reliving the horror of my encounter with the mistress of the house, and the next moment two guards armed with swords and javelins were at my doorway, demanding that I accompany them. In fact, as I later discovered, five hours had elapsed since I fled my mistress's chamber, but I was so confused by the situation that I had lost all track of time.

In the intervening five hours I had sat alone in my quarters, thinking about the bizarre events of that afternoon, desperately trying to find reassurance. The encounter with my mistress had been traumatising because of the lengths she was prepared to go to. Reliving the incident mentally was unsettling enough, but contemplating what might have happened was even more harrowing. Fear flooded my soul. What would she do next?

I imagined the best-case and worst-case scenarios, but neither gave me comfort. I imagined she would try to have me replaced as overseer, but wondered what rationale she would use. I was certain that she would never tell her husband what had happened, but feared she would seek revenge in some way.

The thought of being bound in chains never even crossed my mind.

I had been escorted down to the courtyard where I found an incensed Potiphar waiting for me, his dishevelled wife also present. Then I realised the enormity of the situation. The guards who came for me bound me in chains under my master's fiery gaze then threw me at his feet. With great difficulty I picked myself up from the ground, wincing in pain as the rough edges of the manacles dug into my flesh, drawing blood. I thought about my arrival at El Akhet over four years ago. It felt like I had come full circle.

'Why?'

The question was asked in a voice raw with emotion – pain, anger and confusion vying for supremacy. I could understand his anger, but the pain was a revelation. I was seized by a compulsion to set the record straight and clarify that I was the victim in the saga, but an even more powerful compulsion told me to keep quiet. I went with the latter, knowing that only God could instruct me to do something that went against common sense.

'I gave you everything,' continued Potiphar. 'You

had access to all my affairs and carried my signet ring to execute business on my behalf. I treated you more like a son than a slave, so why would you throw dung in my face?'

Tears gathered in my eyes as he spoke. I longed to defend myself but yet again a powerful inner restraint prevented me.

'You could have had your pick of the female servants and slaves with my blessing, if your urge was that strong,' he continued in a voice that was edging towards anguish, 'but why my wife? Why would you be so brazen?'

My silence seemed to aggravate his pain, and his contorted expression made me realise the torment he was going through – which his beloved wife had orchestrated for her own selfish purposes. If she had kept quiet, he would have been none the wiser and she could have spared him all this agony. He loved her, despite her inability to provide him with children, yet she despised him. I knew that, if it came down to it, he would believe anything she said and my version of events would be swept aside because he was too blind to see the truth. Even if he would have believed me, I had no intention of exposing her infidelity; it would break him. A broken-hearted man is a handicap to himself and others, and I did not wish that for him.

'How did you think you would get away with it?' asked Potiphar, shaking his head in disbelief. 'Did you think that you could buy her silence? What with? Youthful vigour? Did you imagine that she would fall in love with you after you had forced her to lie with you?'

I stared past him at my accuser, who was still sobbing. Her crocodile tears threatened to flood the Nile. As our eyes met, she slowly and deliberately winked at me. I stared aghast unable to react in the way all my senses were urging me to. Who would believe me? Her confidence stemmed from the fact that she knew her husband trusted her beyond all reason.

'You leave me no choice,' he said, pacing around me. 'Under Egyptian law, your offence is one for which the death penalty is reserved.'

My heart leapt within me and my muscles tensed in trepidation. To my surprise, his wife's eyes widened in terror and her lips parted, as if she were about to speak.

'However,' he went on, 'in view of your diligent service in my business affairs, I have decided to be merciful. I have also considered the fact that nothing actually happened between you and my wife, thanks to her bravery in fighting you off. So I am sentencing you to an indeterminate term of incarceration in the Den of Confinement, starting from this evening. You will remain there for as long as I remain captain of Pharaoh's guard. That is your punishment.'

I did not know whether to be grateful or despondent. As captain of Pharaoh's guard, Potiphar could have sentenced me to death and executed me that very evening; on the other hand, he could remain captain of the guard for a very long time because it was a life appointment that depended on the tenure of the Pharaoh who appointed him. If he outlived the Pharaoh, then a new Pharaoh could choose to leave him in office or replace him. I noted the relief in Potiphar's wife's eyes as her husband finished speaking. Her mouth clamped shut. She clearly didn't want me to die, but she had no qualms about me rotting in an Egyptian prison, which is what the Den of Confinement was. As part of his role, Potiphar oversaw the administration of this prison and had the unilateral power to sentence and confine anyone.

'Take him away!' said Potiphar, turning away from me.

The guards hauled me away in front of the other servants and slaves, who were returning home from the festival. I could see the bewilderment on their faces. Abali stepped forward in consternation, quizzing me with his eyes, but one of the guards shoved him roughly out of the way. I was tempted to turn around to look back at the residence one last time, but I resolutely refused this option.

Just when I believed I was rising in stature and drawing closer to the day of my release, I found myself once again an innocent victim of another's hatred.

*   *   *   *   *   *   *

The Den of Confinement

The Den of Confinement or 'the Tomb', as it was more commonly known, was the place reserved by the Egyptian penal system for those who were deemed undesirables. On the outskirts of Waset, the Egyptian capital, it was a massive stone fortress built by the same workforce responsible for the pyramids. Its site on the Nile's western bank was adjacent to a complex necropolis containing cemeteries and tombs for the wealthy, hence its nickname. Large hieroglyphs were engraved on the high walls and the entrance, which was between two stone columns, had large sculptures of Egyptian gods on either side. The idea was that whoever ended up in the Tomb was subject to the will of the gods.

As the supreme authority, Pharaoh could sentence

anyone who displeased him to spend a season in the Tomb. There were no sentencing guidelines to govern the execution of this authority, but it was subject to whatever Pharaoh or his nominees decided. In addition, the penal system did not have a hierarchy of prisons or places of incarceration, as imprisonment was more like a waiting room for more substantial sanctions. The Tomb therefore catered for a variety of different societal misfits, including criminals awaiting final punishment, soldiers who had broken rank, indentured slaves who had offended their masters, and serial debt defaulters. It was also a class-conscious system that seemed to favour the rich and influential. A scribe's or priest's slave who offended them could expect to spend time in the Tomb, as would a slave who owed more than he could afford to repay.

The Tomb was overseen by Potiphar, the captain of Pharaoh's guard, and he presided over judgements, sentences and executions. As a judge, he was supported by a council of priests and scribes, but as an executioner he acted alone, exercising Pharaoh's authority. Anyone Potiphar sent to the Tomb had no right of appeal: he could unilaterally decide to execute anyone he felt still posed a threat to the Egyptian empire, despite their incarceration. The day-to-day running of the Tomb was down to a prison governor nicknamed Keeper of the Tomb or just the Keeper. The Keeper reported to Potiphar and was supported by a couple of scribes and a detachment of armed guards.

The Tomb was split into a criminal wing and a domestic wing. The criminal wing was the maximum security section reserved for those accused of crimes against Pharaoh and the state, while the domestic wing was the minimum security section, housing indentured slaves accused of offences against their masters. The main distinction between the two was that the maximum security section had armed guards stationed there around the clock, while the minimum security section had none. For my alleged offence I was sent to the maximum security section.

On arrival at my new residence after a tedious and agonising journey from Men'at Khufu, my wrists and ankles were raw and sore from the hot, crudely fashioned manacles and all my limbs ached from the effort of walking in chains. Each step was physically and psychologically tortuous. I struggled to blank out my thoughts to avoid them straying to the circumstances of my incarceration. Fixing my mind on the things I believed to be more edifying, I kept up my spirits by recalling the dreams God had given me. Even though such a future now seemed virtually impossible, in light of my current predicament, I drew strength from replaying the images over and over again in my head.

After the guards at the Tomb took custody of me, the Keeper appeared – a short, rotund man with facial skin as smooth as a baby's and chubby cheeks. He offered no name and was not addressed by one; everyone simply called him the Keeper. The Keeper never smiled, and his sullen expression made him hard to read. He signed the requisite papyrus to officially take custody of me, then had one of the armed guards escort me to my cell in the maximum security section. As we walked along the poorly lit, dingy corridor, the squeaking of rodents mingled with the dull chorus of my chains scraping along the floor.

As we passed the cells, each with a narrow iron gate, I noticed the faces of the inmates. They were a shuddering diversity of defiance, anger, bitterness, hostility and despondency. Some of them looked utterly hopeless and helpless, stripped of confidence; these faces narrated their own stories and previewed their obituaries, giving me a deep feeling of foreboding. The stench of death was everywhere and I considered that the Den's nickname was well deserved.

My cell was on one of the upper floors and, like all the others we had passed along the way, was behind a bolted narrow iron gate that afforded no privacy. The cell was for two people. When the guards opened the gate I froze at the sight of my cell mate, a powerfully built, dark-skinned hunchback, whose grotesque facial features – bulbous nose, thick lips and wide-eyed stare – crowned my macabre experience. He was on his feet by the gate as it opened and he eyed me in fascination as I was shoved in. His body odour was nauseating and his heavy breathing reminded me of a camel's. Breathing through my mouth, I surveyed my environment. My heart sank. There were no beds, just three rough stone walls, an uneven floor, a single window too narrow for anyone to squeeze through, and a bowl on the ground for passing waste.

One of the guards unchained me, taking off my wrist and ankle manacles, while another aimed his javelin at my menacing cell mate, as if keeping him at bay. Despite my relief at being freed from the irons that chafed my skin, I was concerned about being left alone with a man who seemed to instil fear even in prison guards. The gate slammed shut behind me. As the bolts were slid in place, my anxiety heightened. I stood facing the window on the opposite side of the room, keeping my back to my cell mate in the hope that he would ignore my presence. However, the sound of feet shuffling towards me crushed my fragile expectation, prompting me to edge nearer the window.

The window was narrow, permitting a bird's-eye view of the mountainous ranges of the eastern desert in the distance and the nearby surrounding tombs. Noisy vultures circled above and, as I followed their flight path, I noted the deep gully to the rear of the building where a small group of men were unloading what looked like the lifeless bodies of ex-inmates from a mule-drawn cart and dumping them into the bowels of the gully. The stench from the gully hit me and I felt like throwing up. I considered the health implications of having an open burial ground right beside the prison and began to fear for my mortality. The thought of living with the combined odours from within and without filled me with dread.

'They call me Raamah. I am Cushite,' said a guttural voice in crude Egyptian.

The sound of his voice startled me, and I jumped. Turning around slowly, I confronted the menacing hulk of a man. His massive hands looked like they could squeeze the life out of me. I swallowed and summoned the courage to look in his eyes. Although they appeared to bulge out of his skull, there was something intriguing about them, and the more I stared, the more I saw inquisitiveness rather than aggression.

'My name is Joseph, I am Hebrew,' I answered hesitantly.

'And what is your crime?'

I thought about this, trying to consider the most balanced response – one that told the truth without blowing up the offence.

'I am accused of trying to forcefully lie with my master's wife.'

Raamah did not even blink. Instead he stared unnervingly into my eyes. 'I do not believe it,' he said at last in his gravelly voice. 'A good-looking boy like you does not have to forcefully take what women will willingly offer him.'

Despite his logic, I was grateful that someone believed in my innocence – even if he lacked the capacity to do anything about it. Summoning courage, I ventured to make some enquiries of my own.

'What about you?' I asked casually. 'What are you accused of?'

'Killing a slave girl who spurned my advances.'

My fears rose to the surface again and I instinctively stepped backwards till my back touched the wall.

'Did you?' I asked timidly.

'Does it matter? After all, you just found me guilty.'

His response made me think. I realised that my reaction had been unwittingly judgemental. He backed away to the other corner of the cell and lowered himself to the floor, where he curled up and rested his head on his folded arms. Despite his grotesque appearance, he appeared to have a gentle soul.

'I am sorry,' I said quietly.

'Just stay out of my way,' he grunted, 'or I *will* harm you.'

His reaction to my judgement of him had created an invisible social divide. He was probably used to disgusted stares, as well as being treated with fear and contempt. In response, he had developed a hard shell as his defensive mechanism. He was clearly a misunderstood soul, in need of sensitive handling, but my reaction had just reinforced his perception. It had probably cost me the chance of building a friendship with him.

The rest of the day was spent in virtual isolation, with Raamah ignoring my existence and keeping to his corner of the cell, and me looking for every opportunity to repair the damage. Sporadically, I thought about my family, wondering about my father's health, Benjamin's welfare, and whether my other brothers were remorseful about what they had done to me. I did not know whether I could ever forgive them but I still craved their repentance; just knowing that they were full of regret would aid my healing.

As evening fell, a guard appeared at the door with two bowls of watery soup and two chunks of hard bread. He reached through the bars of the gate, placed the food on the floor and departed without saying a word. I watched as Raamah roused from his slumber and reached for one of the bowls and a chunk of bread. He emptied the bowl and gnawed the bread in less than a minute, then sat staring at me.

I tasted the soup and spluttered as the cold, bland broth touched my tongue. I tried the hard chunk of bread, which looked mouldy, and gave up after several attempts to chew my way through it. Leaving both items on the floor, I retreated to my corner, where I sat with my back to the wall. At one point, sleep began to call for me. As I drifted in and out of slumber, I was vaguely aware of Raamah crossing the room on all fours and reaching for my soup and bread.

* * * * * * *

Seven months later

I stared down at the bowl of watery lentil soup in my bowl and instantly lost my appetite. This was a daily ritual with me, and one that was affecting my health.

During the first seven months of my incarceration, my weight had plummeted dramatically, to the stage where my ribs were exposed and my sunken eyes were almost obscured by the sharpness of my cheekbones. All the muscle I had developed at Potiphar's house had shrunk so that my upper arms, thighs and calf muscles, which had previously been a source of pride, were now pitiable.

We were fed twice a day. I was eating a meal every other day, and then only because I had to, to preserve my strength for the hard labour we were made to do. The Tomb had a basic structure for all inmates: those in the minimum security wing remained in their wing carrying out basic tasks, while those in maximum security worked in a local stone quarry a short distance from the building.

At sunrise, as the orange bowl of the sun rose above the surrounding mountain ranges of the eastern desert, armed guards appeared with manacles, which they placed on our wrists and around our necks, so we could be chained together. They then led us to the courtyard, where there was roll call, before escorting us out of the building and to the stone quarry, which I later discovered belonged to the Tomb. We toiled all day extracting stones from the quarry, only pausing for water and a short break. Never before in my life had I worked so hard. The stones we extracted were sold to the owners of the surrounding cemeteries, who used them to create bespoke tombs.

Prison life comprised of working six days in the quarry from sunrise to sunset, then having a day off to recuperate. I was not proficient in the art of extracting stones and, despite my best efforts, I was unable to excel. Part of the problem was my poor energy levels resulting from my self-imposed starvation. The uneaten food did not go to waste because Raamah was always on standby, despite his hostility, to help himself to my rations. Even on days that I managed to eat, he still hovered around me, ready to pounce. How I survived these seven months, I have no idea. It must have been by the grace of the God who miraculously sustained and empowered me to cope with the rigours of my prison schedule without fainting.

To ensure that we kept to the production schedule, the quarry foremen, under the Keeper's instructions, whipped us. Pain is neither an incentive nor a motivation, but a deterrent. There is no way to deter an exhausted person from taking a rest. I observed many of my fellow inmates flagging under the brutal labour and being carried off the site to recover; occasionally some were pronounced dead.

If heat exhaustion did not take its toll, then the whipping did. Each night as I lay down, bruised and aching, I remembered to give thanks to the God who had seen me through the day. A major challenge for me was dealing with the bitterness and self-pity that warred in my soul.

The images of my brothers – particularly Simeon, Levi, and the sons of Bilhah and Zilpah – often passed through my mind, and at such times thoughts of revenge surfaced. I reasoned that if they had not sold me, I would never have experienced the inhumane treatment of slaves and all the other circumstances that ultimately landed me in the Tomb. However, whenever these thoughts came, I tried to neutralise them by focusing on my dreams and what they had promised me.

During the first month of my stint in the quarry, I

discovered that some of the inmates had developed a code for communicating with each other. I began to learn it, partly out of curiosity and partly from survival instinct. They tended to use a combination of crudely scrawled hieroglyphs on stones with hand and eye signs that resembled hieroglyphs. As I gained proficiency in their secret dialogue, it became clear that a plan was being hatched – and that my cell mate was at the centre of it.

If Raamah had been unpopular outside the Tomb, within it he was an icon. His bear-like features meant that he was called upon as a henchman by many inmates in their dealings with each other. 'Accidents' often happened, such as a stone being 'accidentally' dropped on an inmate's foot, immobilising him, or a person being shoved down a dry water cistern in the quarry. All these were arranged.

Over the preceding seven months, Raamah's hostility towards me never materialised as physical violence, but the psychological torment was enough to keep me out of his way. He would glare at me for no reason, then start mouthing words in his native Cushite dialect. His bizarre behaviour merely increased the quality and frequency of my prayers, as I sought protection from him.

As the months passed, there was a growing unease among my fellow inmates in the maximum security wing. The food rations worsened in quality and our personal hygiene suffered due to communal baths decreasing in frequency from weekly to fortnightly. Considering the hot and sticky conditions under which we toiled, this was inhumane. To further aggravate the situation, the number of physicians assigned to attend to our healthcare needs dwindled, and injuries such as cuts, gashes and bruises was left to inmates to treat. Some inmates who had developed a specialty in treating such injuries took it upon themselves to assist others, but poor hygiene was a critical problem, often resulting in infected wounds, which led to death. The rodent infestation problem escalated during the seven months and a plague began to spread, which was worsened by our poor immunity from illness.

There were rumblings among inmates regarding the dwindling state of affairs. Despair and frustration were rife because the Keeper did not seem to be bothered about our welfare. I began to hear rumours of a planned revolt or protest, but the details were sketchy. Depending on who I spoke to, it was either going to take place at the quarry or within the Tomb. The only detail that everyone seemed to agree on was that my cell mate, Raamah, was the brains behind it. This news concerned me – partly because, having shared a cell with him, I did not credit him with any sort of political intelligence. I was also concerned that his idea of a protest could spill over into a bloodbath, given his fiery temperament and short fuse, coupled with a mouth that seemed disconnected from his brain. He was more comfortable letting his fists do the talking and, whenever he did, it was usually a monologue.

One evening, on the last week of the seventh month, as the inmates headed back from the quarry to the Tomb, I noticed one of the inmates surreptitiously passing a thin metal tool to Raamah, which he secreted beneath his loincloth. Several of Raamah's associates made hand signals which I recognised and deciphered. The inmates' secret plan involved Raamah playing a pivotal role in their revolt. This probably explained why he had been passed the tool. The level of security at the quarry was high, and while we were unchained so that we could perform our tasks, we were closely watched by armed guards and placed in chains again at the end of our shift. However, because we were in chains, the guards paid less attention to us and body searches were infrequent.

My nervousness escalated as Raamah passed the security checkpoints outside the Tomb and entered the premises, the concealed tool beneath his loincloth. Concerned about potential violence, I once again considered whether I should alert the Keeper. If Raamah and his comrades were plotting their revolt this evening, there could be deaths. Since I was his cell mate, I was afraid of being caught in the middle of any violent confrontation.

As we trudged into the Tomb's central courtyard for our fortnightly communal bath, where we washed using the large water troughs, it was obvious that trouble was imminent. Standing in the courtyard with chained manacles around my ankles, I closed my eyes and lowered my head to say a quick prayer for guidance. Lifting my head, I sighted a guard walking around the periphery of the courtyard. As he drew closer, I signalled to him, indicating that I wished to use the conveniences. The guard beckoned me over and I shuffled towards him. He led me to a secluded corner where there were large reinforced bowls. As we walked, I tapped him on the arm. He turned.

'I need to speak to the Keeper,' I hissed urgently. 'I think there's going to be an uprising by some inmates.'

The guard grabbed my arm and yanked me towards him. 'Who are they?' he asked ferociously, his voice so loud I felt it could be heard across the courtyard.

'Let me speak with the Keeper,' I said, refusing to

give in to his intimidation.

Noting the defiance in my sunken eyes, he backed down and led me towards the Keeper's office near the front of the building. When we arrived, we found the Keeper studying a handful of papyrus documents. To my frustration, the guard waited for him to finish reading before sharing my information with him.

The Keeper rose to his feet as the guard finished speaking. His crow-like, beady, brown eyes scrutinised my face perniciously.

'Who are those behind this?' he asked.

'I do not know all of them,' I said, 'but I know one of them is carrying a weapon.'

'Which one?'

'Raamah.'

'The hunchback?'

I nodded.

The Keeper turned to the guard who had escorted me. 'Bring him to me,' he snarled.

I watched with a sinking feeling in the pit of my stomach as the guard drew his sword and headed out of the office towards the courtyard. Raamah would most likely have seen me leave the communal area, and he would suspect me of raising the alarm.

'Why are you telling me this, Joseph?'

I was surprised that he knew my name, as he always dealt with inmates via his administrators or guards.

'Because, while I empathise with the reasons for the revolt, I have no wish to see any bloodshed,' I answered as boldly as my weariness permitted.

'And what are the reasons for the revolt?'

'Well, I suspect they are to do with our deplorable living conditions.'

His silence confirmed my fear that he was unwilling

to either compromise or commit to making improvements. A stalemate would inevitably prolong the situation.

'Raamah speaks for all of us,' I added, hoping that would get him to engage.

His beady eyes studied me closely. 'You know what will happen to you if Raamah finds out you betrayed him?'

I nodded. A convenient accident in the quarry would be arranged, and all inmates would look the other way. But I had faith in God.

'I will try my best to protect you,' he said vaguely, 'but I cannot guarantee anything.'

'I understand.'

I realised the reason for his evasiveness. With a finite level of resources, he had no way of absolutely ensuring my protection. Those finite resources were also the reason for our worsening living conditions.

My contemplation was fractured by the sudden distant roar of male voices, followed by the sound of the guards' gong, which was their official alarm in the event of an incident. Against this backdrop, my ears picked up the sound of running feet heading in our direction. My breathing quickened.

'Keeper! Keeper!'

We turned toward the doorway to see the captain of the prison guards, urgency and apprehension printed all over his perspiring face. Behind him was the guard who had just left to apprehend Raamah, who also looked distressed.

'What is it?' asked the Keeper, with upraised hands.

'The revolt has already started!' said the captain of the guards. 'The inmates have managed to free themselves from their chains and have taken over both the maximum and minimum security wings!'

'But how?' asked the Keeper, looking around perplexedly.

I recalled the metal tool that had been passed to Raamah; it was most probably a key. While we were bathing he must have freed himself then passed the key around to others until there were enough of them free to mount a takeover.

'I do not know,' answered the captain, 'but they have taken some of our men hostage and sealed themselves in the communal recreation area.'

The communal recreation area was an open section that separated the maximum and minimum security wings. There was a gate leading to the area which one had to pass through to gain access to either wing. The inmates effectively owned the Tomb, although they could not escape because of the armed guards outside.

'And I presume Raamah is the ringleader.'

'Yes, Keeper,' answered the captain in a subdued voice.

'Are any of your guards harmed? Has anyone been killed?'

'Not as far as we know, but I am expecting casualties.'

'Have they made any demands?'

'Not yet, Keeper, but you know Captain Potiphar's instructions regarding the handling of inmate revolts.'

'Not to give in? Yes, of course I know that!'

'I suggest we call for reinforcements from the garrison to break in and seize control, killing anyone who opposes us.'

My already racing heart gathered even more momentum. I knew that Raamah would be one of the first to die and that many others would be killed at random in the most gruesome way. I had heard stories of how the guards would slowly torture inmates to death before beheading them and placing the severed heads in the quarry as a deterrent to others. I felt the urge to do something to avert the bloodshed, but had no idea what influence I could bring to bear in the circumstance.

'That seems like the only option,' said the Keeper, stroking his chin pensively. 'How many of your men are being held?'

'I estimate about ten, but there may be more – I have not had time to do a head count.'

'They are already dead men,' said the Keeper balefully.

'There does not need to be any loss of life,' I interjected, unable to keep quiet any longer. 'I think I have a solution.'

All three men turned towards me with expectant expressions, confirming my suspicion that they were open to any plan that could avoid violence. Buoyed by their lack of indignation, I took a deep breath, knowing that I would have to make things up as I went along.

'Let me speak with them,' I offered.

'Speak with them?' asked the captain of the guard.

I nodded. 'Let me find out their reasons for revolting and any list of demands they might have.'

'That is pointless, Hebrew!' said the captain, looking aghast. 'We cannot meet their demands, no matter what they are.'

'As the captain of the guard, you are in charge of security,' I said quietly, realising that what I was about to say would not go down well. 'If Potiphar discovers that the uprising happened because your men failed to carry out a proper body search of the inmates, you may be held to account.'

The captain's face clouded over. I drew back, but he controlled himself and his rage went no further than his face. My words were deliberate, and they seemed to be having the desired effect.

'And what happens when you find out their demands?' he asked in a restrained voice.

'You review them, but attach conditions such as the guarantee that your guards will not be harmed in any way and that property will not be destroyed.'

'And you expect them to listen to you after you betrayed their confidence?' asked the Keeper, staring at me as if I had taken leave of my senses.

'They never took me into their confidence. I stumbled on their plan by chance. Besides, what do you have to lose?'

The Keeper considered this and nodded. He had nothing to lose if I died in the process: after all, I was just another inmate to him.

'Unchain him,' said the Keeper, eyeing the manacles around my ankles.

The captain hesitated, his expression conveying his displeasure.

'If he gets into trouble, at least he can run,' explained the Keeper.

The captain instructed the other guard to unchain me then to escort me to the gate of the communal recreation area. Before I left the office, the Keeper drew me to one side for a private word.

'I have been watching you since your arrival,' he said quietly, 'and have noted your diligence and discipline, which are exemplary. Your conduct today confirms that you are also a brave and honourable man.'

I nodded, unsure whether his assessment required a

verbal acknowledgement. I did not feel brave; in fact, I felt quite the opposite. I left the Keeper's office in the company of the guard, limping as I waited for the circulation to return to my legs, and headed across the courtyard to the gate. There were at least twenty armed guards outside the gate. As we approached, I became the focus of their attention. With every step, I knew I was drawing closer to a destiny I had not foreseen, and my only confidence lay in the detail of my dreams, which had not yet come to pass. I was quietly confident that God, who had earmarked me for greatness and revealed my destiny in those dreams, had a plan to bring it to fruition in the appointed season.

At the gate to the recreation area, the guard with me spoke forcefully to his tense-looking comrades, explaining the situation to them. They quickly dispersed, giving me access. Using a small rock I picked up from the ground, I banged as hard as I could against the metal frame. My exertions eventually attracted attention and a gruff voice asked who it was. I announced myself as Raamah's cell mate, then waited. After a brief pause, another voice spoke, which I instantly recognised as Raamah's. My anxiety heightened.

'What do you want, Hebrew traitor?'

'I am here to explore options for resolution.'

'You mean you are here to spy on behalf of the Keeper.'

'No, I am here to avert unnecessary bloodshed. If you let me, I wish to discuss a way forward which is in everybody's interest.'

'And why should we listen to you?'

'Because you have nothing to lose.'

There was a lengthier pause, then Raamah spoke

again. 'Tell the guards to lower their swords and move to the centre of the courtyard. Warn them that if they try to follow you in, we will start killing their friends.'

I turned around to convey his instructions, but the guards were already retreating to the designated spot, their weapons lowered. I heard the bolts at the other side of the gate grate as they slid back, and realised that this was the moment of truth. Although I did not have a final strategy, I had the bones of a plan that I thought would work. I only prayed that it was acceptable to both sides.

The gate opened a fraction and I eased my slender frame through the gap. As I stepped through, the gate slammed shut again and two burly inmates slid the bolts back in place. The recreation area was full of inmates from both wings, some standing, others seated in groups. In the dwindling light I sensed their hostility as they looked in my direction. Raamah was waiting near the gate with a sword in his hand, undoubtedly liberated from one of the hostages, and his powerfully built frame looked ready for war.

'So what is this plan of yours?'

* * * * * * *

Raamah and I sat alone in a ground-floor cell in the minimum security wing. It was furnished with two beds covered with straw mats. Each of the cells in the minimum security wing had access to a communal washroom where inmates could bath in relative privacy. The ambience in the cell was far better than ours, and I felt deprived.

We sat on the beds facing each other, an oil lamp between us providing the only light in the cell. At my request, he had arranged for the privacy as I felt more comfortable discussing my proposal, which I was still working out in my head, without the distraction of a lynch mob. Heading to the cell, some of the inmates from the maximum security wing pushed or shoved me, making clear their intent if I were ever let loose in their midst: for now, I enjoyed Raamah's protection, but for how long?

'What were you hoping to achieve with this protest?' I asked, figuring out that it was better to tailor my solution to the specific concerns.

'We are tired of these inhumane conditions,' muttered Raamah, toying with the sword in his hands. 'I have been here three years and things have not improved! Look at our food! The water is unhygienic, we sleep in rat-infested cells and are only allowed to bath once a fortnight, even though the Nile is but a few miles away.'

'And you believe a revolt will make the Keeper suddenly improve conditions?'

'Yes!' thundered Raamah, surging to his feet before slowly sitting down. 'We want Pharaoh to hear about these conditions. If our revolt gets to his ears, he will hold Potiphar to account, and hopefully Potiphar will put pressure on the Keeper to make improvements.'

I shook my head gently at his naivety. I did not know how such matters were dealt with back in his home country, but in Egypt any protest that threatened the state would be crushed and a brutal example would be made of all ringleaders. If the revolt had resulted in the loss of any Egyptian's life, the perpetrators would be dealt with like prisoners of war and executed. I had learnt a lot about the Egyptian justice system from my dealings with the official scribes who worked under

Potiphar and who drafted all the penal laws. Thanks to my role in Potiphar's household, I also understood budget management and accounting.

'The Keeper has a budget,' I explained as simply as I could, 'which is the total amount of money he has to spend on running the Tomb. This budget is allocated to the Keeper by Potiphar from his own budget, which is fixed by Pharaoh's accountants. The Keeper is therefore limited to whatever allocation he receives from Potiphar.'

'Then maybe our revolt will persuade Potiphar to increase the Keeper's budget.'

I shook my head again, but this time emphatically.

Raamah grimaced.

'By the way, how are the guards?' I asked. 'Are any injured? Are they all alive?'

'Three are injured, mostly cuts and bruises, but they are all alive.'

'You need to release the injured guards so they can receive treatment.'

'And why are you so concerned about their welfare?' His tone was accusatory.

'Because it will make it easier to get a deal done.'

Raamah pondered the matter and then nodded. 'You can take them with you when you leave,' he mumbled.

'Good,' I observed, 'and now where is your list of demands?'

Raamah stared at me blankly, making it obvious that the thought had never crossed his mind. His rage had been his fuel.

'No problem,' I said, not wishing to waste any more time. 'If you can find me a sheet of papyrus, a brush and some ink I will draw up the list.'

* * * * * * *

The Keeper studied the list on the papyrus sheet I handed to him on my return, shaking his head as he read it through.

'I cannot possibly agree to this list of demands,' he said at last. 'I have a very limited budget and, rather than increasing, it is shrinking. The poor harvest this year has affected everything.'

Having drawn up the list, I understood his concerns. The list covered improvements to food, sanitation, healthcare, accommodation, clothing, recreation, work shifts and visitation rights. The improvements looked like a tall order, but during my time with Raamah I had given a lot of thought to how they could be achieved in both the short term and the long term.

'Maybe I can help,' I said, handing him a second papyrus document that I had prepared after drawing up the list of demands.

He studied the second document with as much intensity as the first and at intervals he looked up at me incredulously before continuing to read. When he finished reading through several times, he looked up at me and shook his head in awe.

'You want to convince me that this is achievable?'

'Yes,' I answered. 'The savings I have outlined can be achieved in the first and second year. After that, regardless of what happens to the harvest, these savings can be sustained and even increased. It is about eliminating waste and increasing productivity.'

'But I don't know where to start. I am no good with figures.'

'I can assist if you want,' I murmured. 'I achieved similar savings when I ran Potiphar's household, and I will apply the same principles here.'

'So you are the young Hebrew man who ran Potiphar's household,' said the Keeper, staring at me reverentially. 'I have heard about you, but did not make the connection until now. What strange misfortune has brought you here?'

I held my silence, unwilling to bring up matters that were too painful to relive. Besides, I understood that the Keeper was unlikely to be objective when the architect of my misfortune was his employer's wife.

'It is settled,' said the Keeper, clapping his hands. 'You shall run this cost-saving project – after all, you are more qualified than me or any of my staff to do so. I will make you the overseer of prison welfare and will pass my budget to you. You can have a skeleton staff, chosen from among the inmates, to assist you, and you can inform them that we will be looking into their list of demands.'

'Maybe it would be better if it came from you,' I said, struggling to understand my sudden reversal in fortune.

'No, you tell them in your new capacity as overseer,' he insisted. 'I want them to know that I have heard their cry and that I have appointed you in response to their requests. You will then identify and round up the ringleaders so the captain can dispense the appropriate punishment, to stop this from happening again.'

'I cannot do that,' I said, shaking my head. 'It will defeat the whole purpose of my appointment.'

His chubby face became flustered. 'Joseph, I do not follow you. An overseer has to command respect among his fellow inmates, and the only way that can be achieved is if they know that you work for me and have my backing.'

'I appreciate that,' I answered carefully, unwilling to upset him, 'but part of our grievance is with the brutal corporal punishment we're subjected to. You may not realise this, but it does have an impact on our productivity.'

'How?' He seemed genuinely interested.

'A bruised, injured inmate is less productive both physically and mentally.'

The Keeper appeared to chew on this. When he eventually nodded, I recorded another victory and gave thanks to the God who had kept inspiring me.

'Your strategy relies on having inmates who are healthy and motivated enough to contribute to the improvement of their community,' I clarified. 'To achieve that, we have to start cultivating the sort of behaviour that supports productivity.'

'But we have to make an example of Raamah and his associates.'

'Then you have to make an example of me too,' I said, staring at him intently, 'because I am one of his associates.'

'Solidarity is all well and good,' said the Keeper with a sigh, 'but I need to be able to update Potiphar about the events of this evening.'

'Why?' I asked, rising from the stool on which I was perched. 'Does he know about the inmates' revolt yet?'

The Keeper shook his head, but his eyes were suspicious.

'Then why bother him with the details? Apart from a few injured guards, who have now been released by Raamah as an act of good faith, there have been no fatalities and no damage to property. And very soon all the inmates will be back in their cells.'

The Keeper sighed again. 'Okay,' he said heavily, 'if

you can end this revolt and persuade the inmates to go back to their cells, I will not escalate the incident.'

'Thank you,' I said, but my real gratitude was to the one who inspired me.

OPEN DOORS

Revelation 3:8

The inmates' revolt ended as quickly as it had begun. Acting on the Keeper's instructions in my new role as overseer, I approached Raamah and his small band of associates in the communal recreation area, where I informed them in private about the deal I had struck on their behalf. Raamah couldn't believe that I had been able to achieve such a deal without strong resistance, and openly declared that he believed it was something to do with the might of my God, for which he received no argument from me.

I explained my strategy, clarifying that all inmates would have to contribute their quota in order for us to achieve the improvements. I told them to end the revolt because it had achieved its objective. Reassured that there would be no consequences for their actions, Raamah announced the end of the revolt and introduced me as the newly appointed overseer tasked with improving conditions within the Tomb. I then addressed the inmates collectively and instructed them to return to their cells before personally releasing the remaining guards being held hostage.

True to his word, the Keeper did not impose sanctions on the ringleaders, and managed to persuade the captain not to report back to Potiphar. The captain could not hide his displeasure at either the cover-up or my appointment, and even though he never said a word whenever we met, his countenance spoke volumes. Determined to make progress, I set about establishing my new team, which included Raamah as my chief enforcer. I aimed to establish a new regime of discipline without whips or fists. It was a unique situation for Raamah, but he grew into his role and by the end of the first year was already exhibiting more appropriate behaviours.

My action plan for addressing the inmates' challenges was similar to the business model I had developed in my father's house, as well as Potiphar's: I tackled waste and placed the emphasis on quality rather than quantity. I introduced a leaner business strategy that cut out many layers and processes, as well as a fair bit of red tape, and streamlined productivity to ensure we could achieve more with less.

I started by negotiating with all suppliers of goods and services, examining the quality of their offerings compared to similar goods and services in the marketplace, as well as reviewing areas where services overlapped and operations were duplicated. My review revealed that some suppliers had been ripping us off for years with substandard goods and services. We dropped some suppliers because of the poor quality of their goods and services, and their refusal to improve; others who were satisfactory were allowed to participate in competition against new suppliers. The introduction of competitive bidding achieved better value for money across a wide variety of goods and services, producing instant savings.

To achieve value for money, I dropped a number of services that I thought unnecessary, then arranged for skilled inmates to set up an internal workforce to deliver those services instead. For instance, I created a sanitation team to tackle the hygiene problem and gave them free rein to consider the problem and come up with solutions. To their credit, the team came up with a strategy which saw the open burial site moved from the gully behind the Tomb to a plot of land further away. They arranged for a deep pit to be dug and introduced cremation, where the bodies of non-Egyptians were dumped in the pit and burned. The rat infestation was dealt with by the introduction of Persian and Anatolian cats, which were allowed to roam freely within the grounds of the Tomb and gorge themselves on the troublesome rodents. The team introduced a new way of emptying cell waste, where inmates volunteered, on a rota, to clean out each other's cells and dispose of the waste in clay barrels mounted on carts. The barrelled waste was carted out to farmlands in the western bank area and sold as manure by farmers.

I set up another local team to cover the personal hygiene issue and organise the digging of more wells to cover the water supply requirements for inmates. I also entered into a number of deals with neighbouring cemeteries within the western bank necropolis to irrigate byways to channel water to our arid fields; this sustained our crops. The increased water supply ensured that within six months of the project commencing, inmates were able to have a communal bath every other day.

I dealt with the dietary problem by sourcing food directly from farmers and wholesale traders, then entering into arrangements with Cushite and Nubian caterers to prepare a variety of nutritional meals under a set menu of their choice. This was very well received, and I made sure that the quality of food was the same for inmates in maximum and minimum security. As a result of the improved diet, my weight stabilised, as did that of so many other inmates.

In response to the demand for visitation rights,

which were previously only enjoyed by some inmates in the minimum security wing, with the Keeper's help I developed new guidelines for all inmates. The guidelines set out the rules of entitlement and aligned these to the inmates' conduct. Inmates whose behaviour was unacceptable lost all visitation rights, but those who were consistently well behaved were permitted one visit by either friends or family every two months (in the case of minimum security inmates) or three months (in the case of maximum security inmates). Well-behaved inmates with young children could apply for an extra visit every two months. These measures went a long way to improve social relations in the Tomb.

To address the boredom that seemed so prevalent among inmates, and which gave rise to all sorts of mischief, I managed to persuade the Keeper that it would be a good thing for us to introduce a variety of entertainment. He reminded me that the Den of Confinement was not a hostel but a place of incarceration for those whom society deemed undesirable, and that such privileges would not go down well with the administration. He suggested running the idea past Potiphar first, at which stage I got cold feet and considered withdrawing it.

I did not want my former master to know about my involvement, in case he challenged my appointment as overseer. I informed the Keeper about my change of heart, but he, being a shrewd and insightful fellow, said nothing. I was therefore surprised when he summoned me several weeks after I first mooted the suggestion, to inform me that he had received permission from Potiphar to purchase board games for recreational purposes and to encourage a curriculum of sporting activities among the inmates to boost their fitness. When I enquired how he had been able to achieve such success, he confided in me that he had sold the idea to Potiphar as being his own. At this point, he opened up making it clear that Potiphar knew about my elevation and had approved it. He informed me that all Potiphar knew was that I had been supporting him in his transformational agenda, and told me not to worry. I found this confusing, but was relieved that there would be no backlash from my previous master.

By year two, I had tackled clothing and accommodation, and with some of the first year's savings procured new kilts and tunics by sourcing textiles from the manufacturers and then arranging for several tailors to make the clothes. By using one colour scheme and the same style, we were able to use our bulk purchasing power to drive down the unit cost of these items. Accommodation was subjected to extensive internal repairs to cells, and mats were introduced for beds.

I also negotiated with a new set of physicians living on the eastern bank to set up practice on the western bank in order to visit the Tomb every other day on a rota.

Probably our finest achievement was the renegotiation of contracts for the supply of quarry stones. As the owners of cemeteries and tombs within the western bank necropolis were reluctant to increase the price they paid, we partnered with the administrators of the quarry to start selling stones to builders of homes on the east bank, which was a more affluent region. We were able to offset the cost of ferrying the stones across the Nile to the other side by charging more for the stones. These accomplishments gave me the confidence to gently advocate for a more restrained regime in relation to the whipping of inmates, reserving it for acts of rebellion and insubordination. At my request, the Keeper placed an age restriction on inmates assigned to quarry work, thereby ensuring that older inmates were given less physically demanding tasks. I also recommended that inmates work in designated shifts on a rotational basis and that they had every other day off to enable them to recuperate.

Not being whipped, coupled with working shifts, meant that inmates' productivity increased exponentially. Inmates still wore chains on their ankles between the Tomb and the quarry, but these were better constructed and less damaging to the joints. Within a short time, the mood of inmates going to the quarry changed. No longer was the air rent with the sound of wailing and the crack of the foremen's whips. The quarry business was soon producing profits equivalent to the Keeper's annual budget, so he was always left over with a surplus – which he conveniently failed to inform Potiphar about. I was sure he was siphoning off some of the profits, because his personal appearance and the quality of his clothing improved significantly, but because inmates were so well catered for, his fraud had no effect on their welfare.

During this time, I began to have dreams again, and in them I saw events occurring in the Den of Confinement as well as in Egypt. Sometimes I featured in the dreams, but most times I did not. Whenever I awoke I prayed to the God of my fathers for insight, and he would give me an interpretation of the dreams.

In some cases, the dreams concerned particular inmates and I would discreetly share the dream with them, but others concerned my security, and God began to reveal to me plans by the captain of the guard to undermine me. The knowledge I gleaned from these dreams enabled me stay one step ahead of him, which became frustrating for him. On one occasion, after yet another foiled scheme, he could not help but remark that I must have access to some mystical power.

* * * * * * *

During my second year as overseer, I received a surprise visit from Abali, who had travelled all the way from Men'at Khufu to see me. He had turned up one afternoon while I was teaching a group of inmates how to write. I was thrilled to see him after two and a half years. Abali looked extremely well, in his prestigious tunic, and he brought many gifts for me from other servants in the Potiphar household. After exchanging pleasantries, he informed me that he had been appointed overseer of the Potiphar household, although he had less authority than I had enjoyed. He believed that his appointment had come about because he had been my assistant, and expressed his gratitude for all I had taught him, including how to read and write, which was his most valuable skill.

It was from Abali that I learnt about Onamun's death following a sudden illness just after he had finished building his retirement home. This news saddened me, as I had hoped to see him again one day. Abali also informed me that Potiphar had become quite withdrawn since my imprisonment, as if he regretted what he had done. I found this genuinely concerning and promised to keep him in my prayers, as I bore him no ill will.

As for Potiphar's wife, Abali had nothing good to say about her. Rather than propositioning him, she was making his life a living hell by comparing everything he did to how I used to do it. Abali believed she was prejudiced against him because of his racial origin, but I urged him not to dwell on this, to avoid becoming bitter. Before he left, I asked that he visit me again and regularly, as I had no one else outside the prison, and he promised he would. However, that was the last time he visited.

* * * * * * *

Two years later

I stood up, confronting Raamah, trying to restrain the tears that threatened to fall from the corners of my eyes, and swallowed hard to rid my throat of the lump lodged there. Following the Keeper's decision two years ago to introduce an inmate review system, administered by himself and the captain of the prison guard, inmates who had been held for longer than five years were considered for release. Although I had been consulted and had suggested that this be applied to all inmates, regardless of whether they were held in maximum or minimum security, Potiphar had instructed that it be confined to those in minimum security. Raamah had been my able assistant since the system of reforms commenced five years ago, and his conduct had been so transformed by the level of trust placed in him that the wild mountain goat had become as docile as a lamb. I had recommended that his incarceration be reviewed, even though he was in maximum security. To my surprise, Potiphar had approved the recommendation, but made it clear to the Keeper that this was to be the exception rather than the norm.

The Keeper had assured me that he would push to see that the review occurred at least once a year and that at least three maximum-security inmates got the opportunity to leave. The reason he proposed to give Potiphar for the policy was that it would reduce overcrowding and costs. This development excited me, because I began to see an end to my plight and the possibility of an early discharge. Though it was going to be conducted on a sporadic basis, the review system gave me hope and improved my spirits. I was confident that, after Raamah, I would be next on the list.

I could see the tears glistening in Raamah's eyes and understood what was going on in his heart. The Tomb had been his habitat: a place where he had achieved notoriety for his aggression and then had attained respect because of the authority he wielded under my command. Leaving the Tomb would be a surreal experience for a man who had effectively become institutionalised.

'I will never forget all you have done for me, Master Joseph,' he said, addressing me in the reverent manner that had become his custom. 'Nobody has ever treated me as humanely as you have.'

I nodded and looked away, my eyes pricking with tears. I was going to miss him.

Raamah took the reins of the mule which I had given him, with the Keeper's blessing. I had suggested that it would be unfair to release inmates back into society without any form of sustenance until they found employment, and we had come up with a package to assist them. Each departing inmate was given a mule and enough food to last a fortnight. In addition, we made arrangements with some of our suppliers to employ the inmates for a short while until they were able to find other work. This ensured that they were not at risk of slipping back into their old life.

The bakery that supplied our bread had agreed to accommodate him for a while but, beyond that, Raamah had plans of his own. He planned to train as a riverboat captain and work hard to purchase a boat so that he could ferry people up and down the Nile, reckoning that his challenging features would be less of a problem in that line of business. It also helped that, despite his disability, he was an excellent swimmer.

We hugged warmly and parted before a fresh wave of emotion swamped us. Behind me a small crowd comprising more than half of the inmates came forward to wish him farewell. We waved as he mounted his mule and trotted off through the open gates into his future without a backward glance. I understood. In his sandals, I would have done the same. Looking back prolonged the pain of leaving. As the crowd dispersed, I caught the disparaging eye of the captain of the prison guard. He was openly opposed to maximum security inmates gaining their freedom and had protested directly to Potiphar, who opted to support the Keeper. I knew that the captain held me responsible and that his hatred for me had increased.

'You think you have won, Hebrew,' he said, drawing close to me.

'I was not aware we had a contest,' I murmured, taking care not to project disrespect as this would only play into his hands.

'You know what I mean,' he said, placing his hand menacingly on the hilt of the sword strapped to his waist. 'But this is not over, and it is only over my dead body that another inmate will be released from maximum security.'

'Those are strong words, Captain,' I observed quietly, 'and I pray that they do not come to pass.'

Leaving him seething by the gate, I returned to my office and began to dream of going home to Hebron. I had spent just over ten years in Egypt so far: four and a half years in Potiphar's house and five and a half years in the Den of Confinement. My youthful exuberance had long since departed and I had become a man, seasoned by a wealth of life experiences. I wondered whether my father was still alive and, if he was, if he would recognise me. I also thought about Benjamin. Would I ever see him again? Would we ever again be as close as we had been before my enslavement? I wondered about my other brothers and how they would react to my return: would they lie to my father or confess and beg for my forgiveness? If they asked for my forgiveness, would I grant it? It was a confusing mix of emotions.

A month later, I was summoned by the Keeper to his quarters. As I entered, his grave expression gave me a feeling of impending doom. I listened with a heavy heart as he told me how Raamah had been caught in a compromising situation with a young Midianite girl whom he had been trying to lie with against her will. Before the city's crime enforcement guards could arrive to take him into custody, an angry mob of Midianites had stoned him to death, in accordance with their custom. However, the news had reached Potiphar, who was livid, and immediately cancelled the inmate review system for all maximum security inmates to prevent a repeat offence.

My heart sank into a pit of despair as I left his presence. I could tell that the Keeper was not pleased with the development, and that he was equally sad about Raamah's demise.

As I headed back to my quarters, I began to blame myself for the state of affairs that had resulted in Raamah's death. If I had not recommended his release, he would still be alive. I wondered about the temptation that had dragged him to his death, and struggled to reconcile it with the behaviour he had shown before his release. Raamah had never denied killing the slave girl who had allegedly spurned his advances, but nor had he admitted it. It was something we never spoke about. I began to see a flaw in my plan: I should have tried to get him to speak about that incident, and if he admitted his guilt, I could have ensured that he was completely rehabilitated before recommending his release. Inside my quarters, which were now in the minimum security wing, I found the captain of the guard waiting, a sardonic grin on his smoothly shaven face.

'Hebrew, did I not tell you that it would only be over my dead body that another inmate would be released from maximum security?'

I chose not to respond. A violent emotion was rising up within me, about to give birth to a rage I feared I might have no control over. He chuckled gently and headed towards the doorway. As he drew level with me, he leant close and whispered the words that chilled my soul for many days after.

'You will never get out of here.'

That night as I lay in bed mourning Raamah, a deeply misunderstood man who had known little peace or joy in his life, I drifted off into a deep sleep. As I slept, I dreamt. In my dream, I saw the captain of the guard handing some stones to a mysterious group of people who were hiding in the shadows, then pointing at an old eagle with a deformed wing that had just been released from a wooden cage, but was struggling to fly. The men with the stones began to pelt the defenceless bird until it collapsed on the ground and lay still. I woke up from my dream in a sweat, breathing heavily. As the interpretation of the dream came flooding into my mind, sorrow swept over my heart. On the one hand, I was reassured about my late friend, but on the other I was enraged that his life had been snuffed out.

*   *   *   *   *   *   *

About a month after the news of Raamah's death, I sat in my quarters playing a board game called Hounds and Jackals with one of my assistants when the captain of the guard appeared in the doorway, accompanied by two well-attired Egyptians who looked like dignitaries. One of them was slender, elegant and middle-aged with clean-shaven features and kohl around his eyes. He wore a knee-length tunic with exquisite gold embroidery and a broad necklace of bronze beads. His curved nose had an arrogant tilt.

The other man was shorter and more robust. He was also clean-shaven, wearing striped headgear and a tight-fitting tunic that was dampened by patches of sweat. His eyes were fidgety and it was difficult to hold his stare even for a second. They wore well-made sandals, making it clear that they were very important people.

I sprang to my feet and bowed. The shorter man acknowledged me with a nod, but the other eyed me as if I were a dead bug plastered to the sole of his elegant sandal. I surmised, from their appearance, that they were attached to Pharaoh's palace, and began to guess at their professions, concluding that the shorter one was a scribe and the taller one was a member of Pharaoh's Council of Administrators. I turned to the captain of the guard, who was looking extremely uncomfortable, and knew that all was not well.

'These are two of Pharaoh's high officials,' he said reverentially, 'and they have been placed in my personal custody by Captain Potiphar, on Pharaoh's command.'

I nodded, still struggling to understand the reason for his discomfort.

'I am therefore placing them in your care,' said the captain. 'I would like them to share your quarters so you can attend to their needs.'

I knew he meant that I should serve them. While I did not have a problem with that, as I already saw myself as a servant to all, I still wanted to understand the circumstances surrounding their presence in the Tomb. Although we have had a number of inmates who had served in Pharaoh's administration or household and had displeased him, they were lowly personnel who had no real status. They were accorded no special favours and were usually placed in the minimum security wing unless their offence had a criminal element to it. Very few of Pharaoh's personnel who were sent to the Tomb were guilty of serious criminal offences, as the punishments such people received were usually more brutal, including maiming, mutilation, and, on occasion, death.

I wanted to ask the captain what they had done, but I could see from his mood that he had no intention of discussing their offences with me. I gestured to my quarters and invited them to come in, as both men were still hovering around the doorway. The shorter man took the first steps and sat on the spare bed, but the other man remained where he was, looking around him disdainfully.

'May I introduce you to Pharaoh's chief baker,' said the captain, gesturing to the stockier man on the spare bed, 'and his chief cupbearer.' He turned to the lankier man next to him, grinning fawningly.

These were clearly two very powerful officials. The chief cupbearer led a retinue of cupbearers and was one of the closest officials to Pharaoh. He was effectively the person who protected Pharaoh from being poisoned by tasting all his beverages before he drank them. The chief cupbearer had access to all kinds of antidotes to poisons, and was assigned a personal physician whose job was to administer the relevant antidote as quickly as possible. It was a vicious cycle; if the physician failed to find the right antidote on time, the chief cupbearer's life would be at risk. The chief baker ran the royal bakeries and ensured that Pharaoh and his household had access to freshly baked produce on a daily basis.

'Well, Joseph,' said the captain, backing out of the quarters, 'I will leave them in your capable hands. I have a lot to do.'

He bowed to the cupbearer and headed out as quickly as he could, almost falling over his own feet. His awkward behaviour, amusing as I found it, concerned me. Why was he so subservient to the cupbearer? A glance at their wrists and ankles indicated the absence of manacles. There were no tell-tale marks indicating that they had worn manacles at any point.

'I am sure you would like to freshen up,' I said pleasantly. 'I will arrange to get you some water and show you to the communal washroom.'

'Communal washroom?' asked the cupbearer, looking aghast.

'Yes, we use communal facilities,' I said, 'but I will arrange for you to have the space to yourselves whenever you need to bath.'

The cupbearer nodded stiffly, but remained by the doorway. He was clearly struggling to adjust to his surroundings, and I suspected that he had been removed from office very swiftly without time to prepare mentally. The baker, on the other hand, had adjusted, which meant that he had probably seen it coming. I instructed the inmate who had been playing Hounds and Jackals with me to fetch water from one of the wells and arrange for the communal washroom to be vacated so they could bath. After my assistant had departed, I confronted the cupbearer, determined to pacify my curiosity.

'What is Pharaoh's chief cupbearer doing here?' I asked, meeting his frosty gaze.

The cupbearer's eyes flashed and he opened his mouth with the obvious intent of rebuking me, then shut it again.

'He failed to properly identify ingredients used in wine that he knew would give Pharaoh an allergic reaction,' said the baker, jumping in, much to my relief. 'Unfortunately, after drinking it, Pharaoh suffered an allergic reaction. Pharaoh would have had the cupbearer's tongue cut out but for the intervention of the queen, so he was sent here instead to await Pharaoh's judgement.'

The cupbearer glared at the baker, but said nothing. I empathised with the cupbearer. Surely it had been a momentary lapse? He was clearly proud of his role and I was sure he had performed it efficiently and effectively.

'And what about you?' I asked, turning to the baker.

'While Pharaoh was recuperating, he ate a piece of his favourite barley bread and discovered a weevil in it,' mumbled the baker, avoiding my gaze. 'Even though it was freshly baked, his servants carelessly stored it next to some grains that contained weevils, but I got the blame.'

His shifty eyes made me question his version of events. Even though I could not dismiss his account, I had my doubts.

*   *   *   *   *   *   *

One year later

One of the changes I had introduced to encourage a more sociable atmosphere was communal eating, as servants had done in Potiphar's house. Rather than inmates being confined to their cells for meals, they all ate in the open courtyard, where they were served by the caterers. My investigations had revealed that most inmates became suicidal or depressed due to spending too much time on their own. Although we still had the odd suicide or case of self-harming by inmates, the numbers had greatly decreased. I normally ate with the other inmates, but since the arrival of the baker and the cupbearer, at the Keeper's request, I started having my meals with them in my quarters.

It had been a year since their arrival, and they had coped with the experience differently. The cupbearer was very much a loner who kept to himself, speaking to no one other than the Keeper and me. Despite the privilege of not having to work in the quarry, he was perpetually morose and abrasive. The baker, on the other hand, was a more sociable animal who appreciated his elevated status within the Den and mingled freely with other inmates. With the Keeper's permission, he was able to bake his own bread which he shared with me and the cupbearer. Occasionally I played board games with them but, whenever the cupbearer condescended to join us, it was a joyless event.

One morning, while I was serving my cellmates with their morning meal, I noticed their faces. The cupbearer was no bearer of joy but at least he had never betrayed any signs of depression or despondency. Studying their faces as I served, I recognised that they were genuinely deeply troubled, and my curiosity prompted me to enquire.

'Why are you both looking so worried this morning?' I directed my question at the cupbearer.

'We had troubling dreams last night,' said the baker, electing himself spokesman, 'and though we have discussed them with the Keeper and the captain of the guard, neither of them can tell us what they mean.'

I wondered why they had bothered sharing their dreams with two people who had never demonstrated any gift of dream interpretation. I asked them the details of their dreams.

'My God specialises in dream interpretation,' I said, sitting down next to them, 'so why don't you tell me about your dreams?'

To my surprise, the normally reserved cupbearer opted to speak first. His enthusiasm was completely out of character.

'In my dream I saw a grapevine in front of me,' he began, 'and the vine had three branches that had begun to bud and blossom. As I observed the branches, they began to produce clusters of ripe grapes. Since I was holding Pharaoh's cup in my hand, I took the grapes and squeezed their juice into the cup and then placed it in Pharaoh's hand.'

As he spoke, God was giving me His interpretation of the dream. Under my breath, I gave thanks to God.

'This is the meaning of your dream,' I said solemnly. 'The three branches you saw represent three days. Within three days, Pharaoh will elevate you from this place and restore you to your former position as his chief cupbearer, and once again you will serve him and be the custodian of his cup.'

I paused as urgency gripped me. I began to see a divine purpose to the events of this morning. When the cupbearer's face lit up with joy, I decided to make my pitch.

'Remember me when things turn out well for you,' I went on, 'and please do me a favour – mention me to Pharaoh so that he may release me from this place, for I was unjustly snatched away from my homeland, the land of the Hebrews.' I paused to quell my emotions. 'Even though I am now an inmate here, believe me, I have not committed any offence to justify it.'

'You need to interpret mine too!' interrupted the baker before the cupbearer could respond to my passionate request.

I nodded and turned my attention to him, mindful of the need to remain neutral.

'In my dream I had three white baskets stacked on my head,' he said breathlessly, a glitter in his eyes. 'The top basket was full of all kinds of pastries for Pharaoh, but some birds appeared and began to eat the pastries!'

He looked at me expectantly. However, the interpretation that came to me was concerning.

'This is what your dream means,' I said, in a grave voice that matched my expression. 'The three baskets are three days. In three days Pharaoh will lift your head and will hang you from a tree and the birds will come and strip away your flesh.'

As the ominous words departed my lips, I felt a deep sorrow for him. My agony increased as I noted his crumpled expression. To all intents and purposes he was as good as dead already: his mood deflated and the effervescence that had been his hallmark evaporated. For the rest of the day, the dour cupbearer took on the exuberance of the baker and the latter adopted the cupbearer's melancholic mask.

Three days later, on Pharaoh's birthday, when a banquet had been arranged for all his officials and servants, the captain of the guard appeared early in the morning with a detachment of armed guards and informed the cupbearer and baker that they had been summoned to Pharaoh's presence with immediate effect. I watched quietly, unable to say anything in the captain's presence, as the two officials were escorted out of my quarters for the last time. Later that day, I learnt from the Keeper that, while the chief cupbearer had been restored to his post, the chief baker had been hanged on a tree. A crowd had gathered to watch birds of prey nibble at his flesh, just as God had revealed to me.

A GOLDEN OPPORTUNITY

Proverbs 18:16

Two years later

On the evening before the thirteenth anniversary of my time in Egypt, I sat by myself in a corner of the prison courtyard, deep in thought, observing but not registering the activity all around me. Having been fed, inmates were using the last scraps of daylight to play board games including Senet and my favourite, Hounds and Jackals, while drinking non-alcoholic ginger-flavoured beer. There was laughter all around me, but my heart was heavy.

I had woken that morning with an unusual heaviness in my head and chest, which I initially attributed to insufficient sleep, but eventually discovered to be linked to my state of mind. One of my duties as a scribe was to keep a record of all activities and events, with the requisite dates and sometimes the times according to the sundial. It was in the course of going through the week's records, checking for any inaccuracies, that I noted the date and realised that today was the eve of my thirteenth year in Egypt.

The realisation of this milestone occupied my thoughts for the rest of the day. As my mind roved over the events that defined my life in Egypt, I recalled the names and faces of the key players. In particular, I recalled how I had interpreted the dreams of Pharaoh's chief cupbearer and chief baker, and my expectations for release from the Tomb.

It had been two years since the cupbearer left my quarters to return to his post at Pharaoh's side, but in all that time nobody had shown up from Pharaoh's palace to demand my release from the Tomb or invite me to state my case. After waiting for six months, I concluded that I had been forgotten and lowered my expectation. Realising that I had been forgotten brought up memories of my brothers' betrayal. I became emotionally fragile and bitter, but managed to overcome this by redirecting my thoughts to God and reliving the dreams he had given me. The more I focused on God, the stronger I became until I had successfully erased the cupbearer from my mind.

The captain of the guard took much delight in taunting me whenever our paths crossed, frequently reminding me that I would spend the rest of my useful life locked away, but I always ignored him, knowing that only God could make such definite pronouncements about my future. My dream had revealed the captain's role in Raamah's death. I knew why he had done it: however, I still had a spark of hope that my God would not forsake me in my hour of need, and that the captain would not have the last laugh.

Only the Keeper remained a source of encouragement, frequently complimenting me on even my smallest accomplishments and extending to me all sorts of benefits and kindness. For instance, his wife would bake my favourite honey-flavoured bread embellished with assorted fruits and send it to me via her husband. She saw me as the saviour of her marriage, because she now got to see a lot more of her husband who was able to visit home more frequently. I also happened to hear that, on account of all the profits from the quarry, Potiphar had granted him permission to use stones mined from the quarry to build a family home.

The most aggravating thing about the last two years of my incarceration was the news that my friend, Abali, had been granted his freedom by Potiphar. Because the captain of the guard frequented Potiphar's house, he updated the Keeper on the affairs of the household. Abali, like Onamun, had been given a generous allowance to build himself a house and start a modest trade, and Kaa had been promoted to overseer in his place. I thought back to my encounters with Potiphar's wife and endured mental agony as I considered how her lust had robbed me of freedom and the chance to return to my homeland.

'What is bothering you?' asked the Keeper, joining me. 'You have not been yourself all day.'

I read the anxiety in his eyes and was grateful for his concern, but didn't know where to start. How could I tell him about my agony at having spent thirteen of the most productive years of my life in forced servitude in a strange land? How could he understand my state of mind? I decided to keep it simple.

'I am pining for my family,' I said quietly. 'Almost everyone here gets to see a member of their family regularly, but I have not seen mine for over thirteen years.'

'I see,' answered the Keeper, nodding gently. 'It has been a long time.'

I felt like saying that that was the understatement of the year, but wisdom silenced me. He returned to his wife and children every other day, thanks to my able oversight of the Tomb's affairs, but I did not even receive a visit from those I considered my friends, like Abali and Kaa. A pernicious voice whispered something about fair-weather friends, but I blocked it before the thought could take root.

'I don't even know whether my father is still alive,' I continued, 'and have no idea whether his household is in the same place. We are nomadic people; constantly moving but never straying from the land that God gave us.'

'But don't you think that the god you serve, who has shown you so much favour all these years, will preserve them until the day of your reunion?'

The Keeper's words pierced deep, embedding themselves in the core of my heart. My father had tried to teach us the importance of trusting God in the dark, like little children, even when we didn't know where we were or what was going on. I recalled all the stories my father had shared with us about his time in our grandfather's house in Mesopotamia, when he had relied on the grace of God, particularly when all around him looked bleak.

I knew that God had been with me for every one of those thirteen years in Egypt and that it was His presence that had sustained me – and elevated me to positions of responsibility in Potiphar's house and in the Den of Confinement. I knew that my efforts alone could never have secured my promotion. It had been His wisdom working through me that had produced all the innovative solutions; solutions that I had received the accolades for. He had been with me from my youth and He was still with me.

'I know it is not my place to say so,' said the Keeper, leaning closer, 'but I believe you will see your family again. If your god is a god of justice, he will fight your corner and reward you for your humility and service.'

I sighed and nodded.

'Just look around you, Joseph,' said the Keeper, gesturing to the inmates. 'Was this the atmosphere you encountered when you first arrived?'

I surveyed the inmates' faces and it gradually dawned on me. I had served all those placed within my care and, through me, God had added value to their lives.

'Their lives will never be the same again,' said the Keeper, who seemed to be enjoying his efforts at lifting my spirits. 'You made that happen – remember that.'

'Thank you,' I said, feeling strengthened.

After his departure, I let my tears flow as I pondered God's faithfulness to me.

* * * * * * *

I was awoken on the morning of my thirteenth anniversary by a pair of rough hands that grabbed my shoulders unceremoniously and shook me vigorously until I opened my gummy eyes. Staring up in confusion at the barely visible figures surrounding my bed, I panicked and opened my mouth to cry out. Before a sound could escape my larynx, a large hand clamped itself firmly over my mouth, muffling my alarm. The unexpectedly aggressive treatment was reminiscent of my days under Onamun at Potiphar's home, as well as in the stone quarry under the brutal guards, and those unpleasant memories reinforced my terror. I thought about the captain of the guard. Where was he? Then I remembered he had taken a week off to visit a sick relative in Lower Egypt.

'Joseph,' said a familiar voice that I instantly recognised as the Keeper's, 'do not be alarmed. These are members of Pharaoh's elite guard. He has sent for you.'

I nodded stiffly raising my hands in a peace gesture, and the guard removed his hand. As my blurry eyes cleared, I counted four dark-skinned guards, all wearing the impressive uniform of the infantry charged with Pharaoh's personal protection, and a middle-aged Egyptian male official wearing a long tunic. He held a similar garment over one arm and a pair of sandals in his hand. In the background I could see the Keeper. His pensive expression worried me.

'You need to get shaved and dressed,' said the official. 'Pharaoh demands your presence immediately.'

I lowered my hands and quickly got up off the bed. The fact that they had brought clothes for me confirmed that my appearance was important, so I decided to have a quick bath. After my bath, one of the elite guards produced a razor and began to shave off my overgrown beard, then proceeded to do the same to my lion's mane of dark hair. By the time he had finished, I was smoothly shaved. To my discomfort, he began to apply kohl to my eyes. I then dressed hurriedly in the tunic and sandals and allowed the guards to steer me towards the front gates. The sun had just begun to rise when we emerged from the minimum security wing, and the courtyard was still deserted. Apart from the four elite guards, Pharaoh's official and the Keeper, the only other people awake were the six nightshift Tomb guards.

At the gates, the Keeper halted and reached out a hand to grip my shoulder. He said nothing but his eyes seemed to wish me good luck. I could understand why: when Pharaoh summoned an inmate, it was usually because that inmate's fate had been decided – a pardon, mutilation of some form, or death. Those who were pardoned or executed were never seen again, but a number of inmates had returned with gruesome forms of scarring or mutilation, usually facial. It really depended on Pharaoh's mood. I wondered whether the cupbearer had eventually remembered me and put in a good word for me with his employer, and my mood brightened.

Outside the gates, several chariots waited. I was made to mount one of them, with a guard at the reins. Once on board, and holding the handlebar, I was driven at speed towards the banks of the Nile. This was my first ride in a chariot of any description and the sensation of speed was mind-numbing, especially as my freshly shorn head was exposed to the elements. The ride was a short one, terminating at the western bank near a mooring point, where a majestic boat was waiting. I recognised the boat as one of those in Pharaoh's fleet, because of its canopy supported by four beams and the colourful hieroglyphs inscribed on its bodywork.

We transferred to the boat which was manned by ten oarsmen, mostly Nubians. We were soon joined by the other three guards and the official, whom I was convinced was a scribe, because of his attire and the stains on his fingertips. The boat cast off shortly after we boarded and sailed in the direction of Lower Egypt, affording me a sublime view of the city of Waset at sunrise.

The journey across the Nile was short: the boat speared its way from the west bank to the east bank and headed for a grand-looking mooring point flanked by large statutes of lions at rest. Towering above the mooring point, overlooking the Nile, was Pharaoh's magnificent palace. Most of its walls were painted in vibrant colours and plastered with colourful frescoes.

I had seen Pharaoh's palace a number of times, but at sunrise it looked especially glorious, with the golden sun crowning its terrace and casting a reflection of the palace over the mirror-like surface of the Nile. We disembarked and the scribe led us up the broad stairway towards the palace, then down a long paved route bordered by statues of lions and pointy-eared hounds.

This building was the most famous landmark in Waset. Despite my nervousness, I could not help soaking up the beauty of the exotic plants and trees in the palace garden. There were several pools in which exotic fish swam. With the sun reflecting off the building's walls, the whole effect was stunning. At every entry point stood armed soldiers, all looking alert, creating a sense of formidable security. Despite the early hour, servants were about, carrying out chores. As we passed, they paused to look at us.

Arriving in a courtyard, bordered by colourful pillars adorned with frescoes and hieroglyphs, I saw a familiar figure. It was Pharaoh's chief cupbearer. My pulse soared. The self-important official who had apparently forgotten about me for over two years was now my reception committee. The official who had brought me from the Tomb halted a short distance from the cupbearer, but gestured for me to keep on walking.

'Joseph,' said the cupbearer, as we stood face to face, 'it has been a long time.'

I simply nodded, rendered speechless by events.

'Pharaoh is in urgent need of your powers,' went on the cupbearer. 'He has had strange dreams which none of the wise men or magicians have been able to interpret. But, I remembered what you did for me and mentioned this to him.'

'Any ability I have is from God,' I murmured. 'Where is he?'

'He is in the grand hall with his officials,' said the

cupbearer. 'I will take you to him.'

He led me through the main building into a grand hall with huge columns and a polished stone floor that was slippery to walk on. At the end of the hall stood about ten men in a horseshoe formation, all dressed in long tunics and facing a vacant throne that sat at the top of a short flight of marble stairs.

'I never forgot about you,' said the cupbearer awkwardly, as we approached the gathering, 'but having been pardoned by Pharaoh I didn't want to push my luck by mentioning your predicament to him – particularly as you are a Hebrew. Looking back, I regret my cowardice.'

I did not respond. I was in awe of my surroundings and the fact that I had been summoned to Pharaoh's presence, but at the same time I was anxious. What would happen? Would I be able to help Pharaoh unravel the meaning of his dreams? The opportunity was unnerving.

Officials turned towards us as we halted behind them. Potiphar was among them! I froze as our eyes made contact, then averted my gaze. Instinctively, I still thought of him as my master. When I looked up, he was still staring at me. I bowed and swung my face away. All the officials turned around again as Pharaoh arrived from a chamber to the right of the throne, accompanied by two Nubians who were fanning him with ostrich feathers attached to long reeds. Pharaoh was a short, portly man with a prominent nose that curved over his upper lip. His expression was grave.

'Has the Hebrew arrived?' asked Pharaoh once he was seated on his throne.

'Yes, Your Highness,' answered the cupbearer, gently pushing me forward.

I stepped forward self-consciously and approached the steps to the throne, so I had to look up at the supreme ruler of the Egyptian empire. I met his inquisitive gaze and respectfully lowered my eyes. Having not been instructed on the correct etiquette, I had to follow my instincts.

'Last night I had a dream, but none of my courtiers or wise men have been able to interpret it,' said Pharaoh slowly. 'However, I have heard that you have the power to interpret any dream.'

'I am merely a vessel,' I replied, 'but I serve a God who can interpret any dream. If you share your dream with me, He shall provide the meaning.'

'In my dream,' said Pharaoh, 'I was standing on the bank of the Nile. Seven well-fed, healthy cows came up out of the river and began to graze on the marsh grass. But after them, I saw seven thin, unhealthy-looking cows come up out of the river. These were the most malnourished-looking cows I have ever seen in Egypt. As I watched, the seven thin cows ate the seven fat cows, but afterwards they were as malnourished as before. At this point I woke up, but as I was trying to gather my thoughts I fell asleep again. This time, I had another dream. In it I saw seven healthy heads of grain, growing on one stalk. But then seven blighted, shrivelled heads of grain appeared, which had been blasted by the east wind, and they devoured the seven healthy heads of grain. I told these dreams to my magicians, but they could not interpret them.'

As Pharaoh was speaking, my God began to speak to me, providing me with insight, so as Pharaoh finished his narrative I had a clear idea of what the dreams meant. Silently, I gave thanks to God then lifted my head, making eye contact with Pharaoh.

'Both of Pharaoh's dreams have the same meaning,' I said. 'God is revealing to Pharaoh what he is about to do. The seven healthy cows and the seven healthy heads of grain represent seven years of prosperity, while the seven thin cows and the seven unhealthy heads of grain blasted by the east wind represent seven years of famine. These years will occur in the order I have just described; God is revealing to Pharaoh in advance what he is about to do.'

Pharaoh was leaning forward, his chin resting on the clenched fist of one hand. It was clear that I had his full attention, which could be construed as a sign of trust.

'The next seven years will be bountiful ones and there will be great prosperity throughout the whole of Egypt,' I went on. 'But after this season of excess shall come seven years of famine – they will be so severe that the years of plenty will be forgotten. The famine shall consume the land, erasing all memory of the bountiful years. The fact that the two dreams are similar is confirmation that God shall definitely bring these events to pass – and very soon.'

The officials standing behind me began to murmur among themselves like bees as they heard these words. I paused until Pharaoh's raised hand silenced them. Their panic was palpable, as were their trepidation and helplessness, but even as they spoke God laid a strategy in my heart.

'To be adequately prepared for these events,' I continued, 'Pharaoh should find a discreet, wise man and set him over the entire land of Egypt. Pharaoh should then appoint officers to supervise the collection of one-fifth of all the crops produced during the seven good years. Let these officers gather all this food and store it in new granaries which Pharaoh shall construct in different cities. Let Pharaoh's soldiers guard the food. If you do this, there will be sufficient food to sustain the population during the seven years of famine.'

As I finished speaking, Pharaoh's eyes lit up and the tension drained away from his face. The murmuring behind me resumed, but now the speakers seemed to be in a buoyant mood. It was clear that my God-given strategy was well received. As I silently thanked God, I wondered whether this might be an opportune moment for me to state my innocence before Pharaoh and throw myself on his mercy. I was conscious of Potiphar's presence and the effect this may have on him, but I was past caring. All I wanted to do was go home to my family – or what was left of it.

Pharaoh rose to his feet and came down the steps to where I was standing. He placed a hand on my shoulder before turning me around to face his officials, who fell silent.

'Can we find anyone in Egypt like this?' asked Pharaoh. 'A man in whom the spirit of his God so clearly resides?'

Their faces confirmed Pharaoh's assessment. As my eyes met Potiphar's, I could see that his eyes sparkled with tears, although I could not tell whether they were of gladness or regret.

Pharaoh turned to me and looked up at me intently. 'Your God has shown you all that is about to transpire; there is clearly no one wiser or more discreet than you in Egypt. Therefore you shall preside over my court and instruct all my officials and servants. Only in matters pertaining to my throne shall I outrank you.'

I almost fell over in shock, overcome by a sudden dizzy spell. Nausea gripped my stomach and the sensation rose to my throat, almost suffocating me. My brain struggled to process the information I was hearing, and sweat sprang out over my forehead and armpits. I opened my mouth to say something, but I could not speak. My stifled vocal chords committed an act of treason. What was I hearing? What was happening? It was such a surreal moment that I felt as if I was floating, in a trance.

'Joseph,' continued Pharaoh, 'today I have set you over all the land of Egypt.'

As he finished speaking he removed his signet ring, one of the core symbols of his authority, and slipped it onto one of my quivering, clammy fingers. As I gazed down at my shaking hand, now adorned with greatness, Pharaoh clapped his hands loudly. Within minutes two servants appeared and bowed low before him. He issued a quick instruction which I failed to understand. They darted off to comply and returned moments later, one of them carrying one of the most elegant linen tunics I had ever laid my eyes on. The garment was embroidered and had been dyed in several different colours. I stood, still trembling, as my tunic was removed and replaced with the more regal one. Tears welled in my eyes as I recalled the colourful coat my father had given me over thirteen years ago.

It was as if I had come full circle.

I was vaguely aware of Pharaoh removing a gold chain from around his neck and reaching up to place it around my neck. The only thing that prevented me from falling to my knees and crying out at this great honour was my awareness of my environment, and my audience. Like a man in a dream, I was aware of my emotions but unable to connect to what was happening in any real, meaningful way.

'These are only small tokens of my gratitude,' said Pharaoh, stepping backwards, 'but from now on you shall be arrayed even more splendidly than this and you will be presented in a manner befitting of my second-in-command – my vizier.'

He headed back to his throne and I was immediately surrounded by his awe-struck officials who had keenly observed my impromptu investiture. In the midst of the euphoria my foremost thought was that I would not be spending another night in the Den of Confinement.

THE SOUND OF MUSIC

Psalm 40:1-3

'Bow!' yelled my driver as my gold-plated horse-drawn chariot ripped through the dusty streets of Men'at Khufu, scattering startled pedestrians out of our path. As they scuttled for safety, I saw in some faces the almost instantaneous transition from curiosity to disbelief – curiosity about the identity of the dignitary invading their tranquillity, then disbelief when they realised who I was. The reaction of every person, whether Egyptian or foreigner, was to immediately bow on one knee or stoop, as commanded. My entourage of six armed members of the Egyptian elite guard, riding behind me in chariots, was assigned by Pharaoh to ensure compliance with my driver's instruction.

Although the news regarding the meteoric rise of a Hebrew immigrant from inmate at the Den of Confinement to Pharaoh's second-in-command had begun to filter out to cities within Upper and Lower Egypt, nobody really knew who I was. Even though Men'at Khufu was the most influential commercial centre in Upper Egypt, with access to trade routes linking to the Red Sea, this was my first visit here in an official capacity. The last time I was here was almost eight and a half years ago, when I was led out in chains to commence my term in the Tomb. I had been led out in shame and obscurity late one evening for a crime I did not commit – but now, by the grace of God, I was returning in splendour and prominence at noonday as the vizier over Egypt – a role that I did not merit.

Pharaoh could easily have assigned me to work

under one of his high-ranking officials, as I had done in Potiphar's household, and I would still have been grateful to get out of the Tomb. Provided I was given a reasonable degree of autonomy, I could easily have conducted the role of supervisor over Egyptian agriculture in a subsidiary capacity and still achieved a favourable outcome. But to elevate a foreigner to such high office from such an ignoble status was unheard of. To tell you the truth, I would have been grateful if I had merely been given my freedom and allowed to return home to Hebron. The chain of events that had led to my new status was surreal, and I was still struggling to wake up from what felt like a protracted dream.

It had been almost two months since my appointment. Already we had received reports from farmers, particularly in the Lower Egypt region, of amazing conditions for planting and of arable land replacing areas previously deemed infertile. It was as if some miraculous fortune had touched the land and provided farmers with increased planting options. Provided they had enough seed, they were guaranteed a full harvest with minimal loss of crop. To ensure that we could maximise this opportunity, I made plans to order more seed from Canaan, Mesopotamia and Anatolia, which were within easy reach of Lower Egypt, and also initiated a plan to train more people as farmers. If God had promised seven years of bountiful harvest, then there was scope for us to maximise this by increasing the volume of seed being planted.

Men'at Khufu was more of a trading centre than an agricultural community, but my plan saw a seven-fold increase in farming activity in the region. My 'Back to the Land' initiative – a seven-year initiative to develop an agricultural workforce ready and able to exploit the expected seven-year period of plenty – was just one of the many bright ideas that the Lord had blessed me with during those two months, and I was determined not to waste any time. As we raced between Waset and Men'at Khufu, I had felt uneasy. When we arrived, my anxiety increased. In addition to a custom-built chariot, I had access to a magnificent eight-oar boat for longer journeys. I had briefly considered using this for the trip to Men'at Khufu, but discarded the idea as travelling by chariot gave me the opportunity to survey potential farmland.

On this trip I intended to meet with regional rulers and high officials to discuss my 'Back to the Land' initiative and review the steps they had taken to implement it in Men'at Khufu. I knew that Potiphar was going to be there, as well as many of his neighbours from El Akhet whom I had got to know when I was overseer of his household. It promised to be an interesting reunion, because I was returning as their master. There would be no vote on my initiatives; it was not a democracy.

My inauguration as vizier had been conducted according to Egyptian tradition and presided over by the chief priest of the city of On, Potipherah. I had some reservations about this, but submitted to as it was essential to my investiture. Potipherah was the high priest of the sun god Ra, and one of Pharaoh's closest advisers. Even though the city of On was in Lower Egypt, Potipherah retained a residence in Waset from where he performed his administrative role. He had been present as one of Pharaoh's high-ranking officials when the Lord interpreted Pharaoh's dream through me. Days after my inauguration, I had heard whispers that his daughter was one of the women being lined up to be my wife. My misgivings about participating in a ceremony where the sun god Ra was the spiritual overseer were assuaged by a word I received from God while in prayer. God assured me that He knew my heart belonged to Him.

Probably the most significant change associated with my elevation was my change of name. Pharaoh bestowed upon me the name Zaphnath-Paaneah, meaning 'the one who reveals secrets', and this was the name all Egyptians addressed me by.

To establish me as Pharaoh's vizier, Pharaoh passed an edict that no man could refer to my past ever again, and at Pharaoh's command all records regarding my slavery and imprisonment were deleted. Even though, officially, I was essentially a new man with no past, the indelible record in my memory could never be expunged.

From my first day in office as vizier, the perks and privileges kept rolling in: many of Pharaoh's officials, whether under compulsion or of their own free will, sent me all sorts of expensive gifts. By the end of the first month, I had a stable full of the finest pure-bred Arabian horses; made-to-measure tunics with exquisite tailoring; bales of expensive textiles, mostly linen and silk; jewellery of gold and precious stones; innumerable pairs of high-quality sandals; bowls full of spices and cosmetics; male and female slaves; reams of high-quality papyrus sheets and several inks and dyes; and enough furniture to fill several palaces.

In addition, I was given my own private quarters within Pharaoh's palace while the house he had designed for me was being built. I was pleased to discover that the house would use stone from the quarry at the west bank that I had helped revive during my tenure in the Tomb, as it was of the very best quality. The same artisans who had worked on Pharaoh's palace were assigned to finish off the interior of mine.

I often recalled my first night in the guest quarters of Pharaoh's palace, bathing in a sunken marble pool filled with perfume-spiced waters, having my body massaged with exotic fragrant oils to relieve my aching muscles, sitting back in a comfortable armchair while gorgeous women gave me a manicure and pedicure, and lying down, alone, on the largest, most comfortable bed I had ever slept in while a pair of Nubian fan-bearers cooled me down through the night with fans made of ostrich feathers.

My first morning was equally memorable. I was assigned several slaves whose primary task was to attend to my oral hygiene, grooming and clothing. After my makeover, I could barely recognise myself in the mirror. The combination of my hairless body and my make-up made me look so convincingly Egyptian that I shuddered. From that day forward, I never again grew a beard or cultivated bodily hair – Joseph of Hebron had become Zaphnath-Paaneah of Waset.

* * * * * * *

The meeting with the Men'at Khufu regional task force was held in the largest, most prestigious hall in the city. When we arrived, we found a large reception committee waiting. Alighting from my chariot, I recognised some of the faces staring at me. Among them, I saw the face I would never forget: the face of the woman whose lies had sent me to prison. She had aged but, like a fine wine, her features conveyed an elegant maturity. She lowered her gaze demurely as I glanced in her direction, and, like everyone else, she knelt. Unwilling to embarrass her or make her feel uncomfortable, I kept my gaze straight ahead so that as I passed, if she looked up, we would not make eye contact.

I sensed her shame, trepidation and mental torment: this was the moment she had dreaded since hearing about my promotion. I did wonder, though, whether she had ever told her husband the truth. While my emotions were still raw, I bore neither of them any malice, for I could see unfolding in front of me a life of greater purpose. My main preoccupation was to get on with the task I had been appointed to perform.

As I approached the entrance to the hall, I saw Potiphar waiting to receive me with the regional administrators. Despite his erect posture, his eyes were lowered. As I came within a few feet of him, he and the other officials went down on one knee with lowered heads. My heart almost stopped beating. The reversal of fortune that I had been struggling to come to terms with suddenly struck me like a thunderbolt and I shuddered, goosebumps smothering my body.

I stood by him, making no effort to enter the hall, waiting for him to look up, but he remained in the same position. Part of me wanted to stoop and lift him up to assure him that nothing had changed between us, but another part instructed me to let protocol prevail. I stood there, undecided, until the voices in my head stopped and a new voice – a smaller, quieter one – spoke. It told me that when Potiphar was my master, protocol demanded that I bowed to him, but now that I was his master, protocol demanded that he had to bow to me. Satisfied with this reasoning, I walked on.

The hall was arranged in much the same way as the hall where Pharaoh held court, with a throne and some chairs laid out to the left and right in front of the throne. I imagined that this was where the regional administrator governed his province.

I headed to the throne, ascended the steps and sat, facing the Men'at Khufu officials and their wives, who formed part of the welcome committee. Potiphar and his wife were seated to my right. Out of the corner of my eye I noticed the tightness of her grip on his arm: she was tense. Though I was in the city to promote the task force and inform the people about my new initiative for tackling the skill shortage in agriculture within the region, I felt I had to resolve the issue between me and Potiphar's wife.

One of my first steps as vizier was to create a project team and a task force. The project team comprised people I had chosen, while the task force was made up of regional officials and officials from Pharaoh's court. The project team's remit was to deliver my pet project, 'Back to the Land'. Heading the project team was Abali – now a free man – whom I had sent for. I called the project team the 'Raamah Squad', in honour of my late friend, and with Potiphar's cooperation I secured the release of a number of inmates from the Tomb, whom I had been mentoring during my time there. These men formed the core of the Raamah Squad.

The task force, on the other hand, had to organise the gathering of a fifth of all the wheat and grain produced in each of the seven years and to store this in specially constructed granaries. These granaries had all been designed to suit the region in which they were situated, to guarantee the preservation of grain, regardless of climate. Under the task force, I had established sub-committees and groups, such as regional pest control teams to control any rats or mice in the granaries, teams of scribes dedicated to recording the dates and source of grain, and stock-taking teams, assigned to weighing the volume of grain stored in each granary. These teams met each month to compare notes and ensure that they were working in a synchronised manner. My plan was to meet up with these regional groups each month so that any concerns regarding our storage policy could be addressed quickly. All these were early initiatives, but I was keen to reinforce my strategy by travelling around the regions to share the message with regional administrators.

As I had done in the other regions I visited, I outlined my strategy for food storage with the regional administrator for Men'at Khufu and his officials. I also shared with them my vision for increasing the capacity and capability of the agricultural sector's workforce through 'Back to the Land'. As in the other regions, my presentation was well received by the audience. At the end, I descended the throne and exited the hall, acknowledging the people as they knelt before me.

Once outside, I gave some quick instructions to the head of my protection team and my driver before mounting my chariot and heading away from the venue. My driver rode furiously towards El Akhet, two of the three chariots in my entourage in pursuit, but halted at a designated spot overlooking the Nile. I had chosen this location for its remoteness from any residential buildings.

El Akhet has many beautiful public spaces, but this park boasted a perfumed kaleidoscope of wild flowers and a cluster of exotic trees. I had retreated here during my time as overseer of Potiphar's household, when I just wished to be alone to commune with God.

I waited under the cool shade provided by the overhanging date and palm trees until I heard chariot wheels pounding over the dusty road. Shortly afterwards, the third chariot in my entourage appeared, carrying two of my security detail, closely followed by a chariot carrying Potiphar and his wife. I had asked two of my men to escort them here because it was far away from prying eyes and eavesdropping ears. I alighted from my chariot and instructed my driver and the security detail to move well out of earshot, so that although they could see us they could not overhear our discussion.

Potiphar and his wife bowed to me. As they rose up, I noticed that she was trembling severely, almost to the point of convulsion. She still held on to her husband's arm and he in turn reached across to place a reassuring hand over hers. Although Potiphar maintained the stance of a military man, I could see the discomfort in his eyes and the pained expression on his face. This worried me. I did not wish to have this sort of effect on them – or anyone else, for that matter – but I had to resolve the issue.

'Do you know why I sent for you?' I asked, staring at them intently.

'To seek your revenge?' answered Potiphar, briefly meeting my stare.

'No – there is no basis for revenge,' I said gently, heaving a sigh as I spoke. 'The records have been erased. There is no evidence either that I served you as a slave or that I spent time as an inmate in the Den of Confinement.'

'But you must feel bitter after what you've been through. Surely you blame me for what happened?'

I shook my head slowly. 'You reacted honourably to what you perceived the situation to be.'

Potiphar nodded and his face brightened. 'In my position, would you not have done the same?'

'In your position, I would not have acted without all the facts.'

'But you were a slave!' exclaimed Potiphar unguardedly.

Our eyes met briefly, but he quickly lowered his gaze – the way I used to do when confronting high-ranking officials. He was a decent man, and I had no intention of robbing him of his dignity in front of his petrified wife, who appeared more fearful than remorseful. As he would be working under me for at least the next fourteen years, I needed to lay the matter to rest to spare him any more discomfort.

'Every slave has a story,' I murmured, fixing them with a wistful stare, 'and you need to know mine. I come from a wealthy, prosperous family in Canaan. My mother died while I was very young and my father did everything to ensure my happiness. However, that happiness was stolen thirteen years ago when I was betrayed by my brothers, who hated me because my father favoured me over them. They conspired to kill me, but the God of my fathers intervened. Instead they sold me to some passing Ishmaelite traders from Midian. Those traders brought me to Egypt and sold me to you.

'Despite the injustice of my circumstances, I served you faithfully and you rewarded me by promoting me to overseer in your home. After the incident your wife accused me of – which I was innocent of, by the way – you could have had me beheaded or castrated, in line with Egyptian law but, because God was with me, you

260

sent me to the Den of Confinement. God preserved me in that evil place and gave me favour with the Keeper, who showed me kindness and made me overseer. If I had not been in the Den I would not have met Pharaoh's cupbearer and interpreted his dream. Even though he forgot about me, God did not abandon me – and at the right time He brought me out of the Den and presented me to Pharaoh.'

I watched them as I spoke, noticing the grim expression n Potiphar's face and the gentle tears that trickled down his wife's flushed cheeks.

'After interpreting Pharaoh's dream,' I continued, 'I expected that he would set me free and permit me to return home to my family, but again the God of my fathers intervened. He facilitated my promotion to this high office in a land where I am a stranger. If I was to ignore His involvement in my affairs, I would abuse the opportunity He has given me to serve, and pursue my own agenda, but I cannot.'

As I finished speaking, my accuser's sorrow overflowed like the Nile during a flood and I, who had instigated her discomfort, became uncomfortable. She covered her face with one hand and stood sobbing, almost doubled over. Her husband, on the other hand, appeared more controlled, although his expression remained serious. A voice in my head urged me not to let my guard down or take any notice of their body language, as it was all an act, but I was convinced that their pain was genuine and their sorrow sincere.

'Can you ever forgive us, Joseph?' asked Potiphar croakily, teetering on the brink.

'There is nothing to forgive.'

'And you bear no bitterness?'

I shook my head emphatically. 'I cannot pretend that

I am still not hurting, but healing is something the God of my fathers specialises in.'

'You are indeed an honourable and wise man,' said Potiphar, straightening up and drying his tears with the back of his hand. 'Pharaoh has chosen a man worthy to occupy the position of vizier, and I pledge my support to you all the days of my life. From this day, my friends will be your friends and your enemies will be my enemies.'

My former master fell to one knee and tugged at his wife's arm for her to follow protocol. She complied, bowing from the waist. This was a pledge of loyalty, not an imposition, and it touched me deeply, as I had neither expected it nor sought it.

'Thank you,' I said as they rose to their feet. 'Your support is appreciated. Now, you'd better leave before the other officials wonder where you are.'

I watched them walk back to their chariot, two sober figures with a lot on their minds. As Potiphar steered the horses away, his wife turned around, gratitude clearly imprinted all over her face, and mouthed the words 'thank you'.

Her words meant a lot, even though it was not the apology I had been expecting. I didn't know whether she had ever told Potiphar the truth about what had happened between us, but that was academic now. It was enough for me that she recognised my chivalry in not dragging her reputation through the mud and destroying the marriage that she had once treated with contempt. After they had ridden away, I stood gazing across the Nile at all the boats that sailed past in either direction, and let my thoughts travel. Watching the display of affection between Potiphar and his wife stirred something within me, and my thoughts strayed to my impending marriage to a high-society Egyptian bride, chosen for me by Pharaoh.

* * * * * * *

My future wife's name was Asenath, and she was the daughter of Potipherah, the priest of On. I had heard whispers about her being on the shortlist of potential brides for me, but one evening in my third month as vizier, as I was preparing to go to bed after a gruelling day touring granaries and farms in Upper Egypt, I was informed by my personal aide that I had visitors. As my house was not yet ready, I still resided in the guest quarters of Pharaoh's palace and so was used to interruptions at odd hours. Without enquiring about the identity of my guests, I changed into a decent tunic and went out to see them. There I was confronted with a vision of such beauty that all traces of my lethargy evaporated.

She was a paragon of beauty from her dark, shoulder-length hair, adorned with golden beads and a lotus flower at one side, all the way down her voluptuous form to the pink tips of her delicate feet, which peeped out beneath the hem of her sheath dress.

The first thing I noticed was her strangely familiar eyes, brown and almond-shaped, above cheekbones that betrayed dimples either side of them. Not even the kohl bordering them could mar their innocence. Her pert nose had a cheeky tilt and her full lips looked as if they were designed for smiling. Her long neck proudly displayed a broad gold necklace and her light-skinned complexion was unblemished. Her linen dress clung to her like an outer skin, accentuating her slender waist and ample bosom.

She looked quite young but her calm demeanour betrayed a maturity far in excess of her years. Above all, there was a trace of purity embedded in her stare that I found extremely appealing.

I was so captivated by her gorgeous face that I almost failed to notice the elderly man standing next to her. Staring more closely at him through the yellowish gloom created by the oil lamps, I recognised the high priest of On and immediately deduced that this had to be his daughter, Asenath. My heartbeat slowly increased in intensity until I could hear it thumping in my ears, and my mouth became dry. I swallowed. My reaction was uncharacteristic and I started to feel guilty. Why was I reacting to her in this way?

'We are here at the request of our Pharaoh,' said Potipherah.

He was not here at Pharaoh's request, but more likely at his command. Among the upper echelons of Egyptian society, all marriages were arranged by the father of the bride and her husband-to-be. Unlike in my culture, where marriage was accompanied by much feasting and celebration, in Egypt it was more of a contract between two parties, and the subject of that contract was the bride. The bride would simply arrive at her husband-to-be's house with her personal effects and would be handed over to him when the contract had been agreed. It focused on property rights and arrangements for the care of the bride.

Most brides were married-off quite young, as men preferred women who were innocent in the ways of the world. However, the situation was different when the father of the bride had been commanded by Pharaoh to give his daughter in marriage to a high-ranking official. In such instances the father was merely the courier and had to cede all his rights of fatherhood to Pharaoh. Even though the father physically gave the bride to the new husband, he was acting on behalf of Pharaoh.

'I thank you for honouring me in this way,' I answered.

The high priest bowed in acknowledgement and from beneath his tunic he produced rolled-up papyrus sheets, which I suspected contained the contract.

'Asenath has been chosen as your wife,' said Potipherah, handing me the papyrus sheets, 'and once we conclude the contract she will remain with you in that capacity.'

I accepted the papyrus sheets and glanced in Asenath's direction as I unfurled them. Even in the poor light I could see that she was pale. I realised she was nervous. It was not uncommon for a bride who had never lived away from her parents to be uneasy about the marriage arrangements, especially where she had not been asked for her opinion or she was getting married to a man who was considerably older than she was. I recalled my father's story about how my grandmother, Rebecca, had been brought to my grandfather Isaac, a man she had agreed to marry without ever having seen him. At least she had been asked for her opinion, but I feared that Asenath had merely been informed. As I read through the contract, which listed all the property that Asenath arrived with, I began to feel like a slave trader. With a heavy heart I reached for the lacquered storage box where my scribe kit was kept. The contract, which was inscribed in hieroglyphs, simply required me to enter the details of my property on the date Asenath arrived in my home and it would be complete, but I hesitated.

'Is there a problem, vizier?'

'Could I spend a short time alone with your daughter before I complete the contract?'

He frowned, and I realised that by not clarifying my intentions I had created the wrong impression.

'No,' I said, raising both hands to reassure him, 'I merely want to speak with her, nothing more, if that is all right with you.'

He turned to Asenath, seemingly communicating with her telepathically before turning back to me, looking much more relaxed. He nodded and stepped outside the chamber. Once he had departed, I put the papyrus sheets down and gestured to a pair of chairs in one corner of the room. Asenath walked gingerly towards the chairs with her head lowered and sat on one, avoiding my gaze. I sat opposite her and reached out to touch her dainty hands, which rested on her lap. At my touch she lifted her head slightly so that her lovely eyes were visible, but her lips were quivering.

'My name is Joseph,' I said gently, smiling benevolently, 'and I come from Canaan.'

Her gaze narrowed suspiciously. 'I was told that your name was Zaphnath-Paaneah.'

Her melodic voice sounded to me like a guileless song.

'That is my official name,' I replied, 'but if we are to be married I want you to call me by my birth name – Joseph.'

She nodded, then lowered her head.

'You are very beautiful,' I said, unsure what to say next.

She nodded, but made no effort to raise her head.

'Are you ready for this?' I asked.

'Ready for marriage?' she asked, glancing up at me. 'Yes, my father informed me about the arrangement a month ago. Many girls my age are already married with children, so I am ready.'

'Well, I am not,' I said quietly, 'and that is why I need you to be patient with me.'

As I spoke, her brown eyes widened in surprise. 'You have never been with a woman before?'

I shook my head, lowering my eyes for effect. 'I am counting on you to teach me all I need to know. Will you do that for me?' I lifted my eyes slowly and stared imploringly at her.

A faint smile rippled across her lips and her facial muscles relaxed. Perhaps it was the discovery that she was dealing with a novice like her. I couldn't read her mind, but sensed that her tension might have been down to apprehension about not measuring up to her perception of her new husband's high standards.

'I will try,' she answered shyly.

'Thank you,' I said, heaving a sigh. 'That makes me feel a lot better.'

That seemed to further reassure her, but she bit her lip. She hadn't finished.

'It is unusual for a man as mature as you not to have been with a woman.'

'Yes, but that is because I have been saving myself for the right one.'

'And how do you know if I am the right one?'

'Something about you reminds me of my late mother,' I murmured. 'She died when I was very young, but I will never forget her eyes – they were always kind.'

Asenath sat upright and a warm glow spread across her features. I had told the truth – her eyes did remind me of my mother's – but I discovered that I had just paid her the greatest compliment.

'I am happy to have been chosen to be your wife,'

she said after an interval.

'And I am happy to have been granted the honour of marrying you,' I answered, 'but one thing worries me.'

'What?' she asked anxiously.

'We worship very different gods, and I fear that my worship may offend you.'

'That will not be a problem,' she answered quickly. 'We have many gods in Egypt and I am happy for you to worship your god.'

'But my God does not tolerate the worship of any other deity,' I said, turning away to gaze at the hieroglyphs on a nearby wall.

There was silence as Asenath considered my words. I studied her closely, anxious to know whether I had just destroyed the foundations of the relationship I was trying to cultivate. She was the daughter of the priest of On, who worshipped the sun god Ra, and she would be expected to continue worshipping Ra. I wondered if I should have waited until after we were married before discussing the issue.

'I cannot worship a god I do not know,' she said with a heaviness that sounded fatal.

'I understand,' I said, surrendering to the inevitable.

'Will you teach me about your God?'

The question was soft, but emphatic.

'Nothing would give me greater pleasure,' I answered, beaming at her.

* * * * * * *

After completing the contract, as Potipherah took his leave, some young maidens came into my quarters bearing all Asenath's possessions. At that stage, reality dawned on me. I was a married man.

My marriage to Asenath marked a new phase in my journey. She was a breath of fresh air in my life and I was grateful to God for her companionship. In the past, I had friends – such as Abali and Raamah – but never a confidante with whom I could share my heart.

The challenge was making the effort to ensure that my time with her did not clash with my dedicated time with God. It had been much simpler when I was on my own, but now I had to prioritise my time. Over the first few months, I took time to tell Asenath about my culture and my faith. I shared with her the history of my people, starting from Abraham, and tried to explain the relevance that God played in our lives. She in turn spoke about her family and her devotion to the sun god Ra, to whom she had been dedicated as a child. I realised that we were poles apart in some areas but closer in others. Because of my hectic schedule, to ensure that she did not get bored, I asked her to supervise the final touches to our future home, something she relished. I wanted our home to have a woman's touch, and left her to resolve the décor.

Several months after our marriage, when she informed me that she was carrying our child, I discovered a rapture that I never believed possible. The thought of being a father was the most exhilarating experience I had ever had. After Asenath had told me the news, I amused her with my euphoric dancing, which lacked the coordination of the Nubian and Cushite entertainers who regularly performed before Pharaoh. But my joy was to reach even loftier heights when one night, six months later, as I knelt by the window of my sleeping chamber to give thanks to God for seeing me through another challenging day, Asenath knelt next to me and asked if she could join me. After that night, we prayed together every day.

I was in the fields around Waset surveying the harvesting of grain when one of Pharaoh's elite guards arrived on horseback to inform me that Asenath had gone into labour and was with the royal midwives. I arrived home shortly after she had given birth to my first child – a gorgeous baby boy, the sight of whom drew tears of ecstasy to my eyes. I was looking at the first member of my new family and, in his innocent eyes, I saw my destiny. As I held him in my arms that first night and gazed up at the clear sky with the full moon overhead, I named him Manasseh, meaning 'to forget', as I believed that God had made me forget all my troubles and those who had betrayed me in my father's house.

From time to time I paused to remember my father's home, but each time, as images of my brothers hovered into view, I quickly blocked them out. Several times I felt a strong urge to seek Pharaoh's permission for me to return to Hebron for a short time to try to track down my family, as I was missing my father and Benjamin, but each time I pulled back. Apart from the fact that I was extremely busy travelling across Upper and Lower Egypt, a trip to Hebron would be a painful one; one that I did not feel able to face just yet. There were still too many conflicting emotions.

Instead, I took refuge in my schedule and convinced myself that I was too busy to make the trip. Having longed to return home the whole time I had lived in Egypt, now that I had the opportunity to visit, I had cold feet.

* * * * * * *

'Most honourable vizier, we have a problem,' said Abali one day as I alighted from my chariot outside the central granary in Waset.

The granary was one of the largest and oldest in Egypt, dating back hundreds of years, having once been the preserve of the priests, holding grain meant only for them. To increase its capacity, I had commandeered it by suspending the privilege of temple granaries across the country until further notice. It had been an unpopular law, but the priests and their followers were forced to abide by it.

'What is it?' I asked after moving out of my driver's earshot.

'It's Men'at Khufu,' answered Abali, fixing me with a troubled stare. 'Khamsin has started playing up again and the volume is dropping.'

Khamsin was the regional administrator in Men'at Khufu responsible for overseeing grain collection within his region, but because he was a stubborn fellow progress was slow, making his region the poorest-performing in Upper Egypt.

Even though he was happy to receive me when I turned up to inspect, he always had an excuse for why targets had either not been met or why there was a delay in meeting them. I later learnt that he was the younger brother of the previous vizier of Egypt and, before my appointment, had been actively lobbying to succeed him.

'By his refusal to perform, he indirectly challenges Pharaoh,' I said with a heavy sigh. 'I have been patient with him, but my patience is wearing thin.'

'Then you ought to get him deposed and let a more compliant person take his place.'

I pondered Abali's practical solution then shook my head. Although I had the power to force regime change in Men'at Khufu, I preferred to avoid skirmishes wherever possible. With the extremely tight timetable I was working to, my project would be affected if I got embroiled in battles with members of my leadership team.

'Week after week, month after month, he challenges you to act – yet you hesitate.'

'I have always preferred for my detractors to fall on their own swords.'

'Only honourable men do that.'

'No – sometimes God gives men a helping hand.'

Abali nodded. Since becoming my second in command, he had embraced my way of thinking and sought to understand my faith in my God. He knew the high esteem in which I held my God and, out of respect for me, sought to do the same. I could, however, see that he was gradually losing his confidence in his pagan culture and opening himself up to the possibility of a monotheistic faith.

'Well, let's pray he does it soon, because we are at risk of missing our monthly target.'

'I will speak with Khamsin.'

'Again?'

'He deserves one last chance.'

* * * * * * *

Khamsin looked across the table at me. The table was covered with stacks of silver and gold pieces. He was a short, round man with an over-inflated ego, who had never accepted my appointment. He had become regional administrator by betraying the confidence of the previous office holder, who was dissatisfied with Pharaoh's regime but had been indiscreet with his remarks. That administrator had been executed and Khamsin installed in his place. It was clear from Khamsin's conduct that he now wanted my job. From the grapevine, I learnt that he had begun the process of building up support among other disaffected officials, who believed that every office in Egyptian government should be held by Egyptians.

I had travelled down to Khamsin's administrative quarters in Men'at Khufu for a face-to-face meeting, and had chosen – against the advice of my bodyguards – to travel alone by chariot. I was hoping that my lack of entourage would ease tension, paving the way for a non-confrontational meeting. When I arrived, I found Khamsin counting tax revenue with a couple of his officials. While his officials had knelt in the customary manner, Khamsin's knee had barely touched the floor. I asked them to leave, as I desired privacy and they hurried out.

'Most honourable vizier, what brings you to my insignificant region?'

I detected his sarcasm.

'I have concerns about your performance in the monthly storage records. Your region is at the bottom of the list.'

'Well, I can assure you that I am doing all I can to galvanise local support for the task force's storage strategy, but there have been setbacks.'

I met his sly smile with a stern stare. 'What exactly is the problem?'

'I have difficulty recruiting enough labourers.'

'That is because your 'Back to the Land' programme is also underperforming.'

'Maybe the problem lies with the concept.'

'Or maybe it lies with your implementation of it.'

We were straying into territory that I wished to avoid.

'Is the honourable vizier questioning my loyalty?'

I shook my head slowly. 'Your loyalty to your ideology is not in doubt.'

He appeared to digest my inference and his smile became bitter.

'Does the honourable vizier have a solution?'

'Yes. I recommend a change of heart.'

'And failing that?'

'A dignified exit.'

'For me or for you?'

'I am determined to improve performance in this region,' I answered, 'and would much prefer if you were fully on board as a partner.'

'Honourable vizier, I am an Egyptian and I am committed to serving my people, but under the right leadership.'

I noted the defiant glint in his eye and nodded. He had thrown down the gauntlet and it was pointless engaging with him anymore.

'Thank you for your honesty,' I said, turning to depart. 'You have made it easier for me to do what needs to be done.'

'Have a safe trip back to Waset!' he called as I left his office.

* * * * * * *

As I rode along the dusty, undulating road between Men'at Khufu and Waset, wishing I had had the good sense to travel down by boat via the Nile, which was the most convenient mode of transport, I heard the thundering of a multitude of horses' hoofs. Turning around, I noticed the party of men on horseback who were rapidly gaining on me, generating a cloud of dust behind them. I carried on driving my chariot, thinking nothing of the pursuing riders, as this was a popular commuter and trade route in Upper Egypt. If I wished to outrun the horse riders, I was perfectly capable of doing so, as the two stallions drawing my chariot were Arabian racehorses. However, I was not too far from the town of Shashotep on the Nile's east bank, where I planned to rest and water my horses and inspect the temple granary dedicated to the ram-headed god Khnum, which I had commandeered.

The sound of the pursuing horses grew louder until I noticed that they were directly behind me. I moved my chariot to one side to give them access. One of the riders drew alongside me as if to overtake, but out of the corner of my eye I saw that he was brandishing a sword. Instinctively I swerved my chariot off the road.

The thud of a spear landing next to me in my chariot made me aware of the danger I was in. Ignoring my heavy heartbeat and racing pulse, I spurred my horses on along the uneven ground. Driving by instinct, I managed to evade the spears being hurled at me and stay ahead of my pursuers till we got to the outskirts of Shashotep.

My personal guards, along with my chariot driver, were waiting for me at an agreed rest point between Shashotep and Waset. I began to regret not bringing them as far as the outskirts of Men'at Khufu. I had played into the hands of my detractors. I suspected that the assassins had been sent by Khamsin to ensure that I never made it back to Waset alive, and the effrontery of the attack told me how much of a threat he perceived me to be. Egypt had a history of viziers being murdered for political reasons, and even pharaohs were not immune from assassination – if enough disaffected officials thought it worth the gamble. While I had confidence in my horses' pace, I prayed out loud for God's intervention and, despite the urgency of my situation, peace flooded my mind. This enabled me to think through my options, weighing the pros and cons. As long as I stayed ahead, I stood a chance of getting to the temple of Khnum, where the temple guards would defend me and repel the threat, but I was still too far from my destination for that to be a genuinely viable option.

As I attempted to leave the road to evade a spear that came whistling past, one of my chariot's wheels struck a rock and came off the axle, causing the chariot to lean severely to one side. My sweaty palms began to lose their grip on the reins and, as I struggled to maintain my balance, I felt a great strain in my arms and lower back. The one-wheeled carriage bounced violently along the bumpy road, jolting me around. Sweat dripped into my eyes, mingling with dust and blurring my vision.

In my attempt to avoid careering into an oncoming mule-drawn cart, my chariot smashed into another rock. This time I was thrown clear of the chariot, landing heavily on my side. I lay there on the barren ground, bruised and cut, watching my unmanned chariot race towards the horizon.

I waited for my assassins to dismount their horses. There were four of them, all tanned and dressed in clothing that identified them as Hyksos mercenaries.

The Hyksos are a Canaanite tribe who once ruled

Egypt. After they were ousted, survivors earned a living as mercenaries and assassins, often employed by wealthy and influential Egyptians to undertake all sorts of clandestine activities. They were the scourge of caravan routes, where they raided caravans, often killing anyone who resisted them. These ruthless swords-for-hire killed without thinking and I knew that I could expect no mercy from them. Two of them were armed with sickle swords and another carried a cudgel. The fourth was unarmed, but from the way the others reacted to him and his swaggering gait, I could tell he was their leader. The unarmed mercenary stepped forward and hovered over me, his callous surveying me like a predator assesses its prey.

The peace I felt within had not completely departed, but I struggled to comprehend the present situation. I thought about my dreams and about how God had placed greatness and influence within my grasp. In spite of the danger facing me, I did not get an impending sense of death. As we eyeballed each other, I heard wooden spoke wheels racing across the uneven ground, coupled with what sounded like the pounding of horses' hoofs, mingled with neighing.

The Hyksos mercenary standing next to me must also have heard the sounds because he spun around, obviously startled. As I stared in the same direction, I observed as one after the other his three companions fell to the ground groaning. The sound of their bodies hitting the ground was buried beneath the noise of what looked like five chariots racing towards us in a huge cloud of dust. The fourth mercenary, seeing that he was alone and outnumbered, hurried towards his horse, mounted it and galloped away in the opposite direction, facing Shashotep.

As the chariots drew nearer, I saw Potiphar in the lead chariot, driven by one of his guards, armed with a bow and arrow. The other chariots that emerged from the dust were also occupied by his guards, and in each carriage there was a guard armed with a bow and arrow. At Potiphar's command the other chariots continued towards Shashotep, in pursuit of the fleeing mercenary, but he halted next to me and alighted. I glanced at the slain mercenaries' bodies, noticing the shafts of the arrows embedded in their bodies, and heaved a sigh.

'Are you all right, honourable vizier?' asked Potiphar, coming to kneel beside me.

'I am all right,' I answered, getting up from the ground, ignoring the throbbing aches and pain. 'Thank you – you came just in time.'

'I heard from someone close to Khamsin that shortly after you left him, some Hyksos mercenaries arrived at his home,' said Potiphar, gripping my arm so that I could stand upright, 'and because I know his reputation I rode out to warn you.'

'I am grateful,' I said, dusting my clothes off, 'and I am in your debt.'

'No, you owe me nothing,' said Potiphar, going down on one knee. 'It is my job to protect you, so your God can continue to use you to protect our people.'

His response overwhelmed me. It was at times like this that I was reminded of the degree of influence that God had given me.

'Don't worry about Khamsin,' said Potiphar, leading me back towards his chariot and helping me mount. 'I will take care of him as soon as my men return with the one who will testify against him.'

I did not say anything; I knew the penalty for rebellion. It seemed that a change of regime would take place without me having to lift a finger.

The Hyksos mercenary was captured and he in turn identified Khamsin as his employer. Potiphar executed Khamsin that same day, beheading him and leaving his body in the eastern desert for wild beasts to eat. Before sunset fell over Men'at Khufu, with my approval, Potiphar appointed one of his scribes as Khamsin's replacement. As part of his oath, I received from him a commitment to meet, and even exceed, all our targets. In the following months, Men'at Khufu regularly outperformed other regions engaged in the 'Back to the Land' and food storage strategies.

THE BUCK STOPS HERE

Matthew 25:21

Seven years later

I stood in what had once been the marshlands of the Nile Delta near the city of On, staring at the rotting carcasses of a dozen cows in an advanced stage of decay, pinching my nostrils to keep out the putrid stench emanating from the lifeless beasts. All manner of scavengers had gathered on the remains for a final celebration of life, including flies, maggots, beetles and ants, and overhead vultures circled, waiting for our departure. Abali and Kaa, who were standing next to me with the regional administrator for the city, appeared to have a stronger constitution: they stood gazing impassively at the death in front of them.

For the past couple of weeks, scenes like this had been appearing in areas that were traditionally watering holes for flocks, signalling an end to our seven years of bountiful harvest. Watering holes were drying up everywhere in Lower Egypt in areas that were renowned for their inexhaustible water supply, and well-irrigated farmlands were becoming wastelands as the Nile evaporated. I had become well acquainted with the stages of decomposition because the fields and farmlands I inspected all contained the cadavers of lifeless animals. In the more arid Upper Egypt regions it was not uncommon to see dry remains that had rapidly passed through all the stages in less than half the time.

Sandstorms were becoming more frequent, driven by easterly winds from across the Red Sea and Arabia, and these winds brought with them all manner of winged predators, including locusts and grasshoppers, that feasted on what was left of the decomposing crops from the last year of harvest. Wells dried up in villages and irrigation paths were reduced to sand-filled gullies. As the water level in the Nile succumbed to the ravages of famine, water became an expensive commodity, which also had an effect on the production of beer and wine.

At home, families restricted themselves to washing their faces and private regions every other day and only having full baths every month, with much less water than before. The 'Back to the Land' programme ended abruptly, and all those who had been trained as farmers were redeployed to work in food distribution centres and retrained by Abali and his team to become proficient in apportioning wheat and grain.

Fortunately for us, God had given us a great head start. The past seven years had been gruelling ones – a mixture of reward and challenges. I had busied myself with collecting and storing grain from the successive seasons of bumper harvests, and training hundreds of new farmers across Egypt to add to the workforce. As the original granaries became full to capacity, we had built new ones. To ensure that there was no delay in the process, I had a network of builders who specialised in rapidly erecting these structures according to the architectural designs I gave them. As soon as we knew that a granary was half-full, a new one was erected within weeks. Initially, we kept count of the volume of grain that was being stored, and I recorded this in my regular updates for Pharaoh, but within a couple of years it became impossible to keep this up as the grain stored became as voluminous as the sand on the banks of the Nile.

During this period, Potiphar worked closely with me to arrange a security detail for each of the granaries to ensure that they were impervious to break-ins by unscrupulous entities. We established the granary guard, who were armed to protect the stored grain, and Potiphar gave instructions that anyone caught breaking in should be put to death. Potiphar was also instrumental in ensuring that farmers supplied us with one-fifth of their harvests, as prescribed in the Food Preservation Edict, issued by me in Pharaoh's name. Any farmer who failed to comply risked forfeiting his land – and spending time in the Den of Confinement.

Khamsin, the ex-regional administrator for Men'at Khufu, was not the only tough nut we had to crack during the seven years; there was a handful of other dissidents who privately objected to my appointment and did all they could to frustrate my efforts by encouraging resistance by regional administrators. However, because God was with me, all their efforts backfired. In some instances they squabbled among themselves, unable to agree, and, in others, they betrayed each other and their schemes were exposed. Within the first year, several high-ranking officials were executed by Pharaoh. After that, I received complete loyalty. My father-in-law was also a useful resource, by virtue of his religious influence, and he was able to drum up loyalty both for me and my plans.

The news of Pharaoh's dreams was a closely guarded secret throughout the country: very few people outside Pharaoh's immediate circle of influence knew about the seven bountiful years or the seven years of famine, and for them the excessive gathering and storage of grain was baffling. We dealt with enquires by informing people that Egypt was seeking to become the world's largest distributor of grain to fund a prosperous future.

In addition to gathering wheat and grain, we had created new reservoirs near the Red Sea and Nile Delta based on principles gleaned from Mediterranean cities. These reservoirs contained vast reserves of water which would be used to irrigate new grazing ground under a new programme aimed at enriching the soil of these lands to ensure plant growth. The plan was to ensure that surviving flocks could be led to these places and sustained during the seven years of famine. Only the very healthiest flocks would be preserved, while others were to be milked, slaughtered and converted into dried meats, which could be stored. Because very few Egyptians worked as shepherds, the arrangements were made with foreigners dwelling in the land.

One of the new grazing lands I created was in a town known as Goshen. I ensured that it was well supplied with the largest of all the reservoirs. I planned to develop Goshen into a paradise for shepherds and collect a levy from them for grazing their flocks there, because I was thinking beyond the famine. After the seven lean years, there would be the need to rebuild and we would need structures in place to facilitate this. One of the privileges of my role as vizier was the ability to acquire land on behalf of Pharaoh, and I set about acquiring Goshen, territory by territory, until by the end of the seven years of plenty, the town and all the surrounding lands belonged to Pharaoh.

* * * * * * *

'Joseph, you have done exceedingly well,' announced Pharaoh while he reviewed my budget report, as he had done for the past seven years.

I bowed in response, while my colleagues murmured in approval.

'I approve your budget,' went on Pharaoh, 'and now issue a decree that no one shall be able to buy or sell food in Egypt without your permission. As you have gathered the food, no one is better qualified than you to supervise its distribution.'

Again, there was a chorus of approval and I bowed in acknowledgement.

Though my budget did not provide an accurate breakdown of the volume of grain and wheat in each of the granaries in Upper and Lower Egypt, because of the impossibility of that task, my mathematical breakdown estimated that there was more than enough food to last Egypt more than fourteen years – if it could be preserved that long. Expert advice from my food hygiene team cautioned against storing grain beyond eight years, so my recommendation was that food distribution started from the oldest stores – which contained food stored in the earliest years – as this was most susceptible to decomposition. Any excess capacity would be sold to foreigners, who I predicted would arrive in Egypt to buy food. My predictions were based on news from Midianite, Anatolian and Mesopotamian traders, who said that the famine had spread to their lands as well and they were less prepared than Egypt for the downturn. Bearing this in mind, I created a tariff for food prices which would increase throughout the seven years as the famine got more intense.

The food would be sold at the lowest price to the poor in Egypt and at a slightly higher price to the wealthy, who could afford to pay more. The highest prices were reserved for foreigners, depending on the relationship between their countries and Egypt.

Countries identified as friends of Egypt would pay the lowest price on the foreign nation tariff, while more distant countries would pay the most. We would not sell food to hostile nations unless they entered into peace treaties with Egypt and agreed to provide military assistance to Egypt in the event of war. Food would be used to secure their loyalty.

I also gave myself a special allocation of grain which I could distribute at no cost to anyone I considered a future ally of Egypt. Food would be used to buy friendships and new trading deals. Pharaoh approved my recommendations without questioning any of them, and gave me an allocation of one-fifth of all the stored grain for my discretionary distribution strategy.

To sweeten the budget, I introduced a food subsidy in favour of all high-ranking officials and their households. My rationale was that, as servants of the Egyptian state, they were entitled to be subsidised by the state. I extended this benefit to all regional administrators in Upper and Lower Egypt and their own high-ranking officials, and received their overwhelming vote of confidence. To ensure that labourers from the 'Back to the Land' programme, who had retrained as food distribution officers, were also taken care of, I created the state distribution strategy. This entitled them and their families to an allocation of grain. I also extended the allocation to retired state servants, such as the ex-Keeper and the former captain of the guard at the Den of Confinement, who had both now retired, as well as to the family of Pharaoh's late chief baker, as I heard that they were suffering terribly and in great need of assistance.

At the end of Pharaoh's council session, I was literally mobbed by the high-ranking officials, including magicians and priests, all expressing their gratitude for my strategies that had, in their words, saved Egypt and its posterity. Some called me the greatest vizier Egypt had ever had, and some paid me the ultimate homage by going down on one knee before me in the outer courtyard. Soaking up their adulation, I suddenly recalled one of my dreams again and wondered whether the sun, moon and eleven stars I had seen were in fact Egyptian officials.

In the weeks following that council session, I set up food distribution centres in every region across Egypt, manned by the regional administrators and their officials. I also set up three distribution centres to cater for foreigners. These were located in major cities within Lower and Upper Egypt. The Central Distribution Centre at Waset catered for those coming from Cush or Nubia, while another at Men'at Khufu addressed the needs of traders from across the Red Sea. The Men-nefer centre catered for those coming from the northern countries and from across the Mediterranean. Each of these centres was manned by one of Pharaoh's high-ranking officials, who reported directly to me.

When the local population began to cry out to Pharaoh as the famine gripped the nation, and starving families saw their children tottering at the brink of death, he directed them to my office, making it clear that I had the final say in all matters relating to food distribution. At this point, we implemented our regional distribution strategy.

* * * * * * *

One year later

On a day I usually set aside as a day of rest to be with

Asenath, Manasseh and Ephraim, I found myself in the distribution centre in Men'at Khufu, overseeing the distribution of grain to people of different nationalities. Potiphar, the official in charge of that centre, in addition to his full-time role as captain of Pharaoh's guard, had fallen ill, requiring me to step in. I had briefly considered delegating the job to Abali but, since he was not one of Pharaoh's high-ranking officials, that was not an option.

The distribution centres were run from makeshift canopies attached to granaries. The granary in Men'at Khufu was one of three new ones that had been built following Khamsin's death, and it contained grain gathered during the first of the seven generous years of harvest. This was the grain that we were distributing to foreigners. On arrival, the purchaser would join a queue and, when it was their turn, they would approach the official in charge with their request and the tariff price. The tariff was posted on the walls of all granaries but, as all caravans trading with Egypt had its details, word soon spread to other countries. The grain was distributed in sacks provided by the purchaser and were only filled once payment had been received. The money received was collected by accounting scribes whose responsibility was to reconcile money received with the volume of food distributed. Specially made scales were used to weigh each full sack before it was handed over to the purchaser, and we operated a rationing system to ensure that rich purchasers did not place excessively large orders for hoarding and reselling. Once a granary was depleted, rather than replenishing it, we simply moved the centre to another.

Promising my wife that I would make up the lost time to her another day, I turned up at the Men'at

Khufu centre to find a long queue of traders and civilians. Abali and the other officials supporting me were also waiting. Before opening for distribution, I took stock of the grain. While Abali and other officials dealt with the customers, my role was to approve each transaction of more than ten full-size sacks of grain. Most of the time, I sat in my ebony armchair, one of my servants holding a shade to protect me from the sun's rays while customers bowed to me before commencing their transactions.

The morning passed fairly uneventfully and very few transactions came my way for approval – until the arrival of ten bearded men on mules whose clothing identified them as hailing from Canaan. I was helping myself to some dates and other dried exotic fruits from a platter proffered by a servant when a familiar voice from the past slashed through my thoughts, making me drop the fruits. My servant began to apologise profusely, but I silenced him with a raised hand and looked towards the voice, which had come from one of the ten Canaanites.

The voice was one of the last voices I had heard as I was lowered into the pit in Dothan over twenty-one years ago. It was a voice I had often replayed in my thoughts as I recalled the lowest point in my life. Every time I heard it, it ushered heaviness to my soul. As the ten men approached Abali and his team, I studied their faces closely. Judah! My heart almost stopped beating. He had not really changed much, apart from the greying hair. His was the voice I had heard a moment earlier, and seeing him after all these years triggered painful memories. I found myself shaking. Why was I reacting like this? Was I not the second most powerful man in all of Egypt? I steadied my nerves and galvanised my thoughts until I was once again the vizier of the most powerful nation on Earth.

From that point, I was calm enough to identify all ten of my brothers, despite their more mature features. With the exception of Benjamin, who was conspicuously absent, the rest were there – Reuben, Simeon, Levi, Judah, Dan, Naphtali, Gad, Asher, Issachar and Zebulun. Benjamin's absence prompted a momentary anxiety. Where was he? Had they dealt with him in the same way as they had me? What about my father? Was he still alive? I desperately needed to know.

'Abali!' I called out, mustering every ounce of authority I could. 'Bring those men to me!'

With the assistance of several of my guards, Abali herded my ten brothers together like sheep and summoned them to my presence. As they approached, Judah leading the way, my pulse rate soared. I was confident that they would not recognise me because of my make-up, hairless head and Egyptian accent, but I still felt apprehensive. I had dreamt about this, and couldn't quite believe it was finally happening.

I watched impassively as all ten prostrated themselves on the ground before me, their faces to the ground. I fought to keep my emotions in check. My mind replayed the dreams of the sun, moon and eleven stars bowing to me, as well as the eleven sheaves of wheat bowing to mine. As I witnessed the fulfilment of my visions, the thumping of my heartbeat heralded a defining moment in my journey. Inwardly, I began to worship God as I saw the unfolding of the twenty-one-year-old mystery.

When my brothers eventually rose to their feet, I saw the humility and trepidation in their eyes and felt empowered. I needed answers to my questions but, to get them, I needed to remain covert.

'Where are you from?' I asked, leaning forward menacingly from my elevated position, so that my icy kohl-adorned eyes assaulted theirs.

'We are from the land of Canaan,' answered Judah, who was multilingual, 'and we have come to buy food.'

'And through which route did you come?'

'We came via the Horus Way into Lower Egypt.'

This was the route I had been brought along by the Ishmaelite traders. It avoided travelling across the Red Sea. It was the shortest overland route from Canaan to Egypt. But it made no sense for my brothers to have travelled south to Men'at Khufu when there was a distribution centre in Men-nefer close to the Nile Delta. I decided to probe further.

'Why did you not go to the Men-nefer distribution centre to buy food?'

'We did, but there was an extremely long queue and many of those ahead of us had been waiting for days, so on the advice of one of the officials we decided to travel down here.'

I knew he was telling the truth: I had received reports from Men-nefer about the lengthy queues of foreigners from Mesopotamia, Assyria, Anatolia and the Aegean Isles. I was already contemplating converting one of the regional food distribution centres meant for the locals as a means of increasing capacity.

'I do not believe you!' I roared, striking one fist into the palm of my other hand. 'You are spies who have come to assess the vulnerability of our land!'

On hearing my charge, my guards reached for their sickle swords and spears and surrounded my brothers, who huddled together in terror.

'No, my lord!' cried Judah, raising imploring hands.

'Your servants have simply come here to buy food. We are all brothers, from the same household, and we are honest men. I can assure you we are not spies.'

'I am not convinced.' I grunted, sitting back with an air of finality. 'I believe you have come to spy on our land to determine how vulnerable we are.'

'My lord,' said Judah, looking distraught, 'your servants are twelve sons of the same man living in the land of Canaan. We left our youngest brother at home with our father, but our other brother is no longer with us.'

'I am still not convinced that you are not spies,' I said aggressively, 'but I will give you the chance to prove that you are not. Unless your youngest brother comes here, I swear on Pharaoh's life that you will not leave this land! One of you will go and fetch your brother while the rest remain in detention so that I can determine whether or not you are telling the truth. By the life of Pharaoh, if you do not present your brother to me I will treat you as spies!'

I beckoned to Abali, who was standing nearby, and when he bent close to me I whispered in his ear.

'Throw them in the Den of Confinement,' I said. 'I do not trust them.'

'For how long, honourable vizier?'

I pondered for a moment. 'Three days,' I answered, 'but tell the Keeper to place them in the minimum security wing and to treat them well. He is to keep them apart from the other inmates and they are to have the very best diet.'

'As you have commanded, honourable vizier,' said Abali, kneeling in line with protocol.

Seeing the slumped shoulders and morose faces of my ten brothers as my armed guards herded them out of my presence, I felt a twinge of guilt, but quickly smothered it. There was no malice in my actions, only a quest for the truth. I had now learnt that both Benjamin and my father were alive – but I needed visual proof. The three-day interval would give me time to formulate a plan of action. But I also figured it would give my brothers time to experience the apprehension that grips a vulnerable man when he is placed in the bowels of uncertainty.

* * * * * * *

On the third day, Abali presented my brothers before me at the distribution centre in Men'at Khufu. Even though they appeared well cared for, their subdued mood revealed their mental turmoil. Here they were in a strange country with the misfortune of being the prisoners of the second most powerful man in the land, facing the prospect of execution for an offence they were innocent of. Their fear of death was real, as was their belief that without a miracle they might never see their loved ones back in Canaan again. Abali had learnt from the Keeper of the Den that they had been extremely sober during the three days and had hardly spoken to each other.

'Because I am a God-fearing man,' I said, as they assembled, 'if you do what I ask, you shall live.'

I gave them time to chew upon my words.

'This is what I have decided,' I said, rising up and descending the steps from my seat to their level, so I was standing in their midst. 'If you are honest men, men of integrity, choose one of you who shall be remanded in the Den of Confinement while the rest of you return home with enough grain for your families, and then come back here with your youngest brother so I can verify whether you have been telling me the truth. Agree to this and you shall not die.'

I looked at them in turn, but none of them dared to meet my stare directly, quickly lowering their eyes in deference. I stepped away from them to give them time to confer and went to inspect the accounts that were being recorded by one of my scribes, making sure I was within hearing range.

'We are clearly being punished for what we did to Joseph,' said Levi.

'I agree,' cut in Zebulun. 'Even though we saw what torment he was in when we threw him in the pit, we still chose to ignore his cries for help.'

'Yes,' said Asher. 'That explains why this calamity has befallen us.'

'Did I not warn you all?' said Reuben, wading in. 'Did I not warn against harming Joseph? But you would not listen! Now we have to answer for what we did, because his blood is crying out for justice.'

Hearing them debating the crisis and reliving the incident, I suddenly became overcome with emotion, and it all came rushing to the surface like lava from a volcano. I turned away from the scribe and hurried to a deserted part of the granary, where I let my tears flow. After a few moments, I composed myself and returned to where they were gathered.

'Have you decided?' I asked, scowling at them.

They looked at each other, clearly undecided and unable to select a candidate. I stepped forward and pointed at Simeon, who appeared to be the least contrite of them. One of my guards seized him and led him away. I studied their faces as Simeon was chained and bundled onto the back of a mule-drawn cart, noting the anguish in their eyes. I had never witnessed this collective empathy before: while it was welcome and refreshing, I could not help wishing they had felt that way towards me. Part of me still craved their love and loyalty, despite my good fortune.

I resumed my seat and summoned Abali. When he came over, I instructed him to fill each of my brothers' sacks with grain and to restore each man's money in his sack. I also asked him to provide them with enough grain for their journey back to Hebron, which I estimated to take seven days. As I spoke I noticed the quizzical frown on Abali's face, but he dared not question me. He went away to execute my order and I watched as my brothers' mules were laden with sacks of grain and enough food and water for their return journey. I made sure that each of them was given breakfast from my personal provision. After they had eaten, I watched as they rode away from Men'at Khufu in the direction of the eastern desert route, which was the fastest way to the Nile Delta.

The likelihood of my brothers returning to Egypt depended on whether they had been telling me the truth about my father and Benjamin still being alive. If they were telling the truth, then their return to Egypt would depend on how quickly they ran out of food, how much value they placed on Simeon, and, most importantly, whether my father would release Benjamin into their care.

The grain they were carrying would last them at least a year; I had, unknown to them, exchanged their original sacks for stronger, larger ones. I had also filled a sack for Simeon's family that had been placed on his mule, which was now in Levi's custody. If they ran out of food they had two options: either purchase food directly from Egypt at a controlled price or find a middleman in Canaan to buy Egyptian grain from, at more than five times the price. The latter option was unlikely because my father was a firm believer in value for money, but if it was a choice between starvation and value for money he might be forced to jettison his principles.

While Reuben and Judah could try to persuade my father to let them return to Egypt for their brother, the very fact that Benjamin had not accompanied them on the first trip was an indication of my father's affection for my younger brother. Did my father trust my brothers enough to release Benjamin into their care?

UNEASY LIES THE HEAD

Romans 13:3

One year later

'Joseph!'

I woke from a deep sleep, disorientated, and stared around me in confusion. Asenath's alarmed voice had penetrated the deepest part of my unconsciousness and hauled me back to reality. While everyone else called me 'Zaphnath-Paaneah' or 'honourable vizier', she insisted on calling me Joseph in private.

The sun had begun to rise and through the sheer gauze of our drapes I could see the distant orange ball above the grey, white and blue clouds that formed a layer beneath it.

'What is it, my love?' I asked, struggling to focus on her concerned face.

'You were talking in your sleep,' she said, placing a delicate hand on my bare shoulder. 'Is everything all right?'

I let her words sink in. This was not the first time, but this episode had clearly been concerning enough to warrant her urgent intervention.

'What was I saying?'

'You were calling out some names over and over again and pleading with them.'

'What names?' I asked, even though I suspected I knew who they were.

'Simeon and Levi,' she answered. 'Are those not the names of two of your brothers?'

I nodded. I had shared my story with Asenath during the early days of our marriage and she had memorised the names of my family members. Having adopted my God as her God, she was equally keen to adopt my family culture. I had therefore discussed my family's history, starting from Abraham, so she could understand the rich heritage into which our sons had been born. In sharing my history, I had spared no detail, including the ignoble acts of Simeon and Levi at Shalem when their thirst for vengeance had wrecked such havoc in the City of Shechem.

Some of the women and children who had been taken as part of their plunder had been sold in slavery, while the single women had become their concubines. I had shared with Asenath Simeon and Levi had played a key role in my own saga. I had, however, not shared with her the fact that all my brothers had shown up in Egypt a year ago to buy food from me, because I could not risk the news slipping out and reaching the ears of my father-in-law. She was also not aware that I was holding Simeon in custody. I knew Asenath was devoted to me and our sons, but she still had a very close relationship with her mother, who was not known for her discretion.

'Maybe I was reliving past events again,' I murmured, reclining against the headboard.

'But why now? It has been almost twenty-two years.'

I shrugged. 'Maybe I am just missing my family.'

There was silence. 'I thought the boys and I were your family.'

I turned toward her and noticed her crestfallen expression. 'You are,' I said quickly, reaching across to plant a kiss on her forehead, 'but I still long to see my father and Benjamin.'

'Then why not seek Pharaoh's permission to visit them?'

This was not the first time she had suggested this, but I had always played down the significance of such a trip at a time when Egypt and the world stood on the brink of extinction due to the brutal famine.

'But the work is not done and there are still five years of famine.'

'You have trained officials at regional and national levels and delegated authority to them. The work will carry on without you.'

'But Pharaoh needs to be updated weekly.'

'I believe you are looking for a reason not to do what is in your heart. Why?'

I wanted to offer another excuse, but her enquiring gaze silenced me. She knew me better than anyone in Egypt, because she had studied me; it was pointless trying to justify my reasons to her.

'Maybe you are afraid of what you will find.'

I sighed heavily. She knew me too well.

'Joseph, do not fear,' she said, snuggling up next to me. 'God knows how you feel and He will provide the balm to soothe your pain.'

I was about to thank her for her concern, but was interrupted by the slapping sound of bare feet running across a hard floor. Looking up, I saw our two sons racing into the chamber towards us, Ephraim leading the way and his older brother Manasseh in hot pursuit. The boys jumped on our bed and we reached forward to cuddle them. They were excited whenever I was at home, because it meant we could indulge in some of our favourite pastimes, such as playing board games, fishing and hunting.

'Daddy, can we go hunting this morning, please?' asked Manasseh.

Asenath cleared her throat emphatically. I chuckled.

She did not approve of me taking the boys hunting, even though they always stayed in a secure horse-drawn carriage protected by four of my personal guards, watching while I chased prey in my chariot, killing them with my bow or a spear. I was about to accede to Manasseh's request when I suddenly recalled my itinerary for the day. I was billed to visit the Den of Confinement, as I did almost every fortnight, to check up on Simeon. Hunting would have to wait.

* * * * * * *

I peered into Simeon's cell through the bars in the door watching him pacing around in circles, speaking to himself. With dark-ringed, sleep-deprived eyes and an overgrown beard, Simeon looked like a man battling with depression. Even though our faces were clearly visible through the bars of the door, he made no effort to communicate with us or even acknowledge our presence, making me wonder about his mental state.

On my fortnightly visits, I always conferred with the Keeper of the Den about Simeon's welfare and observed him discreetly. But, I never attempted to make direct contact with my brother, even though I longed to. As far as the Keeper was concerned, Simeon was a potential spy from a foreign nation and was still under investigation. The Keeper had been instructed to treat him well in accordance with my instructions because he was from a foreign nation which might one day be an Egyptian ally. My visits were to check that my instructions were being complied with, but also to see how my brother was coping.

On some of my visits, I would find him playing board games with the guards or eating and drinking with them. For the most part, he seemed to be adapting well. Simeon was the most rugged of my brothers, and one who could hold his own in a fight, but his mental state was an unknown factor, until now. This was the first real test of his mettle. Part of me was curious to see how he handled himself. It had been roughly a year since my brothers returned to Canaan. For Simeon, the biggest challenge in the Den must be wondering whether or not they would return for him. I had been expecting my other brothers to return with Benjamin within a couple of months, but their failure to return was worrying. It also left me with the problem of what to do with Simeon, because he could not remain here forever.

I watched Simeon for a while longer then turned to the Keeper, who was standing beside me with two of his guards.

'He is starting to lose his mind,' I observed.

'It is a phase, most honourable vizier,' answered the Keeper. 'He will recover.'

I thought back to my days in the Den and knew that, while some inmates did indeed recover, there were those who eventually became lunatics and had to be executed. Not everyone adapted well to life behind bars.

'How long has he been like this?'

'Since your last visit, I have noticed he has become increasingly reclusive and withdrawn, preferring to remain alone in his cell.'

This bothered me, and I almost felt sorry for him. Due to pressure of work, my previous visit had been a month ago. I suspected that Simeon had been counting on our brothers returning before the end of the year, when their grain would run out, but their non-appearance had created doubt in his mind that he would ever see them again. Even though part of me empathised with him, I was keen to see whether he had any genuine remorse for his brutal history.

'He keeps on speaking about betrayal and innocent blood.'

'His guilty mind is turning on itself,' I murmured.

'His guilty mind?'

'He has become his own judge and executioner.'

'Oh, I see. So what do you wish to do with him, most honourable vizier?'

I had determined to keep Simeon behind bars until my other brothers returned, but in his current state I was no longer keen on that plan.

'Keep him in for another two weeks,' I said, 'and if you do not hear from me, then let him go and give him enough money and provisions to return to his own country.'

'As you wish, most honourable vizier,' answered the Keeper.

* * * * * * *

One week later

I studied the twenty square boxes on the surface of the Aseb game board that lay on the stool between me and Pharaoh, trying to decide my next move. We both enjoyed Aseb. Each player moves their game pieces, which are shaped like lions, across three rows of four squares, relying on the numbers they obtain from throwing polished knucklebone dice to determine the distance of each move. The remaining eight squares extended beyond the original twelve, and progress along this path determined who won.

Out of courtesy, I always let Pharaoh win, but there was another reason: by letting him win, I fuelled his desire to keep playing Aseb with me, rather than Senet, in our weekly private meetings. Senet was linked to Egyptian worship of their gods and the journey into the afterlife, which conflicted with my beliefs, whereas Aseb was less ritualistic.

'You have something on your mind, Zaphnath-Paaneah.'

Pharaoh's voice cut through my concentration.

'May Pharaoh live forever,' I said, erasing my wrinkled forehead. 'I am only thinking of the best way to match your excellence at this game.'

'That may be so, but still I detect a distance in your stare.'

'May Pharaoh live forever – I am merely searching for wisdom.'

Pharaoh had the ability to read people's expressions: this was how he determined which of his officials was loyal or potentially treacherous. For this reason, all his officials contrived to wear pleasant or bland expressions whenever they were in his presence. Despite their best efforts, he always managed to detect their inner thoughts and act according to his perception. I never had cause to work on my facial expression when I was in his presence, but today was different because I had come with an unusual request.

Following my visit to the Den the previous week, and having seen Simeon's mental deterioration, I was determined to release him, but to send some guards to track his movements, in the hope that he would lead them to my family in Canaan. Thereafter, I wanted to ask Pharaoh's permission to travel to Canaan to visit my father for a few months. All the time we played

Aseb, my thoughts were on the best way to present my request so that it would be accepted. I was head of the Egyptian food programme, and Pharaoh counted on me. Even though I had effectively delegated, he would not be comfortable with me being out of the country.

We played on in silence, with me eventually losing – legitimately on this occasion, because my mind was all over the place. At the end of the game, as I picked up the pieces to store in the compartment beneath the game board, my gaze met his. I quickly lowered my eyes. I had noted the concern on his face and I knew he was not convinced about my state of mind. Knowing his suspicious mind, I had no wish to leave him guessing.

'May Pharaoh live forever,' I said, after packing up the game. 'I have been thinking about the welfare of my family in Canaan and wondering how they are coping because of the famine.'

'Ah!' said Pharaoh with a satisfied gasp. 'But of course! I knew there was something on your mind. The famine is over the face of the whole Earth, and it will have reached your family. Do you wish to send them food?'

I sighed inwardly. His suggestion seemed to rule out any possibility of me leaving Egypt to visit them. If I was able to send food to them, there would be no need for me to visit them. Pharaoh was shrewd, but he was not emotional. He knew I was missing my family, and that I would cherish the opportunity to visit them, but once I ventured out of Egypt I was outside his control – and he liked to be in control. His suggestion was therefore a pragmatic compromise.

'May Pharaoh live forever,' I answered in a subdued voice. 'Pharaoh is indeed kind and merciful to his servants – however, I have no idea where my family is. I have been away from home for over twenty-two years. Being a nomadic people, they would most likely have moved their tents.'

'We can send a party of trackers to locate them and give them food.'

I was inclined to ask if I could join the party, but wisdom silenced me. Trackers were Cushite and Nubian men who had the ability to track people and were often used by Pharaoh, along with bounty hunters, to locate criminals or political adversaries who had fled Egypt. Trackers could find my family, but I had no wish for such a cold engagement. Besides, it could take months, and I wanted a quicker solution that involved using Simeon. If the trackers could follow Simeon to Canaan, he would lead them to my father's house; at a later date, I would seek Pharaoh's permission to visit them.

'May Pharaoh live forever,' I said energetically. 'I thank Pharaoh for his kindness. With his permission, I will select and instruct the team of trackers.'

Pharaoh nodded benevolently. As our eyes met briefly, I noticed the twinkle in his. He had not only won the game of Aseb but, in his official capacity, as far as he was concerned, he had won our battle of wits. However, my ambitions were not quashed, merely deferred. I would arrange with the trackers to pose as traders and supply them with grain which they could sell to my family at a reasonable cost to ensure their preservation through the famine. The plan forming in my head included instructing the trackers to find a way of returning my family's money to them. Even if my father never sent my brothers back to Egypt, I was determined that they would not starve.

* * * * * * *

I was emerging from the Waset distribution centre, having checked the sales accounts and taken stock of the grain, when I heard galloping hoofs and the clattering of a chariot being driven at pace. My guards instantly went on alert, surrounding me with drawn swords and spears. As the speeding vehicle approached, I saw Abali at the reins and instructed them to stand down. Due to my status, I had eight men around me and two archers on the granary's roof scouting the area. Though my protection detail was almost as impressive as Pharaoh's, my trust was always in God.

'They are here, most honourable vizier!' exclaimed Abali as his chariot pulled up in a cloud of dust, his horse pawing the ground. He clambered out of the carriage and immediately knelt.

'Who is here?'

'Those men from Canaan – the brothers of the man you placed in custody.'

My heart leapt within me and in my joy I pushed through my guards to Abali. 'Where are they now?'

'The ten of them are on their way to Waset under armed escort, but I hurried on ahead to alert you.'

Abali's initiative never ceased to amaze me. A year ago, I had instructed him to inform me the moment my brothers returned to Men'at Khufu so I could return there to meet them, expecting that it would only be a matter of months at worst. By bringing them to Waset, he had saved me a lengthy trip.

'You said ten men – are you sure there are ten men?'

'Yes, most honourable vizier. There is another man with them – a younger man.'

I felt my excitement heighten, but just as suddenly it dropped. What if they had found some young Canaanite man to impersonate Benjamin, in the belief that I would not be able to tell the difference? I decided to defer my euphoria until I had laid eyes on my younger brother. It had been twenty-two years since I had seen him, but I was confident that I would recognise him from the one feature that almost never changed – his eyes.

'How far away are they?'

'Less than half an hour.'

I turned to one of my guards. 'Go to my house,' I said urgently, 'and summon Kaa.'

For the past nine years Kaa had been the overseer of the affairs of my house – a gift from Potiphar when I was elevated to vizier. Though I had given him his freedom, Kaa had stayed on to work for me as a salaried servant. I relied on him for all my domestic affairs, just as Potiphar had entrusted his affairs to me all those years ago. To reward Kaa for his faithful service after five years, I had found him a wife – a young maiden named Kiya who was Asenath's handmaiden. Like her husband, Kiya had stayed on as Asenath's handmaiden.

'So, most honourable vizier,' said Abali, after my guard had departed, 'what about the one in custody?'

'Pick him up, bring him to my house, and hand him over to Kaa.'

Abali remounted his chariot and hurried off to obey my instructions, while I headed for the canopied elevated area reserved for the senior official to await my brothers' arrival. I tried to focus on other matters, but I kept conjuring up scenarios in which an impostor was presented to me as Benjamin and I was either forced to prematurely reveal my identity and expose their charade or accept him as genuine, sell them food, then send a team of trackers after them. I was still immersed in my thoughts when one of my guards arrived. He walked in and knelt.

'The party from Men'at Khufu has arrived, most honourable vizier.'

'Send them in,' I said, gripping the arms of my chair till my knuckles whitened.

Despite the build-up of pressure in my chest, I remained seated, using the brief period of solitude to compose myself. Moments after my guard stepped out, my brothers shuffled into the canopied area, their body language conveying a level of sobriety and humility that looked genuine. When they arrived, my eyes scanned their ranks until I isolated the unfamiliar face of a man who had not been with them the first time around. Standing beside Judah was a bearded young man with a shock of dark, wavy hair. Squinting to get a closer look at his face, I noted his eyes, and they instantly reminded me of the two most important women in my life. While the older nine men went down on one knee in homage, Benjamin hesitated, then hastily copied their example when he realised he was the only man standing. I acknowledged their presence with a casual wave of my hand, but inside I was an emotional wreck.

One by one the ten men rose to their feet until all my brothers were standing before me, looking subdued. I looked at Benjamin's features and went limp. It had been twenty-two years since I last looked into his eyes, but he looked exactly as I had imagined he would. His resemblance to my younger self was uncanny, and for a moment I imagined I was gazing at an old image of myself. With what little strength I could summon I beckoned to Kaa who strode over with alacrity, kneeling beside my chair.

I quietly instructed him to take all ten men to my home and reunite them with their brother. I also instructed Kaa to get my cooks to slay the fattest calf in my flocks and prepare the meat according to Canaanite tradition. In addition, I requested assorted bread, fruits, nuts, choice wine and ginger beer to be laid out for the ten men in my banquet hall, because they would be dining with me that afternoon. Kaa nodded. I watched as he summoned my brothers to follow him in an authoritative voice that seemed to heighten their anxiety.

After they had gone, I remained seated, staring into the mass of Cushite and Nubian people queuing up outside to buy grain. Once again, God had been faithful. His intervention spared me any elaborate planning. Despite my apprehension, my brothers had kept their promise to return with my younger brother, but how had they persuaded my father to release him into their care? Silently I prayed to God for guidance in how to deal with them, then rose up to go home, barely noticing those who knelt as I walked past.

* * * * * * *

When I arrived home, Kaa met me at the front entrance, greeted me in the customary manner, then drew me to one side.

'I have done as you asked, most honourable vizier,' he said, 'and their meal is being prepared. However, one of them, who calls himself Judah, tried to give me some money for the grain they say they bought last time they were in Egypt, but which he said may have been mistakenly replaced in their sacks. Fortunately, Abali had already mentioned what happened the last time they were in Egypt – how you instructed him to replace the Canaanites' money in their sacks – so I told them not to be afraid because we had received their money. I suggested that their God must have placed the treasure in their sacks as a gift.'

'Well done, Kaa,' I said, patting him on the back. 'What about the one I sent Abali to fetch from the Den?'

'Abali brought him home and he has re-joined his brothers. All eleven have washed their feet and are waiting in the banquet hall for you.'

'Good – it is all going according to plan.'

'Most honourable vizier,' said Kaa ponderously, hinting that he was about to ask a question he had no right to ask. 'Abali and I were wondering whether by any chance you know these men. Are they perhaps childhood friends or family from your community in Canaan?'

Unlike Abali and other members of my staff, Kaa was forthright, which could be irritating at times. Although I did not doubt his loyalty, I only shared information with him that he needed to know. I was tempted to dismiss his question, but realised that he was not the only one asking questions about my bizarre handling of the brothers. News would have travelled regarding my treatment of the Hebrew men I gave free grain to, but whose brother I detained in the Den.

'I know their father,' I answered, unwilling to either lie or divulge the truth.

His curiosity partially assuaged, he knelt then left my presence. I remained outside the front door of my house, composing myself. It was helpful that Asenath was out of town with my boys, visiting her parents and supervising the construction of our second home in Goshen, because she would have asked a lot of awkward questions.

* * * * * * *

The banquet hall of my palace was a grand affair with enough architectural splendour to rival Pharaoh's. It had walls covered with colourful frescoes produced by the finest artists in the country and murals painted across the ceiling. It had been decorated under Asenath's supervision and every beam and pillar was wrapped in colourful textiles with patterned hieroglyphs. The floor was of the highest quality stone. It was polished to a mirror-like finish with patterns embedded which showed prominent Egyptian landmarks including pyramids from Giza, obelisks, sculptures and Pharaoh's palace hieroglyphs. Cushions and patterned hand-woven pile rugs from Mesopotamia lined the floor, creating a communal area where my family often had our meals, reclining on cushions.

Before joining my brothers, I went to my sleeping chamber to change my clothes, opting to wear a striped golden head-dress, one of my most impressive jewelled broad collars and, around my waist, a white linen wrap embroidered with gold. My wrists were adorned with gold bracelets and my feet shod in a pair of delicate sandals decorated with gold textiles. I intended to cement the image in their minds of a powerful, influential Egyptian lord who had the power of life and death, as indeed I did, because it was essential to the next phase of the plan that had been forming in my head all morning. Despite their suitably humble demeanour, there were some things I still needed to know, and I did not wish them to become too comfortable in my presence.

When I presented myself to them, ushered in by Kaa, who announced me, I could see the awe on their faces. I knew my garments and jewellery conveyed the right message, and my overall appearance conveyed all the splendour associated with my office. They were standing in the hall gathered around Simeon when I walked in. As soon as they heard Kaa, they bowed to the floor before me for what was the third time.

I looked down at my father's sons who had dominated me in Dothan and thrown me into a pit, and wondered whether they had ever taken the time to contemplate what destiny lay ahead of that vulnerable seventeen-year-old boy. When I had shared my dreams with them, they had fought against something they could never defeat – my God-given destiny. As far as they were concerned, I had probably died in slavery, working in quarries where life expectancy was less than thirty, which is why they believed my blood was crying out for justice.

My brothers rose from their prostrate position and Judah, their spokesman, stepped forward, gesturing to several baskets on the floor, which were picked up by Reuben, Levi, and Simeon, who appeared to be in a healthier state of mind now that he realised he had not been abandoned.

'Sir, we brought some gifts for you,' said Judah, 'a little token of appreciation, but I also wish to thank you on behalf of my brothers for taking such good care of our brother, Simeon.'

I examined the contents of the open baskets. One was stacked with the choicest fruits from Canaan;

another contained jars of what looked – and smelt – like balms, honey, spices and myrrh; and the third contained assorted nuts and almonds. These were highly valuable gifts because of their rarity, but I understood that their wider motive was to soften my heart towards my brothers.

'Thank you for your gifts,' I said, 'but how is your father – the old man you spoke of the last time you were in Egypt? Is he still alive?'

'Yes, sir, our father, your servant, is alive and well.'

On Judah's signal – a raised hand – all of my brothers bowed low again before me. I had a fleeting recollection of my dreams. I waited for them to rise to their feet again and directed my attention at Benjamin.

'Is this your younger brother – the one you spoke about?' When my eyes met Benjamin's, he squinted at me, looking unsure. 'May God be gracious to you, my son.'

I tore my gaze away from Benjamin's, unable to stay any longer, and hurried out of the hall to my sleeping chamber upstairs, where I was able to hide and sob silently, but bitterly. The sight of Benjamin had been too overwhelming.

After a few minutes I stopped crying, washed my face, composed myself and went out to re-join my guests. On arriving in the banquet hall, I called out to Kaa to take charge of the gifts from my eleven guests then arrange for our meal to be served.

As Kaa did this, I arranged for my brothers to be seated in order of age, with Benjamin closest to me and Reuben furthest away. I watched them marvelling among themselves about how I had got the order right – this was the order my father used whenever he shared a meal with us. As the food was rolled out, my Egyptian staff left the banquet hall to go to an adjoining chamber where they were served their own meal, because in Egyptian culture it was an abomination for them to eat with Hebrews. I was counting on my brothers not noticing this.

I sat near Benjamin, but higher up, on a lacquered chair next to an ebony table. When the food arrived, I was the first person to be offered the platters. I distributed the food among my brothers, starting with Benjamin. The dishes included dates, figs, fruits from the Mediterranean islands, assorted spicy breads, grilled fish, roasted meat, wine produced at my personal winepress and beer brewed by me. All drinks were served in the finest bronze goblets, but I drank from my bespoke solid silver cup, which Pharaoh gave me at the end of the seven years of bountiful harvests. Throughout the afternoon, platters of food kept on rolling in and I distributed the food among my brothers, but gave Benjamin more than double the amount that I gave the others.

* * * * * * *

While my brothers were feasting and making merry with all the food and wine at their disposal, I left the hall and summoned Kaa. We withdrew to an adjoining chamber which overlooked the massive fish pond to the rear of my home.

'Fill the men's sacks with grain,' I said quietly, 'as much as they can carry, then put every man's money in the mouth of his sack.'

'As you request, most honourable vizier,' he answered.

'Also, I want you to put my silver cup in the sack

belonging to the youngest man, along with all his money.'

I handed Kaa my silver cup which was engraved with the words *Zaphnath-Paaneah, Vizier of Egypt*. He stared at me as if I had taken leave of my senses. He knew that it was my most prized possession because it was one of only two in Egypt, the other belonging to Pharaoh himself. The weight of the cup was equivalent to forty shekels of silver. Having studied me for a moment to ensure he had not misheard me, he nodded, went down on one knee, then departed to carry out my bizarre instructions. He had worked with me long enough to know when not to question my decisions. I watched him saunter away before returning to the banquet hall to re-join my brothers, both questioning and rationalising my motives.

BACK TO EDEN

Proverbs 24:13

I stood on the balcony of my sleeping chamber which overlooked the rear of my home, which was bordered by the eastern bank of the Nile. The sun was a fiery red-orange ball against the greyish-blue dawn, and a flight of kites flew in a perfect formation headed north. Hopefully, they would find more accessible water at the Nile Delta, where it merged with the Mediterranean. I gazed at the drastically lowered water level along the eastern and western banks – they revealed the reddish mud that was usually out of sight, and I realised that this was an image I would be seeing for the next five years.

Rain clouds had not gathered over Egypt for the past two years, and the drought was eating corrosively into the river, which had previously sustained so much wildlife. I soaked up the early morning before returning to my chamber to get dressed for the day. Without Asenath and my sons, the house was quiet – too quiet. Their presence made the massive palatial house a home, and I missed them.

I had not slept a wink the previous night, but tossed and turned, replaying scenes from my homeland, which were faded in parts, wondering about the chain of events that had led to my arrival in the land of the pharaohs. Downstairs in my vast guest chamber, my brothers had settled down for the night. According to Kaa, they were sleeping peacefully, thanks to the wine they had imbibed. The merriment had continued into the evening. To stir up the mood, I had sent for some musicians and professional dancers to entertain my guests. Throughout the festivities I had longed to speak with Benjamin about Hebron and our family, but had to restrict myself to general conversation about the strategies we employed in preserving food and explaining some of the customs of the land.

Kaa informed me that they would be leaving first thing in the morning via the eastern desert, and confirmed that all my instructions had been carried out to the letter. Despite my reservations about the necessity of my plans, I believed that this was the only way to get the answers I needed. I dressed then headed out of my chamber and across the wide hall to another balcony overlooking the front of the house, arriving just in time to see my stable hands bring out my brothers' mules, which had been fed and watered and laden with sacks of grain. The grain was from my personal granary; only Pharaoh and I enjoyed such a luxury.

Shortly after my arrival, my brothers emerged from the building with Kaa and two of my guards. I drew back so they could not see me. Anticipating that my brothers might wish to thank me for my hospitality, but wanting to distance myself, I had told Kaa to inform them if they asked that I was not to be disturbed. From my vantage point, I watched them mount their beasts and ride off through the gates, noting that Benjamin rode on a mule alongside Judah. The previous evening Judah's eyes had continuously been on Benjamin, and I suspected that my father had placed him in charge of his youngest son.

I heard clapping behind me and turned to see Kaa, who knelt perfunctorily then joined me on the balcony.

'How long will it take them to reach the eastern highway?' I asked.

'At the pace they are going, another hour at least,' Kaa answered.

The eastern highway that linked Waset to Men'at Khufu was outside the city limits, and ran on to Mennefer and the cities in the Nile Delta, including On.

'Okay, give them an hour's head start,' I said distantly, 'then pursue them with at least ten of my guards, all armed. When you overtake them, ask them why they have rewarded my goodness and kindness to them with such evil by stealing my precious silver cup, which I drink from and use to predict future events. Stress the nature of their wickedness in stealing my cup.'

Kaa was silent, but I could tell he was full of questions. Protocol prevented him from probing my motives, but he was clearly uncomfortable. In Egypt, stealing was an offence punishable with incarceration, maiming or even death, and as I was the vizier, stealing from me carried the highest penalty. He knew that he would surely find the cup in their possession and that my brothers would be forced to return with him to Waset for trial and judgement. Having no idea of my ultimate motive, Kaa was probably thinking about the cruelty in my instructions. After his departure, I remained where I was, gazing over the city, the most modern metropolis in the world. It was a great city and I was one of its most influential citizens, but behind its splendour was famine – and behind my significance was a fractured heart.

* * * * * * *

About three hours after my discussion with Kaa, I was seated in the ceremonial hall in my palace, conducting state business with Abali and my scribes, when my head steward walked in and knelt before my throne.

'Most honourable vizier, I have returned with the Hebrews,' he announced, rising to his feet. 'They are waiting outside in the courtyard.'

Kaa looked troubled. This was clearly difficult for him.

'What happened when you caught up with them?'

Kaa cleared his throat then narrated how he had caught up with the eleven men on the outskirts of Waset along the eastern highway and confronted them about the theft of my silver cup. They had denied any wrongdoing and said that whoever was found in possession of the cup would die and that the rest of them would become my slaves. Kaa had revised their self-imposed sentence by stating that whoever was found with the silver cup would become his servant, while the rest of them could go free. The brothers agreed and speedily brought down their sacks for inspection. Kaa had started with Reuben's sack and had gone through each of my brothers' sacks until he ended up with Benjamin's sack, where the cup was found. When he discovered the cup, all the brothers began to lament their fate and shred their tunics in anguish.

'Bring them in,' I said quietly.

Kaa left to fetch my brothers. As we waited, my expression became cold. This was the climax of my strategy and was critical to determining my future relationship with my brothers. Moments after Kaa departed, he returned with the eleven agitated-looking Hebrew men in ripped tunics. They threw themselves down before me on the cold marble floor and remained prostrate before my throne.

'What have you men done?' I asked frostily. 'Do you

not know that a man like me can predict future events?'

'What can we say, my lord?' asked Judah, raising his head to look at me imploringly. 'What explanation can we give or what excuse shall we proffer? How can we clear ourselves? God has uncovered the offence committed by your servants and we have all returned to become your slaves. Even though only one of us was found with your cup in his possession, we are all your slaves.'

'No!' I barked, almost making him jump out of his skin. 'I am a just man and would never conceive of such injustice – only the man who stole my cup will become my slave. As for the rest of you, you may get up and return to your father in peace.'

At this stage, Judah carefully rose to his feet and slowly approached my throne, bowing each step of the way until he was at the foot of the steps.

'If I may, my lord,' he said, in a broken voice, 'please permit your servant to speak a word in your ears, and may your anger not be unleashed on me even though you are as powerful and influential as Pharaoh himself.'

I nodded, inviting him to speak.

'My lord,' went on Judah, 'if you recall, you previously asked your servants whether we had a father or a brother, and we informed you that we had a father who is an old man and a younger brother who was born to him in his old age. The brother of this young man, who was born of the same mother, is dead and he is the only surviving child of his mother. For this reason, he is greatly loved by our father.

'If you recall, you said to your servants, "bring your younger brother to me so that I can see him with my own eyes." We said to my lord, "the young man cannot leave his father, for his father would die." And then you said to your servants, "Except your youngest brother comes down with you, you shall never see my face again." And when we came home to your servant, my father, we informed him of your words. When our father later said, "go back again and buy us some food", we said, "we cannot go back unless you let our younger brother go with us. We will not see the man's face except our youngest brother goes with us." At this point, your servant, our father, said to us, "As you know, my wife gave birth to two sons, and one went away and never returned. Undoubtedly, I believe he was torn to pieces by some wild animal because I have not seen him since then. Now, if you take his brother away from me and some harm comes to him, you will send an elderly, white-haired man to his grave grieving."

'Now, my lord, when I return home to your servant, my father, and the young man is not with us, bearing in mind that our father's life is bound to the young man's, I know what will happen – he will surely die and your servants would have sent an elderly, white-haired man to his grave grieving. What you do not know is that I, your servant, guaranteed the young man's safety and assured my father, saying, "If I do not return him back to you, I shall bear the blame forever." Now, my lord, I plead with you to let me remain here as your servant instead of the young man, and let him return home with my other brothers, for how shall I face my father without the boy in my company? I cannot witness my father endure the anguish of another loss!'

As Judah spoke, there was a gradual build-up of agony in my heart. It suffocated me, and his words systematically broke down my defences. Hearing about my father's suffering due to my death, and how he had clung to Benjamin like a compensatory lifeline, was excruciating. I knew that in my absence Benjamin would be his favourite, but I had no idea how strong that bond had become. My pain morphed into palpitations and blood filled the vessels in my head until it felt as if it was ready to explode. When Judah finished his impassioned plea for mercy, I rose to my feet and roared, no longer able to bottle up the volcanic emotions welling up inside me.

'Everyone except these men should leave my house right now!' I bellowed in a voice empowered by turmoil, not rage.

As Abali, Kaa and my scribes heard my command, they scrambled to their feet and bolted out of the ceremonial hall as if they were being pursued by Assyrian invaders. After they departed, I noticed that my guards were still at their posts so I roared at them and they hastily departed, although with more decorum. Standing at the top of the steps in front of my throne, looking down at the terrified eleven Hebrew men cowering beneath me, I let out another roar which worked its way from the pit of my stomach all the way out of my lungs until the sound produced by my vocal cords bounced off the walls of the hall and echoed around my home. As the roar died, a flood of tears gushed out of my eyes. It was as if my heart was determined to quench the famine in my soul. My wailing continued, unbroken, for more than ten minutes and my body convulsed under its intensity. It was the pent-up frustration, bitterness, anguish, rejection and pain of over twenty-two years, all unleashed in one moment. I ditched all the dignity and grace of my office and shed all protocol as I wept. When my tears permitted my eyes partial vision, I descended the steps like a man drunk on strong wine.

'I am Joseph!' I announced, pausing next to an astonished-looking Judah. 'Is my father really still alive?'

None of my brothers answered me – they were all in shock at my changed appearance and behaviour. Even Judah, who had been the emotionally composed advocate for mercy, was speechless.

'Come near to me, please, do not be afraid,' I said to the men who were still lying on the floor in supplication. They slowly got up and drew closer to me, probably encouraged by the absence of armed guards.

'I am Joseph, your brother – the one you sold into slavery in Egypt!' I said breathlessly. 'Now, do not be angry with yourselves for selling me into slavery in this place, for God sent me ahead of you to preserve your lives.'

I paused to catch my breath, still fatigued from my wailing. 'Draw closer,' I instructed softly, 'look at me carefully. I am Joseph.' Despite my hairless appearance, I could see the flicker of recognition in their eyes, as one by one they overcame their hesitancy and focussed.

'The famine that has ravaged the land these past two years still has another five years left,' I continued, 'during which there will be no ploughing or harvesting. But God sent me ahead of you to deliver you from the famine and preserve your families and many others. Therefore it was not your actions that brought me here, but God's. God has made me an adviser to Pharaoh, his most senior official and the vizier of Egypt, second in command only to Pharaoh himself.'

I looked at their stunned faces as they gradually started to recognise me and believe what I said, and wished I could have preserved their expressions forever as a memorial. They were priceless.

'Hurry now to my father,' I said, gripping Judah's

shoulder, 'and tell him, "This is what your son Joseph says – God has made me the vizier over all of Egypt, so come down to me without delay." And you and your families should move to the region of Goshen so that you, your livestock and everything you own will be close to me. There, I will keep you for the next five years of famine so that you, your households and your livestock will not starve to death.'

Their stunned response prompted me to continue.

'Look! You can see for yourselves that it is really me, and so can my brother Benjamin. You can hear my voice and verify that it is me. I need you to tell my father of my status in Egypt and describe everything you have seen – now you must hurry back to Canaan and bring my father here!'

As I finished speaking, I embraced Benjamin and began to weep with ecstatic joy. My younger brother, losing all inhibition, returned my embrace and wept out loud. We remained like this for what seemed like eternity before gradually pulling apart, still gripping each other's arms.

As we reluctantly parted, I turned to my other brothers, who had gathered around us, and started embracing them one after the other, kissing them and weeping as we hugged. I was in no hurry. After all this time, I felt that I had the right to savour my family reunion. Tears of joy were soon replaced with broad grins, laughter and excited chatter as we enjoyed each other's company.

* * * * * * *

I stood before Pharaoh's throne, having bowed before him in the customary manner, and prepared to explain myself. The full council was present in his ceremonial hall, and there was an excited buzz among them as I walked in. Half an hour before, my reunion with my brothers had been interrupted by the arrival of two of Pharaoh's guards, to inform me that I was summoned to Pharaoh urgently. I immediately suspected that the news of my emotional reunion had reached Pharaoh, particularly as I had sent one of my brothers to search for Abali and Kaa to inform them about the development.

'Zaphnath-Paaneah, we hear your brothers have arrived from Canaan,' said Pharaoh cheerfully, 'and that they have come to buy food.'

'May Pharaoh live forever,' I replied. 'Yes, this is true, and I seek Pharaoh's pardon for failing to inform him immediately of the circumstance.'

Pharaoh waved aside my apology and rose to his feet with a benevolent smile.

'Tell your brothers this is what they should do,' he said. 'Saddle their mules and hurry back to Canaan to get your father and their families, then come back to me, for I will give them the very best land in Egypt and they shall eat the best of what the country has to offer. Tell them to take wagons from Egypt to bring their wives, children and your father from Canaan and not to worry about bringing their personal possessions because the best of all that is in the land of Egypt is yours.'

I thanked Pharaoh for his generosity and returned home, elated by the reception I had received and grateful to God for His overwhelming kindness. Even though I was vizier and had autonomy in most matters, I never did anything without first seeking Pharaoh's approval, and he was kept informed of all my affairs.

He trusted me because of my transparency in all matters.

Even though I had not informed him yet of my intention to settle my family at Goshen, I knew that when the time came he would not object. It was with his permission that I had begun the construction of a second home in Men-nefer, a short distance from Goshen, to provide me with a base from which to administer the Lower Egypt region. My second reason for this home was to enable Asenath to live closer to her family in the city of On, as I was often away from home on state business and she needed company. Looking back now at that decision, I could see the mysterious wisdom of God at work in what had appeared at first to be merely a pragmatic solution.

Thrilled by Pharaoh's approval of my proposal to relocate my family to Egypt, I set about making hasty arrangements for their trip. Through Kaa, I procured twelve large wagons, each attached to four mules, to carry my brothers' wives and children, with one reserved for the sole use of my father. In addition, I provided each of my brothers with food for the journey and new tunics. I also gave Benjamin three hundred pieces of silver and five new tunics made from the highest quality fabrics.

For my father, I sent ten male donkeys loaded with the finest Egyptian products, including spices, myrrh, silver, gold, jewellery, textiles and the finest wine. I also sent him another ten female donkeys loaded with the grain, bread and meat he would need for the journey. For security, I instructed Kaa to escort my brothers to the Lower Egyptian border with a detachment of my armed guards.

I accompanied them from Waset to the outskirts of

Men-nefer via the eastern desert caravan route. Here, we parted company. I planned to head alone to the city of On to tell Asenath in person what had happened.

'Please ensure that you don't fall out with each other on the way,' I said, as my brothers prepared to continue on across the eastern flank of the Nile Delta. 'This is a time for unity – let us forget the past and move on.'

After receiving assurances from Judah that there would be no bickering among them, I watched their caravan crawl along the beaten track towards the Horus Highway until it was out of sight, then headed towards the city of On.

* * * * * * *

Asenath's eyes conveyed genuine joy as I told her about my reunion with my brothers, starting from their appearance at the distribution centre in Men'at Khufu and ending with my great reveal in Waset. We were on the balcony of her quarters in her father's palace. Several times I noticed a frown sweep across her face as I went over the details of my scheme, particularly when I mentioned the decision to detain Simeon, but at the end of my story, she showed no trace of disapproval. She understood that detaining Simeon had been the only way of guaranteeing that my brothers would return with Benjamin, and that my actions had not been malicious.

She was particularly pleased that I had visited Simeon frequently to check on his welfare. My father-in-law was already aware of the family reunion, as he had been among the high-ranking officials present when Pharaoh permitted me to bring my family to Egypt. However, Potipherah had not informed his daughter about the development, preferring to wait for me to tell her in person.

'So, what are your plans for them?' she asked, with feverish enthusiasm.

'Well, I'm thinking of settling them in Lower Egypt, because they're shepherds by profession and, as you know, it's against the law for shepherds to reside in Waset.'

'Do you have anywhere in mind?'

'Goshen.'

'Near us?'

'Yes. The land is fertile for their livestock and not too far from the Horus Highway leading to Canaan – this way, we can both be near our families.'

Her teary eyes conveyed a joy that confirmed I was making the right decision.

'I can't wait to meet them,' she said, dabbing at her eyes with a linen cloth. 'I'm especially looking forward to meeting your father and Benjamin after all you've told me about them.'

I did not respond, but something in my pensive expression must have alerted her to my state of mind.

'Are you apprehensive?'

I nodded slowly. 'I understand that my father has aged considerably since I left home,' I said, 'and I am concerned that he will not be strong enough to make the journey.'

'Where is your faith in God?'

Before I could respond she continued. 'Do you think that this reunion would be possible without him?'

She was right. My apprehension was misplaced. It was God who had preserved my father's life and orchestrated the events culminating in my family reunion. The timing was no accident, and neither were the circumstances. If the distribution centre at Men-nefer hadn't had long queues, they would not have come to Men'at Khufu, and if Potiphar had not fallen ill, I would not have been covering for him that day. Without His involvement, I would never have known about my brothers' trip to buy food in Egypt. If God had worked everything out so strategically, why would He not preserve my father's life on the journey between Canaan and Egypt? As I thought about God's mercy and kindness, peace began to seep into my soul.

'You will surely be reunited with your father,' said Asenath, embracing me tightly.

'Thank you,' I whispered, placing my head against her chest.

* * * * * * *

In the days following my brothers' trip back to Canaan, I commissioned the building of new houses for each of my brothers and their families, as well as a grand dwelling for my father. To ensure that quality was not compromised due to the tight timeline, I used Minoan builders from the island of Crete. The buildings were designed by the Minoans and made of imported timber and local basalt instead of mud bricks, which were not very durable and tended to wash away in the rain. I specified red-tiled roofs and flagstone floors for the houses as well as stone-slab pathways, connecting the houses and sewage facilities. To ensure that the houses would be ready for occupation by the time my family arrived, I got the Minoans to double their workforce and work round the clock. Although I had not discussed the Goshen settlement with Pharaoh before beginning construction, I was confident that he would approve.

In addition, I got Egyptians to dig two wells in the region for my family to use to water their livestock, and built several new granaries, a bakery, a brewery, a community hall and a large stable for horses and mules. Because the land was near the Nile I was confident that when the rains returned the wells would be full and the land would be well irrigated from the Nile. All I needed to do after the famine was extend the channels to the fields where I intended my brothers to graze their livestock.

I wanted to ensure that my family had the infrastructure they would need to rebuild their lives. Because of my commitment to the food distribution programme, I entrusted the Goshen project to Kaa, who relished the responsibility and authority it entailed. I visited occasionally to check on progress, but otherwise left it in his capable hands. I also stepped up work on the completion of my palatial home on the outskirts of Men-nefer.

* * * * * * *

About two months after I parted company with my brothers along the eastern desert highway, I rode my chariot at a furious pace towards Goshen, my armed guard struggling to keep up in their chariots. A day earlier, my brother Judah had arrived at my home in Waset to inform me that my father was approaching the Egyptian border and needed directions to Goshen. Because I was tied up with state business at the time, I instead sent Kaa to accompany him. The community had been completed on schedule and all buildings were habitable. Each building was inscribed with the name of the brother to whom it belonged, so there was no scope for confusion. At my request, the Minoans had created larger dwellings for my father and Benjamin, locating these in the most prominent location.

Leaving Abali in charge of my administrative affairs in Waset, I headed down to Men-nefer by boat to inform Asenath of my father's arrival. At her request, I had left Asenath and my sons in our Men-nefer residence, which was now completed. These days I spent my time commuting between Men-nefer and Waset on official duty, mostly travelling by boat along the Nile. After I told Asenath the news, I mounted my chariot and made a beeline for Goshen.

On Asenath's advice, I wore a generic tunic that was less Egyptian in style, and kept my face make-up free. I also covered my clean-shaven head with a short braided wig. In her opinion, I had to make the right impression, and appearing before my father after twenty-two years looking like an Egyptian would be too much of a shock for him.

As I rode towards Goshen, my heart pounded in my ears, drowning out the sound of my chariot's wheels and my horses' galloping hoofs. What would my father look like after all this time? Would he recognise me? If he recognised me, would he disapprove of my appearance? These questions and more whipped around my mind until my thoughts became foggy. I cried out to God for clarity, and eventually He gave me the ability to focus. The last thing my father would care about was my appearance. At the outskirts of Goshen, I slowed my pace, enabling my guard to catch up, and rode sedately along the beaten track towards the small settlement I had created for my family. At the outskirts of the community, we passed large flocks of sheep, goats and rams, occupying the fields on both sides of the road. Ahead, I saw the caravan of mule-drawn wagons and donkeys near the cluster of Minoan-styled buildings, and halted my chariot.

I leapt out of my chariot and raced past the buildings, edging my way through the beasts, women and children, towards the elderly man who was being helped off one of the wagons by Benjamin and Reuben. As my father's sandaled feet touched the ground, he supported himself with the staff he had carried ever since the angel of God dislocated his hip and turned instinctively in my direction.

'Father! Father!' I cried out, tears streaming down my cheeks at the sight of my father.

I halted a few feet away from him, soaking up his appearance, noting the thinning lion's mane of white hair, his tanned, leathery complexion, his twinkling brown eyes beneath thick white brows, his curved nose and cotton-wool white beard. At that moment, I became a seventeen-year-old boy again. It was as if we had never been separated.

'Joseph?'

His voice was instantly familiar, and as comforting as I remembered. He squinted at me with a twinge of uncertainty.

'Yes, Father, it is Joseph.'

'Joseph!' he exclaimed, as recognition appeared to come flooding in.

Slowly I walked towards him, conscious that a small crowd was watching me, but not really seeing anyone else. My tunnel vision was fixed on the man who had been the centre of my world. Carefully, gingerly, I embraced him, afraid that his frail form would not be able to withstand the firmness of my hug but, without warning, he dropped his staff and embraced me tightly, with an intensity that almost choked me. In his enthusiasm, he almost lifted me off my feet as he had done when I was a boy. As if on cue, we began to weep. Despite his age and bent frame, he was still a tall man. As our cheeks brushed, his cotton-soft beard against my smooth skin, our tears seemed to mingle. I clung to him, crying my heart out as I returned to my childhood, blocking out the intervening years.

'You were only supposed to go as far as Shechem,' my father said, his voice choked, 'but when I saw your tunic I thought I had lost you forever!'

'I am here, Father,' I mumbled. 'I was kidnapped by traders and sold as a slave in Egypt, but God has been with me.'

'My son, Joseph! What have you been through?' He sobbed even harder. 'Joseph! Joseph! Oh, my son, Joseph!'

'I am here, Father.'

'God has been so merciful to me!'

We clung to each other for support and wept for what seemed like an eternity. I lost all track of time. As our sobbing subsided and our tears dried up, we slowly came apart, still gripping each other's arms.

'Let me look at you, my son,' said my father croakily. He stared into my eyes and shook his head slowly. 'Now I am ready to die, since I have seen your face and know that you are still alive.'

The rest of the afternoon was taken up with introductions to the members of my extended family whom I had not yet met. Over sixty people, as well as my brothers' wives and servants, had accompanied my father from Hebron in Canaan. Most of them were strangers to me. Later that day, I sent Kaa to my home in Men-nefer to bring back food and wine to the community hall in Goshen, and thereafter we feasted, sang, danced and made merry till evening.

*　*　*　*　*　*　*

After I had escorted my father to his new residence and left him there to rest, I summoned my brothers, together with their wives and children.

'I will inform Pharaoh that you have arrived from Canaan,' I said once they were all assembled, 'and that you are shepherds by trade. I will also mention that you have brought all your livestock and possessions. When Pharaoh sends for you and asks what your occupation is, inform him that you come from a long line of shepherds and have been in the profession since your youth. This will ensure that he allows you to remain in Goshen, because shepherds are an abomination to the Egyptians.'

The following day, I brought my father to my house in Men-nefer and introduced him to Asenath. At his request, I left them together to chat, and was delighted to see how well they seemed to get along. I had been apprehensive because of Asenath's background, but my fears were clearly misplaced. Later that day, Asenath accompanied me to Goshen where I introduced her to my brothers and their families; again there was much warmth and cordiality between my family and Asenath, who had insisted on wearing traditional Hebrew clothing so she blended in. Asenath distributed many gifts, including clothing, cosmetics and jewellery to my brothers' wives, and this act of kindness created a solid bridge of fellowship between her and the other women.

Three days later, I presented my father and five of

my brothers – Reuben, Judah, Gad, Dan and Benjamin – to Pharaoh. They stuck to the script I had given them. When Pharaoh asked them where they would prefer to live, they requested the land of Goshen. As expected, Pharaoh granted their request, but he also appointed them as shepherds over his own livestock. The occasion ended with my father having a brief chat with Pharaoh, before blessing him. As we left Pharaoh's palace in Waset, I felt a peace that I had not known since my arrival in Egypt, and felt the last fragments of bitterness in my soul slowly dissolve.

A MATTER OF HONOUR

Luke 12:48

With my family settled, I was able to focus on the task confronting me. The low water level in the Nile Delta, and the lack of rain, was affecting the everyday lives of the locals. Rainfall in Egypt traditionally occurs in Lower Egypt, and sporadically in Upper Egypt, which is surrounded by desert. All agricultural production was carried out around the Nile, but the river was too low to irrigate the surrounding fields, so the soil hardened and eventually fragmented, revealing cracks and ruts where there had previously been grass. The marshlands in Lower Egypt were also badly affected: areas that were usually impassable due to their swampy soil were now usable paths.

Surprisingly, Goshen survived the worst of the famine, and even produced enough wild grass for livestock to feed on, although the soil was still not good enough to plant crops, due to the lack of rainfall. As a result, I fed every member of my family from my private allocation of grain, and deposited enough in their granaries so they could enjoy a sense of independence. I put Benjamin in charge of food distribution to ensure that each family was fed according to their numbers. I continued to provide bread and grain for my father.

Two years into the famine, the Egyptians and Canaanite dwellers spent huge sums of money buying food from our granaries because the agricultural sector was effectively dead. During this period, I collected and accounted for the entire revenue generated by the sale of grain and deposited the same with Pharaoh, who was flabbergasted by the wealth that was pouring into his coffers. If he found the two-year revenue overwhelming, the next five years were to prove even more prosperous: when the Egyptians and Canaanites ran out of money to buy grain in the third year, all the Egyptians in the Upper and Lower regions of the land approached me to make a new arrangement for them to obtain grain, to prevent people dying of hunger.

Moved by a need to preserve the people's dignity, I requested that they give me their cattle in exchange for sufficient grain to see them through the year. With the help of my officials, I devised a barter system that provided a tariff for calculating the value of different types of livestock against the weight of grain. We bought horses, sheep, goats, rams, cows and donkeys according to their tariff value.

Not all livestock or animals were worth much; many had been so ravaged by the famine that they could barely stand. Nevertheless, our tariff created a value for such animals, allowing us to exchange them for grain. Any animals that were worth saving were sent to animal recovery units, which used livestock rehabilitation techniques similar to those I had created for Potiphar, and nursed back to health. Animals that were too ill or diseased were humanely put out of their misery and left in the deserts to feed wild beasts. Healthy livestock were sent to Goshen, where my brothers and their servants grazed them as part of Pharaoh's livestock. Likewise, any animals that had been nursed back to health ended up in Goshen.

At the end of that year, the people showed up again, demanding food even though their money was spent and their livestock had become Pharaoh's. They were desperate. They offered both themselves and their land in exchange for grain to make bread. Realising that Egyptian citizens would die if we didn't do something, we came up with a strategy to ensure we could distribute food to people for the duration of the famine without them having to pay.

I introduced a new land-use edict that enabled me to take ownership of land in exchange for grain. All landowners were required to have title deeds drawn up for their land. They had to deposit these at their regional food distribution centre, where they were registered by the scribes, then they were given a regional number for themselves and their families. They wore the number on a copper token, and they were required to present this at their local food distribution centre whenever they needed grain. We gave them enough grain for three months, depending on their number, and every three months they returned for a refill. We drew up a rota to keep track of those we had distributed food to, so we could guard against fraud.

Under this new strategy, I bought all the land in Egypt for Pharaoh and sent him the title deeds for storage. To ensure that we could meet the people's needs, I moved them out of rural areas to the major cities in their region. The only land we did not purchase was that belonging to the priests because they were each assigned a portion of grain by Pharaoh and therefore didn't need to sell their land. I went from region to region, informing the people of the new rules regarding land use and ownership in Egypt.

I told the people that I had purchased their land for Pharaoh, along with their services. As part of my strategy, I distributed seed to people for them to sow at the end of the famine, then told them they had to give Pharaoh one-fifth of their yearly harvest, but they could retain four-fifths. Out of their four-fifths, they were to reserve some for seed and eat the rest with their families. The gratitude of the people confirmed the success of my strategy. Wherever I went, they thanked me for saving their lives and pledged their loyalty to Pharaoh.

All foreigners were still required to bring either money or livestock in exchange for food. Many made the effort to bring livestock. Throughout the famine, I fed the people. At the end of the seven years, the first rains fell. For almost a week, the rain was torrential: the Nile rose to its previous level and even overflowed its banks. Within days, the marshlands in Lower Egypt had been restored. Within a month, most dry fields were covered with green grass and the cracks in the soil had begun to heal. To ensure that farmers could plough the soil, we released healthy cattle and donkeys to them in exchange for a larger portion of their first year's harvest. A year after the end of the famine, foreigners had stopped coming to Egypt to buy food, and life more or less went back to how it had been.

* * * * * * *

Twelve years after the famine, Goshen had become one of the most prosperous cities in Lower Egypt, on a par with Men'at Khufu. The few buildings I had erected had been swallowed up in a larger metropolis. My industrious brothers had created a livestock bazaar for trading animals, which was visited by traders from all over Crete, Canaan, Anatolia and Mesopotamia. Their profits enabled them to diversify into sales of jewellery, which led to the construction of an even larger bazaar that attracted women from all over Egypt. In addition, they built homes to rent out and created guest houses for travellers, where their wives served authentic Hebrew cuisine. Many foreigners living in Egypt chose to relocate to Goshen because it felt more cosmopolitan than other Egyptian cities, and there was less of an Egyptian presence.

Judah rose to prominence within the community as its unofficial governor, and placed himself in charge of revenue collection. Because of my status, Egyptian officials did not challenge his activities, even though I could tell they were uncomfortable with the arrangement. My family started swelling in size: in a very short period, my brothers' wives trebled their number of children. This was coupled with their older children marrying Canaanites from the Hebron area who chose to relocate to Goshen and raise families there. My brothers' children and grandchildren soon formed a large community.

In the midst of this post-famine prosperity, my father sent for me through Benjamin, whose subdued face gave me a hint of what lay in store. I arrived at my father's house in Goshen, where I learnt that he was still in bed, even though it was noon. However, the moment his servant informed him of my arrival, he rose up. When we entered his chamber, we found him sitting up on the bed fully clothed, leaning on his staff. I bowed down before him then sat next to him on the bed. Though he was lean and wiry, and his hands trembled, I felt that he looked well for a man of over a hundred and forty-seven years old. In the seventeen years he had lived in Egypt, he had aged, but not as rapidly as I had expected. With the exception of his failing eyesight, he looked no different from when he first arrived.

'My son,' he said shakily, 'if I have found grace with you, please place your hand beneath my thigh and honour my last request. I need you to promise that you will not bury me in Egypt. I wish to be buried with my fathers. When I die, I want you to carry me out of Egypt and bury me in their resting place.'

This tradition was effectively an oath: a serious, inviolable commitment.

'I will do as you request,' I answered solemnly, my hand placed beneath his right thigh.

'I need you to swear to me.'

'I swear, Father, that I will not bury you in Egypt, but will carry your body to the burial place of your fathers.'

Looking satisfied, my father bowed and began to pray and worship, leaning against the headrest of his bed. As I watched him, I knew the end was near. I had to prepare myself emotionally for the moment when we would part from him for the last time.

* * * * * * *

The moment I had been expecting arrived while I was attending a state function in Men-nefer with my sons Manasseh and Ephraim on behalf of Pharaoh. Kaa arrived to tell me that my father's health was rapidly failing. Excusing myself from the event, I departed with my sons for Goshen. When I arrived, I found my brothers waiting outside the door of Father's chamber, looking tearful, although none was openly weeping. We exchanged hushed greetings and I ventured into the chamber with my sons, fearing what I might find.

The scene within resembled the one from my last visit a week ago, except that my father was paler than normal. When I walked in, he was sitting on the edge of the bed, leaning on his staff. Even though his eyesight was failing, I knew he was aware of my presence. My sons and I bowed low then rose to our feet, facing him.

'God Almighty appeared to me at Luz in the land of Canaan,' said my father wheezily, 'and He blessed me, and said to me, "Behold, I will make you fruitful and multiply you and I will produce from you a multitude of descendants and create from you a multitude of nations, and I will give the land of Canaan to your descendants for an everlasting possession." Now your two sons, Ephraim and Manasseh, who were born to you in the land of Egypt, are my sons in the same way that Reuben and Simeon are, but any children born to you in the future shall be yours and will inherit land in the area apportioned to their older siblings.

'As for me, when I was returning from Paddan-Aram, Rachel, your mother, died beside me in the land of Canaan when we were still some distance from Bethlehem, and I was forced to bury her along the way, against my wishes.' His voice faltered and he leant towards us. 'By the way, who are these standing with you?'

'These are my sons whom God has given me in Egypt, Father,' I answered.

'Please bring them to me so that I may bless them,' my father whispered.

I edged my sons forward towards their grandfather and made them stoop, even though I knew that his eyesight was extremely impaired due to his age and that he could barely distinguish them. I watched, my heart heavy, as he reached up to kiss and embrace my sons.

'Joseph, I did not think I would ever see your face again, but God has been merciful and has also allowed me to see your children.'

I bowed low, my face to the ground, before standing to position Ephraim's lowered head within reach of my father's left hand and Manasseh within reach of his right hand. This was an important ritual, because it had the power to determine my sons' destiny. The right hand of the father was reserved for the first son, while the left hand was for the younger son. Traditionally, the first-born received the bulk of the blessing.

However, as I watched, my father stretched out his right hand and placed it on the head of my younger son, Ephraim, and placed his left hand on the head of Manasseh, my first-born.

'Joseph,' said my father in his unsteady voice, 'may God before whom my grandfather Abraham and father Isaac walked, the same God who has sustained me all my life even until this day, the angel who has redeemed me from all danger, bless these boys. May they bear my name as well as the names of Abraham, my grandfather, and Isaac, my father, and may their descendants multiply across the Earth.'

As he prayed, I noticed that his right hand was on Ephraim's head, and was upset. I immediately lifted his right hand from Ephraim's head and started to direct it towards Manasseh's.

'Father, you've got it wrong,' I said, trying to mask my disappointment. 'Manasseh is the first-born so you need to put your right hand on his head.'

However, for some reason, my father resisted my efforts to move his hand.

'I know, my son,' he said gently. 'I know. Manasseh will be great, and so shall his descendants, but his younger brother shall become even greater than him, and his descendants shall become a multitude of nations.'

Realising his mind was made up, I let go of his hand and swallowed my discontent.

As I released his hand, my father replaced it on Ephraim's head and continued his blessing. 'The tribes of Israel shall pronounce blessings in your names, saying, "May God make you as prosperous as Ephraim and Manasseh."'

Then my father removed his hands from my sons' heads and looked in my direction. Even though I knew he could not see me clearly, I felt exposed.

'I am about to die,' said my father, 'but I pray that God shall be with you and shall bring you back to Canaan, the land of your fathers. Over and above what I have given to your brothers, I am giving you an extra portion of the territory I dispossessed the Amorite of with my sword and with my bow.'

After pronouncing this blessing over me, my father called out for my brothers, asking them to gather in his chamber so that he could prophesy what would happen to us in the future. One by one my brothers shuffled into the room, looking mournful, each glancing in my direction as they entered, perhaps wondering whether I had at last told my father what had happened at Dothan almost forty years ago.

* * * * * * *

In blessing me, my father spoke in the third person. He described me as a fruitful vine near deep waters, whose branches climbed over a wall. He said even though archers had sorely grieved me and had shot at me and hated me – a veiled reference to my brothers – my bow remained steady and my arms strong because of the mighty God of Jacob, my father, the shepherd and the Rock of Israel who had always helped me and had blessed me with the blessings of heaven above and the blessings of the deep waters and the blessings of the womb and breast. He then emphasised that his blessings on me were greater than the blessings of ancient mountains or ageless hills, and said that these blessings would be on my head, because I was a prince among my brothers.

* * * * * * *

As my father finished prophesying over each of us, finishing with Benjamin, he stared at us with a steely gaze that for a moment reminded me of the father of my youth.

'I am about to die and join my ancestors,' he said in a stronger voice, 'and you must bury me in the cave that is in the field of Ephron the Hittite. This is in the field of Machpelah, situated just before Mamre in the land of Canaan, which my grandfather Abraham bought as a burial site for his descendants. My grandparents, Abraham and Sarah, were buried in this place, as well as my parents Isaac and Rebekah. It is in this place that I buried your mother Leah. It is the plot of land and the cave my grandfather purchased from the Hittites.'

My father looked at each of us with a vivid intensity that made me believe he had regained his sight, then quietly lifted his feet from the ground and lay down on his bed. As we watched, he breathed his last. I moved closer to his bedside and knelt down beside my father, leaning over him. For the first time, I could not feel his breath caress my face. The evidence of death in his still limbs confirmed what had transpired. I cried out and fell upon him, letting my tears fall on his face as I kissed him. In the background, I could hear the wailing of my sons and brothers, but I only had ears for my own sorrow; it felt as if I was the only one who had been bereaved.

∗ ∗ ∗ ∗ ∗ ∗ ∗

In the days following my father's burial, I took the time to reflect on my father's last words to me when he was prophesying over me and my brothers.

As my father finished blessing me, I could tell from my brothers' faces, with the exception of Benjamin, that they were feeling guilt and shame from their actions almost forty years ago.

Shortly after my father had arrived in Egypt, I had told him – under pressure from him – what had happened when he sent me to check on my brothers in Shechem. I had stressed that I had forgiven them and bore them no malice, because I could perceive a greater plan at work. My father's last words reflected his thoughts during our chat: at the time, after I had told him what had happened, he said nothing, but had instead lifted his legs up onto his bed and gone to sleep. To my relief, he never raised the subject again, either when we were alone or with my brothers present, and I believed that he had forgotten it.

His burial had taken place as he had requested, in the cave in the field of Machpelah near Mamre in the land of Canaan. With Pharaoh's permission, I had accompanied his embalmed corpse. It was my first trip out of Egypt since I had arrived. Although I was impressed with the rate of development in the Canaanite region, my sorrow dampened my enthusiasm. This was not how I had imagined my homecoming.

The burial had been a grand affair, attended by all the high-ranking officials from Pharaoh's court, as well as all my brothers and our wives and older children, in a great procession of chariots, mule-drawn wagons and armed horsemen. After we had mourned my father in the customary manner, I returned to my duties in Egypt, as I had promised Pharaoh, and my brothers returned to Goshen. However, their body language on the return journey bothered me: it seemed as if there was a distance between us that had not been present when our father was alive. It was as if his death had erected a wall that had no right to exist.

I discussed my observations with Asenath, who had accompanied me to Canaan for the burial, but she said she had not noticed any difference in the attitude of my brothers' wives, whom she had shared a wagon with during the journey. She advised me to dismiss my suspicions and build on the family ties I had worked so hard over the past seventeen years to forge. However, my suspicions were confirmed when I sat one day in my official chamber at my Men-nefer residence. Kaa showed up, looking contemplative in the way he did when he wished to draw my attention to something but was trying to judge my mood first before speaking. He bowed then rose to his feet, avoiding my gaze.

'What is on your mind?' I asked, looking up from the papyrus document in my hands.

'Well, most honourable vizier,' said Kaa, pacing around, 'I was summoned to Goshen today and spent some time with your brothers.'

'Is everything all right with them?'

I had not seen them since my father's funeral a month ago, due to my work and having to spend more time in Waset.

'They asked me to give you a message, most honourable vizier,' said Kaa carefully, still avoiding my gaze, 'but I am not sure I am the right person to communicate it as I am not a member of your family.'

'You are,' I said impatiently. 'After all, you were overseer in my house for many years and you know everything about my affairs. Now, what is the message?'

Kaa looked as if he wanted to continue dancing around the issue, much to my irritation, but to my relief he sat down and his eyes met mine.

'They said I should say, "Before he died, your father instructed us – being the servants of the God of your father – to ask you to forgive us for the wicked way we – the servants of the God of your father – treated you and the grievous wrong we did to you, so we beg you to forgive our cruelty to you." That's the message.'

Kaa's words took a while to sink in but, when I digested them, tears clouded my eyes and I lost all strength in my limbs. My instincts had been right about their mood. While I did not know precisely what was at the root of their impassioned plea, I guessed that they were feeling vulnerable and insecure without my father to restrain me from taking revenge. I knew my father had not said any such thing; knowing him, he would have told me himself. My brothers had made up these words – and I suspected Simeon was the brains behind this because, of all my brothers, he was the only one to have been remote from me since his arrival in Goshen. Maybe he recalled how I had thrown him in the Den of Confinement and imagined that I had a similar plan for all of them. They were no longer young men, and the thought of being separated from their families or being killed was harder for them to bear. While I could understand their trepidation, it bothered me.

'Take me to Goshen,' I said, rising to my feet with the little strength I had left.

'Do you wish to see your brothers, most honourable vizier?'

'Yes.'

'Well, in that case you do not need to make the journey,' said Kaa, also rising to his feet, 'because your brothers are waiting outside.'

'Send them in!' I exclaimed, recovering from my fatigue.

Kaa bowed and bolted out of the chambers as if his clothes were on fire. He returned moments later, followed by eleven middle-aged men, ten of them looking downcast. As they saw me, they prostrated before me, on the cold marble floor. Judah, who was at the front, raised his head so I could see the strain etched into his face.

'We are your servants!' he cried, looking more distraught than I had ever seen him.

'Yes!' called out Simeon behind him. 'We are your servants!'

Before I could react, all my brothers were loudly declaring that they were my servants and crying out for mercy.

'Why are you afraid?' I asked, staring at them, flabbergasted by their fatuous chanting. Why were they acting this way? Did they truly believe I had evil plans in store for them? After all I had done for them! It was distressing. 'Am I God? Do I stand in his place? Your actions were driven by an evil motive but God intended a good outcome so that He could save the lives of many people. Please do not be afraid of me; I am committed to sustaining you and your families for as long as I live. Now please get up, I beg you. It pains me to see you this way.'

Reassured by my words, they rose to their feet. I hugged each of them and spoke personal words of assurance until their tearful faces were beaming with a mixture of joy and relief. I asked Kaa to send for my overseer. When he arrived, I asked him to produce my very best wine, which I was saving for a special occasion. I spent the rest of the afternoon drinking and chatting with my brothers, sharing happy memories of our father. By the time they eventually left, they were different people.

As we socialised, my mind drifted to an incident my father had told me concerning the deceitful manner in which he had obtained the blessing attached to the first-born child, even though Uncle Esau was his older twin.

After the deception, Uncle Esau had sworn to kill him, leading my father to flee to Mesopotamia. Over twenty years later, my father returned to Canaan. However, he still feared Uncle Esau, so he prepared a lavish gift for his older twin in the hope of pacifying him. When they eventually met – and I still vaguely recalled that meeting – rather than killing him, Uncle Esau reached out to my father with love and compassion.

My father explained that he believed Uncle Esau had partially recovered from the pain of the deception because God had blessed him in my father's absence. The evidence of this, according to my father, was the fact that Uncle Esau initially refused to accept my father's peace offering, on the basis that he had more than enough wealth, and only reluctantly accepted it due to my father's persistence.

Before now, I had never fully grasped the lesson my father had been trying to teach me but, sitting with my brothers, it suddenly began to make sense.

After their wagons had departed, I went upstairs to the balcony overlooking the rear of my house where Asenath and I liked to spend our evenings watching the sun set over the Nile. I found her waiting for me. We sat side by side, gazing across the river, neither of us speaking, soaking up the breath-taking view. As the sun sacrificed its glow to the moon's luminescence, she broke the silence.

'What is on your mind?' she asked, her voice almost a whisper.

'Ephraim comes before Manasseh.'

'You have lost me.'

'Their destinies lie in the order of their names.'

'This is about our sons?'

'I named our first son Manasseh and the second Ephraim because I believed that God makes you fruitful after helping you recover from the pain of your past, but my father was right. It is the other way around: Ephraim comes before Manasseh.'

'I am still in the dark.' Her lovely face looked perplexed.

'I learnt from my father that God first makes us fruitful. This helps us recover from the pain and suffering of our past.'

She appeared to mull over my words for a moment, then I saw her eyes brighten. 'So that is why you were able to forgive more easily.'

'Well, my father certainly seemed to think so.'

'So, do you finally have peace?'

'I never lost it.'

THE LAST WORD

Joseph was born to solve a problem that posed a risk to God's master plan of redemption; that problem dictated an earthly solution in the form of a man.

Even though God owns the whole earth He relies on men to perform His will in it. He has restrained Himself from directly controlling affairs in the earth because to interfere would be to contradict His original purpose which was for man to exercise dominion in the earth. God, however, retains a power of intervention which enables him to step in and takeover whenever there is a state of affairs which runs contrary to His master plan of redemption. Those interventions can be direct or indirect. God's direct interventions are what we refer to as miracles. Whilst all miracles are inexplicable, some are overt and obvious to everyone, most are covert and can only be perceived by those with spiritual insight.

The fall of mankind resulted in an altered state of affairs in the earth and the idyllic nature of the Garden has never again been replicated due to Satan's corrupting influence. To counteract Satan's strategy, rather than relying on his power of direct intervention, God has a pattern of calling people to fulfil His will and their destiny. This pattern is otherwise known as His indirect intervention. All God's interventions are addressed at tackling anomalies in the earth.

One of the anomalies in the earth is a condition known as famine. Famine is earthly barrenness, where things God ordained to live and be fruitful become unproductive and die. Famine contradicts God's plans for the earth. In particular, famine contradicts God's plans for human beings. God had a plan to create a nation called Israel that would be the womb of redemption (root of the Church of Jesus Christ). Israel was to be a nation of people who would descend biologically from a man named Abraham and his wife Sarah. The nation was to be constructed around twelve tribes named after the twelve sons of a man named Jacob, Abraham's grandson.

The nation of Israel was in its pre-natal stage when Joseph was born in Paddan-Aram in Mesopotamia and comprised Jacob, his wives, concubines and his children. When Jacob settled in Canaan, his family comprised three women and thirteen children making a total of seventeen people. At the time of Joseph's calling, when he was aged seventeen years old, these seventeen people had increased in number, as his brothers got married and had children of their own, but it was still a nation in its infancy.

God knew that there was going to be a natural threat to the survival of Israel and that in its infancy it had to be preserved. That threat was the threat of famine. A global famine orchestrated by Satan would wipe out the nation of Israel in its infancy and derail God's master plan of redemption. It is not clear why God permitted the famine to occur across the whole region necessitating Jacob and his family to migrate to Egypt. It would have been simpler and fully within God's capability for the famine to have been averted. However, the famine was one of those inevitable occurrences that had to happen and God needed to preserve Israel through it. Even as salt is a preservative so also was Joseph used as a human preservative to ensure Israel's posterity. Under Joseph, Israel became a nation and was preserved from extinction.

When we consider that each person's destiny is interlocked with other people's destinies, like cells in a body, it becomes easier to accept why Joseph had to get to Egypt and why slavery was the only way he could have been prised away from Jacob's protective grasp.

God had determined that Israel would grow as a nation, but that such growth could not be achieved in Canaan. If the nation had remained in Canaan, more than likely a pattern of migration may have emerged. With the sons of Jacob scattered across the region, functioning in individual family communes, the nation of Israel may never have come into being. The famine may have been the reason why some of Jacob's other sons didn't leave home. The old adage there's safety in numbers comes to mind here.

God has the privilege of knowing future events because He is omniscient (knowing all things past, present and future) and omnipresent (occupying all domains past, present and future). Because He has no past, present or future, God is able to put in place plans to counteract contradictory events that have not yet occurred in the earth realm. Put another way, God knows all things that are ever going to happen, when they are going to happen and how they are going to happen. Because He also knows the consequences of those occurrences He has put in place a strategy to counteract their negative impacts and part of that plan incorporates people; people like Joseph.